Watch Them Fall

A native of Dundee, Marion studied music and worked for many years as a piano teacher and jobbing accompanist. Now a full-time writer, Marion lives in North-east Fife, overlooking the River Tay. She is the author of the bestselling DI Clare Mackay series, which has sold over half a million copies. Marion can be found @MarionETodd on X or visit her website https://www.mariontodd.com/

Also by Marion Todd

Detective Clare Mackay

See Them Run
In Plain Sight
Lies to Tell
What They Knew
Next in Line
Old Bones Lie
A Blind Eye
Bridges to Burn
Dead Man's Shoes
Watch Them Fall

MARION TODD

Watch them fall

First published in the United Kingdom in 2026 by

Canelo Crime, an imprint of
Canelo Digital Publishing Limited,
20 Vauxhall Bridge Road,
London SW1V 2SA
United Kingdom

A Penguin Random House Company
The authorised representative in the EEA is Dorling Kindersley Verlag GmbH. Arnulfstr. 124, 80636 Munich, Germany

Copyright © Marion Todd 2026

The moral right of Marion Todd to be identified as the creator of this work has been asserted in accordance with the Copyright, Designs and Patents Act, 1988.
All rights reserved. No part of this publication may be reproduced or transmitted in any form or by any means, electronic or mechanical, including photocopy, recording, or any information storage and retrieval system, without permission in writing from the publisher.
No part of this book may be used or reproduced in any manner for the purpose of training artificial intelligence technologies or systems. In accordance with Article 4(3) of the DSM Directive 2019/790, Canelo expressly reserves this work from the text and data mining exception.

A CIP catalogue record for this book is available from the British Library.

Print ISBN 978 1 83598 322 5
Ebook ISBN 978 1 83598 323 2

This book is a work of fiction. Names, characters, businesses, organizations, places and events are either the product of the author's imagination or are used fictitiously. Any resemblance to actual persons, living or dead, events or locales is entirely coincidental.

Cover design by Blacksheep

Cover images © Depositphotos, Shutterstock

Printed and bound in Great Britain by Clays Ltd, Elcograf S.p.A.

Look for more great books at
www.canelo.co | www.dk.com

Claire MacLeary, this one's for you; because, without your kindness, the other Clare (Mackay) wouldn't have seen the light of day. Thanks so much for your support and friendship.

Day 1: Tuesday, 10th February

Chapter 1

'Body found at the harbour,' DI Clare Mackay said as Detective Sergeant Chris West emerged from the station kitchen, coffee mug in hand. He stopped for a moment and took a draught, slurping noisily.

'Suspicious?'

She smiled. 'That's for you to find out, Sergeant. Take Natalie, please. It'll be good experience for her.'

'Patch?' His face fell at the mention of the new detective constable. He slurped his coffee again. 'Hope you're not expecting the two of us to fit in the same car. She's as broad as she's long.' He glanced at her, clearly expecting her to return the smile and his face fell. 'Joking, obviously.'

Clare regarded him steadily. 'If I ever hear you say anything like that about another officer...' She stopped, her eye travelling past Chris.

He turned, following her gaze and a flush spread up his neck. DC Natalie Patchett had just come out of the locker room. She was what Clare's mother would have called *big-built* but she used this to her advantage as a weightlifter, competing at national level. Clare had heard she was hoping to represent Scotland at the next Commonwealth Games, hence her nickname, *Patch the Snatch*.

She was about to order Chris to apologise when Natalie cut across her. 'Good job it's all muscle then.' She appraised Chris with a critical eye. 'I'd say you're around seventy per cent biscuit. Sarge,' she added.

If Clare had any fears about Natalie holding her own in the team they melted as Chris's face fell to his boots. 'Seventy-five, actually,' she said. Natalie's lips twitched but she said nothing. 'Get a pool car,' she told Chris. 'Patch will join you in a minute.' Then she jerked her head at Natalie, and headed for her office.

Natalie followed Clare in and motioned towards the door.

'Yes please,' Clare said. 'And take a seat.'

She studied her new DC, waiting while she closed the door and made herself comfortable. Patch's corn-coloured hair was short and spiky, her eyes blue and arresting. She was muscular, certainly, impressive biceps bulging out of her short-sleeved top. But, Clare knew she was fast as well. Her beep test scores were probably the best in the station.

She'd been a cheerful addition to the team two weeks earlier and her work had been excellent so far. But Chris's remark concerned Clare and, noting Patch's wary expression, she wanted to be sure there wasn't more of it going on. She smiled, hoping to put Patch at her ease.

'How are you settling in?'

Patch's smile was polite but guarded. 'Fine, thanks. I like it here.'

'Getting on okay with the team?'

She nodded. 'They're a good bunch.'

Clare hesitated. 'Chris – what he said…'

Patch shook her head. 'It's fine. I don't let things like that bother me.'

'All the same, it shouldn't have happened. I'll be speaking to him about it.'

Patch's brow clouded. 'I wouldn't want the blame for him getting a bollocking.'

Clare waved this away. 'You leave him to me. I know where he hides his Wagon Wheels.'

Patch laughed and Clare went on. 'What about the rest of the team? Anyone else think they're a comedian?'

'Nah. They're no problem.'

Clare studied her face for any sign she was keeping something back but her eyes were clear and guileless. 'Fair enough, Patch. I won't keep you. But my door's always open. Remember that.'

She watched her go then sat on, thinking over Chris's careless remark. It didn't seem to have upset Patch but maybe that in itself was a problem. Was the fact that Patch ignored these comments allowing them to be normalised? On an impulse she turned to her computer and navigated to the training section. She sat tapping at the keyboard for a few minutes then pushed it away.

It was turning into one of those days. Al, now a superintendent, had left that morning for his new job at Tulliallan Police College, creeping out of bed before six. He'd be back on Thursday night to work from home on Friday. It was nothing new. Not really. He'd worked away in the past. But this was longer term – for the next three years at least – and she wasn't sure how she felt about that.

'You sure you're happy about this?' he'd said when the email had arrived, an array of attachments detailing the terms and conditions.

'Of course.' Her tone was brighter than she felt. 'It's made for you, Al. You have to take it.'

And so he had.

At the time it had seemed months away. Something to worry about in the future. But the weeks had gone by and now it was here. It was here and she wouldn't see him until Thursday night. She felt oddly adrift – lost in a situation of her own making. It was as though the stability she'd built with him, the foundations of a future life together had shifted, the ground beneath her a little less certain now.

Superintendent Penny Meakin had offered her Al's old job. She'd thought about it – talked it through with him, weighing up the pros and cons. But it had been lip service. Nothing more. She'd always known she wouldn't take it. Admittedly, the promotion would have been nice. Nine to five even nicer. But stuck in an office over in the large Bell Street block in Dundee? Leaving Chris and Max, Sara and Jim? No more morning chats with Zoe, her admin assistant, munching hunks of her latest tray bakes? No. Even when she'd told herself it was a good move she knew it wasn't for her. The money was rubbish too. Another thousand or so for all that responsibility.

She shook her head, recalling this now. And yet a tiny voice whispered she'd made a mistake. She'd missed a chance and most likely pissed off Penny into the bargain. Her reaction had been a mixture of disappointment and annoyance. The disappointment, Clare reckoned, was more to do with having to find someone else to fill the role, rather than it not being Clare. Had it been a cowardly decision on Clare's part? Changing jobs was never easy. If she wanted to progress, wasn't now as good a time as any? And, if so, what was stopping her? Was there a danger she was becoming too comfortable here in St Andrews? Maybe she should look for a new challenge. Stay fresh.

An alert pinged from her computer and she turned back to the screen, her eye running over details of a planned protest march, a week on Saturday. It had stemmed from a planning application for fifty luxury houses on the edge of town. Clare thought the protestors had a point. St Andrews was already one of the most expensive places in Scotland, available properties snapped up by investors with deep pockets. As often as not they were let to students – those with wealthy parents who could afford the inflated rents. The town was becoming unaffordable for young folk trying to hit that first rung on the housing ladder. She'd heard her own officers complain about it. But would a protest march achieve anything? Maybe if the press showed up. The problem with that was—

The phone rang, cutting across her thoughts. Chris.

'Might be suspicious,' he said. 'But it's hard to tell. He's been in the water a few days at least.'

'He still in there?'

'Nah. Couple of fishermen heaved him out before we arrived. Apparently he was floating face down and they thought they might be able to save him.'

'Okay,' Clare said. 'Ask a uniform to stay with him for now and I'll call Neil at the mortuary. Any ID?'

'Yeah. Wallet with bank cards in a zip pocket. Name of Dennis Gibb.'

'Address?'

'Can't tell. His licence is starting to peel. I'll check mispers when I'm back.'

Clare ended the call and swiped through her contacts until she found the number for Neil Grant, the pathologist. Policing the protest march would have to wait.

Chapter 2

'Reported missing a week ago,' Chris said, scrolling through the missing person report for Dennis Gibb.

'By?'

'Son. Steven Gibb. He only saw his dad occasionally so wasn't sure how long he'd been missing. But at least a week.'

'He's been in the water all that time?' Clare said.

'Suppose so, although he wasn't in bad nick. Hands a bit wrinkled, body swollen with gases but surprisingly intact otherwise.'

'Any sign of injury?'

He shook his head. 'Couldn't tell.'

'Hmm, okay. Where did he live?'

Chris squinted at the monitor. 'Kenly Cottage. Looks like it's south of the town.'

'Near the hotel maybe,' Clare said, thinking of the Kenlybank Hotel, the scene of her first murder case in St Andrews. Five years ago now. Where had the time gone?

'And the son?'

'Kilrymont Road. Want us to call round?'

She smiled. 'Please.'

'Fair enough. I'll take Patch.' He gave her a smile that might have been an apology and she felt a twinge of guilt. There was no badness in him. He was just a bit thoughtless. Quite how he'd react when he learned she'd put him forward for a refresher on diversity training she wasn't sure. But she had Patch to think of as well. No matter how understanding she'd been over Chris's tactless remark, Clare was determined there wouldn't be a repeat.

She glanced at her watch. 'I'm going to head home soon.'

He eyed her. 'You gone part-time?'

'Al – he left for Tulliallan this morning. So I need to pick up Benjy.'

For a minute he didn't speak and she had the impression he was trying to find the right words. 'You'll miss him,' he said, eventually.

She avoided his eye. 'He'll be back on Thursday night.' Then she rose from her seat. 'Let me know how you get on with the son.'

She wandered back to her office, returning to her plans for the protest march. The original application had been for a march from the West Sands to the town hall in Queen's Gardens where the developer was holding an exhibition – an attempt to sell the benefits to the townsfolk. But Clare had objected on grounds of traffic and the organisers had agreed to reroute, finishing the march at the top of North Street, in front of the war memorial. She'd have the street closed from early morning and set up barriers to keep the marchers from fanning out. The top of North Street was wide enough for the numbers they expected. But manpower would definitely be an issue. She'd two officers off sick, not likely to be back in the next few weeks, and a mile and a half's march was a lot of ground to cover. She had to hope they'd be peaceful and good-natured.

By half past four, with Chris and Patch still out, she shut down her computer. 'I need to pick up Benjy,' she told Jim Douglas, her desk sergeant. 'But I'll work on from home for another couple of hours.'

—

Benjy came charging out of the door when she stopped at her nearest neighbour Moira's cottage, a red dinosaur toy clamped in his jaws. Moira had been Clare's dog-walker since she'd bought Daisy Cottage just over four years ago and Benjy adored her. With Al's new job, Moira had agreed to keep Benjy at her cottage while Clare was at work. She'd been consumed with guilt when she'd dropped him off that morning but she knew he was going to love his days with Moira and her husband. She just hoped he wouldn't prove too much for the couple.

'Come away in.' Moira stood back and Clare battled her way past Benjy, seemingly intent on wrapping himself round her legs. 'Cup of tea?'

Clare shook her head. 'I won't keep you. You'll be wanting the place back to yourselves.'

The door to Moira's sitting room stood open, warm light flooding the hall and Clare followed her through, instantly feeling the cares of the day melt away.

It wasn't a large room and there were too many nicknacks for Clare's taste but there was a homeliness she recognised from her own parents' house. Perhaps the contentment that came with a lifetime of growing into each other was absorbed by the walls surrounding them. A fire burned in the grate throwing heat out into the room, a stack of neatly cut logs in a basket to the side.

Bill sat in an armchair, legs stretched out in front, a folded newspaper on his lap. The fisherman's rib jersey he wore daily was discarded at his side. He looked up as Clare entered and a smile spread across his face. 'Clare,' he said, easing himself forward, preparing to rise.

Clare gestured for him to stay seated. 'Don't get up, Bill. I'm not stopping. I'll just take Benjy out of your hair.'

'Sure we can't persuade you?' he said. 'Moira's made a huge chicken pie. Plenty to spare.'

She was sorely tempted. The smell of cooking was wrapping itself round her heart, and her stomach rumbled on cue. But this was only day one of Benjycare, as Al had christened it, and she didn't want to impose on the couple. 'It's a lovely offer,' she said, 'but I'd better get home. Thank you, though. It's very kind.'

Moira disappeared for a moment and returned with a small tinfoil package. 'Something for afters, then,' and she followed Clare back out to the hall. 'Same time tomorrow?'

Clare studied her face. Was Moira tired? The light in the hall wasn't as bright as in the sitting room but she wasn't sure. 'Was it okay today?' she said. 'Benjy, I mean. You must tell me if it's too much.'

Moira waved this away. 'He kept Bill company in the garden this morning, then I took him for a long walk this afternoon. It did us both the world of good.'

Clare eyed her for any sign she was being polite but Moira genuinely seemed to have enjoyed the day. She could only hope it would carry on that way. She thanked Moira, clipped Benjy's lead on and led him out to the car.

Five minutes later, she drew up outside Daisy Cottage. Her heart lifted when she saw lights on in the front room. Al must have come back. Maybe he'd negotiated a few more days working from home. There was no sign of his car, though, and she wondered if he'd nipped out. But as she put her key in the door she sensed a stillness and she remembered the timer switches he'd installed. *So you're not coming home to a dark house.*

It was warm too, the heating timed for her arrival. Casting an eye round the room she saw he'd set the woodburner and she considered putting a match to it. And then she thought *what's the point? It's only me.* For a moment she thought back to Bill and Moira's home. It had a warmth that was so much more than the heat from the fire. But, here, tonight, standing in her own cottage kitchen, the sense of it being a home was absent, somehow. She was tired from the day's work, from the early rise as Al had left for Tulliallan, but she couldn't shake off the feeling that something was missing — something more than the man she'd become used to sharing her cottage with.

She gave herself a shake. It was only the first week of his new job. Time to get a grip. She drew the kitchen curtains, shutting out the darkness and pulled open the fridge door. She could boil some pasta, open a jar of sauce, chop a few vegetables. But she was vaguely unsettled by this new regime, this new way of working. Benjy at Moira's instead of Moira calling in twice a day to walk him; Al away from Monday to Thursday. This was her life now and she'd have to get used to it.

She felt a paw on her leg and realised Benjy must be hungry. She lifted his water bowl and filled it at the tap then she took a bag of his food from the cupboard and filled the other bowl. For once he didn't fall on it straight away, eyeing her as if waiting for permission. *That was new,* she thought. Maybe he too was feeling the lack of Al around. She smiled at him. 'It's just you and me, kid,' she said in a mock American accent and she nodded at his bowl. 'Go on.' He hesitated, looking up at her then the lure of the food was too much and he tore into it.

Clare watched him emptying his bowl then she took out her phone and found the number for her favourite Chinese takeaway. Phone call done, she took a bottle from the wine rack, uncorked it and carried a large glass through to the sofa to await her food. With Al gone she'd have to get used to cooking for herself. Tomorrow. She'd cook something proper tomorrow.

Day 2: Wednesday, 11th February

Chapter 3

'What the hell's this?'

Clare was on her way to the kitchen when Chris approached, phone in hand. She regarded her sergeant. 'You want to rethink your tone?'

'Diversity training refresher?' He tapped his phone screen. 'Is this about that joke yesterday?'

She stood her ground. 'I don't recall any jokes. I did, however, hear a body-shaming remark about a junior officer. Frankly, Chris, you should have known better.'

He stared at her then exhaled. 'Okay, I'm sorry. I was out of order and I apologised. Patch – we cleared the air in the car. She was absolutely fine.'

'Pretty hard for her to be anything else when you outrank her.' Her face softened. Chris was a big lump at times and it had been out of character. She knew that. He'd meant no harm, but she had a duty of care to all her officers. 'It's like this: Patch might reflect on it. She might go home and speak to whoever she lives with – tell them what you said and they might kick up a stink. Tell her she should complain; and to be honest, they'd have a point.'

'It wasn't like that. Honestly. She's a good cop. We get on.'

'Just do it, Chris. It's two hours, tops. And make sure you ace it. Okay?'

She stood, waiting for his response. Finally he nodded and she motioned towards the kitchen. 'Let's have coffee and you can tell me about yesterday.'

They took their drinks through to Clare's office, Chris pulling up a chair opposite. Clare reached into her desk drawer and withdrew the foil package Moira had given her the night before. She'd been too full of chow mein and had decided to keep it for the following day. She'd planned to eat it with her afternoon cuppa. But Chris looked genuinely miserable so she pulled back the foil to reveal two hunks of sticky dark gingerbread, generously buttered.

He drew back slightly, his expression wary. 'Don't tell me you've been baking.'

She laughed. 'As if. My neighbour made it. But I was too full last night. If you don't want it though…' She stretched out her hand but he was too quick for her, scooping up one of the slices.

The ice broken, she pressed on. 'How did you get on with the next of kin?'

'As you'd expect. Pretty upset.'

Clare thought back. 'Son, wasn't it?'

'Yeah. Wife died a few years ago so it's the son and daughter-in-law.'

'What are they like?'

'Nice. Sort of fit, you know?'

She raised an eyebrow.

'Not that kind of fit. Fit like they run, or go the gym. They were wearing the gear.'

'Jobs?'

'He's a delivery driver and she's a receptionist in a GP practice.'

'Here?'

'Cupar.'

Clare sipped her coffee. 'Any pointers?'

He broke off a piece of gingerbread and popped it in his mouth. 'Not really.'

'Was our victim a drinker?'

'Yeah. A bit. Son thinks he'd likely had a skinful. Wandered down by the harbour on his way home and missed his footing.'

Clare bit into the gingerbread, considering this. 'Where did you say he lived?'

'Wee cottage just outside town on the A915.'

'Eh? That's nowhere near the harbour. Where had he been drinking?'

'They didn't know. The son suggested a couple of pubs on North Street.'

'Wait.' She sat back, thinking for a minute then took out her phone and clicked on a map of the area. 'If you're in a pub here,' she said, tapping the top of North Street, 'which way would you go to reach the A915?' She turned her phone for him to see and he peered at the screen, moving the map around with a sticky finger.

'Suppose I'd cut through one of the lanes to South Street. Then I'd head this way and carry on up the road.'

'Exactly. So what was he doing at the harbour?'

Chris shrugged. 'I dunno. It's not that far. Maybe he wanted a pee.'

'He'd have gone before he left the pub.'

'Unless he forgot. If he was legless…'

They fell silent, enjoying the gingerbread then Clare glanced at her watch. 'Did Neil say anything about the PM?'

Chris nodded, licking his fingers. 'Later today. Tomorrow at worst.'

That was something at least, Clare thought. There was likely nothing in it but she'd be happier if the PM confirmed a high level of alcohol in the victim's system. But, if he'd been sober…

There was a tap on her door and Jim entered without waiting. 'Housebreaking just come in.'

Clare popped the last of the gingerbread in her mouth and took a tissue from a box on her desk. 'Details?'

'Big house out Hepburn Gardens. Owners were away overnight. Came back this morning and called it in.'

'Much taken?'

Jim shook his head. 'They're not sure yet. House that size, it could take a while to check.'

Clare wiped her hands on the tissue. 'Can you spare a couple of uniforms to swing by?'

He hesitated and Clare picked up on it.

'Jim?'

'They implied it wasn't a random attack. They reckon they've been targeted.'

She sat back, weighing this for a moment. It wasn't like Jim to overreact. Strictly speaking she should prioritise Dennis Gibb's death. But, so far, there was nothing to indicate it was suspicious. Chances are he'd had a skinful and wandered down to the harbour for a pee. If he'd staggered into the water maybe he'd been too drunk to clamber out; or the cold had got to him. She glanced at Chris. 'Our body in the harbour – what do you reckon?'

He inclined his head. 'Wouldn't be the first drunk to have an accident.'

She considered this. Even if the PM was done that afternoon it would be the end of the day or tomorrow before they had a cause of death; and Jim did seem concerned about the burglary.

She sighed. 'You'd better give me the details.'

—

The house was a substantial Edwardian dwelling built over two storeys, freshened by what Clare thought was newly applied cream render. A broad drive was bounded on both sides by deep laurel hedges and Clare pulled the car in and off the road. She followed the drive round towards the front door and came to a halt beside a sleek dark blue Lexus.

Chris clicked off his belt and jumped out of the car. Clare followed him slowly, her eyes running over the house. Initially she thought the leaded windows were original but, as they approached the substantial stone porch, she realised they were new, the lead cames replaced with PVC astragal bars. The porch, too, was a recent addition. Clearly money had been spent but she wasn't convinced the changes were entirely sympathetic to the original building.

'Max would hate this,' she whispered, referencing her other DS's obsession with architecture.

'I could stand it,' Chris said and Clare remembered he and his wife Sara were house hunting.

'Any luck with houses?' she asked. The front door opened, cutting short their conversation, a tall suntanned man on the threshold. He was dressed in a light grey business suit, a claret-coloured tie knotted tightly at his neck. He was disarmingly handsome, Clare realised, aged about forty, his dark hair gelled back from his forehead. His beard was neatly trimmed, his blue eyes arresting.

Chris shot her a glance then stepped forward, warrant card in hand. 'Mr Freeman?'

The man studied the card then formed his face into a smile, a well-practised, professional smile, Clare thought. One that said *don't waste my time here. I have empires to build.*

'DI Clare Mackay and DS Chris West,' she said and the man nodded.

'Are your forensic people en route?'

For a moment Clare wondered if she'd missed something. Was there more to this than a simple housebreaking? Jim had said the couple thought they'd been targeted. It was certainly a house that screamed money; but was this man suggesting the thieves had been more interested in its occupants than the contents?

She returned his smile. 'We often find forensic tests aren't useful. Most houses have multiple sets of fingerprints. Unless the thieves are known to us, it's unlikely to be helpful.'

His eyes narrowed and he seemed about to speak.

'Maybe we could come in?' Clare suggested. 'Have a proper chat.'

He stepped back to admit them then closed and locked the door. 'We're in here.'

They followed him through to a bright sitting room with high ceilings and an original fireplace. A selection of traditional art hung on pale lemon walls, the bay window framed by richly patterned curtains. The cream carpet was thick underfoot and Clare motioned to their shoes. 'Would you like us to…' but he waved this away.

'Least of my worries.'

She studied his expression and took in his body language. There was no blueprint for how victims of burglary reacted but this man seemed more impatient than shocked. She turned to sweep the room and her misgivings grew. There was something off, here. Something that didn't quite fit. There certainly was evidence of a break-in. That much was clear. The drawers of an oak desk stood open, the contents upended onto an immaculate carpet that showed no sign anyone had been tramping over it. A rose-gold iPad caught her eye; surely the first thing the thieves would have taken. A well-stocked cocktail cabinet also appeared untouched. She wasn't about to bring SOCO out for a straightforward burglary but something told her there was more to this.

The door opened and a slim dark-haired woman came into the room. She went straight for Clare, her hand outstretched. 'Erika Freeman,' she said. 'And you've met my husband, Rex.'

Rex, eh? Clare thought. The king in his castle, right enough. And this, surely, was the queen. Clare's eyes were drawn to her hair, short at the back but a sweep of chestnut brown on top, sitting in beautifully styled layers. It was the kind of hair she'd have loved herself. Erika's make-up and clothes were no less immaculate, her shell-pink blouse falling in soft folds over designer jeans. She might have walked off the set of a magazine photoshoot. Clare took her hand, noting the expensive rings and manicured nails. There was money here. No doubt about that. 'DI Clare Mackay,' she said, 'and this is my colleague DS Chris West.'

Erika smiled and Clare thought her reaction was more natural than her husband's. There was the hint of a tremor in her voice, a nervousness in her eyes. Maybe the burglary had affected her more than it had Rex. 'Would you like some tea?' Erika said. 'Or coffee?'

'Tea would be lovely,' Clare said. 'Milk, no sugar for us both.'

The man indicated a large cream sofa, brightly coloured scatter cushions arranged along the back. 'Make yourselves comfortable,' and he followed his wife out.

Clare waited until he'd closed the door then she turned to Chris. 'Any thoughts?'

'No damage,' Chris said. 'And they left the booze.' He was quiet for a moment. 'Insurance job, maybe? Claiming for jewellery? Could be they've cash-flow problems.'

'Possibly. Did Jim say how they got in?'

'Back door lock. Looks like they took a hammer to it.'

Clare studied the room. It was certainly the kind of property housebreakers went for. Set back from the road, screened by hedges and completely private. But, if the couple were right and they had been targeted, what had the thieves been after?

A selection of framed photos was arranged on a small table in the corner of the room and Clare wandered across for a look. An ornate silver frame caught her eye, a photo of two women – one slim with dark hair, clearly the woman they'd just met. The other was older and almost certainly a relative. They were smiling, both of them, but Clare thought the older one didn't look well.

The door opened again, Rex holding it for his wife who carried a tray of mugs. Erika set the tray down then her gaze travelled to the photo Clare had been studying. 'My lovely mum,' she said, a catch in her throat. 'We lost her a few weeks ago.'

Clare gave what she hoped was a sympathetic smile. 'I'm so sorry. You must miss her.'

Erika nodded but didn't reply, busying herself handing out tea in china mugs. Clare thanked her then eased herself down on a cream sofa, taking care not to spill her drink. She put her mug on a coaster and smiled at the couple. 'If you could tell us what happened.'

Erika looked to her husband and he took the cue.

'Bit of a shock, as you can imagine.'

'Of course,' Clare said. 'You were away overnight?'

Rex nodded. 'We'd been nominated for an award. Architectural,' he added. 'Last night was the awards ceremony.'

'Congratulations. You're architects?'

'Developers.'

'We didn't win,' Erika said, 'but it's always a good do.'

'Where was it?'

'Glasgow. We decided to stay the night, enjoy a few drinks.' She waved a hand round the room. 'What a mistake that was.'

'Which hotel?' Chris asked.

Rex raised an eyebrow and Chris hastened to reassure him. 'Just routine. It's unlikely we'd need to contact them.'

He held Chris's gaze for a moment and Clare thought she understood. He wasn't used to having his movements questioned. He was the alpha male – the one who asked the questions. Perhaps he enjoyed seeing his employees scrabbling for answers. They were in Rex's house today – his domain. But investigating crime was Clare's and she could see he didn't like being the one having to account for his movements, even as a victim.

'We do need to be thorough,' she said, giving him a sympathetic smile. 'It's surprising how the smallest piece of information can be useful.'

This seemed to mollify him and he gave them the name of the hotel.

'What time did you arrive home?' Clare continued.

'Just before ten,' Erika said. 'It's a busy time for us so we had an early breakfast and left before rush hour.'

'Do you have an office?'

Rex shook his head. 'We work from home.'

Clare noted this down. 'Could tell us what you found when you arrived.'

Erika's face creased and Clare wondered if she was about to cry. Maybe Rex was a safer bet. 'Mr Freeman?'

He hesitated, as if the memory was one he didn't wish to recall. 'Front door was locked, as usual. But there was something different. We both felt it, didn't we?' He stretched out and took Erika's hand. 'Even before we came in here.'

Erika's eyes were brimming now and Clare's heart softened. It wasn't just the damage to the back door, the loss of possessions. It was the effect on victims' peace of mind, the invasion of what should have been their safe space – their home. Rex leaned forward and picked up his wife's mug.

'Drink this,' he said, a tender note to his voice. 'It'll help.'

Clare gave them a moment then she prompted again. 'Which room did you enter first?'

Rex was still focused on Erika. He watched until she'd taken a drink of tea then he turned back to Clare. 'This one. I saw straight away someone had been in here. So I went through to the back of the house and saw the door. That's when I dialled 999.'

'And did you check the other rooms?'

He nodded. 'They'd been through the cabinets in the dining room. And the office. That was turned upside down.'

'What about upstairs?'

'I had a quick look,' Rex said, 'but I don't think they'd been up there.'

Clare sensed Chris adjust his position and she knew what he was thinking. Burglars went for small stuff. Things they could carry easily and sell quickly. They took phones, tablets and, when they thought there was money – real money – they went for jewellery. This house with its new windows, that porch, the tidy garden and the freshly rendered walls, it reeked money. There would be jewellery here and any self-respecting housebreaker would know that. Surely they'd have gone upstairs?

'So only the downstairs rooms?'

'Seems that way.'

Clare studied him for a moment. It was as though he was irritated, rather than upset. Impatient more than angry. Was it because the house wasn't crawling with SOCOs? Special attention for a special couple? Did he think they weren't taking it seriously enough? She supposed every victim of burglary felt the same. They all wanted whoever had been in their house to be caught. But they rarely were.

She gave him a reassuring smile, trying to keep him onside. 'I know this is tedious but, the more information we have, the better.'

He held her gaze for a few moments then his face softened. 'Sorry. I know you have to do this. It's just...'

'I understand. But the sooner we do it, the sooner we can leave you in peace.'

He made no reply and Clare went on.

'Do you have an alarm?'

He shook his head. 'Ironically we've someone coming to give us a quote next week. We've only been here a few months.'

'Any CCTV or other cameras?'

'No. I never thought we'd need it.' He glanced at his wife. 'Might be worth getting the alarm company to quote for that as well.'

Erika nodded, woodenly, as though it scarcely mattered now.

'Can you tell us what's missing?' Clare went on.

The couple exchanged glances and Rex's hand went to his chin. Clare waited. What was going on here?

'I'm not sure anything's been taken,' he said, eventually.

Clare raised an eyebrow but said nothing.

'I don't think whoever broke in wanted to steal anything. Well, not valuables, at least.'

'Then what?' Clare asked.

'Information.'

She studied their faces, trying to form her next question. Rex saved her the trouble.

'As I said, we're property developers. We specialise in the domestic market. The demand for homes is at an all-time high. Doesn't matter how bad the economy is, people still need somewhere to lay their head.' He smiled at his wife. 'And that's where we come in.'

It was starting to ring a bell. The exhibition in the town hall, the protest march. Were the Freemans behind the controversial development? She tried to think of a tactful way to ask and, again, Rex cut in.

'And, yes. It's our development that's caused some disquiet in the town.'

'And you think it's connected to the burglary?'

'I'm sure of it. There's been a lot of disinformation, you see.'

'Oh?'

'We've been accused of using sub-standard materials, shipping stuff in cheaply from China, cutting corners, tax dodges, creative accounting – you name it, Inspector, we've been accused of it. I'm guessing whoever broke in was looking for proof.'

'It's all rubbish,' Erika burst out. 'An absolute pack of lies. People with money want to live here. It's a beautiful town. Some people,' she emphasised these two words, 'some people don't like that. They resent anyone who works hard and makes a success of their lives.'

Touched a nerve there, Clare thought. She studied Erika's face. Her cheeks were pink now. 'Who do you think is responsible?'

'We don't know their names,' Rex said. 'But that protest group – the ones who've organised the march. I'd start with them.'

They left soon after, having looked round the house and confirmed nothing had been disturbed upstairs. As they walked towards the car, a red Nissan pulled into the drive, crunching over the gravel. It came to a halt in front of the porch, the handbrake jerked on. Clare recognised the occupant as a reporter from STV news.

'What the hell's he doing here?'

'Heard there's been a spot of bother,' the reporter said, clicking to lock his car.

She regarded him, unsmiling. 'What exactly did you hear?'

'Break-in. So, what's the scoop? Much taken?'

Clare ignored the question. 'Who told you that?'

He smirked. 'You know what they say about journalists and their sources. So, can I quote you?'

She jerked her head at Chris. 'Come on. We've work to do.'

She jumped into the car and threw it into reverse, narrowly missing the reporter. Rex and Erika were standing on the threshold, Rex smiling at the man.

'No prizes for guessing who his source is,' she said, crunching the car into first gear. 'Let's get back to the station. There's something about the air here that doesn't agree with me.'

Chapter 4

Clare stood waiting for the kettle to boil, her mind back at the harbour. She was wondering how Dennis Gibb had ended up in the water, when Chris and Max wandered in. 'I had a look at the plans,' Max said as Chris searched the cupboards for clean mugs. 'The housing development,' he added. 'Just out of interest. Way out of my price league.'

Clare hesitated. Once Max began talking about architecture and houses, it was hard to stop him. But there was certainly something very odd about that burglary. 'What did you think?'

He considered. 'I'd say they're throwing a lot of money at it but very little taste. They're ticking all the right boxes: triple glazing, ground source heating, lots of insulation. Pretty much everything to get it past the planning department. But they're basically putting up enormous boxes. A house can be as ugly as you like but stick in a spa bath and a state-of-the-art kitchen, and they'll sell like hotcakes.'

'What about the materials?'

He shrugged. 'Seems okay on paper. You think there's something dodgy?'

'It's possible someone does. It looks like the burglars were after information. There's pretty much nothing been taken.'

'So they say,' Chris put in. 'I'm not convinced they're telling us the whole story.'

Clare nodded. 'I know what you mean. I just don't know what it is they're holding back.'

Chris began spooning coffee into mugs. 'Maybe they've upset someone. Could be the burglary was meant as a warning.

Might even have left them a message – a note or something. Warning them off. If they are into something dodgy, they're hardly going to tell us.'

He had a point. Clare wasn't sure what was going on at the Freemans' but it seemed far from a straightforward burglary. 'He was very keen we bring SOCO in,' she said. 'Now why would that be?'

'Because he knows there's something to find,' Max suggested. 'Say someone visited him at home – threatened him or warned him about something. Their prints would be in the house; and, if they had a coffee, their DNA would be on the cup.'

Clare shook her head. 'Too contrived.'

'I'm not so sure,' Chris said. 'I reckon our Rex has a pretty ruthless streak.'

'Maybe.'

'And that reporter,' he went on. 'We think the Freemans called him, yeah?'

'I'd say so.'

'Why would they do that?'

'Sympathy?' Max suggested. 'The plans aren't exactly popular in the town. That burglary might be just what they need. From what you've said, I'd guess they'd enjoy playing the victim.'

Clare wandered back to her office, thoughts of the Freemans' burglary running round her head. Would it make any difference to the planned protest a week on Saturday? Might they cancel the exhibition in the town hall? She couldn't help hoping they would. She hadn't the resources or the budget to police the protest effectively.

The phone rang, cutting across her thoughts. She glanced at the display and her heart sank. Superintendent Penny Meakin.

'You've had a burglary.'

For a moment, Clare was wrong-footed. Why on earth would Penny be interested in a housebreaking, particularly when nothing had been taken? 'Yes. But it doesn't look as if—'

'The Freemans, yes? The couple behind that new housing development.' It was a statement, rather than a question.

'Yes,' Clare said again. 'Chris and I attended.'

'So I gather.'

'Can I ask what your interest is?'

'Political. Small p,' she added. 'The Freemans are big news at the moment, as you no doubt realise. Their plans, the protest. We need to tread carefully.'

Clare chose her words. 'As I said, Chris and I attended. We took statements, had a look round and assured the couple we'd investigate – as we do with any crime,' she added. 'I can ask the crime prevention officer to call round if that would reassure them.'

'But you haven't instructed any forensic tests.'

'That's correct. We haven't the budget and I doubt SOCO would view it as a priority.'

'With respect, Clare, that's hardly their call. I'd like them in.'

It took Clare a moment to digest this. Why on earth did Penny want a forensic team to go over a house where nothing had been taken?

'The Freemans believe they're being targeted by those who oppose their development,' Penny went on.

'You've spoken to them?' Clare couldn't keep the incredulity out of her voice.

'I have. Mr Freeman called me after you left. He's concerned the motive wasn't theft, but intimidation.'

Clare pressed her lips together, not trusting herself to speak. What the hell were the Freemans thinking, going over her head and phoning a fucking superintendent? It wasn't even as if anything had been stolen. The arrogance of the couple was astounding. What was worse, Penny hadn't sent them about their business. Was she missing something? She took a breath in and out before trying again.

'Chris and I didn't find evidence of intimidation. Is there something I don't know?'

It was Penny's turn to be quiet and Clare seized her chance. 'I've an unexplained death to deal with as well.'

'Suspicious?' Penny's tone was sharp.

'I'm still waiting on the PM results.'

'So not obviously suspicious.'

Clare could feel the colour rising in her cheeks. This was typical Penny – making assumptions. 'Not as yet,' she admitted. 'But it can be hard to tell.'

'Then I'd suggest you focus on the burglary for now. It has the potential to be far more serious than your unexplained death.'

Clare opened her mouth to ask what she meant but Penny cut across her.

'We have reason to believe the protest group may have been infiltrated by those with more extreme views.'

'Extreme? Seriously?'

'It's possible.'

'And you think it's these extremists who broke into the Freemans' house last night?'

'Again, it's possible. Any prints or DNA we can recover from the scene might help us put the culprits behind bars. At least until the protest is over.'

Clare's mind was whirling. Surely Penny wasn't suggesting local protestors might be joined by others hell-bent on violence. 'You really think there's a risk?'

'I do. So you'll instruct SOCO.'

Again, it clearly wasn't a question. Clare sensed Penny was about to end the call but there was so much more she wanted to say. She already had concerns about policing the march. But now? Admittedly SOCO might find evidence to identify the housebreakers but surely there was a simpler solution. She took a deep breath. 'We need to withdraw permission for the march,' she said. 'I can't risk public safety, or that of my officers.'

'Out of the question!' The sharp response took Clare aback. She wasn't a probationer, for God's sake. She was a detective inspector. Surely they could discuss this. She tried again but Penny was in full flow.

'We can't be seen to kowtow to this element, Clare. It would be wholly undemocratic. And besides,' she hesitated, as if choosing her words, 'the Freemans are influential people. They have connections in the press; and we do not want to see the town on the six o'clock news.' She exhaled, as if tired of explaining something to an unreasonable child. 'I'll drum up as many extra officers as I can but the march goes ahead.'

Clare closed her eyes. How on earth was she going to police this march? And how many protestors were they expecting? She was about to ask Penny to put her in touch with officers who'd managed large events when Penny cut across her thoughts.

'In the meantime, call SOCO please. Priority.'

She ended the call and Clare sat on, phone in hand, her mind racing. Suddenly the shape of the day had changed, her to-do list ripped up and thrown away. Her mind travelled unbidden to memories of Al's office, over in the Bell Street station, now occupied by another DCI she vaguely knew. A small voice in the back of her head said it might have been her office. No, it *would* have been her office. Penny had made it clear her name was on the job. All she had to do was apply. And, if she had?

All this – the burglary, the protest march, Dennis Gibb's death – it would all be someone else's problem. Had she done the right thing turning the opportunity down? The anxious feeling gathering in the pit of her stomach said *maybe not*.

Chapter 5

Raymond Curtice, the SOCO Clare worked most closely with, promised to do his best. 'But I have to be honest, Clare. The likelihood we'll pick up anything helpful is pretty low.'

Clare sighed. 'I know. It's a complete waste of time and resources. But it's not my decision.'

'Really? I'm intrigued.'

Clare opened her mouth to relay her conversation with Penny then she checked herself. Much as she wanted to offload to Raymond she wasn't sure how widely Penny wanted the news about the march disseminated. Safer not to mention it. 'It's Penny,' she said, choosing her words carefully. 'She's got a bee in her bonnet about this burglary. Thinks there's more to it than a straightforward housebreaking.'

'And she really thinks we'll find something?'

For a moment, Clare wasn't sure what to say. She hated not being straight with Raymond. They had such a good relationship and he frequently went above and beyond when the need arose. The least he deserved was the truth. But the mood Penny was in…

'I dunno.' Her tone was noncommittal. 'If you ask me she's being completely unreasonable but she's pulled rank so…'

Raymond laughed. 'Okay. I hear you. Leave it with me. I'll bump it up the queue.'

She thanked him and put down her phone.

Chris was in the incident room, scowling at a laptop. He looked up as she approached. 'I hate you for making me do this. What even *is* unconscious bias? I've never heard of it.'

Clare peered over his shoulder, studying the screen. 'It's B,' she said after a moment. 'And D, I think. Yes. B and D.'

'See! You don't even know yourself.' He shoved the laptop across the desk. 'I'll ask Sara. She knows this stuff.'

'She won't tell you.'

'I'll offer to make the tea tonight.'

Clare considered. 'On balance, I'd take that deal.'

He studied her, the hint of a smile at the corners of his mouth. 'Missing the DCI? Or should I say, the Superintendent?'

'I can cook.'

'Yeah, but you don't. I bet you had a takeaway last night.' He saw her expression and laughed. 'I'm right, amn't I?'

She felt the colour rise in her cheeks and she went on before he could press the point. 'In other news, Penny's insisted SOCO go over the Freemans' house.'

He stared at her. 'You're joking.'

'Nope.'

'But they'll never…'

'I know. I said as much. The Freemans work from home. They probably have folk coming and going all day.'

'And if the perps aren't on our system…'

'I said that too.'

Chris's brow creased. 'I don't get it. What's it to her? Are they related, or something?'

Clare sank down next to Chris. 'Our protest march – Penny thinks we're in for trouble.'

'What sort of trouble?'

'Busloads of protestors.'

'What? Where from?'

Clare shrugged. 'Dunno. Edinburgh, Glasgow, Aberdeen – take your pick. The point is her intel suggests a big crowd, intent on trouble.'

'But this town,' Chris said, 'there's folk live right along the route. They'll be sitting ducks and we haven't the manpower to corral a big crowd – unless she has a spare hundred cops she can give us.'

Clare let out a sigh. 'She says she'll do what she can.'

'Hah. I'll believe that when I see it.' He was quiet for a minute. 'I dunno about the march. I still think that pair could be into something dodgy.'

'Yeah. I get that; but Penny seems to think there's a connection. Whatever the motive behind the break-in, she reckons it's the same people planning to bus in protestors.'

Chris exhaled. 'Sounds like an excuse to have Rex's burglary bumped up the priority list. Maybe they've met Penny – one of those black-tie dos. He likely knows there's bugger all chance of finding whoever broke in so he gives Penny a call and turns on the charm. Probably tells her Mrs Rex is hysterical.'

'Then he plays his trump card,' Clare said, taking up the thread. 'Tells Penny he's heard anarchists plan to join the protest.'

'And kills two birds with one stone. He gets his SOCO investigation and a good chance the march will be cancelled.'

'Makes sense,' Clare agreed. 'Only, it hasn't worked.'

'Oh?'

'I asked Penny about cancelling the march.'

'She said no?'

'Afraid so.'

'She does know we've an unexplained death as well?'

'I tried that too. Until we have a cause of death we're to prioritise the burglary.'

Chris's face darkened. 'So now we're wasting SOCO's time on a burglary we've no chance of solving and we've a bloody great protest into the bargain.'

'That about sums it up.'

He glanced back at the screen. 'Suddenly an afternoon doing this malarkey doesn't seem so bad.'

Clare's phone began to ring. Neil Grant, the pathologist. 'Speaking of unexplained deaths,' and she swiped to answer the call.

'Hi Neil.' She clicked the speaker icon so Chris could hear. 'Any news?'

'Your body in the harbour,' he began. 'It's not exactly straightforward.'

Clare motioned to Chris to pass her pen and paper. 'Go on.'

'First of all, he was alive when he entered the water.'

'He drowned?'

'He did. Froth in the airways and his lungs were distended. Classic signs.'

Chris pushed a notepad towards Clare and she picked up a pen. 'Any alcohol?'

'Yes. But, if you're asking if he was too drunk to stop himself drowning, I'd probably say no.'

'How sure can you be?'

'Given the depressed fracture to the back of his skull, I'd say he had a helping hand.'

'He was struck on the head?'

'Several times.'

Chris raised an eyebrow and Clare closed her eyes, taking in the implications. A murder hunt on top of everything else – how on earth would they cope?

'My initial findings will be on the system tomorrow,' Neil went on, 'but I wanted to give you the main points; and there's something else.'

–

They squeezed into Clare's office, Chris and Patch taking the only two spare chairs, Max, the other DS, electing to stand. Patch's eyes were alert, a hint of nervousness in them and Clare wondered if this was her first murder.

'So it's suspicious?' Chris said.

Clare nodded. 'Looks that way. He was definitely alive when he entered the water.'

'It wasn't just an accident?' Max asked. 'Tripped and fell in – too drunk to get himself out.'

'No. He hadn't drunk that much, and his skull was fractured at the base.'

'He could have fallen backwards,' Patch said but Clare shook her head.

'Neil reckons he'd been hit several times. Probably a rock or a large stone. Something with an uneven surface.'

'Any idea when?' Chris said.

'He can't be precise. But, given the temperature of the water and the condition of the body, at least four days ago, probably no more than ten.'

'Figures,' Chris said. 'He was reported missing eight days ago so he probably died the night before.'

'And he's been in the water since then?' Max asked.

Clare shrugged. 'Seems a reasonable assumption.'

'Any idea why he hadn't surfaced earlier?' Patch asked.

'Now there we do have something,' Clare said. 'There was damage to his clothing, as if it had been caught, or was rubbing on something below the waterline.'

'Boat?' Chris suggested.

'Most likely.'

'So he falls in,' Chris continued, 'drowns and sinks, drifting beneath a nearby boat.'

'Almost,' Clare said. 'He had a bit of help there as well.'

'Oh?'

'There's a distinctive mark on his chest – a circular bruise. Neil says from sustained pressure, rather than a blow.'

'He was pushed under?' Max said.

'Pushed, and most likely held under. The mark's around three to four centimetres in diameter. Neil suggested it could be a boat hook pole, or something like that.' She looked round at them. 'Would that fit?'

Patch nodded. 'I'd say so. My dad sails. He has this fancy pole – feeds the mooring line for you.'

Chris raised an eyebrow. 'Translation please?'

'Makes it easy to tie up the boat,' Patch explained. 'But a traditional boat hook would do just as well.'

'And they'd be about that size?' Clare asked.

'Think so.' Patch took out her phone and tapped at the screen. A minute later she held it out for Clare to see.

'Wooden barge pole,' Clare said, squinting at the image. 'Thirty-three millimetres.' She handed the phone back to Patch. 'That would work, wouldn't it?'

Chris nodded. 'I reckon so.'

'Right, then,' Clare said, 'let's work it through. Say Dennis had a couple of drinks, then he left the pub. For some reason he wandered down to the harbour.'

'Maybe his killer led him down there,' Max said. 'Some pretext.'

'Could have offered him a lift,' Chris said. 'Told him his car was parked down there.'

'Okay,' Clare went on. 'They get near to the water. It's dark, deserted. Maybe our killer says there's something floating in it. Dennis goes over to look. Our man picks up a rock…'

'…and clocks him on the back of the head,' Patch said. 'He'd be stunned. Probably wouldn't realise what was happening. A quick shove and in he goes. Easy enough if he wasn't expecting it.'

'Could be the cold water sobered him up,' Max said. 'He starts splashing around, trying to grab onto a boat or the wall. Our man looks round, maybe sees a pole on one of the boats. Tells Dennis to stop panicking. He'll get something to help him out. Dennis thinks he's giving him the pole to grab hold of but he uses it to push him under.'

'That works,' Clare said. 'And, if the pole was long enough, once Dennis had stopped struggling, he could have used it to drive him under a boat. Make sure he wasn't found for a few days.' She sat thinking for a minute. 'Pubs at that end of town – we need their CCTV.'

'That's a lot of footage,' Chris said. 'Easily half a dozen pubs, a window of five days.'

'That's police work, Sergeant. Get hold of the footage please. And let's play safe. Go back ten days. Ask the next of kin for a few photos as well. It'll make it easier to spot him.'

'There are cameras at the harbour,' Patch said.

Clare nodded. 'Get that footage too.'

'We'll have to tell the son,' Chris said.

Clare was quiet for a moment. 'What did you two think of them – the son and his wife?'

Patch and Chris exchanged glances.

'I don't think they were close to Dennis,' Patch said, eventually.

'Oh?'

'I mean they said all the right things. Seemed upset. But you know what families are like when someone's missing. Frantic with worry.'

Chris nodded. 'It's a good point. They didn't act like concerned relatives.'

'So,' Max said, weighing this up, 'were they not concerned because they didn't much care or...'

'...they already knew he was dead,' Patch finished. 'It's possible.' She glanced at Chris. 'What do you think?'

He wrinkled his nose. 'I can't see it. They don't seem the type. My sense is they just didn't get on. I'd say the wife was more upset.'

'Any reason for saying that?' Clare asked.

He inclined his head. 'I could say it's because women are more caring than men. But I've been doing my diversity training so I can confirm that would be a sexist remark.' He beamed round at them.

'And you *are* the station expert on sexist remarks,' Patch said.

Max stifled a laugh and Clare didn't dare meet his eye.

'On that happy note,' she said, pretending to shuffle her papers, 'let's leave it there. Once I have the full PM report from Neil we'll go round to see them. Meantime,' she eyed Chris, 'I think you have some training to finish. Max and Patch, look into Dennis's background please. See what else you can turn up.'

She sat on after they'd left, thinking about Dennis Gibb. Had his murder been a random attack or had someone lured him down to the harbour? And, if it had been premeditated, who had hated him so much they'd wanted him dead? Her phone buzzed and she saw a message from Patch, forwarding a link to the barge pole. She sent it onto Neil, asking if that kind of pole could have made the mark on Dennis's chest. Then she turned back to her computer and began working through her inbox.

–

Mindful she didn't want to take advantage of Bill and Moira's kindness, she shut down her computer just after four, taking plans for the protest march to work on that evening.

It was uncharacteristically mild for February, cheerful groups of crocuses already blooming in a garden across from the station. If it carried on like this it would soon be spring. Her spirits lifted at the prospect. Before Al had left for his first week at Tulliallan, they'd spoken about a spring break somewhere. Paris, maybe. Or Amsterdam. See those famous bulb fields. She jumped in the car and gunned the engine feeling suddenly hopeful. This time tomorrow Al would be on his way back, to work from home on Friday. Admittedly, it had been a short week with him not starting until Tuesday but it wasn't so bad, really. Not when she was busy at work.

She resisted the temptation to go into Moira's warm house, waving away offers of tea and food. Thanking the couple, she led Benjy firmly to the car, securing him in the back seat.

The heating hadn't come on in the cottage and, for a minute, she worried the boiler was playing up. Checking her watch, she realised she'd come home early. She bent and put a match to the stove, kneeling down as the kindling sparked and spit. Benjy, having completed his sniff-check of the house, wandered over and eased himself between Clare and the fire. She heaved herself up onto the sofa and patted the other cushion. He jumped up obediently and they sat waiting for the logs to catch, enjoying the growing warmth.

The flames licked round the logs and, within a few minutes, they were ablaze. Reluctantly she left the fireside and went through to the kitchen, opening and closing cupboards, looking for inspiration. Resisting the temptation to take something from the freezer, she flicked the switch on the kettle and took a bag of pasta from the cupboard.

Ten minutes later, food cooking, she forced herself to take the protest march plans from her bag. She worked on, stopping only to serve up her meal which she ate quickly, her mind still on the plans. It was only when her phone buzzed with a message that she realised it was almost six o'clock. Glancing at the display she saw it was from Chris.

> Six o'clock news
> Third item
> C

'What's that about?' she muttered, hunting for the remote control. She unearthed it down the side of the sofa and clicked just as the bulletin was beginning.

> Watching now

she replied.

> After the bit on water companies

Chris advised, and she sent back a thumbs up.

A few minutes later she saw the reason for his messages.

> *A couple from St Andrews believe they've been targeted by locals who object to their plans to bring much-needed housing to the area.*

The newsreader read on, a photo of Rex and Erika on the screen. Clare groaned as the report confirmed police were taking the burglary seriously and that a link to a forthcoming protest march could not be ruled out.

'That's all we need,' she told Benjy. 'If anything it'll attract even more rabble-rousers.'

The report cut to a grim-faced Rex, standing outside the newly built front porch. He droned on about being victimised, that his wife was too distraught to appear in front of the cameras, how dispiriting it all was. Eventually Clare stopped listening. She could only imagine how other burglary victims would feel, listening to this privileged, manipulative man telling the world how seriously the police were taking the break-in. These days they were lucky if they solved even half the housebreakings in the area. That this couple should receive special treatment really pissed Clare off.

Her phone rang.

'That pair really rip my knitting,' Chris said.

She smiled at the expression. 'You and me both. Let's forget them for the rest of the night.'

'Suits me.'

'Hey, guess what?'

'Astound me.'

'I cooked.'

'Aye right.'

'No, I really did. Pasta and a jar of sauce but I did it all myself.'

Chris laughed. 'Get you, almost like a real grown up.'

'Goodbye, Sergeant.'

'Goodbye, Inspector.'

Day 3: Thursday, 12th February

Chapter 6

Clare dropped Benjy with Moira and made her way through the Bogward Estate. But, as she approached the turn off for the station, her foot hesitated over the brake then changed to the accelerator. She weaved on through the streets until she came to a small parking area at the iconic pier, the site of traditional Sunday walks by students, resplendent in their red undergraduate gowns. This early in the morning there were few cars and she drew into the first space, turning off the engine. Pulling on her gloves she stepped out and was buffeted by an icy blast. The wind must be turning to the east. She zipped up her anorak and walked smartly along Shorehead, bounded on one side by 1960s-built houses, their fronts a variety of pastel hues. The broad pavement bordered the harbour, the only barrier to the drop a succession of lobster creels dotted along the side. But there were gaps between the creels and she stood, visualising Dennis Gibb's last moments; perhaps being led to the edge to see something. A couple of sharp cracks on the back of his head then a push in the small of his back. With a few drinks inside him, he'd have been unable to stop himself falling forward. She stepped between the creels and surveyed the boats moored close to the wall wondering which one he'd been trapped under. Had his body only surfaced when the boat had chugged its way out of the harbour?

One boat caught her eye and she bent for a closer look. A long pole similar to the one Patch had shown her was secured to the side with a pair of stout brackets. Was that the kind of pole used to hold Dennis Gibb under the water? It looked to be the right size. She stood again and scanned the harbour. There must be twenty boats, maybe more. Did they all have these poles? Even if they found the one the killer had used, would that tell them anything? She looked round to see if there was anyone to speak to but this early on a winter's morning the harbour was deserted, the only sound the gentle lapping of waves against the boats. A gust of wind caught her hair, blowing it into her face and she turned away, heading for the car.

—

The post-mortem report was up on the system by the time she reached her office. She scanned it looking for anything Neil hadn't already told her but it was mainly technical detail about the blood alcohol concentration, size and sight of the injury and other information about Dennis's general health. Mindful she'd have to break the news that his death appeared suspicious, she took time to read it over in full, jotting a few points on her notepad.

She found Chris and Sara engaged in a heated discussion in the kitchen.

'It's called attribution bias.' Sara spooned coffee into mugs. 'Ask the boss. She'll tell you.'

Clare held up her hands, palms towards the pair. 'Don't bring me into this.'

'It's your fault,' Chris said. 'You're the one who made me do that stupid training. I bet you don't even know what this attri-thingy bias is.'

' 'Course I do,' Clare said, checking the cupboard for a clean mug. 'Where have all the mugs gone? I bought another six not that long ago.'

'Don't change the subject,' Chris said. 'Go on. Give us an example.'

Clare shrugged. 'I mean, I could. I just don't want to.'

'You're both hopeless,' Sara said. She turned to face them, hands resting on the work surface behind her. 'It's like this: if I arrived late for work every day you might think I was lazy, or scatterbrained, or I didn't care about being on time. You automatically judge me on that. I could be passed over for promotion, given a warning, anything like that. But you might not realise I was caring for someone and was up and down through the night. Or I might have IBS and struggle to get out of the loo in the mornings, or I might—'

'Okay,' Chris said. 'We get the point.'

'Do you, though?' Sara's cheeks were pink. 'You're so quick to judge. *That's* attribution bias. Maybe look for a reason before you condemn someone for their actions.'

'Here endeth the lesson,' Chris said, dodging a swipe from Sara.

Clare eyed Sara, wondering at her reaction. She was quite sure Chris tried his wife's patience at times but it wasn't like Sara to be so ratty. Was there more to it than Chris's diversity training? They were both avoiding her eye and she decided to change the subject. Whatever was bugging them clearly wasn't up for discussion.

'PM report on Dennis Gibb is in,' she said and Chris nodded. 'Could you call the son please? We'd better get round there this morning. And see if the daughter-in-law can be there as well. I'd like to see how they both take the news.'

She left Chris to his phone call and wandered back to her office, her mind on Dennis Gibb. Was there something in his background that might lead them to the killer?

Her office door opened and Chris ambled in. 'Twelve-thirty okay for Steve Gibb?'

'Thanks, Chris. What about the daughter-in-law?'

'She'll be there, too. It's her lunch hour, though, so she won't have long.'

Clare raised an eyebrow. 'She's not taken bereavement leave?'

'Nope. Nor has Steve. But he's on a day off so he'll be home.'

Clare sat back, twiddling a pen between her fingers. 'Should we read anything into that?'

'Nah. I doubt it. If they were involved I'd bet on them playing it by the book, sniffing into hankies, signed off by their GP. I just think they didn't get on.'

Chapter 7

Clare went in search of Patch and found her in the staff room chatting with Gillian and Mandy, two of the uniformed officers. 'Job for you.' She explained she'd been down to the harbour but found it deserted.

'It should be busier now,' she went on. 'Could you speak to anyone who has a boat moored there – fishermen as well. I want to know if anyone's missing a boat hook pole. Get the details – in fact take a statement. If there's a pole missing it could be our murder weapon – or one of them.'

Raymond called as she headed back to her office.

'I've a team heading over to your housebreaking today. Don't ask me what they're expected to find but they'll do what they can.'

'I'm sorry,' she said. 'It seems such a waste of your time, particularly as Chris and I have already tramped through the house.'

'Ach it's fine; and you never know. We might find something.'

The call done, she turned her attention to the forthcoming march, planning where to erect crowd control barriers and highlighting potential break-out points. Engrossed in her task she was surprised when Chris tapped on her door.

'We should probably get going in ten minutes or so,' he said. 'Don't want to keep the wife hanging about when she only has an hour.'

Steve and Jenny Gibb lived in a semi-detached house in the town's Kilrymont Road. It had once been the site of a busy secondary school, the pupils now moved to a more modern building on the edge of town.

'It's so much quieter since they closed the school,' Clare said.

Chris pulled in, jerking on the handbrake. 'Yeah. Quite a change for the folk living here.' He clicked off his seat belt and jumped out of the car. Clare climbed out after him, wondering if he and Sara had sorted out their differences. He didn't seem inclined to talk so she put it out of her mind and followed him over the road.

A curtain moved in a front window and she nudged Chris. 'Is that them?'

He followed her gaze. 'Yeah. Ready?'

'As I'll ever be.'

The house was set back from the road, a drive to the side leading to a single garage with a dark green up-and-over door. The front garden was similar to others in the street, a neat square of grass surrounded by a border of newly pruned roses.

They approached the front door, Clare noting the small glass panels that made these doors a magnet for housebreakers. Her mind drifted back to the Freemans and she wondered if SOCO would find anything useful. The door opened before they could knock, a man in his mid-thirties on the threshold. She saw immediately what Chris meant when he'd described the couple as looking fit. Steve Gibb stood, one hand on the door jamb, not an ounce of fat visible beneath his T-shirt. His tracky bottoms were loose, his trainers pretty new, judging by how clean they were. He wore a sleek Garmin watch on one wrist, a leather bracelet on the other. He was clean-shaven, his curly hair gelled on top, short up the sides. Clare was drawn to his eyes, dark blue with heavy brows above. He nodded at Chris then turned towards her.

'DI Clare Mackay,' she said. 'Do you mind if we come in?'

He stood back to admit them as a small dark grey Fiat pulled into the drive.

'That's Jenny,' he said. 'Must have been held up.'

They waited while a dark-haired woman climbed out of the car, a blue tunic and lanyard visible under her jacket. Like Steve, she was slightly built, long dark hair pulled back in a pony tail. She slammed the car door, clicking to lock it. Then she hurried round the car, her boots clacking on the tarmac.

'Sorry,' she said. 'Caught on a phone call.'

Clare waved this away and they followed Jenny into the house.

Steve showed them into a small sitting room with French doors leading to what appeared to be a dining kitchen.

'I'll just put the kettle on,' and he disappeared through the doors. While he was gone Clare looked round the room, trying to get a sense of the couple who lived there. An electric fire made to look like a woodburner was against one wall, set in a wooden surround. The wall above the fire was dominated by a large photo of the couple locked in an embrace, the background silver-white sand and a turquoise sea. It could have been the Outer Hebrides but, judging by their suntans, she guessed it was a more exotic location. A smaller photo to the side showed them crossing the finish line at a race, smiles broad, arms aloft. Clearly sport played a significant part in their lives.

Jenny indicated a brown leather sofa but she remained standing, as if hoping they wouldn't stay long. Steve returned and offered them tea.

'I don't have long,' Jenny said, before they could answer. 'I need to be back at one thirty and there's roadworks just outside Cupar.'

'This might take a bit longer,' Clare said. 'Would you like one of us to call the surgery? We could explain.'

The couple looked at each other, Steve's brow clouded.

'Why longer?'

'There's a complication with your father's death,' she said.

'What sort of complication?' He spoke slowly and Clare thought she could see the wheels turning.

'We think his death may not have been accidental.'

'Not – what?' Steve's voice rose. 'You mean someone did something to him?'

Jenny's hand was over her mouth now and Clare saw the rise and fall of her chest.

'Maybe we could have that cup of tea,' she said. 'Chris here is a dab hand with a tea bag.' She turned to Jenny. 'He'll give the surgery a call. Let them know you might be a bit longer.'

Jenny's eyes were flicking left and right. 'I don't understand,' she said. 'What happened? Did he not just fall in the water?'

Steve's hands were fists now, the knuckles white. He was staring at Clare, his lips pressed together, and she had the impression he was trying to control himself.

'I know this must be a shock,' she said.

He opened his mouth to speak and it seemed to take him a moment to form the words. 'Someone did this?' There was a catch in his voice. 'Someone deliberately...'

'We think so,' Clare said. From the kitchen she could hear the sound of a kettle coming to the boil. 'Let's have some tea then we can explain.'

Chris made to rise but Steve was too quick for him.

'I'll do it.' And he strode towards the kitchen.

Clare wondered at his haste to leave the room. Was it a coping mechanism? Maybe he was one of those men who thought showing emotion was a sign of weakness.

Jenny's eyes followed him, her face creased with concern. 'Steve?'

He turned back, his hand on the door jamb. 'Erm, sorry, Jen. Want a tea?'

She stared at him for a moment. 'Yes please.'

Chris and Clare exchanged glances and he took the hint, rising to follow Steve to the kitchen.

Jenny sank down on an easy chair and gave Clare an apologetic look. 'He's upset,' she said. 'It's just his way.'

Clare nodded. 'Everyone reacts differently. It must be a shock. For you both.'

From the kitchen Clare could hear the chink of mugs then the sound of the fridge door opening and closing. Tea making was in progress. They returned a minute later, Steve bearing a tray. He set it down and Clare saw there were three mugs and a dark blue water bottle. She waited while he handed the mugs out, watching as he settled on the arm of his wife's chair, water bottle in hand. Jenny cradled her mug and Steve unscrewed the lid of his bottle. Clare waited while he drank then she began.

'I can't go into detail,' she said, 'but we think your father may have been pushed into the harbour.'

Steve blinked a couple of times. 'Someone pushed him in?'

'But it's not even that deep,' Jenny said. 'Could he not get out?'

'We're working on the assumption he entered the harbour sometime late, the night before you reported him missing. If so, the tide was in. That would have made it more difficult for him to clamber out. The post-mortem also showed he'd been drinking. It's possible he wasn't alert enough to help himself.'

Jenny's hand was over her face now, the other hand still cradling the mug.

'Maybe have some of that tea,' Chris said, his voice gentle but she began to shake as the shock of the news overtook her. He leaned over and took the mug from her hand, setting it down on the coffee table.

Clare eyed Steve, waiting for him to comfort his wife. But his face was stony, eyes on the floor. Finally he lifted his gaze.

'Who did this?' His voice was husky, thick with emotion.

'That's what we aim to find out,' Clare said. 'But we need your help. We want to learn as much as we can about Mr Gibb. So the more you can tell us the better.' She softened her expression. 'Is that okay?'

Jenny began to cry quietly, dabbing her eyes with a tissue. The sound seemed to unlock something in Steve and his face crumpled.

'I – we didn't get on,' he said. 'Didn't see eye to eye – but he was my dad,' he finished, a tremor in his voice. He reached for the bottle again and took a long drink. Then he replaced the lid, wiping his mouth with his hand. He cleared his throat and met Clare's eye. 'What do you want to know?'

Gradually, the couple began giving life and colour to Dennis Gibb. Clare learned he'd been a night porter in a few of the town hotels over the years.

'He was made redundant five years ago,' Steve went on. 'The last hotel he worked at closed down. Gave him a decent pay off so he decided to retire.'

Jenny sighed. 'We thought he'd love it. Being able to please himself. But he just sat around all day, watching Sky Sports.'

'Or drinking,' Steve put in. 'He pretty much drank his redundancy.'

'Did he have a favourite pub?' Clare asked and Steve shook his head.

'I heard he'd been thrown out of a couple.'

'Oh?' Clare sat forward. 'Any idea which ones?'

Steve and Jenny looked at each other. 'The Harvest Moon for one,' Steve said and Clare nodded. She knew it, an unremarkable pub near the West Port, well away from the harbour.

'Where might he have gone for a drink, then?' she asked.

Jenny's brow was creased, her eyes narrowed as if trying to remember. They waited and their patience was rewarded. 'That little one off North Street,' she said. 'Down one of the lanes.'

'The Yardstick?' Steve said. 'You think he went there?'

'Definitely. Remember he left his wallet?' Her face cleared. 'Oh, you were away for the weekend.' She turned back to Clare. 'He'd left his wallet there one night and they couldn't get hold of him. My number was in the wallet so they phoned me.'

Clare noted *The Yardstick* on her notepad. 'Was he still a customer – recently, I mean?'

Jenny considered this. 'Yes. I think he might have been and it would fit with him being at the harbour.'

'We'll check it out,' Clare said. She asked a few more questions but it seemed Dennis was a loner, no real friends. Steve and Jenny were his only family. Clare asked for the keys to his cottage and Steve rose from his seat.

'Think they're in the kitchen drawer.' He disappeared through the French doors and Jenny sat on, twisting a gold band round and round her finger.

'Nice photo,' Clare said, indicating the framed shot of the couple on the beach.

Her eyes followed Clare's. 'Our wedding.'

'Abroad?'

'Jamaica,' she said. 'Such a lovely island and a wonderful climate. They have a reggae marathon,' she added.

Clare stared. 'A what?'

A smile crossed Jenny's face. Obviously a happy memory. 'It's a marathon race but with reggae music played along the route. Probably the most fun race we've ever run.'

Clare looked at the photo. 'Was that when you got married?'

'No. Different trip. We ran the race a few years earlier. It was such a lovely holiday. So, when we decided to get married, Steve said wouldn't it be amazing to be married out there. It was a huge surprise, actually. Steve suggested it and, when I said it sounded lovely, he said it was all arranged. All I had to do was agree.'

'Goodness,' Clare said. 'What a wonderful surprise. Did all your friends and family join you?'

Jenny shook her head. 'Steve didn't want Dennis there. They'd fallen out and Steve reckoned he'd get drunk. My dad had just had a heart op and he wasn't fit enough to travel. So we had a quiet wedding on the beach with a couple of local witnesses and a party when we got home. It was a lovely day and our friends didn't have to fork out for air tickets.'

She was smiling brightly at the memory but Clare thought there was something in her eyes. Something troubling her. 'Would you have liked to have had your family there?'

Jenny took a moment to reply and, in that time, Clare had her answer. Steve had railroaded her into the wedding he wanted because he didn't get on with his dad.

'It was just easier that way,' Jenny said eventually.

'What was easier?' Steve reappeared, a set of keys in his hand.

'Our wedding,' she said, her tone light.

He was watching Jenny intently and Clare wondered what Jenny wasn't saying. Then he turned back to Clare. 'He'd have ruined it, you know, my dad.' He shook his head. 'I loved him, Inspector, and I can't bear to think of him suffering, struggling in that freezing water, trying to...' he broke off, his voice husky.

Clare waited and, after a minute, he cleared his throat. 'I really did love him. But I have to be honest. I didn't much like him. He drank, you see? And, when he drank, he didn't know when to stop.'

He resumed his seat next to Jenny, taking her hand in his. 'I wanted our day to be perfect. Everyone has the right to expect that on their wedding day, don't they? If we'd had it here and he'd found out he'd have – well let's just say I wasn't about to let that happen.' He leaned over and kissed the top of Jenny's head, a gesture so tender it brought a lump to Clare's throat. But there was a stiffness to Jenny, something in her demeanour that told Clare there was more to what Steve had said.

She rose from her seat and nodded at Chris. 'We'll leave you now. But if anything does occur to you please give me a call.'

They emerged into the cool afternoon air, the sun already low in the sky.

'What do you reckon?' Chris said, glancing back at the house.

Clare was quiet for a moment. She clicked to unlock the car and jumped in, turning the key in the ignition. 'They certainly didn't get on,' she said, her eyes straying to the house. 'But I can't see either of them shoving him in the water.'

'Might have had a row.'

'True. Fit of temper and he gives his dad a shove. But the blows to the back of the head, the pole – wherever that came from – that's far more than an argument. That's clearly an attempt to kill.'

Chris tugged on his seat belt. 'What about the wife?'

Clare turned to face him. 'She wasn't happy about that wedding, was she?'

'You reckon?'

'Think about it, Chris. How would Sara have reacted if you'd said you wanted a wedding thousands of miles away with a couple of locals as witnesses?'

'Fair point. You think there's something there?'

'Hmm, I'm not sure. And there's something else as well.'

'Go on.'

'If our Dennis was a hot-headed drunk, as Steve claims, how do you reckon he'd react to not being invited to his only son's wedding?' She glanced over her shoulder and pulled out into the road. 'I'm going to say not well.'

Chapter 8

Dennis Gibb's cottage was south of the town, a mile and a half from the harbour where he'd met his end. It was a typical roadside cottage on an elevated site, a low single-storey building with windows either side of a wooden front door. A short drive missing a set of gates led to a wooden garage, its doors secured by a hefty bolt and Clare pulled the car in, off the road. They sat for a minute, surveying the cottage. Perhaps it was knowing what had happened to the owner but it struck Clare as a house that hadn't been loved or cared for – not for a good many years. Paint was peeling off the window frames, the panes obscured by condensation inside and the chimney stack was in need of pointing.

'I suppose we are okay to go in,' Chris said, 'with his death being suspicious.'

'Yeah, we're fine. It's not a crime scene.'

They approached the front door, Chris jingling the keys in his hand. There were several Yales on the keyring and he took a minute trying each in the lock while Clare did a circuit of the cottage. There was a textured glass window on the end wall, a bathroom she guessed and she carried on round the back through a gate, hanging by a single hinge. A small square of grass was bounded on two sides by an overgrown privet hedge, the remains of a wire fence on the other, its wooden poles bent by the prevailing wind.

A clothes rope hung limply between a pair of cast iron washing poles, a set of four wheelie bins to the side. The lid of the blue one was forced up by its overflowing contents, several empty bottles sticking out the side. In front of the bins a steel manhole cover was set into a concrete slab, access to a septic tank, Clare guessed.

An icy gust caught her hair, blowing it over her eyes and she turned her face into the wind to let the hair blow back. She saw now why Dennis Gibb hadn't allowed the privet hedge to spread across the old wire fence. The elevated view towards the town was breathtaking, orange roof tiles warmed in the sun, the glinting waters of the Eden Estuary beyond. The cottage might be forlorn and unloved but it could make a wonderful home for the right person. She took in the back of the building. It wasn't much different from the front except for a skylight in the roof, an attic room, perhaps.

As she stood, guessing what lay behind each window, the back door opened with a loud creak, Chris on the threshold.

'You coming in?'

The wind caught Clare's hair again and she walked towards the door, rubbing her hands together.

'I hope you're not expecting a heat in here,' Chris said. 'It's Baltic.'

She stepped up and into a square sparsely furnished kitchen, scanning the room for an inkling as to how Dennis Gibb had lived. But there was little here to tell them about the man. Opposite the door, a yellow Formica table stood against the wall, a wooden chair at either end. The table was bare, apart from a folded newspaper, open at the sports page. A frying pan sat on a freestanding electric cooker, a box of eggs on the counter top to the side. The wall beneath the window was home to a stainless-steel sink, an empty dishrack on the draining board. A saucepan was soaking in the sink, an oily film on top, the remains of Dennis Gibb's last supper, she guessed – quite literally.

The door to a small passageway stood open, a bare bulb dangling from the ceiling. Chris indicated the door and Clare followed him through to another room. Here there were more signs of life. A bucket of coal stood to the side of a tiled fireplace, a box of firelighters next to it. An easy chair was drawn up to the fire, a pair of tartan slippers in front, ready to be warmed by the blaze. There was a laptop on the floor next to the chair, the cable trailing to a socket on the skirting board.

'We'll take that,' Clare said and Chris nodded, bending to pull out the plug.

A clothes airer stood in front of the window, draped with T-shirts and socks, most of which had seen better days. Clare reached out to touch an off-white vest top. It was hard to tell if it was damp or just cold and she pulled her arms around herself, trying to get warm. There were a few other odd bits of furniture including a narrow bookcase, an assortment of bric-a-brac arranged along the top. Clare couldn't imagine there was anything of value here and there was certainly no sign of a disturbance. Could the attack on Dennis have been random? Just a pub fight that got out of hand? Somehow she didn't think the answer lay in this modestly furnished cottage.

Across the passageway, another door led to a bedroom. By contrast to the sitting room, the furniture here was a matching set: bed, dressing table and wardrobe all in dark wood. Maybe Dennis and his wife had chosen it together when they'd married; and now they were both gone.

'What did the wife die of?'

Chris shrugged. 'Didn't ask.'

She said nothing for a moment, waiting for him to acknowledge the omission. 'Check it, please?' she said eventually.

He glanced at her but he seemed unconcerned. 'Yeah okay.' He looked round the room. 'Box of papers here. Bills I think. Want it?'

'Might as well.' She stood thinking. 'We've not found a phone.'

'On the body. Wrecked after a week in the water.'

She smiled. 'Of course. Let's get his phone records, then. See who he was in touch with just before he died. Bank records too

– and I'd like to know what's in his will – if he made one.' She shivered again. 'Jesus, it's cold in here. Come on.' She indicated the door. 'I could do with a hot drink.'

Chapter 9

Sara was in the station kitchen when they arrived back. 'Kettle's just boiled.'

Clare reached up to the cupboard and took down two mugs, peering at them. 'These are filthy!'

Chris leaned over her shoulder. 'They look okay to me.'

She went to the sink and turned on the tap, waiting for the water to run hot. 'I'll give them a good scrub.'

'I keep mine in my locker,' Sara said.

'You do right.' Clare ran steaming water into the sink adding a good squeeze of Fairy liquid. 'Anything new?'

'CCTV from a couple of pubs.'

'The Yardstick?'

Sara shook her head. 'Said it wasn't working.'

Clare rinsed the mugs under the tap and put them on the dishrack to drain. 'Did you check it?'

'Yeah. They let me have a look. It hasn't worked for weeks, apparently. To be honest, it's not a great setup. Might not have been much use. But I did have a thought.'

'Oh, yes?'

'I could go door-to-door along North Street. Check who has doorcam footage.'

Clare threw her a smile. 'Good idea. You're looking for Dennis, obviously, and anyone who might have been following him.'

'I found a photo of Dennis on Facebook. I'll take copies with me.'

'Excellent!' Clare glanced at Chris. 'Why didn't you think of that?'

Sara beamed and Clare waited for Chris's usual sarcastic quip. He was opening and closing cupboard doors, looking for something to eat, she guessed. Finally, he found a half open packet of custard creams and he popped one in his mouth. Sara was watching him as well but he steadfastly ignored them both.

Clare watched him for a moment longer then busied herself with the mugs. Whatever was going on between them she didn't want to get in the middle of it. She picked up a tea towel and dried the mugs. 'Coffee?'

Before Chris could answer, Clare's phone began ringing. Raymond – calling from the Freemans' house, she guessed. She swiped to take the call, fully expecting him to say they'd found nothing.

'Hi—' she began but he cut across her.

'There's something here you need to see.'

–

'It was Molly who spotted it,' Raymond said, his eyes on the ceiling. 'She noticed it was different from the others.'

'Any prints?' Clare asked and Raymond nodded.

'Not sure we'll be able to find much. Lots of smudging, as you can imagine. It's not easy, working above your head.'

'Do they know?'

Raymond shook his head. 'They're out. Couldn't have them here while we were working.'

'Fair enough. I'll give them a call.'

Clare took out her phone but a movement from the window caught her eye as the dark blue Lexus swept onto the drive. 'Where can I take them?'

Raymond indicated the rear of the house. 'We're not doing the kitchen. There's no sign anyone's been in there. Loads of room, too. The table's huge.'

Chris went to meet the couple while Clare walked down a short hallway that opened onto a bright kitchen. From the dimensions she thought it was close to the full width of the house. Cream units ran along two sides with a sky-blue Aga against one wall. Next to this there were two light oak doors. Larders? A utility room? Might even be a wine store. The house seemed to have everything else.

A wide casement window gave onto a long garden with a hot tub on the patio.

'I'm in the wrong business,' she muttered, turning as the sound of voices approached.

She greeted the Freemans and suggested they sit at the table. As Raymond had said, it was enormous, a light oak top with legs painted a soft green. Bespoke, Clare guessed. It was far too large and lovely to be mass produced.

Rex eyed them, his expression impassive. Erika picked up the kettle and held it under the tap.

'I need a coffee,' she said, setting it down to boil, her back to them. Clare wondered if it was a distraction technique. Something to calm her nerves. If so, what was she afraid of? Surely their worst nightmare had been the burglary. She glanced at Chris who gave a noncommittal gesture.

Erika busied herself taking bone china mugs from a cupboard and opening a packet of almond biscuits. She set these on a tray and carried it over to the table. Rex, still on his feet, moved to the kettle.

'I'll make it.' He turned back to Clare and Chris. 'Coffee all right?'

Clare smiled. 'That would be lovely. If it's no trouble.'

A few minutes later they sat round the table, the Freemans' eyes never leaving Clare's.

'Our Scene of Crimes Officers found something,' she began. 'Something unusual.'

Rex plunged the cafetiere. 'Oh yes?'

'One of your smoke alarms looked different from the others. Had you noticed?'

Whatever the Freemans had expected Clare to say it clearly wasn't this. They exchanged glances then Rex found his voice.

'Different? How, exactly?'

'It's not a smoke alarm for a start,' Clare said. 'It's a replica.'

Rex's eyes narrowed as he processed this. 'I don't understand,' he said, finally. 'What's the point of that? It's not like they're expensive.'

A conversation with one of Clare's officers came into her mind. Complaining about the cost of fitting interlinked smoke alarms in every room. Nearly a hundred quid, she'd said. A lot for anyone struggling with a large mortgage, but for this pair? A drop in the ocean.

'It's what it concealed,' she said, watching them carefully. 'The alarm casing was used to house a camera.'

There was no mistaking the shock on the couple's faces.

'A – camera?' Erika said at last. 'What sort of camera?'

'The kind that records what happens in the room,' Clare said. 'It's a security device.'

'You mean someone's been spying on us?' Rex's jaw was tight, a tiny drop of spittle on his chin. Erika's hands were on her cheeks now, eyes on her husband.

'As to that,' Clare said, 'we can't be certain. There's no SD card built in which is unusual. It'll have to be examined by our technical experts but it's possible it was transmitting remotely.'

She saw Rex flex and unflex his fingers and she had the sense he was battling with his temper. 'This is my home,' he said, finally. 'My home – and someone's put a camera on the ceiling?' His tone was level but the warning note was unmistakable. Clare noticed he'd said *my home,* not *our home.* The Freemans were clearly a powerhouse couple but she had no doubt, if it came to it, that Rex would put his own interests ahead of his wife's. There was an edge to his manner that suggested a streak of ruthlessness.

She hesitated. 'Yes. That's correct.'

The colour had drained from Erika's face.

'Maybe you should have some coffee,' Clare said, pushing a mug towards her.

Erika stared at her then down at the coffee.

'It's them, isn't it?' Rex's voice was rising now. 'Those bloody protestors. They've broken in here and when they didn't find anything they've left a camera, hoping to catch us out. It's a bloody outrage.'

Erika's eyes were on her husband, as though looking for a cue from his reaction. Then she nodded vigorously. 'It must be them. Who else would do something like that?'

'You can arrest them, can't you?' Rex said. 'And stop that march while you're at it. It can't go on now. Not when they're doing stuff like this.'

Clare let him speak, sipping her coffee while he made a succession of demands. She wasn't so sure the break-in was the work of protestors. She reckoned they'd have made it obvious the burglary was a response to his plans. Otherwise, what was the point? But she let him talk on, watching him carefully. Finally he seemed to run out of things to say and he sat back in his chair, fingers drumming on the table.

'As to who's responsible,' Clare began, 'it's too early to say. But our technical team will be in touch as soon as they know anything.'

'I take it the camera isn't yours?' Chris asked.

'Obviously not!'

Chris held up his hands, a conciliatory gesture. 'We do have to ask.'

Rex gave a slight nod. 'Sorry. Of course you do. It's just a shock.'

'And you've no idea who might have installed it?' Chris went on.

'None.'

Clare was watching Erika carefully. It wouldn't be the first time a wife had fitted a spycam to find out what her husband was up to – or vice versa. Clare couldn't be sure but Erika's body language wasn't betraying prior knowledge of the camera. You never could tell, though.

'I'd like to ask your internet service provider for details of recent activity,' she went on.

Rex raised an eyebrow. 'Is that really necessary?'

'It might help us find the person behind the camera, assuming anyone is. It could simply be left over from a previous owner. But, if someone has been using your Wi-Fi we'll be able to trace them.'

Rex shrugged. 'If we refuse I suppose you'll get a warrant.'

'It would be a help,' Clare said. 'Could save us time.'

'Fine, then. Do what you like.'

Clare turned to Erika. Her brow was creased and Clare wondered if she'd been concealing something from her husband. There was definitely something not right with this pair. 'Mrs Freeman?'

She made a noncommittal gesture with her hand. 'Yes, of course.'

Clare took a drink of coffee, letting the question of their browsing history hang in the air. When neither appeared to have anything to add she carried on.

'Have you had any work done on the house recently? Any workmen in?'

The couple exchanged glances. 'Of course,' Erika said, finding her voice. 'We've only been here six months but we've decorated, had the boiler serviced, new light sockets.' Her brow furrowed. 'I'm sure there were others. I just can't remember.'

'And were any of them here while you were out of the house?'

Erika's hand went to her forehead and she massaged her temples, as if trying to clear her thoughts. 'I – erm, maybe. Yes, I think so.'

'What about the smoke alarms? Did you install them?'

'Already here,' Rex said. 'The vendor wouldn't have been able to sell without them.'

Clare sat thinking for a minute. 'If you could make a list of everyone who's had access since you moved in — names and phone numbers — that would be a huge help.'

Rex nodded. 'Of course. You'll want our cleaning lady's details as well.'

'Thanks,' Clare said. 'That would be good.' Rex seemed to have calmed down so she pressed on. 'What about your business — might you have clashed with someone recently?'

He laughed, but his eyes remained cold. 'In this line of work, Inspector, you're always upsetting someone. Half the town seems to be up in arms at the moment.'

'What about rival companies?'

He shook his head. 'Usually by the time a piece of land comes up for sale it's clear which of us has the money. A plot like ours in a place like St Andrews — you won't get your social housing companies bidding for that. They can't turn enough of a profit to justify the price tag.'

'You weren't in competition for the land?'

He considered this. 'I wouldn't say that entirely. There's always someone interested. But we make a point of cultivating relationships with builders and other trades. We make it worth their while to work exclusively for us. That can make it — difficult for other developers.'

Clare had to admire his business acumen. She was starting to see why the couple were so successful. 'Apart from concerns over your forthcoming development, can you think of anyone with a motive to install this camera?'

'Let me save you a job,' he said. 'Haul in the march organisers. Apply a bit of pressure. I guarantee you'll find one of them's behind it.'

He saw them to the door, promising to email over a list of people who'd accessed the house since they'd moved in.

As Clare and Chris walked towards the car, Erika appeared at her husband's shoulder. 'Inspector?'

Clare turned back towards the house. 'Yes?'

'Which room was it?'

She stood, taking a moment before she answered. 'Your front sitting room. The one we sat in yesterday.'

Chapter 10

'What do you reckon?' Chris said as Clare pulled out into Hepburn Gardens.

She was quiet for a moment. 'Not sure. I can't make them out.'

'I think they're hiding something.'

'Agreed.' She slowed at the mini-roundabout to let a van pass, then swung the car round. 'The question is what?'

'Do you buy his theory about the march organisers?'

'Nope. Not for a minute. My guess is he saw an opportunity to get the march stopped, have the protestors thrown in jail.'

'He could have a point, though,' Chris said. 'If Penny's right about the march being infiltrated by activists it could be them. Maybe they were watching the house. Saw the Freemans put cases in the car and thought they'd be away overnight.'

'Could the burglary have been a cover for installing the camera?' Clare said.

'Dunno. Maybe. It would explain why nothing was taken.'

'Let's hope Tech Support can tell us something, then.' She followed the road round and into Argyle Street.

'Fancy a doughnut?' Chris suggested. 'We could stop at Fisher & Donaldson.'

'No time. I want to call into the estate agent's – the one who sold that house. What was the name, again?'

'Feddinch Property Solutions,' Chris said. 'South Street.'

Clare knew it. She crossed the roundabout and drove through the West Port, the sixteenth-century town gate. South Street was bustling with activity, groups of red-gowned students hurrying between lectures, others strolling along, phones clamped to their ears. One or two cafes had tables and chairs on the pavement, a few hardy souls enjoying a coffee in what remained of the low afternoon sun.

'There!' Chris said, indicating a maroon car whose reversing lights had come on. Clare signalled to pull in, hanging back while the car reversed out of the diagonal space.

Her phone began to ring – Patch. She swiped to answer the call, putting it on speaker.

'We might have the boat hook pole,' she said.

'Oh, yes?'

'One of the fisherman – Zac McKiddie. Seems he's had a bit of trouble with students messing about late at night. When his pole went missing he assumed they were responsible. Then he found it floating at the other side of the harbour.'

'When was this?'

'About a week ago,' Patch said. 'He couldn't be exact. But it looks to be about the right size.' She hesitated. 'You want it over to SOCO? It's pretty long.'

Clare thought for a moment. 'Is it still in the water?'

'No. He managed to fish it out and he's been out in the boat with it a couple of times since.'

Chris was shaking his head. 'Chances are any DNA will be gone by now.'

'I agree,' Clare said. 'Patch, could you get photos please? And an accurate measurement, then send both over to Raymond. See if he thinks it could have caused the bruising on Dennis's chest.'

'Will do.'

Clare ended the call and tucked her phone away. 'Ready?'

They climbed out of the car, Clare scanning the street for Feddinch's office.

'Over here,' Chris said, guiding her towards the zebra crossing.

They reached the pavement and Clare stopped, her thoughts back at the Freemans' house. 'Is it possible they put it up themselves? The camera,' she added.

Chris steered her away from an elderly woman, making steady and determined progress with a mobility walker, her head bent against the oncoming breeze. 'I guess. But why lie about it?'

'Maybe they do know who's responsible for the burglary. Maybe they've seen the footage.'

Chris's eyes narrowed. 'Like who?'

'I dunno. A business rival, blackmailer – I wouldn't put it past that pair to try and get round the planning rules. Maybe they're right. Someone is trying to dig up some dirt on them.'

'So, if they do have the footage…'

'Why not share it with us?' Clare finished.

She began walking again, turning it over in her mind. There was definitely something off about the Freemans.

Feddinch Property Solutions was halfway along South Street, the bright shop front glowing in the fading afternoon light. The windows were filled with photographs of houses for sale and they stopped to look at a few.

'The prices round here are astonishing,' Clare said, shaking her head. 'I don't know how anyone gets on the housing ladder these days.'

'Tell me about it,' Chris said. 'We're gonna be stuck in that flat till the end of time.'

The door dinged as Clare pushed it open and they walked into the bright interior. There was a long reception desk opposite the door, with more adverts for houses, left and right. A woman in a navy jumper was tapping at a keyboard and she smiled as they approached. Her name badge read

Melanie

Feddinch Property Solutions

Clare introduced herself and Chris, and asked to speak to whoever was in charge.

'That's Carol,' Melanie said. 'She's the property manager. She's with a client just now. Is there anything I can help with?'

Clare shook her head. 'We'll wait, if that's okay.'

Melanie offered them a drink but Clare waved it away. A phone began ringing and she returned to her duties.

They wandered across to look at the house adverts, Clare indicating a one-bedroom flat with an eye-watering price tag. 'It doesn't even have double glazing.'

Chris made no reply, lingering over a couple of adverts for small houses. Clare saw him take photos with his phone but she didn't press him on it.

After ten minutes browsing houses neither of them could afford, Clare's patience was running thin. She was on the point of asking Melanie to interrupt Carol when she heard the sound of voices. A woman in a yellow raincoat emerged from a door to the right of the reception desk, another grey-haired woman at her back. The raincoat woman turned and held out her hand. After a brief handshake and a promise to *be in touch* the raincoat woman left, giving Clare a smile as she went. Melanie rose and spoke quietly to the other woman who glanced over to Clare and Chris, then disappeared through the door, letting it swing behind her.

'She'll just be a minute,' Melanie said and Clare smiled her thanks.

Five minutes later, they were shown into a wood-panelled office to the rear of the building. The only window had opaque glass, the room lit by a central spotlight. A silver iMac sat on a heavy wooden desk, a mesh-backed office chair behind. Carol Merryweather came forward, hand outstretched and introduced herself as the property manager. She was the model of efficiency, Clare decided, not one of her slate-grey hairs out of place. Clare was struck by how tall she was, almost the same height as Chris. She was simply dressed in a long navy tunic-blouse and dark grey trousers, a silver necklace and earrings the only adornment. Clare noticed she wore a plain gold band on her right hand and she wondered idly if it had belonged to a relative, rather than a symbol of her own marriage. Her mother's ring, perhaps.

'How long have you worked here?' Clare asked, settling herself on a padded chair.

'Ten years as manager, five years as a property assistant before that.'

'You must enjoy the work.'

Carol inclined her head. 'It can be interesting. Challenging, even. But I've always enjoyed working with sellers, helping them make their homes attractive to potential buyers.'

After an exchange of pleasantries, Clare got to the point. 'You sold a house in Hepburn Gardens about six months ago.'

Carol raised an eyebrow. 'I've sold several in that street. One of the most sought after in the town. Do you have the house number?'

Clare looked at Chris and he shook his head. 'A large house in cream render,' she said and Carol nodded. 'I think I know the one you mean.'

'A Mr and Mrs Freeman,' Clare added.

'I remember them well,' Carol said. 'If I'm not mistaken they're the couple behind the new housing development, yes?'

Clare wondered if it was unusual for an estate agent to recall details of a former client's business, six months after a sale had been concluded. Then she remembered the Freemans were a high-profile couple. Glamorous and powerful. In Carol's shoes she'd probably remember them as well.

'Yes, that's them.'

Carol's brow clouded. 'I hope there's no problem. The sale went through quite smoothly. Months ago, now.'

Clare smiled. 'Hopefully not. But I wonder if you could give us some information please?'

'If I can. The file will be archived, though. Might take a bit of time to pull it out. But I'll have most of the details on our database. Erm...' she seemed to consider something. 'If it's confidential we might need a warrant. I'm not sure.' She reached for a mobile on the desk. 'I may have to take advice.'

Clare glanced at Chris. She didn't want to waste any more time on this. They had Dennis Gibb's killer to find. 'Perhaps we could ask a few questions and, if you're not sure, then you could make a call. Check what you can tell us.'

Carol considered this then gave them a smile. 'Ask away, then.'

Suddenly, Clare wondered where to start. Usually she knew the answers they were seeking, the questions falling naturally from that. But this case? A burglary where nothing had been taken, a hidden camera the homeowners seemed unaware of – where on earth to begin? And then her training kicked in. Go back to the start. Take a history in chronological order. Problem was, when had this started? How long had that camera been there? Maybe it would be easier to work backwards.

'Can you tell me which members of your staff visited the house?'

The question seemed to surprise Carol and she sat thinking for a minute. 'Hm. I was probably first to go. I visited the property to get a feel for it, find out how the vendor wanted to proceed, give them an indication of the selling price – that kind of thing.' Her brow creased as if trying to remember. 'It was probably Eric who went next. Eric Richards. He's our photographer. He'd have gone round a day or two later, taking photographs and a video.' She broke off as if thinking. 'Unless he was on holiday. I'd have to check.'

'Is Mr Richards here?' Clare asked.

Carol shook her head. 'Out on a job.' She moved to her iMac and began tapping at the keyboard. 'If you'll bear with me...'

They waited and after a minute Carol pushed the keyboard away. 'I don't think he'll be back today. He should be in tomorrow, though.'

'Would you ask him to call into the station please? We need to check something with him.'

Carol's eyes narrowed. 'Is there a problem with the house?'

Clare studied her, wondering if she knew about the camera. Unlikely, she thought, but they couldn't rule anything out. 'When you visited the house what sort of checks did you carry out?'

'Checks?'

Clare decided there was little point in keeping what they'd found from Carol. 'The smoke alarms,' she said. 'Do you check they're compliant?'

The colour drained from Carol's face. 'There's not been a fire has there?'

'Oh no,' Clare said quickly. 'Nothing like that. But there does seem to be a problem with one of the alarms.'

Carol was watching her carefully. 'I'm guessing a pretty serious problem, given you're here, talking to me.'

'We need to know who would be responsible for checking them.'

'In that case you want the surveyor. We use Grenville Thomas at Pembertons.'

She reached over to a tray, leafing through a selection of business cards. 'Here,' she said. 'You can keep this.'

Clare glanced at the card.

> Grenville Thomas, MRICS
>
> Chartered Surveyor
>
> Pemberton & Co

She slipped it into her pocket then turned back to Carol. 'Just to be clear, you didn't touch any of the alarms yourself?'

'No. Look, can I ask what this is about?'

Clare hesitated. She wanted to hold back as much information as possible, at least until they knew more about the camera. 'One of the alarms was a replica,' she said, avoiding mention of the hidden camera.

Carol's eyes widened. 'A replica? You mean it wasn't genuine? Which one?'

Clare ignored the question. 'You didn't know about it?'

She stared at Clare. 'I mean – how would I know? Did it look different from the others?'

'We don't think so,' Clare said. 'It seems no one's spotted it until now.'

Carol's eyes were flitting left and right and Clare wondered if she was considering whether Feddinch Property Solutions might have been negligent in not spotting the fake alarm. Clare herself wasn't sure. If there had been a fire at the house might someone have been guilty of criminal negligence?

'We'll need contact details for the previous owners,' Clare said, moving quickly on. She didn't want to give Carol the chance to ask any more questions about the alarm. 'Do you know how long they were in the property?'

Carol thought for a moment. 'Not offhand. I can look it up, though.' She checked her watch. 'I'll call you tomorrow, if that's okay?'

Clare reached into her pocket and withdrew a business card. 'Here's my number.' She rose, nodding to Chris. 'We won't keep you any longer. But if you could ask your photographer to call into the station.'

There was a tap on the door and Melanie opened it a little. Carol looked up, one eyebrow raised, clearly surprised at the interruption.

'I'm so sorry to interrupt, Carol but there's an urgent call from…' she tailed off, one eye on Clare and Chris.

'Broomfaulds?'

Relief swam over Melanie's face. 'Yes. They asked if you could phone back as soon as possible.'

Carol's shoulders sagged and Clare nodded to Chris. They rose and thanked Carol, leaving her to her phone call. As they moved through the front office Chris hung back, lingering by one of the *For Sale* adverts. Clare nudged his elbow. 'House hunt in your own time.'

They emerged into the street, Clare surprised to see it was raining. 'This wasn't forecast, was it?'

'Dunno. What's the hurry anyway? There's a house back there might suit me and Sara.'

Clare turned her collar up against the rain. The temperature had dropped and it was turning to sleet now. She made for the zebra crossing and put up a hand, acknowledging a car that had slowed to let them cross. 'How about a murder, a housebreaking, a hidden camera and a protest march. That do you?'

And, with that, she strode off towards the car, Chris trailing in her wake.

Chapter 11

The sleet was coming down hard by the time they reached the station. Clare made for her office, shrugging off her coat. She ran a hand through her hair, wet with sleet and thought about the Freemans' smoke alarm. Who had installed that camera and, more importantly, why?

There was a tap on the door and Chris came in. 'Dennis Gibb's wife.'

'Oh, yes?'

'Just had the cause of death through. Ruptured aneurysm, nine years ago.'

Clare sat back in her chair. 'Not suspicious, then.'

'Nope. Pretty catastrophic. Dennis was there when it happened, apparently.' He shook his head. 'She was only forty-nine. No wonder he drank.'

'What about his will?'

'I left a message with his solicitor; and I've requested his phone and bank records as well. Might be a day or two, though.' He hesitated. 'Not much more we can do tonight.'

Clare glanced at her watch. It wasn't five yet but it had been a busy day and tomorrow might be busier still. 'Go on, then. Get off home. But in sharp tomorrow, yeah?'

Left alone, she sat thinking about Dennis Gibb and his wife. Forty-nine was no age at all. Might he have been different if she hadn't died? Maybe he'd have spent more time at home and he wouldn't now be lying in a mortuary fridge. Her thoughts turned to Al and his new job. They were spending most of their week apart now, him at the police college, her working all the hours whenever a major crime was reported. Were they doing the right thing? Or was life passing them by while they were both too busy to notice?

She took out her phone to check for messages. Al could work from home on Fridays so he ought to be back soon. She had hoped he might be home early enough to pick up Benjy; but there was no message so it didn't look like he would be. Her to-do list was a mile long but it couldn't be helped. She'd have to work on from home.

She logged off her computer and went to the incident room to see who was there. Max and Patch were tapping at laptops and they looked up as she entered.

'I'm heading home,' she said, 'unless there's anything?'

Max shook his head. 'I'm on Dennis Gibb's work history. Patch is checking his social media.'

'Anything interesting?'

'Nah. Pretty dull so far. Worked for a few hotels in the town, one over in Dundee. Mostly temporary contracts. Nothing that looks dodgy.'

'Maybe phone round the last couple,' Clare said. 'Make sure there were no disciplinaries. The son told us he'd been thrown out of a couple of pubs in the town. Could be he was a bit of a hothead, particularly with a drink in him.' She turned to Patch. 'What about his social media?'

Patch moved the laptop so Clare could see the screen. 'The original keyboard warrior,' she said. 'Not backward at giving his opinions.'

'Anyone local involved?'

Patch nodded. 'Think so. I'll have to check everyone he's had a barney with but it's possible.'

Clare smiled. 'Keep at it. Someone was upset enough to push him into the water then use a long pole to make sure he didn't surface.'

Max sat back in his seat. 'Is that confirmed?'

'Not yet. But I'll be surprised if it's not. So if he's fallen out with anyone we need to know.'

She stopped by the deli in Market Street to pick up a pie for their evening meal, adding a bottle of red to her basket.

Benjy was his usual uproarious self, greeting her with one of Bill's slippers in his mouth. As she wrested it from him she thought briefly of Dennis Gibb, his slippers waiting by the fireside. Who had hated him so much they'd wanted him dead? Maybe Max and Patch would turn something up.

She strapped Benjy into his harness and drove the short distance to her own cottage. Her spirits lifted when she saw Al's car in the drive. He was home. It had only been three days but it had felt so much longer. He hadn't drawn the curtains and, as she pulled in alongside his car she saw him bent over the woodburner, matches in hand. 'Come on,' she said to Benjy. 'Let's get inside.'

They lay together on the sofa, toasting their feet at the stove, Benjy squeezed in between them.

'I've missed this,' Al said, one hand fondling the little dog's neck. 'The job's great and all that. But you can't beat your own fireside.'

'I've missed you,' Clare said.

'Missed my cooking, more like.'

'That too.'

'Sounds like you've had your hands full,' he said. 'Has it been manic?'

'It's been okay. Lots happening but we're coping. I could do without this march, though.'

He put down his glass and turned to face her. 'Do you have enough officers? From what I hear you'll need every cop you can lay your hands on.'

She blinked, taking in his words. 'What?' she said, after a moment. 'What have you heard?'

He was quiet, as if weighing how much to say. 'You can't repeat this,' he said. 'Not even to Chris.'

Suddenly her mouth was dry, the tannins from the wine a sour aftertaste. 'I don't like the sound of this.'

'If our intel is correct – and it might not be – there are some pretty radical groups planning to join the march.'

'How radical?'

'The kind you really don't want marching through the town.'

She shook her head. 'Penny said as much. I asked her to let me ban it but she won't hear of it. Spouting all sorts about democracy and the Freemans' influence.'

He hesitated. 'There's a bit more to it than that.'

Her eyes widened. 'What? Tell me, Al.'

'Clare – you really can't repeat this. I need you to promise.'

'I don't believe this! Okay, I promise. Now tell me.'

'Penny's going to put undercover cops in with the marchers. She wants to flush out the real troublemakers. The ones making the bullets for the rest of them to fire.'

Clare sat digesting this, watching the flames as they licked round the logs. Hadn't there been a family-run store set on fire by rioters a few years back? London, somewhere? Was that what they were in for a week on Saturday? It didn't bear thinking about.

'Isn't there some way of weeding them out before the march?'

'Unfortunately not. They're very good at staying just inside the law – the right side of incitement. Typically they wait for the atmosphere to build, for the chants to become shouts then they call out something inflammatory. Next thing you know they've whipped a well-ordered march into a riot.'

'But if she knows it's going to happen…'

He shook his head. 'She wants to nail them. Or, more accurately, she wants to be the one to nail them.'

Clare's lips tightened as she thought of Penny, safe in her fancy office over in Dundee's Bell Street station. She wouldn't be there on the day, trying to hold the line. 'I'm going to speak to her,' she said.

'Clare! You absolutely can't. She'll know it came from me. You promised.'

She met his gaze for a moment and he stared straight back. Then she exhaled, letting her shoulders drop. 'Fine. But – tell me what to do, Al. I can't have a riot on the streets.'

'First, cancel all leave. You've probably done that but you want every single officer in. Ask every station in Fife and Tayside to provide extra bodies. Penny's likely phoned round already but it won't do any harm for you to ask as well.'

Clare nodded and he went on.

'Next, work out how to contain them without risking a crush.'

'Already done. Heras fencing will go up the day before. I'll have officers walking either side and a line at the front controlling the speed.'

'Where's the finish?'

'Top of North Street.'

'Good plan. The road's nice and wide there and you've a couple of escape routes, if necessary.'

They talked on, chatting about whether to use drones and police dogs until Clare realised the fire had died down. She checked her watch and forced herself up and off the sofa. 'I'll take Benjy out.'

Al put a hand on her arm. 'You've had him for the past few days. I'll do it. You get up to bed.'

She didn't have to be asked twice. She put the remains of the pie in the fridge, loaded the dishwasher and climbed the stairs wearily. He joined her ten minutes later, pulling her towards him. She lay there, enjoying the closeness, wondering if she'd get used to him not being there all the other nights. *Enjoy the moment* a little voice told her but Clare had always been a glass-half-empty kind of girl. Lying there, the warmth of him at her back, listening to his breathing as it became slow and regular, she couldn't help thinking another few nights and he'd be away again.

Her thoughts drifted back to the march and suddenly she was wide awake, the impossibility of controlling an angry crowd running round her head. What was Penny thinking, using Clare and her officers to make front-page news in some shitty tabloid?

A gust of wind threw sleet against the bedroom window and she snuggled down, burying her head under the duvet. Al's grip on her relaxed and she closed her eyes, willing sleep to come.

Day 4: Friday, 13th February

Chapter 12

Penny called as Clare was drawing into the station car park. The ground was thick with slush and she was relieved to see a couple of uniformed officers out with snow shovels and grit.

She took a moment to order her thoughts before answering. The last thing she wanted was to give away anything Al had shared the night before. 'Sorry,' she said, after a few rings. 'I was just parking the car.'

'The Freemans,' Penny began. 'Any news from SOCO?'

It took Clare a moment to register the reason for Penny's call. She couldn't believe the forthcoming march wasn't her top priority. Why on earth was she involving herself with the Freemans' burglary?

'Erm, yes,' she said, thinking back to the previous day's events. 'They found a camera hidden in a dummy smoke alarm.'

Penny was quiet for a moment. 'Were they aware of it?' she said, eventually.

Clare stepped out of the car, phone clamped to her ear. Her foot slid on an icy patch and she gripped the car door with her free hand. 'They say not.'

'They say?' There was an edge to Penny's voice. 'You don't believe them?'

Clare locked the car and began making her way across the car park, eyes on the ground for more patches of ice. 'I'm not sure. I don't think they're being entirely straight with us.'

'You think they're hiding something?'

'I think...' what did she think? What was it about the pair that had her senses tingling? 'I think maybe they haven't told us everything.' She pushed open the station door, stamping her feet on the rush mat to dislodge the slush from her shoes. 'It might be nothing to do with the camera or the burglary but I do think they're holding something back.' She was itching to mention the march without causing problems for Al, and then she saw her way in. 'They seem to think the burglary's connected to the march next weekend.' She let this hang in the air as she headed for her office, tapping at the security keypad.

'Yes.' Penny's voice was clipped. 'They said as much to me.'

So, Clare thought, *they'd been back in touch with Penny.* She bit back irritation at the couple going over her head. 'Our unexplained death,' she said, trying to steer Penny away from the Freemans' burglary. 'It's been confirmed as murder.'

Penny was quiet for a moment. 'You have a good team behind you,' she said. 'I'm sure you'll be able to divide them between the two enquiries.'

Clare took a breath. 'I think the burglary should take a back seat. For now, at least,' she added.

'As you said yourself, Clare, the burglary and march could be connected. So we have to make it a priority; and now I must get on. Keep me posted, please.' and she ended the call before Clare could say any more.

She flicked on the light switch and dropped her bag, kicking the office door shut. Steve and Jenny Gibb deserved justice for Dennis's murder but how the hell could she give the investigation her full attention when the Freemans were on the phone to Penny every five minutes? She weighed the phone in her hand, wondering if she should call Penny back. Have another go. But what was the point? She'd clearly decided the burglary was more important.

There was a note on her desk saying Eric Richards would call in just before nine. It took her a moment then she remembered – the photographer from Feddinch Property Solutions. She wondered if he'd noticed the extra smoke alarm. He might, if it had pre-dated the Freemans. Maybe the previous owners had installed the camera then forgotten to remove it when they'd left.

And then there was the surveyor, Grenville Thomas. Shouldn't he have noticed it when he'd inspected the property? She dug in her bag for the card Carol Merryweather had given her. It was only just after eight. Was it too early to call him? She tapped the number into her phone and hit the call button.

The voicemail recording began playing and Clare was about to leave a message when it was interrupted.

'Grenville Thomas.'

She wondered idly how old he was. It was hard to tell from his voice. Thirties or forties, maybe? His tone was brisk, as though he didn't have time to waste. Best get to the point. She introduced herself and explained they were investigating an incident at the Freemans' house.

'I remember it,' he said. 'Lovely property. What sort of incident?'

Clare ignored the question. 'I'd like to ask about the smoke alarms.'

There was the briefest hesitation. 'There's not been a fire, has there?'

She hastened to reassure him. 'Nothing like that. But I do need to know if you checked them.'

'Not required,' he said. 'We do a visual check – make sure they comply with the legislation. But it's not part of our remit to say if they're working. They might be on the day we do our inspection then stop working thereafter.'

'So you wouldn't notice anything amiss with any of the alarms?'

'You mean if one wasn't working?'

Clare hesitated. 'Something like that.'

He considered this. 'They do have a shelf life – typically ten years. They're bought as a set so when one goes they all stop working. But there's usually an audible warning when that happens. Look – what's this about? If there's a problem with the home report...'

'One of the alarms was a replica,' Clare said finally. As per her conversation with Carol the previous day, she wanted to hold back information about the camera.

'Well either it's been changed since I was there,' Grenville said, 'or it's a damn good replica. They all looked the same to me.'

She thanked him for his time and sat thinking, phone still in her hand. It was a few years since she'd sold her flat in Glasgow and she tried to remember the surveyor's inspection. Had she been there at the time? Maybe Grenville had been alone in the house when he'd visited. Carol could have given him a set of keys.

She reckoned most surveyors would have a folding ladder for inspecting attics and the like. Had Grenville been alone long enough to install the dummy alarm? And, if he had installed it, why? Was he connected to the Freemans in some way? Maybe he was involved with the protest group and wanted to dig up some dirt on the couple; and then she realised that didn't make sense. It was the sellers who'd instructed the survey. There was no way Grenville could have known the Freemans would buy the property and he wouldn't have had access to it after the sale had been agreed.

Mentally crossing him off her list she considered the other staff at Feddinch: Melanie, the lady on reception, Carol the property manager and Eric Richards, the photographer. She fingered the note saying he'd call in just before nine. But, like Grenville, his work would have been done before the Freemans had even seen the house. He might have spotted something. But there was no saying how long that camera had been there. It could even have stopped working. Then she gave herself a shake. The Freemans were taking up far too much of her time. She'd a killer to find.

She logged onto her computer and turned to the file on Dennis Gibb's murder. Max had uploaded a statement from Dennis's last employer, Murray Painter. He'd said Dennis could be a bit hot-headed at times but was mainly a good worker. She read on and saw Murray couldn't remember any incidents involving Dennis.

Patch had added a long list of people Dennis had argued with on Facebook, and the topics he'd argued about. Glancing at her notes it seemed he'd had plenty to say on students, golfers, rich Americans, a curry he claimed had given him the runs and even the weather. Dennis, it appeared, had not been slow to give his opinion.

> I'm following them up but nothing so far.

Patch had written.

Clare sat back, turning this over in her mind. Something was niggling away at her, and then she remembered. She opened Facebook and typed *St Andrews* in the search box, narrowing the results to *Groups*. A string of results appeared, everything from book clubs to wild swimming, from photography to university alumni. She scrolled down until she came to the result she wanted.

> St Andrews Residents Against Over-priced Housing

She'd seen the group when she'd been idly scrolling Facebook but hadn't stopped to look. Now, though, it struck her as the kind of group that might attract keyboard warriors – people like Dennis Gibb. The group was *Public* which meant Clare could see recent posts. More importantly, she could see its members. There were almost three hundred and she thought there was a fair chance Dennis Gibb was among them. She clicked on the list of members and started to type his name. There were three people called Dennis but none with the surname Gibb.

It looked as if non-members could post in the group so she typed his name into the group search box. Again, no results were returned and she wondered if he'd used a pseudonym? She returned to the home page and moved to the general search box, typing in Dennis's name. A dozen or more profiles appeared and she began working her way through them. The first three looked to be the wrong age but the fourth one down was more hopeful. She selected the profile and found herself looking at the face of a dead man. It was undoubtedly him. A photo taken with Steve and Jenny confirmed it. He'd used his own name but he wasn't a member of the group; and yet, from what Patch had found, it seemed Dennis would pick a fight about absolutely anything. So why hadn't he joined that group?

A tap on the door interrupted her thoughts and Jim's head appeared.

'An Eric Richards for you?'

Clare nodded and asked Jim to show Eric to an interview room. 'Is Chris about?'

'Just arrived. I'll ask him to join you.'

Eric Richards was perched on the edge of a chair and he rose as Clare and Chris entered. He was about Clare's age, she thought, but his manner and dress made him seem older. He was clean-shaven, his light brown hair parted in the centre. He wore dark trousers and a blue nylon zip-up jacket, elasticated at the waist. He thrust his right hand forward, a nervous greeting, Clare thought and she wondered if he had reason to be nervous. She introduced herself and Chris, assuring Eric this was an informal enquiry.

He seemed genuinely surprised when Clare asked if he'd noticed anything amiss with the smoke alarms at the Freemans' house. 'Like what?'

She chose her words carefully, avoiding any mention of the hidden camera but it seemed nothing had caught his eye. She asked a few more questions then thanked him for attending. Chris showed him out and rejoined Clare a few minutes later.

'I think the Feddinch lot are a no-go,' he said and Clare nodded.

'Maybe the previous owner will know something. Unless...'

Chris waited. 'Unless?'

She exhaled. 'Dunno. Might be nothing. But there's a Facebook group opposing the Freemans' development and Dennis Gibb isn't a member.'

He raised an eyebrow. 'And?'

Clare shook her head. 'Nothing, really. Just that, from what Patch has found, it looks like he enjoyed a good scrap online. Strikes me as the kind of group he'd have joined.'

'Maybe he was in it and fell out with them.'

She laughed. 'Yeah. That makes more sense. So, what now?'

Chris hesitated, a hand rubbing his chin.

'Spit it out, Sergeant.'

'I mean... we'd likely not get a warrant; but I did wonder if we should be investigating the Freemans. We both think they're not telling us everything.'

'Agreed.'

'And if we found out more about their business we might be closer to knowing who has an interest in keeping tabs on them.'

Clare was quiet for a moment. 'Honestly? I don't think Penny would go for it.'

Chris shrugged. 'She's not the only superintendent in town.'

'No, but she'd cut me off at the knees if I went behind her back. She's never off the phone, asking what I've found out about that burglary.'

'Weird.'

'Isn't it? It's like she has a vested interest.'

'Hm. Do you think she does?'

'Eh?'

'Like shares in the Freemans' company or something?'

'Nah. She'd have to declare it and step back from the enquiry.' She was about to say more then she checked herself, almost wishing Al hadn't shared Penny's plans for the march. 'I think it's more likely they're friends,' she said instead. 'Maybe they did meet at some black-tie do.'

'Makes sense. She is a bit of a snob, our Penny. Or she might be planning to retire to St Andrews!'

Clare eyed him. 'Don't even joke about it.'

—

It was mid-afternoon by the time Carol Merryweather called back. 'The previous owner,' she said.

Clare snatched up a pen. 'Go ahead.'

'Professor John Mountfield.'

'Address?'

Carol reeled off the address and a mobile number. 'It's a retirement complex. Lovely flat. We sold one in the same block recently.' She hesitated. 'I hope Eric and Grenville were able to help.'

She was clearly fishing for information.

'Very helpful,' Clare said. 'Thanks again for their details; and for the information on the previous owner. We'll take it from here.' And, with that, Carol Merryweather had to be content.

She found Chris in the incident room, poring over the Companies House website.

'Those Freemans,' he said. 'They've had a string of companies over the years.'

Clare peered over his shoulder. 'What kind of business?'

He scrolled down a couple of screens. 'Would you believe they started out as party planners?'

'I'd believe anything of that pair.'

'After that, they had two companies described as *Leisure Industries*. The last few have been property development.'

'Any other directors?'

He shook his head. 'Minor shareholders but Rex and Erika have the majority shareholding.'

'Okay. Can you make a note to find out if any of the companies went bankrupt or if there were any court proceedings?'

'I can do it now,' Chris said. 'While I'm in the zone.'

'Nah. Leave it till later. We've a call to pay.'

Chapter 13

Professor Mountfield's flat was in a fairly new development, off Abbey Walk.

'I'd no idea this was so extensive,' Clare said, taking in the tall buildings, their cream and ochre render sympathetic to the older architecture of the town.

'Yep. Almost like a village,' Chris said, nosing the car along, looking for signposts.

'Next right.'

Chris indicated a notice. 'Residents only.'

'It's okay. He doesn't have a car. We can use his space.'

They were buzzed into the building, the interior light and airy.

Clare headed for the stairwell. 'I'm guessing you're still shit-scared of lifts.'

'We all have our crosses to bear.'

The professor's flat was on the first floor and they emerged onto the landing, a corridor running left and right.

'Along here,' Chris said, indicating a dark blue door at one end, the number twelve on a plaque to the side.

Clare pressed the bell and they heard a distant Westminster chime and the sound of movement within; and then the sound stopped. There was a spyglass in the door and she guessed they were being observed. She reached for her warrant card, preparing to hold it out but the lock clicked before she could find it and the door opened slowly. An elderly man peered out, the chain still on the door. Clare found her card and held it up to the gap, Chris following suit.

'Detective Inspector Clare Mackay,' she said, giving him a smile. 'We spoke on the phone.'

He pushed the door closed again, removed the chain and stood back to admit them. They followed him into a bright sitting room, winter sun streaming in a pair of windows. It was a pleasant room, simply furnished with a cream-coloured sofa and matching chair. He indicated the sofa and they sat, taking in their surroundings. The walls were hung with watercolours and there were Staffordshire figurines on a mantelpiece over a living flame fire. Bookcases had been built in below the windows and to the side of these stood an old gramophone in a mahogany cabinet. The lid was propped open and Clare saw a vinyl 78 on the turntable, the arm poised to play.

He followed her gaze. 'My grandfather's,' he said. 'I had to get rid of so much when I moved from Hepburn Gardens but I couldn't part with this.'

She smiled. 'It's a beauty. No wonder you kept it.'

'My nephew's just bought an old record player,' Chris said. 'I can't see past downloads myself, but he likes it.'

There was the hint of a smile on the professor's face and Clare suppressed a laugh.

Chris had moved across the room and was studying the gramophone. 'They're quite thick, these records,' he said and the professor rose stiffly.

'I can let you see how it works, if you like?'

He walked slowly over, and Clare took the opportunity to study him. He was in his late seventies, she guessed, his shoulders rounded by age. She thought briefly of her own parents, still in their sixties but only just. Suddenly she was back at Christmas time, her dad in the kitchen at Daisy Cottage, offering to help with the washing up. Clare had surveyed the chaos, not a single space to put anything down and she'd given him a hug, telling him they'd manage. At the time it hadn't registered but now she realised he hadn't seemed as tall as usual. They were almost the same height. She recalled a poster in her

GP's waiting room, some statistic about the elderly losing height more rapidly after the age of seventy. *Old age doesn't come itself,* her dad was fond of saying. How true that was. The professor was explaining the different parts of the gramophone to Chris and she watched them for a minute, wondering how tall this man had been in his younger years.

Finally Chris thanked him and rejoined Clare on the sofa. She waited till the professor had returned to his seat then she began.

'We'd like to ask a few questions about the house at Hepburn Gardens.'

'Yes, of course. What is it you wish to know?'

'Did you have any security arrangements?'

His brow creased at the question, clearly not one he was expecting, and he took a moment before answering. 'You mean a burglar alarm?'

'Anything of that sort,' Clare said. 'Maybe security cameras.'

'Not really. I do hope there hasn't been a burglary.'

'You didn't install any hidden cameras, for instance?'

He blinked a couple of times, as if processing this. 'I wouldn't have known how, Inspector.'

'Might you have brought someone in to do it?'

He shook his head. 'The last person who did anything in the house was the decorator. The estate agent suggested we give a couple of the rooms a lick of paint. Help it sell, you know?'

She asked for details of the decorator and he reeled off the name.

'I don't think I have their number,' he said, but Chris waved this away.

'I've used them.'

'What about the interlinked smoke alarms?' Clare went on. 'Did you install these yourself?'

'No. We always use Farrell's for odd jobs. They've done a few other things for us. Tidy workmen and good prices.'

She knew the firm. She'd seen their vans around the town. Clearly popular with the locals. She took out her notepad and jotted down the name. 'When did they last do any work for you?'

His brow furrowed again and he gave a slight shake of his head. 'My memory these days...'

Clare waited and eventually he spoke. 'A year or two back, I think. My late wife, Barbara...' he broke off for a moment then cleared his throat. 'She died last February, you know? She wanted some shelves put up in one of the bedrooms. I have, or rather, I had quite a lot of books. When I retired I cleared out my office at the university and the books sat in boxes for years. In the end Barbara called Farrell's and they put up some shelves. Ironic, really...' He clasped his hands together and Clare wondered if he was trying to stop them shaking. 'The books had to go when I moved here. But Barbara had enjoyed seeing them on the shelves.' He met Clare's gaze. 'Is that the kind of thing you mean?'

She smiled. 'Yes. That's very helpful.' She caught Chris's eye. There was nothing to be learned here. The professor was clearly incapable of installing the hidden camera himself and she didn't think it likely the decorator or anyone from Farrell's would have done so. But they'd check it anyway.

They rose together and she thanked him for his time.

He led them to the door and as she turned to say goodbye she felt an unexpected lump in her throat. This gentle man with his frailty, smiling at them through rheumy eyes, this was where they were all heading. First it would be her parents and, after a few decades, herself and Al. This power she had right now, this control over her life – it would all go some day and she'd be the one moving out of her lovely home to a flat on the first floor of a retirement complex. It would be her walking carefully to the front door, checking through the spyglass, keeping the chain on; and, if Al – the man she'd grown to love – if he died first, she'd have to do it all without him.

She gave herself a shake. It wouldn't do, this maudlin nonsense. For all she knew this man was happier now than when he'd been rattling around the enormous house in Hepburn Gardens. There was a lot to be said for making life simpler as you got older, something she'd have to think about for her own parents.

'You okay?' Chris said as they walked down the stairs.

She nodded, not trusting herself to speak.

'I could ask,' he said. 'See if they could fix you up with a nice flat.' He appraised her with a critical eye. 'You can't be far off the minimum age.'

'Shut up, Sergeant.'

'Shutting up, Inspector.'

—

Chris called the decorator when they were back at the station.

'Same lad as did our flat,' he told Clare. 'Pretty sound. I can't see him having anything to do with the camera.'

His next call was to Farrell's who confirmed it was almost three years since they'd put up the shelves in the professor's house, the smoke alarms six months before that.

'Chances are any battery in the camera would have run out long since,' Chris said, putting down his phone. Clare nodded. Another dead end.

'Let's get back to Dennis Gibb, then. We've wasted enough time on the Freemans' burglary.'

'I think Sara has some doorcam footage,' Chris said.

Sara looked up at the mention of her name and Clare wandered over.

'You got something?'

She turned her laptop for Clare to see. 'We don't know which pub he was in but Jenny suggested The Yardstick so I've started with properties nearest to that. I managed to get footage from two flats with cameras. Still waiting to hear back from a few others.' She tapped the screen. 'I'm up to ten p.m. the night we think he died. Problem is – Saturday night – the town was jumping.'

Clare smiled. 'It's a lot, I know.' She scanned the room. 'See who else is around to help. We need to follow up anyone heading in the direction of the harbour.'

She left Sara to her task and went back to her office. Maybe Patch would turn up something from Dennis's spats on social media.

–

Clare's mobile rang just after three. She recognised the number – Diane, her friend who ran the Tech Support unit in Glenrothes, twenty miles away.

'Your camera,' Diane began, 'you probably spotted there isn't an SD card but we think it was still transmitting. It's motion activated and there's a fair bit of life left in the battery.'

Clare couldn't hide her disappointment. 'There's no way to tell who's viewed the footage?'

'Sorry. There is one possibility, though.'

'Oh, yes?'

'Can you get hold of the householder's browsing history?'

'We are trying,' Clare said. 'They've given permission and we've contacted their ISP. But they've not come back to us yet.'

'It might help,' Diane said. 'They'd need Wi-Fi to view the footage. Whoever installed the camera might know the house Wi-Fi code. If so, we might be able to pin down their location.'

Clare said she'd chase this up and she ended the call. An email from Raymond popped up and she clicked to read it, hoping his news was better than Diane's.

> We've taken several prints from the smoke alarm.
>
> Swabbed it for DNA as well.
>
> I'll give you a shout if it matches anyone on the database.

She was tempted to reply asking Raymond how long it would take but she knew how busy his team were so she sent back a short message of thanks. She sat thinking for a moment. The burglary was taking up an inordinate amount of time, far out of proportion to the seriousness and she rose tiredly trying to shift her focus to Dennis's murder.

She found Max and Sara in the incident room, trawling through footage taken from door cameras and pub CCTV.

'Nothing yet,' Max said, stretching back and massaging his neck. 'Not even found anyone who looks like Dennis.'

Something was niggling away at Clare and then she remembered. 'That protest group.'

'The one organising the march?'

'Yes. Dennis Gibb wasn't a member.'

'So?'

Clare bit back irritation. Honest to God – could no one else see it? 'Max – look at the number of Facebook groups he's in. A lot of them are about St Andrews. Given he likes a fight and this is the biggest fight the town's seen in years—'

'Why wasn't he a member?' Max finished.

'Exactly!'

'You're thinking he had an interest?'

'His cottage,' Clare said. 'Can we find out if it was part of the planning application?'

Max opened another window on his laptop and typed *Fife Planning Applications* into the search box. A few clicks took him to the council's planning portal. He typed *St Andrews* and waited for the results.

'Dammit. Too many results to display. I'll have to narrow it down. Any idea of the area?'

'I don't know where the development is but Dennis's cottage is south of the town, on the A915.'

'Leave it with me. I'll see what I can find.'

She turned to head back to her office then stopped. 'Patch?'

'Out interviewing folk Dennis fell out with on Facebook,' Max said.

'Ask her to chase up the boat hook pole please. We need to know if it's a match.'

Chris was waiting in her office when she returned. 'Got Dennis Gibb's phone records; and his will.'

'Oh, yes?' She lifted Chris's mug and put a coaster below it.

He raised an eyebrow. 'You're getting very houseproud all of a sudden.'

She ignored this. 'The will?'

'Nothing much. All goes to Steve – the son.'

'Makes sense. What about his phone records?'

'Just going to make a start.'

She eyed his mug. 'Take that with you, and give me a shout if there's anything interesting.'

He shuffled off, mug in hand. Clare watched him go then she turned back to her computer. But she was vaguely unsettled, Dennis Gibb's death preying on her mind. Who had a motive to kill him? Instinct told her to look close to home. Most murders were domestics, the victims killed by their nearest and not-so-dearest. But there was something about this case – something telling her there was more to it. Was it his cottage? Had the Freemans made him an offer? Maybe he'd demanded too high a price. But, if he had, how far would that pair have gone to ensure their plans went ahead?

—

Al was chopping coriander when she walked into the kitchen, the aroma of curry wrapping itself round her heart. Benjy sat at his feet, clearly drawn by the mouthwatering smells. His tail beat the floor when he saw Clare but his face remained upturned for any stray morsel.

Al put down the knife and bent to kiss Clare on the lips, a lingering kiss reminding her how much she'd missed him.

He drew her close and she felt the roughness of his cheek, the warmth of his body. Suddenly, she was so glad to be home.

'You don't have to go in tomorrow, do you?' His voice was soft in her ear. 'I thought we could do a bit of the coastal path. Give Benjy a proper walk.'

She stood, drinking him in for a moment then, gently, she pushed him away. 'I should, really. I've a killer to find.'

'You could lean on your team a bit more.'

She indicated an open bottle of red. 'Pour me a glass. Then we'll see.'

Later, as they lay together on the sofa, toasting their feet on the fire, she considered his words. If she'd taken his job when it had been offered she wouldn't be trying to juggle things now so they could enjoy a day off together. She'd be Monday to Friday, nine to five. For the umpteenth time she wondered if she'd done the right thing. A little voice in the back of her head said not. But it was done now. She'd settled for staying in St Andrews and she'd just have to live with it.

All the same, she deserved a life outside work and the team did have their instructions. Would it really matter if she wasn't there? She could always look into the station on her way back – check there weren't any problems. Her two detective sergeants would be in tomorrow. Maybe she could take the day off.

'So...' She adjusted her position to let him massage her feet, 'Which part of the coastal path do you fancy?'

Day 5: Saturday, 14th February

Chapter 14

They lingered over breakfast, Al studying a map of the coastal path.

'We could take two cars,' he said, turning the map so Clare could see. 'If we parked at the Tayport end of Tentsmuir Forest we could walk through the forest, past Leuchars and onto St Andrews. Maybe leave a car at Balgove and have a late lunch in the restaurant.'

'Or the steak barn,' Clare suggested.

'Sounds good.'

He pushed back his chair. 'I'll do a flask of coffee. Fancy some sandwiches as well?'

—

There was a nip in the air when they finally set out from the Tayport end of Tentsmuir Forest, having left Al's car in the Balgove Larder car park. They walked quickly, passing the old RAF Meteorological station. Clare had used it in a stake-out operation when they'd been hunting a serial killer. She shivered at the memory of the interview, when he'd finally been caught. She'd thought then he was probably the most wholly evil man she'd ever met. He'd been detained in Carstairs, the high-security psychiatric hospital and she hoped he'd never leave its walls.

'Cold?' Al asked, putting his arm round her and she shook her head.

'Nothing a brisk walk won't fix.'

They strolled on, enjoying the low winter sun until their route took them into the forest, the evergreen trees dense above. Al talked about his job at the police college, heading up a new cyber security unit.

'We've been looking at the security of wearable technologies,' he said. Clare listened, happy to see him so enthusiastic about his work. She couldn't remember when she'd last felt like that about her job. Probably just before Penny had been appointed.

Al stopped to check his watch. 'Another hour should take us to Guardbridge. We could have a coffee now or wait till we get there.'

They were nearing the edge of the forest, approaching the RAF base at Leuchars, now an army barracks. 'Let's crack on,' Clare said. 'It'll taste all the better when we get there.'

'How's your job?' he asked. 'I don't mean the murder – just generally.'

The wind came through a gap in the trees and Clare pulled her anorak zip-up to her neck, tucking her scarf in. 'Oh, it's fine, mostly.'

'Mostly?'

She was quiet for a moment.

'Something wrong?'

She forced a smile. 'I wonder sometimes, you know, if I should have taken your job when it was offered.'

He put an arm round her back and she felt the gentle pressure of his hand, a reassuring sensation. She missed this.

'Is it the murder?' he asked.

'The murder, the burglary, Penny – take your pick.'

He glanced at her. 'There are other openings. DCI posts are always coming up. If you're not happy…'

They were out of the trees now, onto the boardwalks that crossed the old marshlands and she considered his words. She certainly could apply for another post. But did she actually want that? Or did she just not want Penny as a boss?

'I think,' she began, then her phone started to ring. From nowhere she felt tears pricking her eyes. They were having such a lovely day – fresh air, time to talk – the break from work she so desperately needed. Al was home and it was the weekend. Was a day away from work honestly too much to ask?

'You going to answer it?' he said and she shook her head.

'No! It's – I should be able to have a day off, for goodness sake!' Her knuckles were white, gripping the phone and she resisted the urge to throw it across the marshland.

'Clare…' Al's tone was so gentle she felt a lump in her throat.

The ringing stopped then seconds later it began again.

She met his eye, hoping for something there, something that would tell her it was okay to ignore the call – to have some time to herself in the middle of a murder investigation. But it wasn't there. They both knew she had to take the call and she swiped to answer, putting the phone to her ear.

—

By the time they reached the road outside the base Chris was waiting, the engine running. He took in her walking trousers and fleece. 'I didn't know it was dress-down Saturday.'

'You're messing with my day off,' she said. 'And it's Valentine's Day. So tell me.'

'Max has gone ahead. I said I'd pick you up. The ambulance is there now but Max says he's cold.'

'Any outward sign of injury?'

'Not that he could see.'

'What's the wife saying?'

'Hysterical, according to Max. Paramedics are treating her for shock.'

Clare sighed and tugged on her seat belt. 'Best get over there, then.'

Chapter 15

The ambulance was still outside Steve and Jenny Gibb's house when they arrived. Clare drew up behind and rapped on the back door. A moment later, it was opened by a green-suited paramedic. She introduced herself and asked if she could see the body.

He stood back to let her climb in. Steve Gibb was lying on a trolley, his face white and waxy.

'He's well gone,' the paramedic said. 'Cold to touch.'

'Any idea what happened?'

He shook his head. 'Wife was pretty upset but, from what we gathered, he'd slept in the spare room. It was only when she went to wake him this morning that she realised.'

'Did she say why he was in the spare room?'

'We didn't ask. That's more your area.'

She thanked him and climbed back out. The door slammed and she gave Chris a noncommittal gesture. 'Apparently he slept in the spare room last night. Maybe that's something to do with it.'

'Might have had a skinful,' Chris said. 'Choked on his own vomit.'

'Could be. No sign, though. My God – is that her?'

Jenny's wails cut through the cool morning air but, before they could head into the house, a car drew up behind the ambulance. A young woman jumped out, medical bag in hand. Clare went to meet her.

'I'm guessing you're the duty doctor,' she said and the woman nodded.

She introduced herself as Dr Garvey. 'I gather the paramedics were concerned.' She started towards the house. 'In here?'

They went up the drive together following the sound of Jenny's sobs, Clare allowing Dr Garvey to go in first. Max was waiting and he showed the doctor into the sitting room where Clare and Chris had spoken to the couple, just two days earlier.

'I'll see her myself first,' the doctor said and she closed the door softly behind her. They heard her voice, calm and measured and, after a few minutes, Jenny's sobs began to subside, replaced by the murmur of conversation.

The layout of the house meant they couldn't reach the kitchen without going through the sitting room so Clare sank down on the stairs, Max and Chris standing with their backs to the front door.

'Tell me from the start,' she said.

'Call came in just before nine,' Max said. 'She'd phoned for an ambulance and they alerted us. I got here first, ambulance maybe twenty minutes later.'

'What did she say when you got here?'

Max exhaled. 'It was hard to make her out at first. She was watching from the window and came out to meet me. Grabbed my arm and pulled me up the stairs to one of the bedrooms. He was under the covers, just a pair of boxers on, clothes on the floor beside him.'

'And he was cold?'

'Yep. I'd guess he died somewhere in the early hours. Depends on the PM, of course. She managed to say he'd gone to bed at the back of nine but it was hard to get much more out of her.'

'Bit early for a Friday night?'

Max shrugged. 'I think they'd had a row.'

'Did she say as much?'

'No. But she kept saying if only he'd slept in their bedroom she might have known he was ill.'

'She thinks it was natural causes? No other substances?'

'Well, about that,' Chris began.

Before he could continue, the door to the sitting room opened. 'I want her to go to hospital,' the doctor said. 'She's pale and clammy, heart rate through the roof. She needs medical supervision.'

'I can take her,' Max said. 'It'll be quicker than waiting for another ambulance.'

'Can one of you sit in the back with her?' the doctor asked.

Max took out his phone. 'I'll get hold of Patch. She's back at the station.'

Five minutes later, Max and Patch led a shaking Jenny to their car, stowing her safely in the back.

'Stay with her,' Clare said. 'She needs to be interviewed asap.'

They waited until the doctor had left then Clare nodded at the stairs. 'Up here, is it?'

'Second door on the landing.'

She followed him up and into a bedroom furnished simply with a double bed, small bedside table and a chest of drawers under the window. The curtains had been drawn back, allowing the sun to stream in, casting a cheerful glow on the walls. On any other day, Clare would have said it was a pleasant, if unremarkable room. But on this crisp February morning, Steve Gibb's last on this earth, it was a room that might hold clues about his death.

The duvet was pulled back, the sheet rumpled where he'd lain. A pair of Hoka trainers, still laced, had been kicked off along with a track suit and T-shirt. A Garmin was on the bedside table, the water bottle they'd seen Steve drink from next to it.

'Got any evidence bags?'

'In the car. I'll pick them up before we leave.'

'Pity he wasn't wearing the Garmin,' Clare said. 'It might have told us when his heart stopped.'

She stood, taking in the room while Chris went to fetch a bundle of evidence bags. When she'd assured herself there was nothing more to be learned, she went back downstairs and out into the crisp morning. They walked back to the car, Chris clutching the bags now containing Steve's clothes and possessions. Then Clare remembered their conversation, interrupted by the doctor.

'You were about to tell me something.'

'Ah yes.'

Chapter 16

'The call came in during the night,' Jim said as Clare settled on a chair beside him. 'It was diverted to Cupar but the night shift sergeant knew we were investigating Dennis Gibb's murder so they sent on the details.'

'And it was anonymous?'

'Aye. An unlisted number.' He tapped a yellow Post-it note. 'I jotted it down in case you want to check it against anything.'

The report loaded and Clare nodded to Chris to join them. He ambled over and she began to read aloud.

'A man called Steve Gibb from St Andrews is a drug dealer. He was out dealing Fentanyl tonight. You'd better pick him up before he kills someone.'

She read it over again and sat thinking for a minute. 'Can we access the recording?'

Jim tapped at the keyboard again. A few minutes later, she heard the non-emergency operator greeting the caller, then a man's voice. There was definitely something odd about it. The operator asked for the caller's name and the call ended.

'That's all there is,' Jim said.

Clare listened again. 'That voice...'

'Weird, isn't it?' Chris agreed.

Clare thought for a moment. 'Could it be one of those apps that changes your voice?'

Chris frowned. 'Play it again.'

They listened once more and he nodded. 'I reckon it's a recording. Notice he doesn't reply to the operator? I think whoever it is has recorded the message then put it through a voice changer app.'

'And what?' Clare asked, 'they dial the call and play it over?'

'Yeah. Pretty easy once you know how.'

She considered this. 'Why would someone disguise their voice?'

'Erm, so we don't know who they are.'

'But it's not like we have a database of voices we can compare it with.'

Chris shrugged. 'Your average druggie wouldn't know that.'

'So you think that's what it is? Steve was dealing, and someone decided to drop him in it?'

'Yeah. I reckon so. It certainly puts another slant on the old man's death.'

Clare was quiet, turning this over in her mind. 'How so?'

'Maybe the dad – Dennis – maybe he was dealing as well. Could be it's a family thing. Dennis upsets someone – let's say he's muscling in on someone else's turf – our mystery caller, for example. They decide to teach Dennis a lesson. But Steve's still at it. Still dealing. Dennis's death hasn't put him off, hence the anonymous call.'

She stared at him. 'Did you just use *hence* in a sentence? Correctly?'

A smirk spread over his face. 'You hate it when I'm right.'

She thought for a moment, her mind back at their meeting with Steve and Jenny. 'I dunno, Chris.'

'What? Don't make it complicated. You're always telling me the simplest answer's usually the right one.'

Her brows knitted together as she tried to process the events of the past few hours. Steve found dead in his bed, Jenny hysterical – more so than she might have expected – and now this. The idea that the Gibb men, father and son, were drug dealers – somehow it didn't add up.

'You know when we visited the house?' she said. 'Not today – on Thursday.'

'Yeah.'

'That wedding photo in Jamaica. Remember they spoke about the reggae marathon?'

'Again, yeah.'

'They're fitness freaks. I don't see them as druggies. Steve was drinking from a water bottle, like he'd just come from the gym.'

'Aye, but you don't know what was in it.'

Clare shook her head. 'Look at his clothes last night. That track suit, the trainers and his fitness watch – I'll be amazed if there are any drugs in his system.'

Chris eyed her. 'Doesn't mean he isn't a dealer.'

'True. But it makes it less likely.'

'Suppose.'

'Which leaves us with two questions.'

'Go on, then. I'll buy.'

'Who made that anonymous phone call, and why?'

—

Clare asked Jim to share the recording with the team and with colleagues across in Dundee's Bell Street station.

'Could be this isn't the first time someone's used a voice changer,' she said. 'If anyone's had a call like this I'd like to speak to them.'

Jim said he'd add the recording to the network and Clare went to the kitchen to make a cup of tea. She filled the kettle then checked her phone while it boiled. Al had reached Balgove and had picked up his car.

> Hope you're not home too late.

his message read.

She tapped out a quick reply saying she'd keep him posted then tucked her phone back in her pocket. Patch appeared and sank down on a chair.

Clare indicated the kettle. 'Want one?'

'Please. Whatever you're having.'

Clare poured water into mugs then set the kettle down. She glanced at Patch. 'You okay? You look bushed.' She handed her a mug and took a seat opposite.

'Yeah, I'm fine,' she said. 'It's just those keyboard warriors.'

'The ones Dennis fell out with?'

Patch nodded. 'String of complaints as long as your arm.'

'About Dennis?'

'Yeah. If he wasn't swearing at them, he was threatening to report them for neglecting their kids, or parking on double yellows, or a dozen other things.' She shook her head. 'They're worse than kids, the whole lot of them.'

Clare laughed. 'Welcome to policing! Anyone stand out?'

'Not enough to kill him.'

'Oh well. Keep trying; and don't let it get you down. It's tedious but we do have to be thorough.'

Patch smiled. 'Ach it's fine. Anyway, bit of good news.'

'Oh?'

'The boat hook pole. Neil and Raymond both looked at the photos and they reckon the shape and size match the mark on Dennis's chest.'

'So it could have been the pole used to hold him under?'

Patch sipped her coffee. 'They wouldn't go that far. Just that the bruising was consistent with a pole of that size.'

'Probably the best we can hope for,' Clare said. 'At least we know what happened, even if we don't know who was on the other end of the pole.' She cradled her mug, taking in her new DC. Patch was cheerful and hardworking but she didn't give much away. Maybe it was the rank. There were still officers in senior roles who treated their unpromoted colleagues with disdain – contempt, even. Was that the reason for Patch's wariness? She took a furtive glance at her watch and decided there was time for a bit of bridge-building.

'How did you get into weightlifting?'

Patch's cheeks coloured and Clare wondered if the question had embarrassed her. Then she smiled. 'At school.'

'Oh?'

'It was one of the PE options. Most of the girls chose tennis or dance. But I was hopeless at those so I went for weights.'

'Were there many girls chose weights?'

Patch shook her head. 'Just two of us. We were in with the boys.' A smile spread across her face. 'They were all so cocky, you know? All that macho stuff. But they weren't so cocky when I outlifted them all.'

'Wow! I bet they didn't like that.'

Patch laughed. 'They did not. Then one of the teachers put me in touch with a trainer at a club and it went from there.'

'And now you're representing Scotland?'

She flushed. 'Not quite. I've still a couple of qualifying events to get through. But I am currently top of my category.' She eyed Clare. 'If you fancy it, I could give you a taster.'

Clare considered this. Was there something more here? Might this be a way for Patch to get to know some of the other officers? 'If I booked one of the gyms would you fancy doing a session for the officers here?'

Patch's face lit up. 'I'd love to. It's such a great exercise. So many benefits.'

'Excellent.' Clare drained her mug and pushed back her chair. 'Leave it with me. Once we get these investigations out of the way I'll sort something out.'

—

Max called on his way back from the hospital.

'They're keeping her in overnight. Just for observation. Should be out tomorrow.'

'There's no chance we can speak to her?' Clare asked.

'Nah. She's been sedated. They said to call tomorrow, around midday.'

Clare ended the call and it rang again immediately – Janey, a detective sergeant from Dundee's Bell Street station.

'I heard you were asking about calls with voice changer apps.'

'Yes.' Clare explained about the anonymous tip off accusing Steve of dealing Fentanyl. 'We wondered if you'd had anything like that recently.'

'Sorry,' Janey said. 'I've asked around and checked with the supervisors at the call centre. There's no shortage of odd callers but it's usually drunks or kids larking about. No one recalls anyone sounding like they'd use an app.'

Clare thanked Janey and sat on, phone in hand, wondering why the caller had used the app. Maybe they were known to the police or maybe it was to disguise an accent. And then something else occurred to her.

Chris was in the incident room chatting to Sara. They were deep in conversation, neither of them smiling. She was about to leave them to it then she thought better of it. This was work. They'd have to sort out whatever was bugging them in their own time.

Chris looked up as she approached and Sara flushed.

'Those voice changer apps,' Clare began.

'Yeah?'

'Could you use it to change gender?'

'So a man sounds like a woman?' Chris said.

'Or vice versa.'

He glanced at Sara who shook her head. 'Sorry, boss. No idea.'

Chris reached into his pocket and dug out his phone. 'Let me check.' He opened Google and began typing in search terms. It took only a minute to find an app that could change a recording to a variety of accents. 'Gender too,' he said, holding the phone out for Clare to see.

She squinted at the screen long enough to assure herself.

'You're thinking it was a woman?' Chris said.

'I'm not sure.' She sank down on a desk. 'Look, I know I said Steve didn't look the type but suppose he had been dealing Fentanyl.'

'Okay...'

'I don't know a lot about it but I do know it's a really strong opioid, far stronger than morphine; and that makes it dangerous.'

'Yeah...'

'I may be way off, here, but if he was dealing and Jenny got to know about it...'

Chris's eyes widened. 'You think it was Jenny? The phone call?'

'Maybe she was desperate.'

'But her own husband? Drug like that – he'd end up doing time. She'd be left paying the mortgage – all the bills.'

'You're forgetting Dennis's cottage. It'll go to Steve. Might be enough to pay off their mortgage. Jenny would know that and if she wanted out of the marriage...'

Chris stared. 'She'd have to be pretty desperate to drop her own husband in it.' He shook his head. 'I can't see it. You saw the state she was in this morning. That wasn't the reaction of a woman who'd planned to see her husband banged up.'

Clare sighed. He was right, of course. But, if Jenny hadn't made that call, who had?

Sara was back at her desk now, her eyes focused on the laptop screen and Clare wandered over.

'Any luck with the CCTV?'

She shook her head.

Clare watched her for a moment but her gaze didn't lift from the screen so she left her to it. She wandered back to her office, her mind on Steve and that phone call. Chris had suggested Dennis and Steve might have been in it together – both dealing. If so, might they have been using as well?

She couldn't recall if Neil Grant had carried out tox tests on Dennis's body and she navigated her way to the post-mortem report, now up on the system. Scrolling through she saw there had been alcohol in Dennis's body but no mention of drugs.

She tapped out a message to Neil, warning him Steve's body was heading his way, adding,

> Could you test for Fentanyl please?
>
> Also, don't suppose you checked Dennis Gibb's body for the same?

As she clicked *Send* Sara's head appeared round the door.

'I might have him,' she said.

'Dennis?'

'Think so.'

Clare followed her to the incident room and they sat in front of Sara's laptop. 'Show me.'

Sara ran a clip of grainy footage. 'This is about half-eleven, the night we think Dennis went into the water. There,' she said, tapping the screen. 'I think that's him.'

Clare peered at the footage. A man was walking past, hands driven deep into his pockets. He was wearing a light-coloured jacket. There was no hood but he had a checked scarf knotted at the neck. She tried to recall Dennis's post-mortem photos but it was difficult to reconcile the image of his water-damaged corpse with this shadowy figure. She looked more closely at the screen. 'I don't know, Sara. It's not clear enough.'

Sara switched to another tab, open at Dennis Gibb's Facebook page. 'That jacket and scarf...' She clicked on a photo and it filled the screen. 'See what I mean?'

Clare did see. The clothes looked similar, the scarf knotted the same way.

'Can you switch back to the doorcam?'

Sara clicked back to the first screen and zoomed in until the image became too grainy to see properly. 'It's the same, isn't it?'

Clare had to agree. The jacket alone wouldn't have convinced her but paired with the scarf, the way it had been tied, it surely couldn't be a coincidence.

'Can you check on the clothing recovered from the body please?' Clare said.

A smile spread across Sara's face. 'Already done.'

'It's a match?'

She nodded. 'And there's more.'

'Go on.'

Sara clicked to continue the video and, a few seconds later, another figure came into view.

Suddenly Clare was alert. 'Play it again – and stop on that figure.'

Sara replayed the footage freezing on the figure maybe ten seconds behind Dennis. Clare stared at the screen, a smile spreading across her face. 'That's a really good spot, Sara. Well done.'

Sara beamed and Clare looked round. 'Chris?'

'Probably in the kitchen. He was going to make a coffee.'

Clare rose without another word and walked quickly to the kitchen. Chris looked up as she entered, guilt written all over his face. She saw him stuff a Wagon Wheel wrapper in his pocket but she ignored this. 'Something you need to see.' She turned on her heel and he followed her back to the incident room.

The three of them sat round Sara's laptop, Clare indicating the figure on screen. 'Recognise these clothes?'

Chris sat for a minute. 'I've seen the shoes before. You can't miss the soles. They're huge.'

'They're Hokas, aren't they?' Sara said. 'You can see the logo.'

'They are.' Clare's expression darkened. 'We saw these shoes this morning – in Steve Gibb's spare bedroom; and see the three stripes down the trouser leg? That's his track suit.'

'So it is.' Chris sat back in his seat. 'He was following his dad.'

'I'd say so.' Clare was quiet for a moment, her eyes fixed on the screen.

'You thinking what I'm thinking?' Chris said.

She met his eye. 'He was so upset when we told him about Dennis being killed. Angry, even.'

Chris shrugged. 'Played his part pretty well. He wouldn't be the first.'

'You think he did it?'

Chris tapped the screen. 'He followed Dennis down to the harbour, possibly minutes before he died. If he isn't the killer, why didn't he tell us he'd seen Dennis heading that way? He might even have seen someone else hanging around.' Chris sat back and folded his arms. 'Nah. He pushed his dad in, all right. I'd bet my Wagon Wheels on it.'

Sara shot him a look.

'If I had any...' he added.

Clare wasn't listening. 'We need footage from any properties further along the road,' she said to Sara. 'Check the harbour too. And tell Max to hurry up with that planning application search. If Steve Gibb pushed his father into the harbour and used a pole to keep him under he must have had a bloody good reason.'

Chapter 17

'Got the browsing history for the Freemans,' Max said.

They were gathered in the incident room, as many officers as Clare could drum up.

'Send it on to Diane, please,' she said. 'Tell her it's priority. I want to know who was viewing that camera footage. I'm still not convinced Steve and Dennis were dealing but I can't rule it out. I'm going to request a search warrant for both houses. If they were dealing, they'll have a stash of burner phones and I want them found.' She checked her notepad then went on. 'Sara needs help checking door camera footage and I want the best shot of the man we think is Steve Gibb printed out. I plan to release it to the press but not until I've shown it to his wife.' She glanced at Max. 'They still saying midday tomorrow for interviewing her?'

He nodded and Clare went on.

'We need to compare Dennis and Steve's phone records. I'll try to get permission from Jenny tomorrow. Save time on a warrant. I want any numbers in both phones checked out.'

Patch raised her hand. 'You want me to look at Steve's social media as well?'

'Definitely – cross-referenced with Dennis's. There might be a vendetta against the family. You'll need help so,' she looked round the room and Gary raised his hand. 'Thanks, Gary. Anyone tagged in photos, friends, contacts – they all need followed up. You know the drill.'

Chris cleared his throat. 'If someone is picking the family off, could Jenny also be in danger?'

It took Clare a moment to register this. Why hadn't she thought of it? If someone was targeting the Gibbs, they had to keep Jenny safe. She might be the only one who could tell them what the hell was going on. 'I'll ask Dundee if they can put someone up in the ward. At least until we know if there's a connection between the two deaths.'

'Could still be natural causes,' Sara said. 'Steve, I mean.'

Clare acknowledged this. 'It's possible, but we can't rule out Steve or Dennis being involved with drugs; and Dennis certainly didn't die of natural causes.'

'If Steve did kill Dennis,' Sara went on, 'maybe he was overcome with guilt and took an overdose.'

'It's possible,' Clare said. 'But we won't know until the PM report's in. Meantime, we treat Steve's death as suspicious.'

Her eye fell on Max. 'Can you look into Steve and Jenny's background please? Extended family, friends, workmates, anyone they socialised with.' Max indicated he would do this and she glanced again at her notepad. Had she covered everything?

The door opened and Jim stood there, notebook in hand. 'Just had Rex Freeman on the phone.'

Clare's heart sank. What now? She forced a smile. 'Yes?'

'Nothing much. A list of folk who've been to the house since they moved in. Mostly tradesman quoting for work.'

Chris took the list from Jim, indicating he'd work through it but Jim stood on, hand on his chin.

'I've had a couple of calls from reporters as well. Seems one of the neighbours took a sneaky photo of Steve Gibb being carried out of his house, sheet over him. Offered it for sale to the papers.' Jim's lip curled at this. 'Now they've been on the phone, asking if it's suspicious.'

Clare clicked her tongue in annoyance. 'Can you get onto the press office please? The usual holding statement – man in his thirties found dead – we're treating it as unexplained etc.'

Jim went off to call the press office and Clare checked her notepad again. 'I think that's everything; but if anything else comes up give me a shout. I'm going to call the drugs squad over in Dundee. See if they know of anyone pushing Fentanyl.'

And, with that, she left the room fishing her mobile out of her pocket as she went.

She sank down behind her desk, mobile still in hand, trying to order her thoughts. Suddenly Dennis's death seemed much more complicated. Had he been involved in drugs? Was someone targeting the family?

'Priorities, Clare,' she murmured, making notes on her pad.

Her first call was to the duty sergeant at Dundee's Bell Street station. 'I've a patient in Ninewells who could be in danger.' She explained about Dennis and Steve's deaths, and the sergeant said he'd have someone at the hospital within the hour. She thanked him and dialled the number for Ninewells Hospital. She asked for the ward Jenny had been taken to but the phone rang out endlessly. Eventually the operator came back on the line and she asked to be put through to the closest telephone to the ward.

'That would be the consultant's office,' the operator said. 'They're only in Monday to Friday. I'll try the next ward along.'

Thankfully the phone was answered and, after explaining the situation, the charge nurse said she'd go straight to the ward and let them know. 'Absolutely no visitors,' Clare said. 'Not without police supervision.'

She called Penny next. 'I may need a warrant,' she began, explaining about Steve Gibb's death. 'I'm hoping the wife will consent to a house search, plus phone and bank records for them both. But, if not, I'll definitely need the warrant.'

'You really think he was dealing?' Penny asked.

'To be honest, I'm not sure. But that phone call, him dying in his sleep – until we have the cause of death I have to treat it as suspicious.'

'When's the PM?'

Clare checked her watch. 'About now. Given the father was murdered, Neil's agreed to prioritise it. I've asked him to test for Fentanyl and other street drugs.'

'You're not attending?' Penny sounded surprised.

'Ideally I would,' Clare said. 'But I'm pushed for time and, to be honest, short of officers.'

'You still have two off sick?'

'Yes. Both have another two weeks on their current Fit Notes. Might be longer.'

'Fair enough. Draw up the warrants and I'll action them.'

Clare was about to end the call when Penny asked about the Freemans.

'I'm guessing not going to the PM will free up some time,' she said. 'Are you making progress?'

For a moment, Clare didn't trust herself to speak. *Free up some time?* Was she having a laugh? 'Sorry,' she said, her tone sharper than was probably wise. 'I've been a bit preoccupied with my two dead bodies.'

The silence at the other end spoke volumes and Clare guessed Penny was waiting for her to apologise, to regret her words. But she wasn't the least bit sorry and she was damned if she was going to say so.

'Delegation,' Penny said finally. 'It's the art of good management.' And, with that, she ended the call.

Clare's heart was beating out of her chest and she took a few breaths in and out. She had a murder, an unexplained death, a burglary where the householders seemed unaware of a hidden camera and, to cap it all, a fucking protest march that was turning into a magnet for rabble-rousers. She'd need half the Force to delegate that lot.

She turned to her to-do list and scored *Warrants* off, half wondering if she'd ever get through a call to Penny without her mentioning the Freemans.

'If I never hear their names again,' she muttered, scrolling through her contacts until she found the number she wanted.

DI Amy Donovan had been with the drug squad for years and Clare reckoned if anyone knew which drugs were circulating it would be her.

'DI Donovan.'

'Amy, hi! How are you?'

They exchanged pleasantries for a few minutes, Amy asking more about Benjy than Clare herself. 'And how's your sexy DCI? Oh wait – he's a Super now isn't he?'

'He's great, thanks.'

'I hear he's through at the college. How's that working out?'

Clare took a moment before answering. How was it working out? She wasn't even sure, herself. 'He's only done a week,' she said, 'but it'll be fine. We'll get used to it.'

Clare heard someone calling Amy's name in the background and got to the point. 'I won't keep you,' she said. 'But I could do with some information.'

'Go on.'

'We had an anonymous call last night, accusing a lad over here of dealing Fentanyl.'

'Fentanyl?' The surprise in Amy's voice gave Clare her answer.

'I'm guessing you've not come across it?'

'Not lately. We are seeing a rise in synthetic opioids but I don't recall Fentanyl being mentioned.'

'Thing is,' Clare went on, 'the lad accused of dealing was found dead in his bed this morning; and his father was pushed into the harbour a couple of weeks ago.'

'Did he survive?'

'Nope. Didn't surface for ten days.'

'And you're wondering if it's all drug-related?'

'We can't ignore the phone call.'

'When's the PM?'

'Right now.'

'They're testing, yeah?'

'They are. Not sure how long it'll take, though.'

'Leave it with me,' Amy said. 'I'll ask around. See if anyone's heard anything. If it comes back positive will you let me know?'

Clare said she would and ended the call.

She was carrying a mug of coffee to her office when Amy called back.

'I've asked around,' she said. 'Nothing to suggest Fentanyl's being used widely. We had one case a month or two ago. Lad brought in with a whole heap of drugs prescribed to his mum. She'd died and he thought he could make a few quid from what was left.'

Clare thanked Amy and promised to let her know the results of Steve's post-mortem. She put down her phone and thought about Steve. It didn't sound like there was a lot of Fentanyl circulating in Dundee. On that basis it was less likely Steve was involved with the drug. Maybe he had died from natural causes? It did happen. Young, healthy people with undiagnosed heart conditions. If it hadn't been for that phone call she wouldn't even be thinking about drugs; and then there was the footage Sara had found, Steve following his father towards the harbour. Had he lost his temper and shoved Dennis into the water? From what Steve and Jenny had said there was no love lost between the pair. But there was a whole world of difference between a family feud and a murder. Maybe he'd panicked when he realised what he'd done, Dennis gasping from the icy waters, saying he'd have him arrested for attempted murder. She imagined Steve picking up the pole and using it to shove his father under, holding him down until there was no more thrashing. And, if he had killed his father, had he taken an overdose out of remorse? She certainly couldn't rule it out.

She was still lost in thought when her office door burst open. She took one look at Max's face and pushed back her chair.

Chapter 18

They gathered round Max's laptop, Clare peering at the document on screen.

'It was the marriage certificate that first alerted me,' Max said. 'Took a bit of time tracking it down and now we know why.'

'So Steve's real name is Brad?' Clare said.

'That was my first thought,' Max said. 'It's not that unusual. Boy at my school was called Jack. We all knew him as Jack. It was only when he won a school prize and his name was called out we realised he was actually called Noah.'

'Could he have changed his name?' Clare said. 'Born Steve, changed it to Brad before his wedding?'

Max glanced at Chris. 'I think you said Jenny called him Steve.'

Chris nodded. 'Yeah, she did.'

'Then I thought it might be the other way round,' Max went on. 'Maybe he was born Brad and changed it to Steve after the wedding. So I had a look and there is a birth certificate for Bradley Gibb. Father Dennis, mother Andrea. Problem is there's also one for Steven Gibb. Same mother and father.'

'Brothers?' Clare said.

'Looks that way.'

'Were they twins?' Chris asked but Max shook his head.

'Born two years apart. One of the press reports has a photo of the boys when they were ten and twelve. If it wasn't for the height difference you would think they were twins. So alike, especially across the eyes.'

'So,' Clare wrinkled her brow, trying to work it out. 'Did Jenny marry Steve or Brad?'

'That's what I wanted to know. So I did a bit more digging.' He took the mouse again and clicked to bring up a news report. Clare sat closer so she could read the headline.

Concern grows for Sheffield man.

She looked at Max. 'This is him? Brad Gibb?'

'Think so. The report mentions his mother Andrea, and his ex-wife, Cindy; and further down it says he has a brother called Steve.'

Chris tapped the screen. 'Almost nine years ago. Was he ever found?'

'Not that I can see,' Max said.

Clare sat back, trying to order her thoughts. 'Is it possible Brad could have stayed under the radar all that time, then married Jenny without coming to the attention of the press?'

Max considered this. 'I don't see why not. It's not as if he'd have set off an alert at the airport. Sounds like he just opted out for a few years. It does happen,' he added. 'Some folk just choose to walk away from their lives.'

Clare sat, taking this in. Was that what had happened here? Brad had just opted out? Or had he been here all the time? Was he the man Jenny had married?

'So which one's our corpse?' she said. 'And if it is Brad, where's Steve?'

Chris rubbed his chin. 'Has to be Steve. The only question is why that marriage certificate shows Jenny married Brad.'

'I'll keep digging,' Max said. 'There's a ton of archive reports on Bradley Gibb.'

Clare wandered back to her office, trying to make sense of this latest development. Whatever the truth of it, one of the Gibb brothers was missing, the other lying on Neil Grant's trolley, having the secrets of his body laid bare.

Max had uploaded Steve and Jenny's marriage certificate to the network and she logged in to study it. The witnesses caught her eye. Errol Johnson and Carlene Brown. He'd added their addresses, both in Montego Bay. Jenny had mentioned the witnesses being local; and that Steve hadn't wanted Dennis there. But had there been another reason? If Steve was really Brad, maybe Dennis would have said something when they were making their vows. Maybe Steve arranged the wedding so no one would question which brother he really was. Might Jenny be able to explain it when they spoke to her tomorrow?

She sat, turning it over in her mind until an alert pinged – an email from Diane.

> I've uploaded the Freemans' browsing history to the network.
>
> Unfortunately nothing that matches with the camera.
>
> Whoever was using it to spy on the Freemans wasn't using their Wi-Fi.
>
> Sorry,
>
> Diane

Clare picked up her phone and tapped on Diane's number.

'You got my email?'

'Yes. You said the battery was still live?'

'It was. Definitely capable of transmitting.'

'So how did they do it?'

'Most likely public Wi-Fi,' Diane said. 'If there was a hotel or guest house nearby – or a public building – they could have piggy-backed onto that.'

Clare thanked Diane and ended the call. In theory she could stand outside the Freemans' house and see which Wi-Fi networks were available. But, even if Penny agreed to a warrant for every network's browsing history, it would be a ridiculous waste of resources, particularly when they had two deaths to investigate. She'd just have to tell her there was nothing more they could do. The Gibb deaths took priority. Of course, there was Dennis's house...

The box of paperwork she'd brought back from his cottage was in the corner of her room and she heaved it onto an empty chair and began leafing through the contents.

An hour later, she sat staring at a letter, an idea forming in her mind.

She found Chris and Max in the incident room. 'Something you two need to see.' She put the letter on the desk in front of them. 'Read this.'

They fell silent, their eyes running over the page.

'Where did you find this?' Max said when he'd finished reading.

'Dennis Gibb's house.' She turned to Chris. 'Remember that box of paperwork I brought back?'

'It was in there?'

'Yep. So we were right. There was a connection between Dennis Gibb and the Freemans. Dennis's cottage is slap bang in the middle of their proposed development and they'd offered to buy it.'

Max's shoulders sagged. 'I should have seen that. I'd downloaded the plans from the council website but, with Steve's death, I never got back to it.'

'What does that tell us, though?' Chris said.

Clare's brow wrinkled. 'I'm not sure. I've been right through the box we took from Dennis's cottage and I can't find anything like a copy of a reply. I'm guessing he didn't want to sell.'

'Might have been an email,' Chris said. 'Or a phone call.'

Suddenly Clare remembered the laptop they'd brought back from Dennis's cottage.

'Did you send that laptop to Tech Support?'

Chris avoided her eye. 'Did you want it sent?'

'Well I didn't want it to prop open my office door! Honestly, Chris. What's going on with you these days?'

His expression darkened and she decided now wasn't the time to have it out with him. 'Find someone to take it down, will you? I'll have to ask Diane to prioritise one of our cases – again!'

He had the grace to blush. 'Sorry. I could take it down, myself.'

Clare thought for a moment. 'Are any of the phone or bank records back?'

He shook his head.

'Then yes please. The sooner they have it the better; and you'd better stop on the way to pick up some cakes. We owe them big time.'

—

She was about to head home when Max appeared at her office door. She motioned him in and lifted the box of papers off the chair but he waved this away.

'I was hoping to knock off soon,' he said. 'Zoe's doing a Mexican meal.'

Clare's mouth watered at the prospect and she wondered if she could persuade Al to do likewise. She had hoped he'd be back from his walk in time to cook something. It wasn't fair really, expecting him to cook all the time. She knew that. But he was so good at it and she *was* in the middle of a murder investigation. 'Go for it,' she said. 'I'll be heading home soon myself.'

'Before I go,' he went on, 'I turned up something else.'

'Oh, yes?'

'Brad Gibb was never found – dead or alive.'

'Yes, we know that.'

'But, he hasn't been declared dead. Not officially.'

Clare sat back, considering this. 'I'm guessing no one applied to the court for a formal declaration.'

'Nope.'

'Dennis's will, though,' Clare said. 'Isn't Steve the sole beneficiary?'

'He is. I'm guessing Dennis didn't realise he'd have to apply for Brad to be declared dead. Maybe he assumed it happened automatically after seven years.'

'Wasn't there an ex-wife?'

'Yes,' Max said. 'Cindy I think. But if they were divorced she probably didn't care enough. I don't think there were any children.'

'So,' Clare said, twiddling a pencil between her fingers, 'for all we know, Brad could still be alive.'

'Yep. He might even be in the area.'

'That footage, though,' Clare said.

'From the door cameras?'

'Yes. We're pretty sure it was Steve following Dennis, aren't we?'

'Certainly looked that way. Are you thinking it could have been Brad?'

Clare thought back to the photo Max had found – Steve and his brother as young boys. *If it hadn't been for the height difference he'd have thought they were twins.* Was it possible Brad had been here in the town the night Dennis died? Could he have been the figure following Dennis to the harbour? And, if so, was he somehow involved in Dennis's death – or Steve's?

Clare exhaled. 'It's a bit of a leap but we can't rule it out.'

She shoved back her chair. 'Think I'll head home too. The more I think about this case the more muddled it becomes.' She indicated the door. 'Go on. Get off home. We'll look at it with fresh eyes in the morning.' She took out her phone and sent a message to Al, asking if he fancied Mexican. Then she gathered up her coat and bag, and headed out to the car.

'So now you have a connection between Dennis Gibb and the Freemans?' Al said, picking up a fajita and folding over the end.

Clare dabbed her lips with a piece of kitchen roll. 'We do.'

He bit into the fajita and chewed for a minute. 'The Freemans wanted to buy Dennis's cottage?'

'Looks that way.'

'Had he agreed to sell?'

Clare shook her head, mouth full of fajita.

'No solicitors' letters?'

'Certainly not in that box of papers.'

'And his cottage is definitely within the proposed development?'

'Yep.'

'What about the other properties?' Al said, helping himself to another wrap. 'Anyone else holding out?'

'Dunno. I'll get Max onto it in the morning. But Dennis's cottage sits by itself – farmland all round. So it's possible his was the only house within the development area.'

'Which gives the Freemans a motive.'

Clare frowned at this. 'It does. But I'm not convinced they'd resort to murder. Intimidation, maybe. But murder?'

Al began spreading salsa on his wrap. 'Who inherits the cottage?'

'Steve's wife.'

'Tidy sum, then.'

'Yes. And I'm guessing they had a policy to pay off their own mortgage if one of them died so, financially, she'll be pretty well off.'

Al eyed her. 'Anything there?'

She considered this. 'On balance, I'd say no. I've still to interview her but she seemed devastated.'

He inclined his head. 'She wouldn't be the first…'

'Yeah, I know.'

'Unless the missing brother's involved.'

Clare wiped her fingers on the kitchen roll. 'There's definitely something iffy there. That marriage certificate for a start.'

'You going to ask the wife?'

'Just as soon as she's fit to be interviewed. I want to know which brother she actually married.'

Day 6: Sunday, 15th February

Chapter 19

The conversation with Al the night before ran round Clare's head as she drove into the station. The letter among Dennis's papers confirmed the Freemans had wanted to buy his cottage and, as far as she could tell, he hadn't agreed to sell. But, if he had sold, he'd have been worth a few quid. Maybe Steve was concerned the money would go the same way as Dennis's redundancy payment – straight down his neck.

Then there was the mysterious Brad. Had he somehow heard an offer had been made for Dennis's cottage and reappeared to persuade his father to sell? Had that persuasion turned to intimidation or even a scuffle at the harbour? And, having dealt with Dennis, had he then turned his attention to Steve? With him out of the way maybe Brad thought he'd inherit Dennis's estate himself? If he had, Jenny might also be in danger. Thank goodness there was an officer stationed outside her room. The sooner they spoke to her the better.

'Got a pretty good photo,' Sara said as Clare popped her head round the incident room door. She moved into the room and picked up a copy, studying it. It showed the same man in three-stripe trousers walking in the direction of the harbour. But the camera was a better one, the image clearer.

'Has Chris seen this?'

'Yeah. He reckons it is Steve.'

'I agree,' Clare said. 'Can I keep this? I want to show it to Jenny when she's fit to be interviewed.'

'Sure. I've sent it on to the press office,' Sara said, 'and I've printed a few more copies in case you want us to go house-to-house.'

'Keep at the social media for now. You're looking for anyone with precons for drugs and any arguments involving Dennis or Steve.' She looked round the room. 'Max?'

'Think he's out with Patch.'

'Where?'

'Not sure.' Sara glanced round. 'Anyone know where Max is?'

'Housebreaking,' Gillian said, looking up from her laptop.

'Another one?'

'Yeah. Somewhere in the town. Didn't catch the address.'

Clare thanked Gillian and headed for her office, her mind on Bradley Gibb. Was he still alive and, if so, where was he? Waiting for her computer to warm up her thoughts turned to Jenny. If Brad was still alive, had Jenny anything to fear from him? She took out her phone and dialled the number for the hospital ward. Again it rang out and when the switchboard operator came back on she said she'd call later. Instead she rang the Bell Street station in Dundee.

'You've an officer up at Ninewells Hospital,' she said, when the operator answered. 'Can you give me their number please?'

A minute later, she was speaking to PC Vanessa Coyne, a uniformed officer she hadn't met. The line wasn't great but she managed a brief conversation.

'I took over at seven this morning,' Vanessa said. 'My colleague said Jenny had been pretty distressed overnight and they'd upped the sedation. She's sleeping now.'

'Any idea when she'll be conscious?'

'No but I'll see what I can find out.'

Clare thanked Vanessa and ended the call. She sat thinking for a minute. Should she arrange a Family Liaison Officer for when Jenny was discharged? Maybe it could wait until they had the cause of death.

She wandered through to the kitchen, already feeling weary. Chris was spooning coffee into a mug. 'Want one?'

'Please. Any biscuits?'

'It's only nine o'clock.'

'I know. I just need something.'

'Only these.' He indicated a plate of Biscoff, his lip curling.

She eyed them. 'You're not a fan?'

He snorted. 'As if. You'd need about ten of them for a decent mouthful.'

'You wouldn't happen to have…'

He glanced at the door. 'Sara's only in the incident room.'

'I'll keep watch.'

He shook his head. 'I'm not letting you see my hiding place.' He poured boiling water into mugs and set the kettle down. 'Tell you what – you promise not to give me any shitty jobs for the next month and I'll bring one to your office.'

Clare added milk to her mug and stirred the coffee. 'Deal.' She hovered at the door, trying to gauge where Chris might have hidden his precious Wagon Wheel biscuits but he stood, arms folded, waiting for her to leave. A minute later, he nudged her office door open with his foot, coffee mug in one hand, a pair of Wagon Wheel biscuits in the other. He set these down on the desk and Clare grabbed at them.

'Oy! One's for me.'

She shrugged and pushed one of the biscuits back across the desk. She bit into hers and, not for the first time, told him what a disappointing biscuit it was.

'I'll have it back then,' he said but she waved this away.

'Any sign of Steve's phone and bank records?'

He nodded. 'Just going to have this then I'll make a start.'

'You need to compare them with Dennis's.'

'Yeah, you've already said.' He slurped his coffee. 'Any word from Ninewells?'

'Still sedated. The cop up there's going to let me know.'

They fell into a companionable silence broken by Clare's phone buzzing and she clicked to take the call.

'Max?'

'It's this housebreaking,' he said. 'Something odd about it.'

'Go on.' She put the phone on speaker so Chris could hear.

'There doesn't seem to be anything missing.'

Chris sat forward in his seat. 'Was there much worth taking?'

'I'd say so.'

He raised an eyebrow. 'Were they disturbed?'

'Nope. Householder was away overnight. Wedding across in Dundee. Apparently she stayed the night at the hotel and she's just arrived back. It was a neighbour who saw the back door lying open. But that wasn't until eight this morning.'

'And there's definitely nothing missing?'

'Don't think she's had time to do a proper check. But her jewellery's all there, an expensive watch too; and there was thirty quid on the kitchen table. That's not been touched.'

'What about electricals?' Clare said.

'She has an internet TV – that's still here. It would be pretty big to carry off but there's a smaller TV in the kitchen. They didn't take that either.'

Clare's mind went back to the Freemans' house. Two burglaries in as many days and nothing taken at either. It couldn't be a coincidence, could it?

'There's a bit of mess, as well,' Max went on. 'Like they were searching for something.'

Clare was quiet for a moment. If these burglaries were connected, it meant the Freemans might be wrong in thinking their break-in was related to the development.

'I don't suppose SOCO would come out?' Max said.

Clare exhaled 'Honestly, I can't justify the cost. The prints and DNA they lifted from the Freemans didn't match with our system. Even if it is the same burglars, bringing SOCO out wouldn't help identify them.'

'Fair enough. I thought it was a long shot.'

'Just have a good look around,' Clare said. 'Gloves on, mind. You're looking for anything they might have dropped. A petrol receipt – that kind of thing.'

She ended the call and returned to her coffee and biscuit.

'Can't be a coincidence,' Chris said.

Clare nodded. 'I agree. The question is why? Why break into two houses and take nothing? And, if they were searching for something, what was it? Did they find it?'

'Could be some voyeuristic thing,' Chris said, crumpling the Wagon Wheel wrapper and aiming it at Clare's bin.

'That's a big word for a Sunday morning.'

He eyed her. 'This is bordering on workplace bullying, Inspector.'

'Noted, Sergeant.'

–

It was late morning by the time Chris lifted his head from Steve and Dennis's phone records.

'There is one number common to both,' he said, jabbing the screen. 'This one here.'

Clare sat down beside him. 'Is it saved as a contact?'

'Nope.'

'Any messages?'

He shook his head. 'Calls only.'

'In or out?'

He peered at the screen. 'Incoming on Dennis's phone, both ways on Steve's.'

Clare sat back. 'You reckon it could be Brad?'

'Yeah. Could be.'

'Let's say he's still alive,' Clare said. 'Maybe he had his dad's number.'

Chris raised an eyebrow. 'After nine years?'

'Why not? I've had the same mobile number for ages.'

He inclined his head. 'Okay. Go on.'

'Say he phones Dennis. Dunno why but maybe he wanted to see him again. Dennis isn't interested and hangs up.'

'Which would explain why he didn't call the number back.'

'But Steve's his brother,' Clare went on. 'Maybe they had more to say to each other.'

'Hence more calls, in and out.' He threw her a glance. 'You mention *hence* and I'll put in a complaint.'

She held up her hands in mock innocence. 'As if.' She was quiet for a moment, her mind running through the possibilities. 'Maybe the two of them had a plan to make Dennis change his mind about selling to the Freemans.'

Chris nodded. 'Yeah, that works. Could be Brad was already down at the harbour, waiting for Dennis.'

'So the two of them pushed him in the water,' Clare finished. She looked at Chris. 'Does that make sense? Or am I grasping at straws?'

He shrugged. 'Makes as much sense as any other motive for murder.'

They lapsed into silence again then Chris sat forward. 'We could check the DNA from the Freemans' house against Steve Gibb's.'

'You think Steve broke into the Freemans'?'

'It's a possibility,' Chris said. 'Let's say the Freemans make Dennis an offer.'

'Which he declines.'

'He does. Maybe he asks for more money and the Freemans say they can't afford it. Then Steve thinks, if he breaks in, he might find something on them. Let's face it, there's no shortage of rumours about them using cheap materials. Steve probably thinks he can force them to up their offer.'

Clare shook her head. 'Won't work.'

'Why not?'

'Because, by the time the Freemans' house was broken into, Dennis Gibb had been dead for over a week; and Steve was dead when the second break-in happened.'

'Dammit. I'd forgotten that.' He was quiet for a moment. 'What about the mysterious Brad, then? If he's been living off grid for the past nine years, could be he's no stranger to a spot of breaking and entering.'

'Yes,' Clare said. 'I can't help thinking he figures in this. That phone call, accusing Steve of dealing – could that have been Brad?'

Chris yawned. 'I dunno. Why would he do that?'

'Maybe he and Steve had fallen out. Say Brad wanted a share of Dennis's cottage and Steve wasn't having it.'

Chris considered this. 'Maybe. But why would Brad surface now, after all these years?'

'Why indeed.' Clare picked up a pen and began tapping it against the desk. 'I think it's time we found out what happened to Bradley Gibb.'

Chapter 20

Clare was studying a copy of the government guidance on policing marches when her phone rang. She glanced at the display and saw it was Neil Grant.

'Got your post-mortem results,' he said. 'I meant to get them to you yesterday but I ran out of time.'

You and me both, Clare thought. 'No problem. What was the cause of death?'

'You were on the money with Fentanyl. There was more than enough in his system to kill him.'

'He overdosed?'

'Looks that way.'

'Deliberate?'

'I can't tell you that, Clare. That's your job. But what I can say is there was grapefruit juice in his stomach.'

'Eh?'

–

'Apparently, if you take grapefruit juice with Fentanyl it can increase the amount of Fentanyl in the body.'

Chris and Max exchanged glances. Max was the first to find his voice. 'What, like it concentrates the effect?'

Clare's brow creased. 'I think so. Neil says it was a pretty hefty dose so he might have died anyway; but with the addition of grapefruit juice he didn't stand a chance.' She took out her phone, scrolling for Raymond's number. 'I want Steve's water bottle checked. If the Fentanyl's in that it's pretty safe to say he took it himself.'

Chris shook his head. 'I disagree. Why add it to a bottle? If it was tablets, why not just swallow them?' He looked to Max as if seeking confirmation. 'I reckon if there's Fentanyl in the bottle he didn't know about it. Someone else drugged him.'

They sat, processing this.

'And there's another thing,' Chris went on.

They waited.

'If there was Fentanyl in his water bottle and we find grapefruit juice as well, we might be looking for someone with medical knowledge. Who else would know about grapefruit juice concentrating the effect?'

'Almost no one,' Clare said. 'Unless they did have medical knowledge.'

He stared at her. 'You still don't see it?'

'What?'

'Where does Jenny Gibb work?'

'A doctor's surgery in – oh…'

'Hold on, though,' Max said. 'That's a pretty obscure bit of information. She's a receptionist, isn't she?'

'She is,' Clare said. 'But they do have some medical training.'

Max shook his head. 'Not enough to know something like that.'

'Unless the surgery had a patient die of something similar,' Chris went on. 'And, if we factor Brad into the equation…'

Clare stared at him. 'You think Brad and Jenny could have planned this together?'

He shrugged. 'Remember whose name's on the marriage certificate.'

They fell silent, considering this. Clare was first to find her voice. 'Are you saying Steve and Jenny were pretending to be married? That she and Brad conspired to kill Dennis and Steve?'

Chris looked from Clare to Max. 'I've heard weirder stories.'

Max inclined his head. 'I mean, it's possible…'

Clare pushed back her chair. 'In that case, the sooner we speak to Jenny Gibb the better.'

Raymond had already sent the contents of the water bottle for analysis. 'Should be with you late today or tomorrow,' he said. Clare thanked him and she sat back to consider what the SOCO team might find. She had to admit Chris was right about Fentanyl in the water bottle. She knew it came in different forms including liquid. But if the Gibb men were dealing, surely the most likely form was tablets.

A knock interrupted her thoughts and Patch appeared, an evidence bag in hand.

'Found this at the house.' She held it out and Clare saw it contained a small device.

'Flash drive,' Patch went on. 'Kicked under a coffee table. I thought it must belong to the householder but she said no.'

'So the burglars dropped it?'

'Must have. Want me to send it down to Tech Support?'

Clare thought for a moment. Strictly speaking it should go to SOCO first for prints and DNA tests. But the samples taken from the Freemans' house showed what a waste of time and money that was. She should follow procedure, really – send it to Tech Support for Diane's team to check it over. There could be malware or anything on it. But if it had been dropped by whoever had broken into the house they might find something on it to identify the burglar. Her eye went to the USB port on the front of her computer. Could she?

For a brief moment, she imagined herself responsible for hackers gaining access to Police Scotland's most sensitive networks. She couldn't risk it. But maybe there was a way.

'Leave it with me,' she told Patch. She waited for her to go then picked up the phone and called Diane. 'Sorry,' she said, as soon as Diane answered. 'You must be sick of hearing from me.'

Diane laughed. 'You're certainly keeping us busy. What have you got now?'

'It's more advice,' Clare said. She explained about the flash drive. 'Honestly, if we could look at it here it would save so much time.'

'True but it might have some malware. You could end up infecting the whole network.'

'That was my worry,' Clare admitted. 'Any way we could get round that?'

Diane hesitated. 'The official answer is you send it to us and we check it over. The unofficial answer is a standalone laptop. Do you have an old one kicking around that's not connected to the network?'

'Should do. Probably in Jim's Cupboard of Many Things.'

'Before you plug the flash drive in, make sure the laptop's definitely not connected to the network. Even if you use it offline, anything that does infect the machine could find its way onto the network if the machine ever does reconnect. If you're not sure about it give me a call. When you've done that you must scan the flash drive for malware. If you find anything send the machine and the drive to us. Don't do anything else. Clear?'

Clare thanked her and went in search of Jim. 'Don't suppose you have an old laptop I could use as a standalone?'

Jim exhaled. 'Oh, I'm not sure. We sent the old ones back when they upgraded the machines.'

A wave of disappointment swept over Clare. Would she really have to send the flash drive to Tech Support? There was no way they'd look at it today, even if she could get it down there. 'Is it worth a look?'

Jim gave her a smile. 'As it's you...'

She'd been in Jim's cupboard a few times but she never ceased to be amazed by how organised it was. Every shelf was labelled, items in clear plastic boxes. She was half tempted to ask if he'd have a go at the under-stairs cupboard in Daisy Cottage. He went right to the back, kneeling down to investigate one of the lower shelves, removing items and stacking them neatly to one side.

'Aha!'

Clare crossed her fingers. Had he found one? He eased back on his heels and hauled himself up, holding onto shelves either side. 'This do?' He held out a grey laptop, the cable dangling. 'If I remember rightly it belonged to your predecessor. He went off sick then he was transferred. Must have been six months later he was back in the town for something and he handed this in. I meant to send it down to Diane but somehow it was missed.'

'Jim! You're an absolute star. Thank you.'

He laughed. 'Just don't ask me to fit it back in here when you're finished.'

Clare offered to have Patch help him repack the shelves but he waved this away. 'I wouldn't trust any of them.'

Back in her office, she plugged in the laptop and called Diane back. 'Would you mind talking me through this? I'd hate to cause a problem.'

Diane directed Clare to the security software on the laptop and asked her to read out the version.

'Way out of date,' she said. 'You'll have to connect to the network to update this then remove the network, to be on the safe side. You might also want to have a colleague witness what you're doing – in case there's evidence on the flash drive.'

She left Clare with instructions to download and install security updates which took almost half an hour.

'It's not exactly lightning fast,' Clare said when she called Diane back.

'Got someone with you?'

'Chris is here,' she said. 'He's going to video what I'm doing.' Chris called hello into the phone and Diane acknowledged this.

She talked Clare through disconnecting it from the network. 'I'd recommend sending the machine to us when you're done. You don't want to risk someone reconnecting. Not until we've checked it over.'

Clare said she'd do that then she glanced at Chris. 'Ready?'

'Gloves,' he advised and she reached into her bottom desk drawer where she kept a box of neoprene gloves. She pulled on a pair and Chris began recording. As soon as Clare plugged in the flash drive the security software got to work, the check taking only a few seconds.

'It says no threats found,' Clare said into the phone.

'Good. Open the drive and tell me what you see.'

It took an agonisingly long time for the drive to open. When it did the screen filled with dozens of icons.

'Loads of files,' Clare said. 'All MP4 by the looks of it.' She scrolled down, her eyes scanning the file names for anything different. 'Yeah. All the same.'

'Video footage,' Diane said. 'I can't tell you how long each clip will be but if they've not been saved with meaningful names it'll be a tedious job for someone going through them.'

'And we're okay to open them?'

'Do a quick check for hidden files, first.' She talked Clare through this then, with a final warning about not reconnecting to the network, she ended the call.

'So,' Chris said. 'What now?'

'Now, Sergeant, we start checking these files.'

Chapter 21

Clare was beginning to give up hope of finding anything of interest when she opened the tenth clip.

'If there's nothing in the next few I'll get Patch onto it,' she said. 'I've too much to do to waste time on this.'

The clip began to play and she stared at the screen. 'Is that where I think it is?'

Chris leaned in. 'Jesus! It's the Freemans' sitting room.' He jabbed the screen with his finger. 'That's their drinks cabinet.'

Clare left the file playing, her eyes trained on the screen. 'What does this mean, though?'

Chris shrugged. 'Maybe whoever broke into the house last night also installed the hidden camera at the Freemans'.'

'But why?' Clare shook her head. 'I can't make sense of it.'

A figure appeared, a young woman in a tabard, pushing a Dyson back and forth.

'I'd have bet on them having a Roomba,' Chris said.

'You can't order a Roomba about.'

'Fair point. I fancied one but Sara said it'd never cope with the biscuit wrappers.'

'She's not wrong.'

The file ended and Clare clicked to play the next. They watched as Rex came into the room, iPad in hand. He sank down on the sofa, eyes on the screen, tapping occasionally at the keyboard. A minute later, he looked up and Erika appeared carrying two coffee mugs.

'It's like watching paint dry,' Chris said.

'It's not exactly riveting.' She clicked to pause the clip. 'I'll ask Patch to carry on.' She made for the door and stopped. 'Last night's burglary – was it near the Freemans' house?'

Chris's brow creased. 'Don't think so. Somewhere on the Bogward Estate. Check with Patch.'

Clare found her in the kitchen, taking a Tupperware box out of the fridge.

'Job for you.'

'Sure.' Patch made to put the box back in the fridge but Clare stopped her.

'Have your break. Then I've a flash drive plugged into a standalone laptop. It's full of MP4 files. I need you to go through them. See if there's anything of note.'

Patch said she'd get onto it after lunch and Clare turned to go.

'I meant to ask,' she said, stopping in the doorway. 'Where was last night's burglary?'

'Radernie Place,' Patch said. 'Just off Bogward Road.'

Clare knew it. 'Who are the owners?'

'Single woman. Carol Merryweather. She was nice,' she added.

—

Clare rubbed her temples, trying to clear a threatening headache. 'Can we make some sense of this please? Between Steve, Dennis and the burglaries, my head's mince.'

They were gathered in her office, Chris and Max perched on chairs opposite. Patch had been relegated to one of the interview rooms to check the remaining flash drive files with strict instructions not to connect to the network.

'Okay,' Max began. 'Let's take the Gibbs first. Do we think Steve killed Dennis?'

Clare nodded. 'I think so.'

'Motive?'

She glanced at Chris. 'It has to be that cottage. There was a letter from the Freemans among Dennis's papers,' she explained to Max. 'They wanted to buy but it doesn't look like Dennis was willing to sell.'

'Did Steve have money worries?' Max asked.

Clare and Chris exchanged glances. 'It could be more complicated than that,' Clare said. 'We're wondering if Brad Gibb might still be alive.'

Max's eyes widened. 'You think he's the one who killed Dennis?'

'I'm not sure,' Clare said. 'We're pretty sure the CCTV Sara found shows Steve following Dennis towards the harbour. But, if Brad is still alive, maybe he was already down there, waiting for Dennis.'

'Jeez,' Max said. 'It's like a Netflix series. Do you really think Brad's not dead?'

Clare spread her hands. 'I honestly don't know. But, given his body was never found and his two closest relatives have just died, we can't ignore it.'

Max exhaled. 'Fair enough. But I'm not sure how we find someone who's been missing for nine years.'

'Nor me,' Clare said. 'But we have Steve and Dennis's DNA so any samples with a fifty per cent match could be Brad. And…' she hesitated, 'we'll have to go back through Steve's social media, phone records, speak to his work colleagues. If Brad is still alive it's possible Steve knew about it. He might even have told someone.'

'What about Jenny?' Max asked.

'Oh, yes,' Clare said. 'We'll definitely be speaking to Jenny.' She was quiet for a moment. 'So that's Dennis. What about Steve?'

'I reckon someone killed him,' Max said.

Chris shook his head. 'Difficult to prove.'

'Maybe; but if he was dealing Fentanyl he'd have known how much to take without risking an overdose.'

'I agree,' Clare said. 'Someone must have slipped the pills into his water bottle. The tablets are soluble so they may not have been noticed, especially with the grapefruit juice to mask the taste.'

'Suppose,' Chris conceded. 'Chances are whoever it was didn't realise there was grapefruit juice in the bottle – or the effect it would have. They probably didn't mean to kill him. That phone call,' he went on. 'The caller accusing Steve of dealing. My money's on a rival dealer. I bet they slipped him a few pills, hoping we'd arrest him and find it in his blood stream. They didn't so much want him dead as want him warned.'

Clare was quiet for a moment. 'I'm not sure,' she said. 'I spoke to Amy Donovan, a DI in the drugs squad over in Dundee. They've not seen any Fentanyl dealing to speak of.'

Chris shrugged. 'Doesn't mean it's not happening.'

'Of course,' Clare said. 'And now we've alerted them I'm sure she'll let us know if they do see it circulating. But, for now, I'm not convinced about a rival dealer.'

'What about Jenny?' Max asked. 'Her reaction to his death was pretty extreme.'

'It was,' Clare said, a troubled look in her eyes.

'That was more than grief,' Max went on. 'She was hysterical – and she'd definitely have had access to Steve's bottle.'

'And she's married to Brad,' Chris added. 'Legally, anyway.'

Clare met his eye. 'I know what we've said about Brad's involvement and his name on that marriage certificate but I really don't want it to be Jenny. Don't ask me why. There's something – oh I don't know – something vulnerable about her. I reckon he railroaded her into that wedding. When we mentioned the photo I'm sure she wasn't completely happy about it.' She turned to Chris. 'Could you imagine Sara agreeing to a wedding like that? No friends, or family?'

He was quiet for a moment. 'I hear what you're saying. But you're letting sentiment get in the way.'

She shrugged. 'Suppose. I just don't want it to be her.'

Chris eyed her. 'You can't be thinking like that. We've a job to do here. It's for her defence advocate to argue the degree of culpability.'

She forced a smile. 'Yeah, I know. Oh, let's leave Steve and Dennis for now – at least until we've spoken to Jenny. Let's get back to the burglaries.'

'Bit of a coincidence,' Chris said, 'Carol Merryweather's house being burgled a few days after the Freemans'.'

'Both houses searched and nothing taken,' Max added.

'And Carol works for the company who sold the house to the Freemans,' Clare said. 'It can't be a coincidence.'

'So what's the connection?' Max said. 'Why were both these houses targeted?'

Clare shook her head. 'No idea. But I'm going to find out.'

–

It was growing dark by the time the call from Ninewells came in. 'She's calmer now,' Vanessa said. 'I think they might want to keep her in another night. She won't eat, barely drinks. Just cries all the time. The psych doc's with her now.'

'Can we speak to her?'

'They said it was up to the psych guy. I'll let you know what he says.'

Clare checked her watch and tapped out a message to Al letting him know she'd be late. She saw the dots indicating he was typing and a minute later his reply came in.

> I'll be here till 7 then I'll have to leave.
>
> I'll feed Benjy and give him another walk. If you're going to be out past 11 you'll need to come back and let him out.
>
> Try not to be too late – for your sake as well as B's.
>
> X

She stared at the message and found herself unreasonably annoyed with Al, telling her not to be home late. Like she had a choice!

It was fine for him, with his shiny new job. Why couldn't he have stayed in his old job at Bell Street? If he had he'd be relaxing in front of a roaring fire instead of packing for another week away. He'd be there when she finally arrived home, his open arms pulling her in, holding her close. He'd warm up some food or pour her a glass of wine and listen as she talked about her day. He'd tell her what Benjy had been up to and they'd laugh at the little dog's exploits, Clare pretending to scold him.

But sitting here now in the quiet of her office, her to-do list growing by the minute, she resented his new role – the orderly nature of it. Why couldn't she have a job like that?

And then she realised who she was really annoyed at. Penny, obviously, Al to an extent. But, most of all, she was angry with herself. She couldn't blame Al for grabbing this opportunity. The job was made for him and it had come with a promotion. Problem was the job Clare had been offered – his job – most definitely wasn't made for her. But, because she hadn't taken it, hadn't had the courage to move out of her lane, she was stuck in a situation of her own making.

Al's first weekend home and she'd barely seen him. And now he'd be gone by the time she finished for the day. How many more weekends would there be like this?

She stared at her phone, willing Vanessa to call, hoping she might still make it home before he left. But her phone remained stubbornly silent. She let her shoulders sag as the anger left her body. There was nothing else for it. This was the path she'd chosen and she'd just have to get on with it.

Chapter 22

It was another hour before they heard Jenny Gibb was well enough to be interviewed.

'The psych doc says she's lucid enough but to go easy. She's still pretty tired,' Vanessa said. Clare thanked her and went to find Chris. He was sitting in the incident room, lost in thought, a laptop open in front of him.

'Earth to Chris?' she said, waving a hand in front of him.

He stifled a yawn. 'Sorry. What's happening?'

'Jenny Gibb,' Clare said. 'Come on. Let's see what she has to say for herself.'

The sun was low in the sky as they headed out of town. They passed the playing fields in front of the Old Course Hotel and Clare's eyes drifted across to the West Sands, beyond the hotel – the starting point for the protest march. Would they have made any progress by the day of the march? It was looking increasingly unlikely.

A black ice warning flashed up on the dashboard, catching Clare's eye. 'Going to be another cold one,' she said, glancing at Chris. He made a noncommittal grunt and they continued the journey in silence. Clearly she wasn't the only one feeling the strain of the investigation.

Ten minutes later, she took the turning for Ninewells Hospital, making for the closest car park.

'I wish it was like this all the time,' she said, indicating the empty spaces.

'Sunday teatime,' Chris said. 'All the sensible folk are at home watching *Antiques Roadshow*.'

'Don't tell me you're a fan,' she said as they descended the steps towards the main entrance.

'Hah. You must be joking. That's more Max's thing than mine. But Sara's mum likes it. Says she's an attic full of treasures. If you ask me, it's all junk.'

They entered the concourse, Clare making straight for the Acute Medical Unit. She'd been there so many times over the years she didn't need to check for directions. A woman in hospital pyjamas, her skin as dark as leather came towards them. She was wheeling a drip stand, her fags and lighter in the other hand.

'If ever there was a time to give up smoking,' Clare said. 'It's Baltic out there.'

Chris shrugged. 'Needs must.'

They weaved their way through the corridors until they arrived at the unit. The smell of cooking was everywhere, a line of heated trolleys stacked against one wall.

A uniformed officer was sitting on a chair outside a room, Vanessa Coyne, Clare guessed. She introduced herself and Chris, and asked when Vanessa went off duty.

She checked her watch. 'Another two hours.'

'Go and get yourself some food,' Clare said. 'We'll be half an hour at least.'

'Not much still open,' Chris said but Vanessa waved this away.

'I've sandwiches in the car. I'll nip out to fetch them.'

They waited until she'd left then pushed open the door to Jenny's room.

She lay propped up, her head on one side, staring into space. She turned a little when they entered then sank back into the pillows. Her cheeks were pale and tear-stained. There was a pulse oximeter on her finger, a monitor by the bed showing her heart rate. She had a cannula strapped to her hand but there were no tubes attached and Clare wondered if they were weaning her off sedation.

'Hello,' she said, her voice soft. 'Remember us?'

Jenny eyed Clare and gave a slight nod.

'Clare and Chris,' she went on, hoping for a response, but still Jenny said nothing.

'How are you?'

Jenny closed her eyes and shook her head.

Clare waited to see if she would speak then she carried on. 'It must have been a dreadful shock, finding Steve. I'm so sorry. If there's anything we can do you only have to ask.'

She raised her hand slightly, and Clare wasn't sure if she was acknowledging this or dismissing the notion.

'Jenny,' Clare tried again, 'we'd like to ask you about yesterday morning, if you feel up to it. Would that be okay?'

They gave her a minute and when she moved her head to face Clare she saw Jenny's eyes were brimming. Chris took a handful of tissues from a box on the bedside cabinet and handed them to her. She took them and dabbed at her eyes.

'Maybe we could start from Friday night,' Clare said. 'I gather Steve slept in the spare room, yes?'

Jenny dabbed her eyes again and nodded. 'We'd argued,' she said, her voice barely above a whisper. She swallowed hard and Clare resisted the temptation to prompt her.

'It was the day after you'd been to tell us about Dennis being killed,' she said eventually. 'We'd both called in sick. My job – you can't do it with your head somewhere else. And Steve, well, he drives and he might have had an accident. So I said we should both stay off. Maybe talk about a funeral, that kind of thing.' She broke off and Clare had the impression she was ordering her thoughts – trying to decide how much to tell them. If so, what was she hiding?

Then her expression cleared. 'In the end, we didn't do any of that. Steve – he was just watching TV and I did a big ironing. Anyway, it got to four, maybe half four, and I asked what he wanted for tea. And that's when he – he said he'd go to the gym.' She began worrying a honeycomb blanket with her fingers, her eyes avoiding Clare's. 'He'd sat on his backside all day and then he decided he was going out.' She flicked a glance at Clare. 'I know it sounds terrible but I was annoyed.'

'Understandable,' Clare said giving her a smile. 'Everyone deals with grief in their own way.'

'Suppose.'

'So he went to the gym, yes?'

She nodded. 'I mean, I think so. That's what he said, anyway.' She hesitated. 'I think he knew I was annoyed because he said he'd bring back fish and chips. Only, he was gone for hours; and I know it sounds heartless, but I was starving. I hadn't eaten since twelve. And, when he did eventually come back he was stinking of drink; and he'd forgotten the food. I was furious. So I said he could sleep where he liked as long as it wasn't with me.'

She started to weep quietly and Chris pushed the box of tissues towards her. She smiled her thanks and took another handful.

'And yesterday morning?' Clare said, her voice as gentle as she could manage.

The tears were streaming down Jenny's face now.

Clare took hold of her hand. 'This must so painful,' she said. 'But the more help you can give us, the quicker we can work out what happened to Steve.'

Her head was down now, shoulders shaking and they watched as she seemed to be struggling with some inner turmoil. Clare glanced at Chris who shrugged. She gave Jenny a minute and tried again.

'Jenny, I know this is dreadful for you.'

'No,' her voice was raised now. 'You don't know. You don't understand. It's not that.'

Clare let her cry, let her talk between sobs.

'It's Steve,' she said, clutching a crumpled tissue. 'It's all my fault.' She raised her face to meet Clare's, her cheeks blotchy with crying. 'It's my fault,' she said again. 'I killed him.'

It took a good ten minutes to calm Jenny down long enough for her to make any sense.

'I was so angry with him,' she said, 'coming in late, stinking of drink. He was in a horrible mood too.' Her face darkened at the memory. 'I'd made myself cheese on toast earlier and he asked if there was any food – like I was his servant or something.' She reached for the water beaker, her hand shaking. She drank, spilling some of it down her front then replaced the glass, wiping at her hospital gown.

'I had this pie,' she went on. 'Five days out of date. He was so drunk I didn't think he'd notice. I heated it then I lifted up the pastry. I put a load of salt and pepper on the filling, to disguise the taste.' She looked at Clare, her eyes pink with crying. 'I only meant to give him a tummy upset. I never dreamt...' She broke off as sobs overtook her once more.

Clare glanced at Chris and saw he was thinking the same as her. There's no way that pie could have killed him. There was no sign he'd been sick or had diarrhoea; and the post-mortem had confirmed the cause of death – an overdose of Fentanyl.

'Jenny,' she said, putting a hand on her arm, 'listen to me, okay?' She waited until she knew Jenny was listening. 'You did not kill Steve. Do you hear me? You didn't kill him.'

Jenny's eyes widened. 'I don't understand. He's dead and I gave him that pie. It must have poisoned him. It's too much of a coincidence.'

Clare gave Jenny's arm a gentle squeeze. 'You didn't. The pie had no effect on him. It didn't cause his death.'

She looked from Clare to Chris and back at Clare again. 'Then what?'

Clare considered her next few words carefully. There wasn't any reason to withhold the truth from Jenny. She'd have to know soon enough. 'Can you tell us what was usually in Steve's water bottle?'

The frown on Jenny's face deepened. 'His bottle? I don't understand.'

'Did he have a favourite drink?' Clare suggested.

'Erm, water, mostly. Sometimes juice.'

'Any particular juice?' Chris asked.

She stared at him. 'Tesco's I think. Why does it matter?'

'If you could just tell us,' Clare said. 'Was it orange? Or – something else?'

'Grapefruit,' she said. 'Always grapefruit. It was too tart for me but Steve liked it.'

'Did he drink a lot of it?'

She thought for a moment. 'It was in our weekly delivery. Two litre cartons, I think.'

'Did he have it on Friday?'

'Honestly? I've no idea. He might have. I could check the fridge.'

Clare smiled. 'No, that's fine.'

Jenny's glance went between Clare and Chris. 'I still don't know why you're asking. Was there something—' She broke off, her brow creased as if trying to work out what they weren't saying. Then she met Clare's gaze, her eyes full of fear. 'Was he poisoned? Was there something in his water bottle?'

Clare watched her, trying to assess if she did know something. Then she gave a slight nod. 'We're waiting for test results but we think so.'

'Someone – poisoned Steve?' Jenny's voice was thick with emotion. 'Someone – did that to him?'

'We're not sure,' Clare said. 'But we can tell you Steve died from an overdose of a drug called Fentanyl.'

Jenny opened her mouth as if about to speak, her eyes flitting back and forth. 'I don't understand,' she said eventually. 'That's a pain killer. The doctors at the surgery give it for end-of-life care. It's really strong. Steve wouldn't have needed anything like that.'

Chris sat forward, his eyes on Jenny. 'It's also a drug that's sold illegally.'

They saw the rise and fall of her chest, the monitor showing her pulse rate climbing and Clare wondered if they'd have to summon a nurse. Jenny's hands were shaking again and she clasped them together, as if trying to control the movement. 'You mean addicts use it? Like heroin? People sell it on the street?'

Chris nodded.

She shook her head, a sharp movement that brought a hand to her temple. 'No,' she said. 'No. Not Steve. He hated drugs. He wouldn't. He just wouldn't.' Her voice was rising and Clare took hold of her hand again.

'It's okay, Jenny,' she said. 'Breathe. Nice slow breaths in and out.'

By some effort of will she persuaded Jenny to breathe along with her, in for a count of four then out for another four. Slowly her heart rate began to fall and Clare gave her a smile. 'Well done.' She decided to leave telling Jenny about the phone call accusing Steve of dealing for another day. There were more pressing questions.

'Can we go back to your wedding,' she said.

Jenny's eyebrows lifted. Clearly a question she wasn't expecting.

'Jamaica, wasn't it?'

She nodded. 'On the beach at Negril.' She smiled at the memory. 'It was so lovely.'

'One of our team was doing the paperwork – for Steve,' Clare said, keeping her tone light. 'And they happened to look at your marriage certificate. Steve's name wasn't on it.'

Jenny's expression clouded. 'Why were you looking at that?'

'Just routine,' Clare said, her tone smooth. 'As I said, there's a ton of paperwork when someone dies suddenly. But we were curious about his name.' She left the question hanging, wondering how much Jenny knew.

'Oh that.' She looked visibly relieved. 'Steve's real name is Brad,' she said. 'Or it was.' A spasm of pain crossed her face as she corrected herself. 'It's Bradley on his birth certificate. But he was Steve all the time I've known him. Even Dennis called him Steve.'

Clare sensed Chris shift in his seat. 'Why was that?' she asked.

Jenny's brow wrinkled, as if she was trying to recall. 'He did tell me but it was ages ago now. I think some disagreement between his mum and dad. His dad had registered the birth, calling him Bradley without telling his mum. Apparently he'd said he liked the name and she said she'd think about it. He thought she'd come round so he went ahead and did it. But she wasn't happy. She'd wanted Steve. So she refused to call him Brad. Even told the school to call him Steve. I suppose it stuck. Obviously, when we were married, the names had to match our birth certificates, but that's all it was.'

Chris sat forward. 'What name's on your mortgage?'

Jenny's face clouded. 'Actually, it's Steve. It's Steve on all our other documents.'

'You didn't wonder about that?' he asked but she shook her head.

'I did ask Steve, after we were married and I saw Brad on the marriage certificate. But he said for mortgages and stuff like that it wasn't as strict. He'd always gone by Steve and he had a driving licence to prove it.' She met their eyes. 'I honestly didn't think anything of it.' She looked from Clare to Chris. 'It's not a problem, is it?'

Clare was thinking quickly. It didn't look like Jenny knew Steve had a brother, let alone that he was called Brad.

The door opened and a nurse appeared, wheeling a blood pressure monitor. 'Sorry,' she said. 'I'll only be a minute.'

They stepped outside and moved along the corridor where they couldn't be overheard.

'You going to tell her?' Chris said.

'We have to. She has a right to know.'

Clare's phone began to buzz and she swiped to take the call. 'Patch?' Her face creased as she tried to make out what Patch was saying. 'Sorry,' she said after a moment. 'I'll move to get a better signal.' She nodded to Chris to wait outside Jenny's door and began walking along the corridor. She pushed open the door to the stairwell then the call cut out. Holding the phone up to try and catch a signal, she headed for the main concourse. It was quieter now and she guessed most patients had returned to their wards for the evening meal. The shops and cafes were shut and she spotted Vanessa sitting on a chair, munching a sandwich. She saw Clare and made to finish but Clare waved this away.

'I'm trying to get a signal. Take your time. We're not done yet.'

As she reached the automatic doors, her phone began ringing again. This time the signal was good.

'That's better,' she said. 'It's hopeless down in the wards.'

'Do you have a minute to listen?' Patch said. 'We've found something else.'

Chapter 23

Clare made her way back through the concourse towards the Acute Medical Unit, the conversation with Patch running round her head. The ward was busier now, beeps and buzzers sounding, staff flying back and forth between bays and rooms. A nurse stood talking to a doctor at the desk while the phone rang out, and she wondered how anyone could concentrate with so much going on.

Chris was leaning against the wall next to Jenny's door and he nodded at her room. 'She's having her tea.'

'That's fine,' Clare said, 'because we have to decide what to tell her.'

'About what?'

'Patch has done some digging. Steve's been married before; and there's no record of a divorce.'

'Eh? He can't be. Even marrying abroad, he'd have to prove he wasn't married already.'

'Well he was married and, so far, Patch hasn't found a divorce certificate or anything to show his first wife's dead.'

'He's a bigamist.'

'Looks that way.'

'Unless he actually is Brad.'

Clare was quiet for a moment. 'I'm not sure how we could find out. Even if we took DNA from Steve's body it wouldn't tell us if he was Steve or Brad.'

'Don't suppose there's any chance of finding the first wife?' Chris asked.

'They're working on it now. In the meantime, we'd better break the news to Wife Number Two.'

Chris peeped through the window in Jenny's door. 'Doesn't look like she's touched her food.'

'She'll have even less appetite when we've finished with her,' Clare said. 'Come on. Best get it over with.'

Jenny was propped up, a pile of pillows at her back, the over-bed table at her front. Clare looked without enthusiasm at the food and she didn't blame Jenny for not eating. 'Not hungry?'

Jenny shook her head. 'They're keeping me in another night,' she said.

'I'm sorry,' Clare said. 'It's not much fun in here.'

'Doesn't matter.' Jenny's voice was flat. 'I've nothing to go home for.' She raised a hand and pushed the table to the side then sank back into the pillows.

Clare shot a glance at Chris. This wasn't going to be easy. She eased herself down on a chair, Chris pulling his up beside her. 'Jenny, we have something to tell you.'

Her eyes searched Clare's face for any clue as to what was coming.

'It's about Steve.'

'What?' There was a tremor in her voice. 'Tell me, please. Whatever it is, it can't be worse than losing him.'

'Dennis and Andrea – Steve's parents – they had two children. Two boys.'

She stared at them, confusion in her eyes. 'No,' she said. 'That's not possible. Steve would have said.'

'I'm afraid it is. Steve had a brother.' She took a moment. 'His name was Bradley.'

There was a sharp intake of breath and the colour drained from Jenny's face. 'You're making it up. It can't be true. It's that thing with the names.'

'It is true,' Chris said. 'Our team back at the station have found two birth certificates. One for a boy called Steven Gibb and the other for Bradley Gibb. Same parents, two years apart.'

Jenny's eyes were full of fear and she pulled the covers up around her neck and shoulders. 'I don't understand,' she managed, her lip trembling. 'Steve said his real name was Brad.' She broke off and Clare saw the rise and fall of her chest. Her eyes moved back and forth, as though searching for the answer in this room. A silence hung in the air, the only sound Jenny's breaths, sharp and shallow. Clare glanced at the monitor again, watching as Jenny's pulse rose and she took hold of her hand.

'Slow breaths,' she said and she breathed deeply along with Jenny until her pulse returned to normal.

Finally, Jenny met Clare's eye. 'Steve lied?' Her voice was little more than a whisper. 'He lied about his name?'

Clare nodded. 'We think so. We're still trying to clarify what happened but I do need to ask if the marriage ceremony you went through was with the man we met as your husband – the man who died early on Saturday morning?'

Jenny's eyes were like saucers. 'You think I lied too? About my wedding?'

Clare hastened to reassure her. 'No, not at all. We're just trying to find out why your marriage certificate has Steve's brother's name on it.'

Her eyes filled with fresh tears. 'Honestly,' she said, her voice husky, 'if I knew I'd tell you.'

'Did Steve never mention having a brother?' Chris asked.

Jenny shook her head. 'No. I had no idea.' Something flicked across her eyes. 'What happened to him – the brother?'

'We don't know,' Clare said. 'It seems he disappeared about nine years ago.'

'Disappeared?'

'Yes. My colleagues have been trying to track him down but there's been nothing for nine years. We're not sure if he died, went abroad or, even, changed his identity; but he's not popped up anywhere.'

Jenny's brow furrowed as she took this in. 'Does that mean he was – what is it they do – declared dead?'

'Not officially. The family have to request it and it doesn't look as if anyone did.'

'So he might still be alive?' Jenny said. 'He might be out there somewhere.' Her breath was coming faster again. 'What if it's him? What if he fell out with Dennis and Steve and he's come back to kill them both? What if I'm next?'

Clare tried to take hold of her hand again but Jenny shrugged her off, pulling the covers more tightly round herself. 'It could be him. Maybe he hated Dennis so much he pushed him into the water – and – and Steve found out so he poisoned him.' Her eyes were full of fear. 'You have to find him.'

Clare and Chris exchanged glances and she saw what he was thinking. Looking at Jenny lying there, this husk of a woman, she wanted so much to reassure her. But could they? Could they really say she wasn't at risk from Brad?

'We'll keep you safe,' Chris said, giving Jenny a reassuring smile. 'There's an officer outside your door here and we'll look after you when you're back home as well.'

Jenny eyed him and he smiled again. Gradually the tension left her body and she loosened her grip on the blanket.

Clare wondered not for the first time what it was about Chris that seemed to calm panic in people, particularly women. Was it because he was big and awkward? Did that make him appear more straightforward? He certainly wasn't a Flash Harry. God knows, there were enough of them around. Sharp suits and haircuts to match. For a brief moment, she recalled Paul Henry, an FLO she'd billeted with a family whose daughter had died. He was all superficial charm and designer cologne. Chris frequently looked as if he'd fallen off a flitting but maybe that was it – the secret to folk trusting him. There was no side with Chris, no hidden agenda. He just told it like it was. And here, in this hospital room, with this broken woman, she was glad it was Chris sitting next to her.

'There is something else we need to tell you,' Clare said.

Jenny eyed her and she wondered briefly if she ought to have entrusted this task to Chris. But she'd started now so…

'Our team also found a marriage certificate for Steve.'

Jenny's brow creased. 'I don't understand.'

'Steve was married eight years ago.'

She stared and for a moment she didn't speak. Then her mouth opened, as if she was about to say something, but the words didn't come. 'Married?' she managed, eventually. 'Married to who?'

'Her name is Amber Morgan,' Clare said.

'Is?'

Clare nodded. 'We think she's still alive.'

Jenny stared. 'Eight years?'

'Yes.'

'So they divorced?' Jenny's eyes were searching Clare's face.

Clare hesitated and, in that moment, she saw the truth dawn on Jenny. 'Oh my God,' she said. 'They're still married. That's what you're going to say, isn't it? Steve's still married.'

'We can't find any record of a divorce,' Clare said, her voice as gentle as she could make it. 'My team are still checking but it does look as if he was still married to Amber at the time he died.'

Jenny's head was shaking, tears spilling. 'No,' she said, her voice rising. 'No, it can't be. He can't have been married to her. He was married to me.' The tears were coming fast, now. 'He was my husband,' she managed, between sobs.

Clare gave her a moment before asking the obvious question. 'Steve never mentioned it?' She hardly needed to ask but she had to be sure.

'Of course not,' Jenny said, an edge to her voice. 'I'd hardly have married him if I'd known.'

There was a tap at the door and Vanessa appeared.

'That's me back on duty,' she said and Clare smiled.

'We'll just be another few minutes.'

Vanessa resumed her post outside the door and Clare turned back to Jenny, giving her an encouraging smile.

'Two more things,' she said. 'If you're up to it.'

Jenny's eyes were focused on the blanket, her fingers picking at a loose thread.

'We'd like permission to search your house,' Clare said.

'What? Why?'

She took a moment, choosing her words. 'As I said, we believe Steve was killed; and now you've confirmed he didn't tell you about his earlier marriage, we'd like to be sure he didn't have any other secrets.' She deliberately didn't mention the phone call accusing Steve of dealing. Jenny's mood seemed to have darkened and Clare didn't want to provoke her any further. 'It might help us find out what happened to Steve.'

'Suppose.'

Clare gave her an encouraging smile. 'Thank you. That's very helpful.'

She was watching them carefully. 'You said there were two things.'

Clare reached into her bag and withdrew the photo Sara had copied from one of the door cameras in North Street. 'Can you look at this please?'

Jenny took it, staring at it for a long moment. Then she lifted her gaze and met Clare's. 'Where was this taken?'

Clare avoided the question. 'Do you recognise this man?'

She exhaled. 'Obviously I do.'

Clare said nothing and eventually Jenny sank back in the pillows.

'It's Steve,' she said after a minute. 'The man I thought was my husband.'

—

They made their way back through the concourse and out into the night.

'What do you reckon?' Clare said.

'Jenny?' Chris began taking the steps to the car park, two at a time. 'I don't think she knew Steve had a brother and I'm pretty sure she didn't know he was already married.'

'I agree,' Clare said. 'All the same...'

'Yeah?'

She stopped halfway up the steps, her breath condensing in the night air. 'I'm not sure she was being entirely straight with us.'

'Really?'

'Yes. When she was talking about Steve going out to the gym – it was almost like she was making it up as she went along.'

'Why, though?' Chris said. 'What would she be hiding?'

Clare met his gaze. 'I don't know. But there was definitely something.' The cold was starting to seep into her bones and she began climbing the steps again, Chris following.

She didn't need to check her watch to know she'd miss Al, now. Even if she headed straight home he'd be on his way to his flat at the police college by the time she reached the cottage. And she really ought to go back to the station – see what else was happening.

'Please tell me we're not going back to the station,' Chris said as if reading her thoughts.

She hesitated.

'Clare, we've been on for nearly eleven hours. I'm dog tired and, frankly, you look like you need your bed.'

The hospital car park was almost empty now, only a handful of cars dotted along its length.

'Thanks very much,' she said as they reached the car.

'Seriously. You look done in.'

She nodded. 'Okay. There's nothing that can't wait until tomorrow.' She started the engine and drew out of the space.

'If you step on it you might just catch the DCI – oops Superintendent, I mean.'

'Nah. He'll be leaving about now.'

Chris's phone buzzed with a message and he swiped to read it. 'Sara's got a casserole in the oven. Come back and eat with us.'

She slowed for the speed bumps that peppered Ninewells Avenue then accelerated towards the roundabout. She was tempted. Sara was a good cook and she was hungry. But if she went back with Chris, sat at their fireside maybe with a tray and a mug of tea, kicked off her shoes, well – she wouldn't want to dig herself out again for the drive home.

And then there was the tension between the couple. There was definitely something wrong. She'd love to think she could help them through it but tonight wasn't the night. She was too damn tired.

'That's so kind,' she said throwing him a smile. 'But I'd better get back for Benjy.'

'We could do you a food parcel?' Chris said. 'Something you could microwave.' There was a gentleness to his voice and she found tears pricking her eyes. What on earth was wrong with her? Most likely a combination of tiredness, worry over this damn march – just six days away now – and her frustration at not being home in time to see Al.

'I'll take that as a yes, then,' Chris said, tapping his phone to message Sara.

'No, honestly,' Clare said. They were on Riverside Drive now, passing the modest Dundee Airport. 'Al will have left me something. But thanks. It was a lovely thought.' She flicked him a glance.

'Don't want you collapsing on us,' he said, and they both understood he was making a joke to cover his concern.

'I promise I'll go home and eat something sensible. Anyway, Benjy will look after me.'

'I always thought it was that way round,' Chris said, and the moment passed.

—

She dropped him at the station and left him de-icing his car. It was no more than a ten-minute drive to Daisy Cottage through the Bogward Estate but she took her time, fearing black ice.

The moon was out and already the roads were glistening with frost. It was going to be a cold one. Her thoughts went to Al and his route through Central Scotland to the police college at Tulliallan. But he was sensible. She knew he'd drive carefully.

He'd lit the lamps at Daisy Cottage, leaving the front room curtains partly open for Benjy. The headlights caught him as she swung into the drive, his nose pressed to the glass, and she was glad she had him at least to come home to.

She climbed out of the car, fishing for her house keys. Inside, Benjy fell on her, and she managed to shove him back far enough to close the door behind her. She was home.

Al had left her the remains of a pasta bake and she put this in the microwave to reheat. There was half a bottle of red next to it and she poured herself a generous glass, sipping as she moved about the kitchen.

In the sitting room she saw he'd lit the log burner but it had died down so she opened the vent and put a log on to revive it. A spitting sound came from the microwave and she dived to open the door. She'd put the pasta on too high.

'Probably should have used the oven,' she told Benjy, putting the container down on a mat to spoon the pasta out. He'd been lying in front of the fire but the log had smothered the embers and he raised himself up and wandered over to the radiator.

She began spooning pasta onto a plate and a spark of cheese sauce landed on her hand. 'Shit,' she said, putting her hand to her mouth. 'Shit, shit, shit!'

Benjy had been circling his chosen spot, preparing to settle himself down but he came padding over now and put his head against her leg. She reached down and stroked him, blinking back tears.

She finished spooning out her meal and carried plate and glass through to the table. Benjy, having assured himself she was okay, returned to the radiator and resumed circling, preparing to lie down.

Clare loaded her fork, trying to work out what she was feeling. The fire had gone out, she'd burned her hand and, somehow, she was laying it all at Al's door. He'd taken a job that meant being away from Sunday night to Thursday knowing full well what her job was like. Whenever there was a major incident the hours were long, often for days, or weeks on end. He must have known there would be nights like this when they'd miss each other by an hour, that they'd spend the majority of their weeks in separate places. Why the hell had he taken the job?

She was being unreasonable. She knew it. But tiredness did that. If she was honest with herself, it wasn't Al's fault. She'd more or less been offered his job and she'd turned it down, displeasing Superintendent Penny Meakin in the process. But there had been something iffy about the whole thing. It was as if Al and Penny had carved it up between them. *You take this job and Clare can have yours.* And that had annoyed her so she'd politely declined. Had it been a stupid decision? Had she turned the job down simply because they thought she'd jump at it? Had she cut off her nose to spite her face, as her mother would have said?

Probably.

From nowhere the log burst into flames, air from the vent suddenly igniting it. Benjy cocked an ear and made his way back over to the stove, settling at Clare's feet. She finished the pasta, drained her glass and put the tray down. Benjy looked up as if seeking permission and she patted the sofa cushion next to her. He leapt up, put his head on her lap and stretched out across the cushion.

Her phone buzzed. A message from Al.

> Back in my flat at the college. Hope you're home safe and sound. Sleep well.
>
> All my love,
>
> X
>
> PS there's a surprise in the fridge. Should be good for a couple of days.

Gently, she removed Benjy's head from her lap and heaved herself off the sofa. In the fridge she found three small ramekins with a pink-coloured dessert. His raspberry posset. He'd promised to make it at Christmas but they'd run out of time. He must have defrosted the raspberries that morning and made it before he left.

She carried one of the ramekins through and ate the posset, ignoring Benjy's puppy-dog eyes. 'Not a single drop,' she told him, scraping the ramekin clean.

She picked up her phone and took a selfie of herself and Benjy, tapping out a message to Al.

> We're on the sofa, enjoying the fire. Thanks for a delicious dinner. Have a great week. Can't wait to see you on Thursday night.
>
> Love you,
>
> X

Then she lay back on the sofa, thinking of the messages they'd just exchanged. They were both trying to make it work. Both sending messages as if it was all okay – as if they could do this. But was it? Could they? She pulled Benjy close, burying her face in his neck wondering how long they could keep it up.

Day 7: Monday, 16th February

Chapter 24

Clare arranged to meet Chris first thing at Steve and Jenny's house in Kilrymont Road.

A neighbour was leading a child clad in a thick winter coat towards her frosty car and she stopped, watching as they made their way to Jenny's front door. 'Terrible thing,' the neighbour said. 'Read about Steve on Facebook.'

The curse of social media. Clare recalled the quote about a lie being half way round the world before the truth had its boots on, and she wondered what the latest gossip on Steve and Jenny was. Probably best not to know. She smiled back at the neighbour but made no comment.

'How's Jenny?' the neighbour persisted. The child was tugging at her mother's hand, whispering they were going to be late.

'Doing well, thanks,' Clare said and she turned away from the woman.

Chris had the key in the door and they hurried in, closing it against prying eyes. Clare stood in the hallway, trying to get a sense of the house without its occupants. Was there anything here other than a young couple's treasured home?

'I take it we're not doing a full search,' Chris said and Clare shook her head.

'No point. A fair number of us have tramped through the house since your first visit with Patch. Besides, unless we suspect

Jenny of putting Fentanyl in his water bottle, this isn't a crime scene.'

'So we're looking for?'

'Evidence he was dealing.'

'Phones, then.'

'Phones, notebooks, anything that could be a list of customers – and drugs, obviously.'

Chris stood scanning the front room. 'I reckon we won't find anything down here. Look how tidy it is? Strikes me our Jenny's pretty houseproud.'

Clare regarded him. 'Bit sexist.'

He laughed. 'You think Steve did the housework?'

'Dunno. Maybe they shared it. I bet Sara doesn't do it all in your house.'

'Fair point. Anyway, you only have to look at how tidily dressed she is.' He nodded his head towards the street. 'And you could eat your dinner off that car out there.'

'Yeah, you're right,' Clare agreed. 'If there was any dealing going on, the evidence won't be in these rooms. Let's start upstairs. Gloves on, just in case,' she added.

They began with the spare bedroom, untouched since their visit on Saturday morning. The sight of the duvet pulled back, the bed creased where Steve had died drew Clare up for a moment, reminding her he was now lying in a mortuary fridge. Chris moved to the small chest of drawers under the window and pulled it forward, feeling along the back for anything that might be stuck there. Then he checked round the window before emptying the drawers, one at a time.

Clare finished checking the bedclothes and she pulled them back up, spreading the bed neatly. She knelt to look under the bed and behind a small bedside table. Nothing. The spare room was as neat as the rest of the house. She rose, hands on her hips and flexed her back.

'I'm getting too old for this.'

'Want me to lift the carpet?'

She scanned the floor. 'Just the edges, although I can't see him storing a burner phone under this. It's too thin.'

'Might be a loose floorboard,' Chris said and she nodded.

Half an hour later, they were satisfied the spare room held nothing of interest and they moved on to the couple's bedroom. Clare studied the room. 'If this was you and Sara's, where would you hide your Wagon Wheels?'

That drew a snort. 'As if I'd risk crumbs in bed. Dead giveaway, that. But, since you ask…' He looked round and his eye fell on a clear plastic tub in the corner of the room. He peered at it then removed the lid. 'Protein shakes. Dozens of them.'

He indicated the tub. 'Good place to hide something – in plain sight,' and he began sorting through the contents while Clare attacked the wardrobe.

It took almost two hours for them to complete the search.

'If Steve was dealing,' Clare said, brushing dust off her trousers, 'he's certainly not keeping his stash here.'

'No extra keys, either,' Chris said. 'So I doubt he has a lock-up. I think that phone call was designed to throw us off.'

'Or to make us think he'd OD'd himself,' Clare said.

'Yeah. Could be. Question is, who had a motive for that?'

'Search me – unless it's Brad.' She stopped half way down the stairs. 'Any progress finding him?'

'Nothing yet,' Chris said. 'I've been back through Steve's social media and spoken to his boss. He doesn't recall anyone turning up at Steve's work, asking for him. Jenny gave me the login for his Facebook as well. No DMs from anyone that could be Brad.'

'We're pretty sure the caller is also the killer, yes?'

'Agreed.'

'So answer me this, Sergeant: who had motive, means *and* opportunity? It's one thing slipping a few pills in someone's drink at a bar but the lids on those bottles are pretty secure.'

'As far as opportunity goes, Jenny had the best chance. But, even with her working in a doctor's surgery, I can't see her getting her hands on Fentanyl.' He began walking down the rest of the stairs, Clare following. 'I keep coming back to Brad.'

They were in the kitchen now, Clare pulling open drawers and rifling through the contents. 'We need those phone records,' she said, picking up a selection of takeaway menus. 'I think Penny actioned the warrant on Saturday. If we chase the phone company, we might get them today.'

'That sounds like a job for Max,' Chris said.

'Hah. You wish.' She closed the drawer she'd been checking. 'I think we're done here, yes?'

'Yeah.'

Chris made for the hall, Clare following. Then she stopped, one hand on the sitting-room door. 'Unless…'

'Unless what?'

'Jenny.'

'What about her?'

'Steve had been dead for hours when we arrived, agreed?'

'Yeah, for sure.'

'And Jenny had phoned it in.'

'Again, yes.'

She stared at him. 'Think about it, Chris. We have no idea how long she waited before making that call.'

His brow creased. 'I'm not sure what you're saying.'

'It's this: maybe Steve was dealing. Maybe Jenny knew about it. Weddings in Jamaica don't come cheap.'

Chris's face cleared. 'Oh, I see. You think Jenny got rid of anything to do with drugs before she called 999?'

Clare looked round at the house. 'It's possible. If she knew Steve was dealing, and he'd OD'd accidentally, or someone had done it to him, she'd know we'd go through the house. She might even have thought we'd seize their stuff.'

'Proceeds of Crime Act?'

'Yes! It happens all the time. She could have read about it in the papers.'

Chris began peeling off his gloves. 'So, she's found Steve, realised he was well gone and she's gone through the house, getting rid of anything that could tie him to drug dealing.'

Clare hesitated. 'I mean, when I think about Jenny, what she's like, I honestly can't see it. Look how upset she was over that out of date pie? But we can't ignore that phone call. Not every dealer has Love and Hate tattooed on their knuckles.'

'You're out of date, Inspector. It's all barbed wire around the face these days.'

'Seriously?'

' 'Fraid so.'

They stepped out into the street, Chris pulling the door closed behind them. 'Back to the station?'

'Definitely. I'm dying for a cup of tea.'

—

Clare was in the kitchen waiting for the kettle to boil when Patch put her head round the door.

'Jenny Gibb,' she said. 'Should be out of hospital this afternoon.'

'Thanks, Patch. Can you make sure Dundee sends someone home with her? If they're struggling we'll do it but they're closer. She's not to be left alone.'

'Will do.' She was about to leave when Clare stopped her.

'How are you getting on with the hidden camera footage?'

'Sorry, boss. There was a bit of bother in the town last night.'

Clare raised an eyebrow. 'It's important, Patch.'

'Yeah, I know. But there was a fight in a pub and the uniforms needed an extra pair of hands. Took longer to sort out than it should have.'

Clare smiled. 'They always do. But get back to that footage please. Top priority.'

Patch escaped with visible relief and Max reappeared.

'Got the phone records for Steve and Jenny,' he said. 'I'll get onto it now.'

Clare carried a mug through to her office and sank down in her chair, mulling over the Gibb family. What a muddle it was. She didn't even know which brother Jenny had married. Had Steve used his brother's birth certificate? Or had Brad spent the last few years pretending to be Steve? And, if he had, why?

The phone rang, cutting across her thoughts. She glanced at the display and her heart sank. Penny. No doubt another call to check on progress with the Freemans' burglary. She swiped to take the call and did her best to sound cheerful.

'I'm mindful this protest march is happening at the weekend,' Penny began, without introducing herself. For some reason this always annoyed Clare. Obviously she knew it was Penny; and Penny would know Clare had her number saved. It just seemed rude not to say who was calling, maybe even ask how Clare was. Then she gave herself a shake. This was Penny. She didn't do small talk.

'I've managed to get you some additional officers,' Penny said. 'They'll report to you at eight in the morning. Anything beyond four in the afternoon will come out of your budget.'

Gee thanks, Clare was tempted to say. Instead she thanked Penny and asked how many there were.

'Twenty – and I have to say it wasn't easy so please make good use of them.'

'Twenty?' It was out before Clare could stop herself. 'Erm, just twenty?'

'Is that not sufficient? How many had you in mind?'

Clare hesitated. She'd been so busy she'd not had time to work out actual numbers. But something north of fifty was the very least she'd expected, particularly in view of what Al had told her. Then she thought, what the hell? Penny was already annoyed with her. She'd literally nothing to lose. 'I was thinking more like sixty plus.'

There was an agonisingly long silence and Clare thought she must have overstepped the mark. She opened her mouth to apologise, but Penny cut across her.

'Have you any idea what that would cost?'

'I've not done the sums, no,' Clare admitted.

'I could tell you but there's little point. Even if I could afford it, I cannot put my hands on that number of officers. Had you given me more notice a few more might have been possible but, at this late stage, that's it, I'm afraid. If you're struggling with how to deploy them effectively I'll be happy to bring someone else in to police the march. Just let me know.' And, with that, she ended the call.

Clare sat staring at the phone, her face scarlet. How bloody dare Penny? She knew they were expecting trouble. She was pretty much banking on it so she could have her undercover officers swoop in and arrest the ringleaders. But what about the rest of them? The crowd whipped up by the people Penny was so keen to arrest? Who was going to stop them rampaging through the town? Certainly not twenty extra officers. She moved to her computer and navigated to the budget folder. Maybe there was some way she could pay for officers from elsewhere.

She ignored the knock at her door. Honest to God, for once could someone else sort out whatever it was? The door opened and she glanced up ready to ball out the knocker.

'The CCTV,' Patch said. 'You have to see this.'

Chapter 25

She managed to find Chris and Max and the three of them made their way to the room Patch had been using to go through the footage. Chris brought an extra chair and the four of them squeezed round Patch's laptop.

She waited until they were all sitting with a view of the screen then she clicked to play the first clip.

'Okay,' Patch began. 'The first thing to say is there must be a second camera at the Freemans'.'

'Eh?' Clare glanced at the other two. 'SOCO only found one in the sitting room.'

Patch shrugged. 'They said the burglars hadn't been in the kitchen, didn't they? That's where it was,' she added.

'Another smoke alarm?' Clare asked.

'Not sure,' Patch said. 'All I can tell is it's ceiling mounted. So probably. The clips alternate between the two cameras and I'm still working through them.'

Clare nodded at the screen. 'Go on, then.'

Patch clicked one of the files which she'd renamed *Tuesday 10th February*. 'I'm going back to Tuesday for the first clip. It's from the camera SOCO found. Recorded just after two in the afternoon – the day before they reported the burglary.'

They watched as the clip began to play. Erika was first to appear, moving to the window and closing the curtains.

'Eyup,' Chris said. 'Please tell me we're not about to see the Freemans having some afternoon delight.'

Patch's eyes were fixed on the screen. 'Keep watching.'

Rex joined her and they moved into the centre of the room. There was no audio but it was clear a conversation was taking place, Rex pointing at something and Erika shaking her head, pointing at something else. This continued for a few minutes then they began moving round the room, pulling out drawers, spilling contents on the floor. Occasionally one of them would stop and speak to the other then they'd return to their task, the room becoming increasingly messy.

'Are they doing what I think they're doing?' Chris said.

The pair stood back to take in their handiwork then moved out of sight, presumably to another room.

'They are,' Clare said. 'They're staging their own burglary. The question is why?'

Patch paused the footage while they digested this.

'Has to be the protest march,' Chris reminded her. 'I reckon it was a put-up job to have the march organisers arrested.'

Clare looked at him for a moment, her mind back at the Freemans' house. 'I think you're right,' she said. 'I bet that was their goal all along. They wanted to be cast as victims and to have us arrest whoever's behind the march; and if the march was cancelled the planning committee might be persuaded there was no real opposition to the development.' She exhaled. 'Crafty buggers.'

'Gotta give them credit,' Chris said. 'They put on quite a performance – all that guff about Erika being too upset to speak to the reporter.'

'We could do them for wasting police time,' Max said.

'We certainly could,' Clare agreed. 'But let's not rush this.' She smiled at Patch. 'Keep at it,' then she nodded to Chris and Max. 'My office.'

They followed her through and drew chairs round Clare's desk. 'Tell you what I don't get,' Clare began. She picked up a pencil and twiddled it in her fingers.

'Go on then,' Chris said.

'That flash drive was found in Carol Merryweather's house, yes?'

'Yes.'

'And we think whoever broke in dropped it.'

'Again, yes.'

'That brings up two questions. Who installed the hidden cameras in the Freemans' house and what were they doing at Carol Merryweather's?'

'She's the estate agent?' Max asked and Clare nodded.

'Could it be something to do with the Freemans buying the house?'

Clare's brow creased. 'I can't see it. Surely, if there was something funny about the sale, they'd have broken into the office, not her house.'

'What about the previous owner?' Max asked but Clare shook her head.

'Sweetest old man you'll ever meet.'

'With respect—' Max began but Chris cut across him.

'Nah,' he said. 'Nothing doing. Even if it was him – and trust us, it's not – why would he break into Carol's house?'

Clare was quiet for a minute. 'Maybe we're looking at this all wrong.'

They waited.

'The Freemans' burglary wasn't real, agreed?'

They nodded.

'Do we think Carol's was?'

They were quiet for a moment. Max was first to find his voice. 'Problem is none of us attended both scenes.'

It was true. Clare and Chris had visited the Freemans, Max and Patch had gone to Carol's.

'My gut says Carol's was genuine,' Max went on. 'I do think someone else had been in that house.'

'Okay,' Clare said. 'So we need to stop thinking about these as two burglaries. Could be there's no connection.'

She looked at them for confirmation but Chris was shaking his head.

'Carol's burglary,' he said. 'Nothing was taken. Don't know about you two but I've attended a fair few burglaries in my time and never one where nothing was taken. Even when they're disturbed most housebreakers will grab something.' His eyes narrowed. 'We might not be dealing with two burglaries but we are dealing with two very unusual incidents, within days of each other.'

They were quiet for a moment, considering this.

'If Carol really was burgled,' Clare said, 'what were they looking for?'

Chris spread his hands. 'Search me.'

'Okay, then,' Clare said, putting down the pencil. 'Let's look into all three of them: Carol, Erika and Rex. See if they have any friends or associates in common.' She turned to her computer. 'I'm going to ask Penny if she'll authorise a warrant for Carol's phone records. Not that she's in the mood for granting my requests,' she added.

Chris raised an eyebrow. 'Bit of a stretch. Carol's a victim, after all.'

'Be a lot quicker if we just asked her,' Max said.

'Yes it would,' Clare admitted. 'But she'd wonder why, wouldn't she?'

'She would. But we could say we've had another burglary and we're checking their phone records for missed calls – something like that. You know the kind of thing – folk phoning up, trying to find out when a house'll be empty.'

'Go on, then,' Clare said. 'Sounds plausible; and it might throw something up.'

There was a tap on the door and Sara came in. 'Call from Ninewells. That's Jenny discharged. Just waiting on her meds from the pharmacy.'

Clare thanked Sara and reminded her to make sure someone went home with Jenny.

'Actually,' Sara went on, 'she's asked if she can see you, boss.'

'Really?' Clare glanced at Chris. 'Did she say why?'

'Something about wanting to explain.'

'Hmm, okay,' Clare said. 'Ask whoever's driving her to give me a shout when they're leaving; and, in the meantime,' she eyed her two sergeants, 'Max, get onto Carol. Ask if we can access her phone records. Then I want the two of you looking for contacts those three have in common. Go back to their schooldays if you have to. I'm sure there's a connection.'

They went off to their tasks and Clare's thoughts drifted back to the protest march. She'd sent an email round all the station inspectors she could think of, begging any spare officers with a promise of returning the favour. So far she'd had offers of ten cops from Methil and eight from Stirling. If what Al had said was correct, it was still nowhere near enough. She opened her planning file and ran an eye down the list of requirements for pre-planned events. The Heras fencing would be up by Friday afternoon and the order restricting traffic was in place. Jim had been in contact with bus companies, and drop-off zones and parking had been arranged. Diversion signs were on order and she'd called in every special constable available for traffic duty. It still wouldn't be enough but she'd just have to work with what she had. She turned to a map of the town and began allocating officers to points along the route.

She didn't hear Sara's knock and looked up in surprise when she appeared in front of her.

'Sorry, boss. I did knock.'

Clare waved this away. 'What can I do for you?'

'Jenny Gibb's on her way. She'll be here in twenty minutes.'

Chapter 26

Jenny Gibb sat behind a desk in one of the small interview rooms, her eyes flicking left and right as she took in her surroundings. She was pale, dark circles beneath her eyes but she seemed calmer than when they'd seen her in the hospital room.

Chris entered with a tray of plastic cups. Jenny accepted hers with a nod but said nothing. Clare eyed her as he handed the cups out. They'd both felt Jenny was holding something back when they'd spoken to her at the hospital. Would she volunteer it now? Was that why she'd asked to see them?

She waited until Chris had closed the door then she gave Jenny a smile. 'You must be glad to be out of hospital.'

She nodded. 'It wasn't great. The staff were lovely but...'

'I know,' Clare said. 'Especially that ward. It never stops.'

Jenny picked up her cup and sipped at it. 'I wouldn't have slept a wink if they hadn't doped me.' Her eyes went to a hospital pharmacy bag on her lap. 'They gave me a pill for tonight. Said I could get more from my GP if I needed them.' She gave a wry smile. 'I think they were too afraid to give me any more.'

Clare eyed her. Jenny had been through a lot and Clare was mindful they had a duty of care. 'Do you feel as if you might?' she said. 'Take pills, I mean.'

She was quiet for a moment. 'No,' she said at last. 'I don't much want to keep going – to put one foot in front of another. It all seems such an effort. But I'm not ready to...'

'If you do have any thoughts like that,' Clare said, 'it's important to let your GP know. They can help – put you in touch with organisations, people who can support you.'

Jenny sipped from the cup again. 'Yeah. They said that at the hospital.' She flicked a glance at Clare. 'Truth is I just want to sleep. Properly, I mean. Not drugged. I'm so tired. I just want to climb under the duvet.'

Clare glanced at Chris. 'We can put this off,' she said. 'Talk another time.'

But Jenny shook her head. 'No. I want to do this. There are things you need to know.' She took a moment, as if ordering her thoughts then she met Clare's eye.

'I had a lot of time to think in hospital. I wasn't doped up all the time and there was no one to talk to. So I started thinking about it all. About Dennis and Steve. The wedding, the different names, all of it.' Her brow furrowed as if she was trying to order her thoughts. 'I think I've worked it out,' she went on, 'and I want to tell you. Because, if it makes sense to you, it must be right.'

Clare wasn't sure about that but she gave Jenny a smile. 'That sounds fine. Take your time.' She indicated Chris. 'This isn't a formal interview, Jenny, but Chris will take notes if you don't mind. Save us trying to remember what you tell us.'

'Of course.' Jenny took a couple of breaths in and out then she began.

'I met Steve almost six years ago. We were in the same running club and our pace was pretty similar so we usually ended up running together. One night we went for a drink after the run and we hit it off.' She smiled at the memory. 'Seems ages ago now.'

They waited and after a moment she went on. 'We'd been dating about a year when…'

Clare gave Jenny a smile. 'Take your time.'

She nodded and swallowed a couple of times. 'I discovered I was pregnant.'

Jenny's cheeks were flushed now, her voice husky.

'How did you feel about that?' Clare asked.

'Shocked,' she said. 'At first, anyway. But excited too. Thinking of us with our own baby.'

'What about Steve?' Chris asked.

A slight crease appeared on Jenny's forehead. 'I was worried about telling him. I wasn't sure he'd want to be involved.' She dabbed at her eyes. 'I mean I was keeping the baby. I knew that much. But I did say to Steve he didn't have to be tied to me; said I wouldn't come after him for money or anything like that. My mum and dad – they'd have helped me. But Steve was thrilled. I mean, like me, he was shocked at first. We definitely hadn't planned it. But once we got over the shock it was quite exciting. We started talking about a nursery, whether it would be a boy or a girl – that sort of thing.'

Clare sensed Chris shift his position and she thought he was wondering the same as her. What had happened to the baby?

'Thing is,' Jenny went on, 'my mum and dad are a bit old-fashioned. They wouldn't have said anything but I know they'd have preferred if we were married before the baby was born; and I said this to Steve.'

'How did he react?' Clare asked.

'Quiet,' Jenny said. 'At first, anyway. He asked if he could think about it for a few days.'

Clare and Chris exchanged glances. Not quite the answer you'd want to a marriage proposal.

'I was a bit disappointed,' Jenny said. 'I kind of hoped Steve would want to get married as well. But that wasn't his way. He went off to the hills for a couple of days. Took a tent and camped out. I was glad, really. I'd rather he worked it out for himself than let his mates tell him what to do.'

'Do you think they'd have talked him out of marrying you?' Chris said.

Jenny spread her hands. 'I've no idea. But I did want it to be his decision. Anyway, it didn't matter because he came back after two days and he had a ring.' She fingered a diamond solitaire next to a gold band and smiled down at it. 'This ring.' She stopped for a moment, as if reliving the memory. 'I was so happy,' she went on. 'It felt like we were going to be a proper family.'

Then her expression clouded. 'I had thought we might have a lovely white wedding. But there was Dennis, and my dad, of course. He'd just had a heart by-pass operation.'

She stopped to sip her drink then replaced the cup on the table. 'I know it sounds silly, but I didn't want to walk up the aisle with a baby bump. So I said to Steve maybe we should just have a quiet ceremony in the registry office, here in the town.' She glanced at Clare. 'The important thing was being married, not how fancy the wedding was.'

'But Steve didn't want that?' Clare asked.

'Oh he seemed okay with it at first,' Jenny said. 'Told me not to book it but to start thinking about what I'd want; then one day he came in and said the wedding was all arranged. I thought he meant the registry office but he said how did I fancy being married on a beach in the Caribbean.' Jenny's face lit up at the memory. 'I couldn't believe it. It was so…'

Clare was watching her carefully. She was saying all the right words, what a wonderful surprise it had been; but something in her eyes betrayed her. Her mind went back to the conversation with the couple, the day before Steve had died. He'd railroaded Jenny into that wedding. She was sure of it.

It was on the tip of Clare's tongue to ask about the baby but Jenny was talking again.

'It was a lovely day,' she said, a smile crossing her face. 'Silver sand, turquoise sea and a warm breeze.' Then the smile froze. 'The name thing didn't faze me at the time. I believed what Steve told me.'

'And now?' Clare asked.

'Now…'

They waited and eventually Jenny went on.

'Now, I think I know what happened.' Her brow creased as if trying to collect her thoughts. 'I think what you said was right. Steve did have a brother called Brad and, somehow, Brad disappeared, or died. Whatever happened, he vanished from their lives.' She glanced at them. 'I mean, you know that already; and now I know Steve was already married. So, when I told him I was expecting, he must have had to work out what to do. It would have taken ages to get a divorce and he knew how much I wanted the wedding before the baby was born.' She stopped for a moment then gave a slight nod.

'I think he must have got a copy of his brother's birth certificate and used that to get a passport in Brad's name. Probably had a friend sign the photos to say it was him.' She shook her head. 'Now I think back, he made a big fuss about keeping all our documents together. He said the Jamaican authorities were really strict about the paperwork and he didn't want anything to go wrong. I suppose that was so he could use this passport – the one in Brad's name.' She broke off for a moment. 'I've been going over it ever since you told me Steve was married. He kept both our passports the whole time we were away. He gave me mine when I needed it but I never saw his.

'The irony is,' she went on, 'it makes me feel even more loved. He went to all that trouble to make me happy, using Brad's name, whisking me off to the Caribbean…' She looked from Clare to Chris. 'Whatever he did, I'll always have the memory of our wedding.' She picked up the cup and held it to her lips, sipping for a few moments then she put it down, her hand shaking. 'We were only home a couple of weeks when I lost the baby.'

'Oh Jenny,' Clare said. 'I'm so sorry.' Beside her, she felt Chris tense and she guessed he found this kind of conversation uncomfortable.

Jenny's shoulders sagged. 'All the expense, the hurried wedding, my parents not being there. It was all for nothing.' She took a tissue from her pocket and blew her nose. 'I wanted to try again, but Steve wasn't sure. He said we should wait until we had a bit more money behind us.' She dabbed at her eyes with the tissue. 'I'll never have his baby now.'

There was a tap on the door and Clare clicked her tongue in irritation. Of all the times. Chris took the hint and slipped out to deal with whatever it was. He was back a moment later and motioned to Clare to join him.

'Sorry about this,' Clare said. 'We won't be long.'

Jenny leaned back in her seat, utterly spent. 'It's fine,' she said. 'I'm in no hurry to go back to that house.'

Outside the room, she glared at Patch. 'This had better be good.'

Patch met her gaze and nodded. 'You have to see it.'

Chapter 27

'Remember I said there was another camera in the Freemans' kitchen?' Patch began and Clare nodded.

'The next two clips are from that camera.' She clicked on a file she'd renamed *Friday, 13th February (1)*.

'I recognise it,' Chris said as the clip began playing. 'Remember we took them in there to tell them about the first camera?'

'I saw that,' Patch said. 'You had three biscuits.'

Clare laughed at this then focused her attention on the screen.

They watched as Erika loaded the dishwasher, Rex putting things in a large fridge. It took Clare back to the day they'd sat round the Freemans' kitchen table and she suppressed a smile at the irony of telling them about one camera while being filmed by another. On the screen the couple suddenly looked up, their eyes on the door to the hallway. Erika said something and moved to the door.

'Doorbell?' Clare said and Patch nodded.

A minute later she returned, a woman behind her. Rex moved to greet the woman and a conversation ensued. The woman was gesturing with her hands while Erika stood, arms folded. Rex moved to lean against the fridge, leaving the woman standing just inside the door. At best their body language implied disinterest, at worst, hostility. After a couple of minutes' conversation, the Freemans exchanged glances, the woman standing as if waiting for them to speak. Then Rex shook his head and her shoulders sagged, an air of resignation overtaking her. She turned towards the door and seconds later Erika led her out. When she returned there was a brief exchange. Rex opened the fridge again and took out a bottle of wine. Erika put two glasses on the table and he filled them. They pulled out a couple of chairs and sat at the table, deep in discussion.

'Play it back a minute,' Chris said, moving closer to the screen.

Patch dragged the scroll bar back to the moment Erika led the woman into the kitchen.

'There,' Chris said.

Clare looked at him. 'Is that who I think it is?'

He nodded. 'It's Jenny Gibb.'

'She's the wife of the man who died, isn't she?' Patch said. 'I sat in the car when Max drove her to hospital. I thought you'd want to see it.'

'Good spot, Patch,' Clare said. 'And you're sure this was last Friday?'

'Definitely.'

'That was the day after we told them Dennis's death wasn't an accident,' Clare said.

'A few hours before Steve died,' Chris added.

'So why was Jenny Gibb calling on the Freemans?'

'Dennis's cottage,' Chris said. 'Has to be.'

'Did Steve inherit the cottage?' Max asked.

'He did.' Chris turned back to Patch. 'What time was that recorded?'

'About half five, give or take.'

He thought for a moment. 'She told us they'd both taken the day off work. They were at home until almost teatime. Then Steve nipped out – remember she said he was going to the gym, and that he'd bring back fish and chips?'

Clare nodded.

'Maybe she took the chance to pay the Freemans a visit, knowing Steve would be out for a while. Let's say she starts thinking,' Chris went on. 'They've a nice house, most likely don't want Dennis's cottage. But, if they sold the cottage, they could pay off their mortgage – or a fair bit of it. Maybe Jenny thinks, if they don't move quickly, the Freemans might change their plans and not need the cottage after all. I reckon Steve was like his dad, a bit of a hothead. He'd likely rub them up the wrong way. But Jenny – she strikes me as the peacemaker. So she goes round to see if they'll budge on price. Maybe told them she'd persuade Steve to sell if they went up a bit more.' He sat back with a wave of his hand. 'I rest my case.'

'You could be right,' Clare said. 'But, judging by their body language, I'd say the Freemans refused.' She glanced at Patch. 'Is that it?'

'One more clip.' Patch opened another file she'd saved as *Friday 13th February (2)*. Once again it opened in the kitchen; and this time there was no mistaking the Freemans' visitor.

'The same trousers,' Chris said.

'The Hokas too,' Clare added.

'This is Steve?' Max asked and Clare nodded.

They watched the exchange and immediately Clare felt it was different from the Freemans' encounter with Jenny. Rex gestured to a chair and Steve sat, the couple joining him at the table. Erika moved to the kettle, filling a teapot which she set down on a tray. She added a plate of biscuits and carried the tray over to the table.

'I could be wrong,' Max began, 'but were they expecting him?'

'I think so,' Clare agreed.

Erika began pouring out mugs of tea but Steve held up his hand as if declining. He felt inside his jacket and pulled something out, setting it down on the table.

'His water bottle,' Chris said, his voice soft.

They watched, fascinated by the exchange, altogether more harmonious than Jenny's meeting an hour or two earlier. Steve seemed to be pleading his case but Rex kept shaking his head. At one point Rex tapped his fingers, as if counting and Clare wondered if he was listing the costs associated with buying Dennis's cottage. Maybe he was explaining why they couldn't budge on price. Steve gestured towards Erika as if appealing to her but Rex simply shook his head again.

'How long does this go on for?' Clare asked.

'Maybe five more minutes,' Patch said. 'I can speed this bit up if you like. It's the next bit you'll want to see.'

They sat, eyes on the screen, as Patch fast-forwarded through the footage then returned it to normal speed. 'Now, watch.'

Seconds later, Steve rose and spoke a few words. Erika pushed back her chair and walked towards the door, gesturing with her hand. Steve left his water bottle on the table and followed her out of the room.

'Where's he gone?' Max asked.

'I think to the loo,' Patch said. 'He comes back a couple of minutes later. But watch what happens next.'

They watched as Erika reappeared at the door, just in sight of the camera. She stood as if listening while Rex moved to a kitchen drawer. He returned seconds later, a small blister pack in his hand. With a glance at Erika he twisted the lid off Steve's bottle and added every pill from the pack. Then he replaced the lid, swirling the contents around. He put the empty pack in his pocket and resumed his seat at the table, Erika joining him. A minute later, Steve returned. He picked up his bottle, glanced at the couple and left.

Erika went out after him, returning shortly after. There was a brief exchange then Rex took the empty blister pack from his pocket, holding it out for her to see. She stared at it for a moment then watched as he dropped it into the pedal bin.

'They go out of the room a few seconds later,' Patch said. 'And that's all I've found so far.'

Chris's eyes were fixed on the screen. 'The Fentanyl,' he said. 'Jesus.' He turned back to Clare. 'I think we've just watched Steve Gibb being murdered.'

'Pick 'em up,' Clare told Max. 'Both of them. Take two cars and keep them apart.'

'You want them arrested?'

'Ideally not. But do it if you have to; and put them in separate rooms.' She nodded at Chris, a sheaf of stills from the video footage in her hand. 'Come on. Let's see what Jenny has to say about this.'

Jenny looked up without enthusiasm as they re-entered the room, her second cup of coffee almost untouched. Then her expression changed. She was suddenly alert. 'Something's wrong, isn't it?'

Clare resumed her seat. 'We do have some new information, yes.'

Jenny's eyes were full of fear. 'About Steve?' Her voice was almost a whisper.

'Partly.' She regarded Jenny. 'Do you know a couple called Rex and Erika Freeman?'

She avoided Clare's eye. 'I'm not sure.'

'Jenny,' Clare waited until she met her gaze, 'I think you do know them.' She fished out the first of the stills, the best shot Patch could capture from Jenny's visit to the Freemans' kitchen. 'I think this is you.'

Jenny's eyes widened. 'Where did you – how...'

'This is a still photo taken from a ceiling-mounted camera in Rex and Erika Freeman's kitchen in Hepburn Gardens. Would you tell us about that please?'

She was quiet, her eyes busy as though recalling her visit, deciding what to tell them.

'Let's start with when you visited,' Clare said.

'Friday.' Jenny's voice was small.

'Time?'

She thought for a moment. 'I'm not sure. Maybe about five.'

'Five p.m.?'

'Yes.'

'And the reason for your visit?'

She ran her tongue round her lips. 'Dennis's cottage,' she said eventually.

'What about it?'

'I knew they wanted it and that Dennis had refused to sell. He'd told us about it. I think he'd told lots of people. Bragging in the pub, Steve said. Apparently he was boasting he could scupper the whole project because he wasn't going to sell. Went on about how the town didn't need any more rich bastards.'

'The Freemans wanted Dennis to sell and he'd refused?' Clare said, and Jenny nodded. This confirmed what they already knew.

'Do you think he hoped the Freemans would up their price?'

But Jenny shook her head. 'Dennis was born in that cottage and he said he would die there. No way was he selling. Steve tried to persuade him but it was no good.'

'Go on.'

'And then Dennis died and I thought Steve would inherit the cottage.'

She flashed Clare a look. 'It probably sounds heartless, with Dennis not long dead. But we didn't want the cottage and the Freemans did.' She broke off and Clare had the impression she was choosing her words. 'And I thought maybe, if we had a bit more money, Steve might agree to try for another baby.' She shook her head at this.

'I said to Steve we should sell to the Freemans. Take whatever they offered. But he said we should hold out – wring as much cash out of them as possible. He thought we were in a strong position. I wasn't so sure. I thought they might build around Dennis's cottage. Surround it with their new houses, you know? So, when Steve went out to the gym that night, I decided to go and see them. Tell them I'd try and persuade Steve to accept a lower offer.'

'How did they react?'

Jenny face clouded. 'They weren't very nice, to be honest. I thought they'd be glad to see me – glad to hear they might get the cottage for a little more than they'd offered Dennis. But they didn't want to negotiate. Said they'd made Dennis an offer and that was the price.'

'How did you leave it with them?'

Jenny shrugged. 'I said I'd speak to Steve again but they said it didn't matter. They'd adjust their plans. They couldn't get rid of me quick enough.'

She fished a tissue from her sleeve and dabbed at her eyes. 'I don't even know if it'll be mine, now – I mean, if Steve's married to someone else...'

Clare decided to press on. The question of Dennis's cottage was one for another day. For now, she wanted to see what Jenny made of the second photo. She sifted through them and withdrew a still showing Steve in the Freemans' kitchen, time-stamped ninety minutes after Jenny's visit. She pushed it across the desk and waited while Jenny took in what she was seeing. Then she raised her gaze to meet Clare's.

'When was this taken?'

'You agree that's your husband, Steven Gibb?'

'Of course it is! But I don't understand. He didn't mention going to see the Freemans.'

'Did you tell him about your visit?'

She let her gaze fall. 'No.'

'As far as we can tell,' Clare said, 'Steve called on the Freemans the same night as you, an hour and a half later.' She watched Jenny carefully. 'According to the video clip it was a longer visit than yours. Have you any idea what they might have talked about?'

Jenny nodded. 'Like I said, he probably asked them to up their offer. Judging by the mood he was in when he came back, I'd guess they gave him the same answer as they gave me.'

Clare had already decided she wouldn't mention the Freemans slipping tablets into Steve's water bottle. Not at this stage.

But there was one more thing she wanted to quiz Jenny about. She leafed through the photos again until she found the one she wanted, placing it on the desk.

'You remember I showed you this photo yesterday?'

Jenny stared at it and Clare thought she saw fear in her eyes. *She's ahead of me,* she thought. *She knows what's coming.*

'Jenny?'

'Yes.' Her voice was thick with emotion. 'I remember.'

'And you agreed it's Steve?'

'Yes. That's Steve.'

'Have you any idea where it was taken?'

Jenny said nothing.

'I'll tell you,' Clare went on. 'It was taken from a door camera on a house near the top of North Street on the night we believe Dennis was pushed into the harbour.'

Jenny began to cry quietly.

Clare gave her a moment then went on. 'Jenny, I have to ask what you think Steve was doing that night.'

The sobs were audible now, a crumpled tissue held to her mouth. Chris picked up the coffee cup, cold and congealed, and went to fetch a drink of water, returning a minute later. He put the plastic cup in front of Jenny and they waited while she took a drink, some of the water splashing on the table in front of her.

'Would you like me to repeat the question?' Clare asked, her voice as tender as she could make it.

Jenny shook her head. 'I can't be sure,' she managed, eventually. 'I'll never really know. But I've always wondered.'

'What have you wondered?'

'About Dennis. Steve – he was furious with him. He said the cottage was a dump – that it was damp, the roof needed fixed and the doors were draughty. He said Dennis could sell it to the Freemans and have a nice little flat somewhere in the town.'

Privately, Clare doubted this, having seen the prices in Feddinch's window but she let it go.

'Steve said if Dennis wouldn't sell he'd make him,' Jenny went on.

Clare sat forward. 'What do you think he meant by that?'

She took a moment. 'I wasn't sure. But when you told us someone had killed Dennis…'

They waited and Clare thought there was a struggle going on in Jenny's head. 'Whatever it is, Jenny, it'll come out eventually,' she said. 'It might help to tell us.'

Jenny nodded and she took a breath in and out. 'I couldn't help wondering – if Steve had something to do with it.' Her shoulders sagged as if the tension had left her body.

'You thought Steve might have killed his father?'

She hesitated. 'I thought maybe he'd given him a shove, you know? And Dennis had overbalanced and gone into the water; and then Steve had panicked and pushed him under.' She stopped for a moment.

'That night – the night we both went to see the Freemans – we'd argued.' She swallowed then went on. 'I asked him if he'd had anything to do with what happened to Dennis – if they'd had a fight. I said I wouldn't tell anyone. But I wanted to know.'

Clare was watching her carefully. 'What did he say?'

Jenny's face was a picture of misery. 'He denied it. Said it was ridiculous. What sort of a wife was I, accusing him of murder? Then he stormed out. But he hadn't looked at me. Hadn't met my eye so I knew…'

Clare let a silence hang in the air before continuing.

'I have to ask,' she said, her voice more gentle now, 'did you not think of coming forward? Telling us what you suspected?' She glanced at Chris. 'We've had a lot of officers working on Dennis's murder.'

Jenny's face was scarlet now. She opened her mouth but the words wouldn't come. Clare sensed Chris's discomfort and she knew what he wasn't saying. They'd pushed it far enough. Jenny was a victim here – a victim of her husband's bigamy and now she was the widow of a murder victim.

'I think we'll stop there,' she said. 'I'm so sorry we had to put you through that, but we're grateful for your honesty.' She rose from her seat. 'If you wait here, I'll have someone take you home and stay with you for a couple of hours. See you're okay in the house.'

Jenny nodded but didn't speak, the sound of her sobs gradually filling the room.

Chapter 28

'I'm going to bring in a family liaison officer,' Clare said. 'I've sent Jenny home with one of the PCs but I'd rather have someone there on a regular basis. Just while we work out what's going on.'

'You're not suggesting she's in danger?' Chris sank down in a chair. 'I thought we agreed Steve killed Dennis.'

She was quiet for a moment. 'Yeah, we did.'

'And the Freemans killed Steve.'

She didn't reply.

Chris rolled his eyes. 'So why does she need an FLO?'

Clare didn't answer.

'You're not trying to overcomplicate this are you? You know the most obvious answer is usually the right one.'

'I dunno, Chris. It doesn't quite add up.' She picked up a pen and twiddled it between her fingers. 'Two questions.'

'Shoot.'

'Where did the Freemans get Fentanyl and why did they put it in Steve's bottle?'

Chris shrugged. 'Guys like Rex Freeman have connections.'

Clare raised an eyebrow. 'Seriously? He's a pretty high-profile businessman. Why would he involve himself with drugs?'

'I dunno. Why does anyone? Money.'

'Yeah, I suppose.' She drew a notepad across the desk and began making a note. 'I'll try Amy over in the drugs unit again. She might have heard something else.' She stopped writing. 'All the same…'

'Go on, then. I'll play.'

'Amy said they'd no reports of Fentanyl circulating.'

'And?'

'What if someone's brought it in from another area?'

'Someone? Oh wait…'

She nodded. 'I can't ignore Brad. His body was never found, never declared dead. Maybe he did hear Dennis had been offered money for the cottage and he wanted his share. He helps Steve kill Dennis and they plan to split the proceeds. But Steve starts playing awkward with the Freemans, holding out for more money. Brad realises the Freemans could just build around Dennis's cottage. Steve's going to blow it. So he has to take Steve out of the equation as well. He supplies the Fentanyl, telling the Freemans he'll settle for the original price. Or even a bit less. If he's been living rough for nine years he'd likely be happy with a lower offer.'

Chris was quiet as he considered this and Clare went on.

'Maybe once the fuss has died down, he'll reappear and claim his inheritance.' She put down her pen and sat back.

Chris shook his head. 'I see what you're saying but it's a bit of a stretch. I know you don't want to hear this but I think you are overcomplicating it. There's not a shred of evidence that Brad's still alive.

'If you ask me,' he went on, 'the Freemans saw Jenny as a soft touch. She admitted she wanted Steve to sell the cottage. Most likely they thought if they got rid of Steve, Jenny would inherit. They send a card, flowers, give it a week or two then tell her the original offer still stands. Maybe throw in another grand out of sympathy.'

'Yeah. You're right. It makes more sense than Brad's involvement.'

His expression was seraphic. 'I try.'

'I'm still not convinced about the drugs, though. I know what you said but it doesn't fit with that pair. They're making a packet from their property business. I just can't see them buying Fentanyl from some skeezy dealer.'

'Maybe they were prescribed it.'

'I doubt it. That's one strong pain killer.' Something was niggling at her but it wouldn't come.

'I still think they could be involved with drugs,' Chris said. 'There's something about money that makes folk like them think they're untouchable – that anything's possible, including getting their hands on restricted drugs.'

The door opened and Max appeared. 'They're out,' he said.

'The Freemans?'

'Afraid so. We've left an unmarked car outside the house so they'll alert us when they return.'

Clare thought for a moment. 'Can you plug the car reg into ANPR?' but Max shook his head.

'There's a window at the side of their garage. Both cars are there.'

'Dammit. Okay. Get onto local taxi firms. Find out if anyone picked a fare up in Hepburn Gardens. If so, get the destination. I won't be happy until we have those two in the station.'

Max went off to phone round.

Chris waited until he'd closed the door then turned back to Clare. 'What I don't get,' he said, 'is where those cameras came from. And why.'

'You and me both,' Clare said. 'I wonder.'

'Uh huh?'

'Do you think we should ask Carol Merryweather to check her smoke alarms?'

'For cameras?'

'Yeah. Remember the thief dropped the memory stick in her house.'

Chris considered. 'Might be an idea. Who attended her burglary?'

'Max.'

'Would he recognise the house from the footage?'

Clare shrugged. 'He might.'

'Could take a while, though,' Chris said. 'Far quicker to go round. Check for ourselves.' He glanced at his watch. 'We could do it now. Wouldn't take long.'

Clare smiled. 'Let's see what tomorrow brings.' She checked her watch. 'I've a couple of phone calls to make then I'll head home. But, if that pair turn up, call me. I'll come back out to interview them.'

'Best stay off the sauce, then.'

She gave a noncommittal gesture. 'It's not like I have a glass every night.'

He rose, pushing back his chair. 'You keep telling yourself that.'

She waited until he'd left then picked up her phone and scrolled through her contacts. Her finger hovered over the number for Wendy Briggs, a family liaison officer she'd worked with on a few cases. Wendy was a safe pair of hands, sharp eyes and a sound judge. She'd be good for Jenny – do a good job. But did they really need someone of Wendy's calibre? She scrolled on until she came to Paul Henry's number. She'd worked with him as well, just the once, and it hadn't been a success. He'd been arrogant, bordering on insensitive and they'd clashed repeatedly. But they'd cleared the air in the end. Was it worth giving him another chance?

'DC Henry.' He spoke quickly, as though trying to convey the impression he was super-busy. Irritation flared in Clare but she bit it back. They'd parted on good terms the last time they'd spoken and she resolved not to be the one to break the peace.

'Paul,' she said, making an effort to sound pleased to hear his voice. 'DI Clare Mackay, St Andrews station. How are you?'

'All good, thanks. How are things with you, Clare?'

Patronising as ever, she thought. 'Pretty busy, actually. I'm after an FLO. You available?'

There was a slight hesitation. 'I'm guessing you couldn't get anyone else.'

'On the contrary. You're the first one I called.'

'Blimey. Erm, okay. Yeah, I could be. What's the scoop?'

It was on the tip of her tongue to suggest he used more professional language but she let it go. She began explaining about Jenny Gibb.

'Sheesh,' he said. 'So she's married her brother-in-law?'

Clare shook her head. 'No. She's not legally married to anyone and it's been a huge shock so please don't mention it.'

''Course not. Just the usual? Eyes and ears open?'

'And keeping the press at bay. We may be in a position to make an arrest for her husband's murder in the next few days so there will be interest.'

'Roger wilco. Tomorrow do you?'

'Yes, that's fine. If you head here for nine I'll take you round. Introduce you.'

She put down her phone, silently congratulating herself for not being narky with him. Frankly, it was a piece of cake compared to her next call.

Superintendent Penny Meakin answered on the second ring, her tone more clipped than usual. 'Clare – not another request for manpower, I trust?'

There was no easy way to do this. She took a deep breath. 'I'd like to request a warrant.'

'For?'

'To search the Freemans' house.'

There was silence at the other end. A long moment but Clare held her nerve. She was well within her rights to request the warrant and she wasn't about to back down because Penny thought the Freemans deserved special treatment.

'I think you'd better explain,' Penny said, eventually.

She listened as Clare recounted the discovery of the footage and, when she did finally speak, her reaction surprised Clare.

'My only concern,' she began, 'is the legality of the footage. It's an unusual situation. Not one that's covered in our standard operating procedures.'

She had a point.

'Arguably,' she went on, 'the Freemans are victims, here. Their privacy has been invaded without their knowledge. On the other hand, we have unwittingly stumbled on evidence that suggests they may be guilty of a crime.'

'We didn't put the cameras there,' Clare said. 'It's not entrapment.'

'True.' Penny fell silent. Clare waited and eventually she spoke. 'I'll grant it. But please don't execute it until you've checked with me. I may have to take legal advice.' She hesitated. 'I assume you plan to arrest them?'

'I'll aim for voluntary attendance,' Clare said. 'But if they refuse, I will arrest them.'

'In which case you'll need the warrant asap. Leave it with me.'

She ended the call and Clare sat on, phone in hand. She'd expected a battle for the warrant, to have to fight her corner. But Penny had come good after all and she was faintly reassured. Clearly the higher up the ranks you went, the more political you became – the more other factors came into play. She knew that much from Al's stint working in Policy, over in Bell Street station, his office a few doors away from Penny's. Her confidence in Penny over this forthcoming march had taken a dent. Clare felt she was in danger of putting her connections above straightforward policing. But she had just restored Clare's faith in her. Maybe there was hope for Penny yet!

—

She was pushing open the door to Daisy Cottage, Benjy squeezing past her legs, when her phone began ringing.

'No luck with taxis,' Max said. 'No fares from Hepburn Gardens at all today.'

'Dammit,' Clare said. 'If they didn't take a taxi where have they gone? Could they be visiting neighbours?'

'Actually Patch spoke to the neighbours. Just casually,' he added. 'Nothing to make them think it was serious.'

'And?'

'One of them saw the Freemans getting into a dark car about two this afternoon.'

'Don't suppose she got the reg? Or anything else?'

'Only that it was a dark saloon. She said they both got in the back so she thought maybe there was another couple in the front. Thing is, they had a small wheely case. I've been trying their mobiles but both going straight to voicemail.'

Clare flicked on the kitchen light and put down her bag. Benjy began lapping noisily at his water dish. 'Dammit. If they're going on holiday...'

'I can't see it,' Max said. 'Remember the exhibition on Saturday. Surely they're planning to be around for that.'

The exhibition! The reason for the protest march. She was starting to wish she'd never heard the name Freeman. 'Good point.'

'Besides, it was one small case between them,' Max went on. 'They'll likely be back tomorrow.'

Clare thought for a moment. 'Max, could you check their social media please? See if they've tagged any hotels. They might have a few favourites they use – spa breaks, that kind of thing. It's worth ringing round. We might just be lucky.'

Max agreed to do this and Clare put down her phone. Benjy was sitting, his face upturned and she relented, opening the cupboard where his food was kept. Mindful of Chris's words she took a carton of juice from the fridge and poured herself a glass. There was a quiche in there too, one Al had bought from the deli in Church Street and she put this in the oven to heat. Then she carried the juice over to the table and sank down, sipping from the glass. It wasn't grapefruit – some mixed fruit variety Al had bought, but she couldn't help thinking of Steve Gibb and his fatal cocktail. Hopefully, the warrant would be through by morning and the Freemans picked up. She was pretty sure Steve had killed his father; and now they had video evidence of the Freemans adding tablets to Steve's bottle. If they could charge the couple with his murder she'd be able to give the forthcoming march her full attention.

She made short work of the quiche and poured herself a coffee, taking this over to the sofa. She was too tired to light the fire, turning the radiators up instead. The remote control lay on the floor where she must have left it the night before and she reached for this, flicking the TV on. Benjy padded over to the fire then, realising there was no heat from it, jumped up beside Clare. She pulled him towards her, relishing the warmth of his body, and closed her eyes. Just for a moment.

A noise from the TV roused her and she realised it was after ten. She'd slept for almost three hours. She pulled herself to her feet and led Benjy to the kitchen door. He escaped to the garden for a sniff and a pee then padded back in, heading straight for his basket. She wrapped a blanket round him and went round the house, putting out the lights.

But the evening nap meant she was wide awake now, thoughts of the Freemans, of poor, sad Jenny Gibb, and that bloody protest march running round her head. Somewhere distant, an owl hooted and suddenly she longed for it to be spring, and for the name Freeman to no longer consume her waking thoughts.

Day 8: Tuesday, 17th February

Chapter 29

Max pressed the mute button on his phone. 'He wants to speak to you.'

'You found him?' Clare flicked on her office light and put down her bag.

'Yes. Good shout on the social media. There's a few hotels in Scotland they use regularly. Just a case of phoning round. Some spa the other side of Glasgow,' he said. 'Eye-watering prices.'

Clare eyed the phone. 'I'm guessing he's not happy.'

'You could say that. Glasgow cops are on their way to pick them up but he's foaming at the mouth.' He hesitated. 'I could say you're not here.'

Clare sighed and put her hand out for the phone. Max unmuted it and she put it on speaker.

'Mr Freeman, good morning.' She kept her tone light, professional.

'Inspector Mackay?'

'Yes. I gather you asked to speak to me.'

'I certainly did.' He spoke quickly. His voice was level but she sensed it wouldn't take much for it to be raised. 'What on earth is so important you have to interrupt our short break? I'm quite sure whatever it is can be dealt with by telephone.'

Clare thought of her many conversations over the past week with Penny. They were two of a kind, she decided. Anyone else might have phrased that last remark as a question but, with Rex, it was a statement of intent. *You try and make us come back,* he was saying, *and it won't end well for you.*

Had Penny not authorised the warrant Clare might have had more of a battle on her hands. But she sensed, this morning, Penny might not be available for Rex's calls. In fact, she'd bet Chris his Wagon Wheels stash Rex had already tried her.

'I'm afraid not,' she said. 'Some information has come to light and I need to discuss it with you in person. Both of you,' she added.

'I really think...' his voice was rising now but she cut across him. *In for a penny...*

'Furthermore, I'd like permission to search your house.'

There was silence for a moment. When he spoke again he enunciated every word with care, as if dealing with a very slow child. 'I presume this is a joke. At least I *hope* it's a joke.'

Max's eyebrows shot up and Clare suppressed a smile. 'As you are aware, Mr Freeman, a hidden camera was placed in your house without your knowledge. We've been working tirelessly to find out who is responsible.'

He tried cutting across her but Clare ploughed on. She wasn't about to let this self-important man get the better of her.

'Our enquiries have unearthed some evidence that means a discreet and careful search of your house has become necessary. A warrant can be requested but I'm sure you're as keen as we are to bring the perpetrators to justice.'

He made a noncommittal sound and Clare knew she had him.

'Do we have your permission, Mr Freeman?'

He sighed heavily. 'I can scarcely refuse, can I?'

'Thank you. That's very helpful. I believe we have your cleaning lady's details. If you have no objection we'll ask her for the key.'

He ignored this. 'If you're still investigating, I'm sure we could continue to enjoy our break. We'll be home tomorrow.'

'That won't be possible,' Clare said. 'The evidence in question needs to be seen by you both today and we can't do that by telephone; and now, if you will excuse me, I have pressing matters to attend to.'

She ended the call and handed the phone back to Max.

'Smooth,' he said. 'I bet he can count on one hand the number of times anyone's spoken to him like that.'

Clare sank down in her chair. 'Maybe I should have been a bit more conciliatory. But I've not had my coffee so…'

Max smiled. 'I'll do you a filter coffee. It's the least you deserve.'

'What does she deserve?' Chris said, pulling up a chair. 'And can I have whatever it is as well?'

'Clare's just wiped the floor with Rex Freeman,' Max said, 'so I'm doing her a coffee.'

Chris turned his best puppy-dog eyes on Max and he relented.

'I'll do a cafetiere.'

Chris waited until he'd left. 'So you found him?'

'Max did. He was absolutely spitting, though.'

'Hah! Wait till he hears about the second camera. Please let me be there when you tell them.'

Max returned a few minutes later, tray in hand. Clare moved a pile of paperwork to make room for it. She waited while he plunged the cafetiere and poured out mugs.

Chris sloshed milk into his mug. 'So what's the plan?'

Clare pulled her mug across the table. 'Max, I'd like you to take a team to the Freemans' house, please – as many as you can lay your hands on. I'll be interviewing them when they arrive so, if there is anything there, I need to know about it asap.'

'Anything particular you're looking for?'

'Pills, specifically Fentanyl. I'm afraid you'll have to do the bins as well. There might be empty blister packs; and the usual – any electronics that could contain information.'

'Paperwork?'

'Definitely. But I want a tidy job. They work from home so let's not give them any reason to complain. Mind you, if we do charge them…'

Max smiled. 'I'll do my best.'

Clare lifted her phone to update Penny but the call went to voicemail. She left a message saying the Freemans had agreed to a search of their house, and hoped that would satisfy her.

—

She'd forgotten Paul Henry was due at nine and was in the kitchen washing her mug when he arrived.

'Don't suppose there's any coffee going?' He gave her a dazzling smile.

She shook her head. 'You don't get any better, do you?'

He laughed. 'You'd be disappointed if I did.'

She indicated one of the wall cupboards. 'You'll find coffee and mugs in there. Help yourself.'

He let the smile drop. 'Seriously, I was pretty chuffed you asked for me.' He inclined his head. 'Was I honestly your first choice?'

'Scout's honour.'

'Cool.' He found a mug and made himself a coffee then followed Clare to her office.

'I'm a bit pressed this morning,' she said, 'so I'll ask one of the others to take you over. But go gently, mind. She's just lost her husband and realised he most likely killed his own father.'

'It's like a Greek tragedy.'

'It is a bit. Only, I've a feeling the worst is yet to come; and with two deaths in the family I want to be sure she's safe so no visitors, or anyone else in that house please.'

Clare let him finish his coffee then she asked Mandy to take him over to Jenny's house. Mandy raised an eyebrow when she saw who the FLO was but she nodded towards the car park and he followed her out. Clare watched them go wondering how he would get on. She had to admit he was marginally less irritating than he'd been the first time they'd met.

'Maybe miracles really do happen,' she murmured, making her way back to her office.

The Freemans arrived as she was about to eat her lunch. She asked the officers accompanying them to bring Erika in first. She didn't want the pair to have any opportunity to chat, although they'd likely have done that before the officers arrived at their hotel. But would they have known about the video evidence? She hoped not.

Erika Freeman wore a long camel-coloured coat that Clare thought was cashmere, a brown cross-body leather bag dangling at her hip. She shoved a pair of designer sunglasses onto her head and Clare saw her make-up was impeccable. She looked as if she'd walked straight off a film set – except for her expression, a mixture of disdain and – was that fear?

She left Chris to deal with her and went to check Jim had arranged solicitors for both.

'Bit tricky,' he said. 'They use the same solicitor, obviously. A woman called…' He checked his notepad. 'Gemma Featherstone. Apparently she's going to sit in with Rex and Erika has requested another solicitor. Someone she knows, I think.'

Erika was led to an interview room, Clare watching her go. She had to admire her composure. Her head was up, eyes straight forward. She wondered briefly if Erika had done any modelling in the past; or perhaps she'd had dance training. She certainly knew how to carry herself; and then she was gone, safely installed in the small room and it was Rex's turn.

He strode into the station, making no secret of his annoyance at this turn of events. 'This really is unacceptable,' he announced to Jim who moved forward to greet him. 'We've lost a valuable night's relaxation at a very expensive hotel; a night we both needed,' he went on, 'given we're victims of a crime. Bloody embarrassing too, in front of our friends.'

Jim displayed exemplary patience as he led Rex to another interview room.

'And I've missed my lunch,' Rex said, as Jim opened the door and ushered him in.

'Better get them a couple of coffees,' Clare said. 'And if there are any biscuits...'

'He's not having my Wagon Wheels,' Chris cut in. 'And that is the hill I will die on.'

Clare eyed him. 'Bit dramatic, Sergeant.'

He snorted. 'Some things are sacred, Inspector.'

Garth Bryce arrived twenty minutes later and was shown into Erika's interview room. After another ten minutes, he indicated they were ready to proceed. Clare had decided against eating her lunch while they waited for Erika and Garth to finish their private chat. Her stomach was unsettled and she realised she was nervous about the interview. Was it because of Penny? She certainly couldn't afford to put a foot wrong with the Freemans. Jenny Gibb deserved justice for Steve's murder. But Clare knew, if she did mess up, Penny wouldn't miss her and hit the wall. On the other hand, they had footage of the couple colluding in Steve's murder. She'd like to see Penny put a positive spin on that one.

Chris had isolated the spycam clips and loaded them onto a tablet to show the couple.

'Makes sense to take her first,' Clare said. 'She wasn't the one who added the pills so I reckon she's more likely to burst.'

They entered the room and greeted Erika and Garth. Clare thanked them for coming and Garth sat up in his seat.

'This is a huge inconvenience for Mrs Freeman, to say nothing of interrupting a much-needed holiday with good friends. I trust the interview won't take long.'

Clare appraised him and decided he was no fool. He was fortyish, she thought, receding hair cut close, emphasising his steely grey eyes. His fine grey suit looked expensive and his open-necked shirt spoke volumes about his self-confidence. He had no need of a tie to stamp his authority on any meeting. She wondered briefly how he knew the Freemans. A business connection? Or maybe he'd gone to school with one of them. He might be a similar age to Rex.

She gave him a smile, cool and professional, determined not to betray the nerves she felt. 'If we're all ready, then…'

Chris ran through the preamble, listing the date, time and their names. As he did this, Clare glanced at Erika. She stared pointedly back, a stiffness in her frame, suggesting this would not be a comfortable interview. The nervous feeling in Clare's stomach grew as she wondered how Erika would react to the video evidence. She forced back nerves, smiled at Erika and began.

'I'd like to take you back to the morning of Wednesday, 11th February. You reported a break-in at your house in Hepburn Gardens.'

'We did.'

'Following this, our Scene of Crimes Officers attended and a hidden camera was found in the ceiling of your front room.'

Garth sat forward. 'What's this?'

Clare explained about the dummy smoke alarm. Garth clicked his pen and began making notes. 'Have you discovered who was responsible?'

'Not yet,' Clare said.

'I'd have thought that was rather more important than dragging my client back from the other side of Glasgow.'

Clare forced a smile. 'I assure you I have officers working on it. But something rather more serious has come to light.'

Garth met Clare's eye. 'More serious than my client's home being broken into, than a hidden camera placed there without their knowledge?'

'Something that relates directly to the *break-in*.' Clare put particular emphasis on those last two words. An expression she couldn't read crossed Erika's face but she said nothing.

'The camera didn't have an SD card,' Clare explained to Garth. 'We believe it was transmitting via public Wi-Fi to a remote location but we have yet to determine that location.'

Garth was watching her carefully and she waited a moment in case he had a question.

'What we have found, is a flash drive with footage from the hidden camera. I would like to play that footage now.' She glanced at Erika, trying to read her. Had she joined the dots? Clare didn't think so. She watched as Erika reached into her handbag, withdrawing a red spec case which she snapped open. She withdrew a pair of tortoiseshell glasses and placed them on her nose. Garth waited until Erika was ready then he nodded at Clare.

Chris clicked to play the first clip, turning the tablet so Erika could see Rex and herself staging the burglary. A mixture of fear and rage crossed Erika's face.

'Stop this,' she said, her voice rising. 'I don't want to see it.'

Garth put a hand on Erika's arm. 'Say nothing.' He eyed Clare. 'I'd like a moment with Mrs Freeman, please.'

They paused the interview and left the pair to talk. 'Can't see her wriggling out of this one,' Chris said.

Clare's eyes were on the interview room door, for any sign they were ready to resume. 'With that one, anything's possible.'

Jim approached. 'The husband's solicitor's here. They've asked if we can start in ten minutes.'

Clare laughed. 'In their dreams. We're not half done with the wife.'

A troubled look crossed Jim's face. 'I could get Max back. Let him make a start with Rex.'

Chris shrugged. 'Might be an idea. The clock's ticking and we've no idea how long we'll be with the wife.'

It was a fair point. Clare thought for a moment. 'Get hold of Max, then. See how quickly he can get back here. The notes for Rex's interview are on my desk.'

Jim went off to call Max and Clare resumed her spot, eyes trained on the interview room door. But it was another five minutes before Garth and Erika were ready to continue. They resumed their seats, Clare studying Erika, wondering what she would say about the footage.

Garth clicked on his pen, a gesture Clare took to mean he had something to say. He waited for Chris to restart the recording then he eyed Clare, his expression serious. 'Mrs Freeman doesn't understand this footage. She believes the whole thing, the hidden camera, this footage, that it's all part of a plot to undermine their business plans.'

'It's that thing,' Erika burst out. 'That deep-fake stuff. Someone's made it look like Rex and I did this ourselves. But we didn't. Why would we?'

Why indeed, Clare thought. 'We can of course have our technical support team examine the footage to determine if it's been artificially created,' she said. 'But I have to say, for something like a local planning application, it's unlikely anyone would go to such trouble.'

'Nevertheless,' Garth continued, 'that is our position.'

'Noted,' Clare said. 'But I must advise that charges may follow in relation to this.'

Neither of them spoke and Clare pressed on. 'There is something else I would like to ask you about.'

Erika shot a look at Garth. The burglary footage had clearly unnerved her and Clare thought she must be wondering what else they knew. *How many secrets do you two have?* she thought.

She took a moment, watching Erika carefully. 'Did you know Dennis Gibb?'

Erika arched a slender eyebrow. 'I don't think so.'

'I'll remind you,' Clare said. 'Dennis Gibb owned a cottage in the middle of the piece of land you are seeking to develop.'

There was no outward sign of recognition. If anything Erika looked bored, as though the question was irrelevant. 'I recall the cottage.'

'Did you approach Mr Gibb with an offer to buy his cottage?'

She inclined her head. 'Almost certainly. We would likely have written to him. Our original plan would not have worked without the land on which his cottage stands.'

Clare nodded at this, pretending to consult her notes. 'Did Mr Gibb agree to sell?'

'You'll have to ask my husband,' Erika said. 'But I suspect not, otherwise we wouldn't be looking at changing our plans.'

Clare eyed her. 'When did you decide this?'

Erika surveyed the room as though it was of more interest than the question. Perhaps she was trying to give the impression it hadn't been an important decision. 'Oh I'm not sure. We have so many business discussions, you see.'

'And how will you change your plans?' Clare asked, 'assuming you are not able to buy the cottage.'

A smile twitched at the corners of her mouth. 'Oh that's confidential, Inspector. It's a highly competitive industry. We can't risk news of our plans leaking out.'

Clare could feel anger rising but she kept her expression neutral. 'I assure you, Mrs Freeman, we have no interest in your plans beyond the scope of our investigation. Any information disclosed in this interview will remain entirely confidential.' She eyed Erika waiting for her reaction but she simply looked round the room, as if affecting boredom.

Clare couldn't wait to see her reaction when Chris played the other video clips. But, she wasn't going to rush it. One thing at a time.

'Are you aware Dennis Gibb died almost three weeks ago?'

Erika formed her face into a mask of sympathy but Garth cut in before she could reply.

'I trust you're not suggesting—'

'Not at all,' Clare said. 'I'm simply checking Mrs Freeman is aware of all relevant circumstances.'

'I am,' Erika said, smiling at Garth. 'Terribly sad.'

'Did it occur to you it might be easier to buy the cottage, now Mr Gibb is dead?'

Erika sat forward and placed her elbows on the desk. 'What you probably don't understand, Inspector, is how complex a large-scale planning application is. Thousands of pages of plans, drawings, letters – there's simply no end to it. I'm afraid I gave the late Mr Gibb's cottage very little thought. I'm sorry for his family, obviously,' she added.

She sat back in her seat and Clare had the impression she was saying *job done* to herself.

'Moving on to Mr Gibb's family, do you know his son Steven Gibb?'

She took a moment before replying and Clare wondered if she was playing for time; perhaps trying to guess where the line of questioning was leading. 'Maybe,' she said, eventually. 'I've spoken to a fair few of the locals. Good PR, you know?'

'What about his wife, Jennifer Gibb? Have you met her?'

Erika spread her hands. 'It's highly possible,' she said. 'But the name doesn't ring a bell.'

Clare spoke slowly, her eyes never leaving Erika's face. 'Are you quite sure about that?'

Erika made no reply and Clare glanced at the tablet Chris had placed on the desk. He took the cue and tapped the button on the front to bring it to life.

'It seems another camera was installed in the house,' Clare went on.

Erika stiffened. 'What camera? Where?'

Clare took a moment, savouring Erika's alarm. 'In the kitchen. Again, ceiling mounted.'

Something passed across Erika's eyes and Clare wondered if she was mentally running through Friday evening's events – wondering just how much they knew. 'When did you discover this?'

'In the last twenty-four hours.' She watched Erika, trying to read her reaction but she had a grip on herself now, her face a mask.

'This next clip was recorded around five p.m. on Friday 13th February.' She nodded at Chris and he clicked to play the footage, turning the tablet again so Erika and Garth could watch. The mask slipped and Erika's face drained of colour as she saw herself lead Jenny Gibb into the kitchen. Clare nodded to Chris and he paused the footage.

'I'd like you to identify the woman in your kitchen,' she said.

Erika's eyes were flicking back and forth, as though trying to decide what to say. In the end she settled for nothing.

'Mrs Freeman?'

When she didn't speak Clare tried again. 'Do you agree the woman in this clip is Jenny Gibb?'

Erika wouldn't meet Clare's eye. 'I suppose it might be. But I barely know the woman.'

'And yet she is in your kitchen.'

She shrugged. 'More of that deep-fake stuff, then,' but her expression betrayed how unlikely she knew this was.

Clare regarded her. 'It sounds like an awful lot of trouble for a business rival to go to.'

'Protestors, then,' Erika said, a catch to her voice.

Clare was watching her carefully. The footage of Jenny had clearly unnerved Erika and she decided to press home her advantage. 'Let me play the rest of the clip. It simply shows a conversation between you, your husband and Jenny Gibb. The sooner we find out the nature of that conversation the sooner we can move on.'

Erika looked at Garth and he gave a noncommittal gesture.

'All right.' She did her best to affect a bored expression but her eyes betrayed her.

They watched as Chris ran the rest of the clip, ending with Erika showing Jenny out of the kitchen. For a moment the room was silent, Erika shifting in her seat. She opened her mouth as if to speak but her voice cracked and no words came out.

Chris was despatched to fetch water and he returned a minute later with four plastic cups on a tray. Erika removed her specs, setting them down on the table and took one of the cups. She drank slowly and Clare wondered if she was playing for time, mentally rehearsing her story. Finally she replaced the cup on the table.

'I do remember Jenny now,' she said. 'It took a minute for it to come back to me.'

'Of course,' Clare said. 'What was the nature of her visit?'

'That cottage. She thought if we offered her husband a bit more he might sell.'

This matched with Jenny's account. 'And how did you respond?'

Erika was into her stride now, clearly believing she was on safe ground. 'We told her we'd offered her father-in-law the best price we could. By the time we paid for demolition, removal of debris and levelled the ground, we'd be lucky to cover our costs.'

Privately, Clare doubted this. She didn't know how much the Freemans had offered Dennis but she was pretty sure this pair knew how to turn a profit. 'Anything else?'

She shook her head. 'That was pretty much it. She asked for more and we said we couldn't afford it. Then she left.'

Clare let this hang in the air, wondering if Erika realised what must surely come next. She saw something flicker in her eyes. Brief, but it was there. Panic.

'We have one more clip to show you,' Clare said with a nod to Chris.

'No!'

They stared at her.

'I don't want to see it.'

Garth put a steadying hand on Erika's arm again. 'I'd advise you to say nothing more, Erika.' He turned to Clare. 'I really think Mrs Freeman has given you all the help she can. This has been a distressing experience. I'd like to terminate the interview.'

Clare indicated Chris should pause the footage. 'That's fine,' she said. 'But we will have to come back to this and I'm afraid

Mrs Freeman will remain in the station while she composes herself.'

Erika's eyes were wild with fear. 'Remain here? Can't I go home?' Her voice was rising again and Clare gave her a moment.

'I'm afraid not. The last bit of footage is rather more serious.'

'Mrs Freeman may exercise her right to leave,' Garth suggested.

Clare met his gaze. She didn't want to have to say it, not while there was a chance Erika might volunteer the truth.

Garth gave a slight nod. He understood. If she tried to leave they'd arrest her. 'Erika?' His voice was gentle, full of concern. 'We can carry on just now or you can take a break. But you will have to stay here in the station.'

Her eyes were brimming and Clare pushed a box of tissues across the table. She waited while Erika took one and dabbed at the corners of her eyes.

'Shall we continue?' she said, after a moment.

Erika nodded.

'Can you please say you're happy to continue?' Clare said. 'For the tape.'

'Yes,' she stammered. 'Get it over with.' She reached for her specs, almost knocking over the half-full cup of water. Chris put a steadying hand on the cup and they waited while Erika replaced her specs, her hands shaking.

Clare motioned to Chris to play the final clip. Again, Garth and Erika's eyes were on the tablet while Clare watched for Erika's reaction. She sat transfixed as if she couldn't tear her eyes away. Perhaps seeing what they had done played on a screen brought home the weight of their actions. Surely Erika must know she wouldn't walk away from this.

Garth's expression was grave and, when Chris stopped the recording, he spoke softly to his client. 'I'd advise you to say nothing,' but Erika shook her head.

'I – I had nothing to do with that,' she said. 'Whatever Rex was doing, I knew nothing about it.'

So, Clare thought, *she's throwing him under the bus to save herself. Interesting.* 'Can you tell us what your husband Rex was doing in that clip?'

'Erika,' Garth said, his voice louder this time. 'Say absolutely nothing.'

It was as if she hadn't heard him. Her eyes were closed, head shaking as though trying to dismiss what she had seen. 'I don't know,' she said. 'But it was nothing to do with me.' She opened her eyes and met Clare's gaze. 'You have to believe me. I didn't know what he was doing.'

'And yet he showed you an empty blister pack,' Clare persisted. 'You saw him swirling the contents of the bottle, trying to mix tablets in.'

'But I didn't see what he did with them. I was looking out for that man.'

'Steven Gibb?'

'Yes, him.'

'Why?'

For a moment it seemed Erika didn't understand. 'Why what?'

'Why were you looking out for Steven Gibb?'

Erika opened her mouth to speak then stopped. *Getting her story straight,* Clare decided.

'I'm not sure,' she said. 'Call it instinct. He'd asked to use the toilet and I didn't trust him. I didn't want him wandering all over our house. I'd told him where the toilet was and I wanted to check he didn't go into any other rooms. Yes, that's it,' she said, her face suddenly relaxing as if relieved to have hit on a plausible story.

'You weren't, for example, making sure he wouldn't return in time to catch your husband putting pills in Mr Gibb's water bottle?'

'Certainly not. Whatever Rex did was nothing to do with me.'

Clare watched her carefully. She'd begun to recover herself. There was just one final question.

'What was on the blister pack?'

Erika stared. 'Sorry. I don't understand.'

'Blister packs,' Clare said. 'They usually have the name of the drug on them. The footage shows your husband holding out the empty pack for you to see. So which pills were they? And where did you get them?'

Erika hesitated and Garth cut across her, indicating Erika's specs. 'As you can see, Mrs Freeman needs reading glasses for close work. Given how small the writing on these packs can be, I doubt she'd have been able to identify whatever it was.'

Erika threw him a grateful glance. 'Yes,' she said. 'I'd no idea what those pills were.'

Clare regarded Erika, her face stoney. 'I have to tell you, Mrs Freeman, that Steven Gibb died a few hours after his visit to your house and we are treating his death as murder.'

Erika put a hand on the table as if steadying herself.

Clare watched her without sympathy and nodded to Chris. 'Interview terminated at one thirty-five p.m.'

Then she pushed back her chair and swept from the room.

Chapter 30

Clare left Chris to tell Erika she would remain in custody, pending further investigation. Jim was waiting for her.

'Max is in with Rex now,' he said.

'Who's with him?'

'Nita came over from Cupar.'

Clare had worked with Nita on a few investigations when she'd needed extra detectives. She was a reliable DC with a sharp pair of eyes and Clare knew she could be trusted with such an important interview. 'Thanks, Jim. How's the search at the Freemans' going?'

'Nothing much so far. But Max brought this back.' He held up a laptop that Clare thought had seen better days.

She stared at it. 'This was in the Freemans' house?'

'Yes. Max said it seemed odd. Everything they have is Apple. iMacs, iPads and a MacBook. He said it didn't fit with the other stuff.'

Clare studied it. An old HP, scuffed along one edge, the logo faded. It certainly wasn't a new machine. 'Where did he find it?'

'That's the odd thing,' Jim said. 'It was on Rex's desk, on top of all the other papers and stuff.'

Clare thought back to the day they'd attended the so-called burglary. She couldn't recall seeing an old laptop on Rex's desk. 'As if he'd been using it recently?' she said and Jim nodded.

'That is odd. Was there anything else lying about – old stuff, I mean? Maybe they were having a clear-out.'

'Not that Max mentioned. He thought you might want to look it over before it goes to Tech Support.'

Clare took the laptop from Jim and headed for her office. Her stomach rumbled, reminding her she hadn't eaten so she went via the kitchen, flicking the switch on the kettle.

Chris lumbered in, a pastie from a nearby convenience shop in his hand.

'You know how much fat's in those things?' she said but he waved this away.

'Gotta die of something. Kettle on?'

'Just boiling it. Want a coffee?'

'Go on, then.' He began opening cupboard doors. 'Any clean plates?'

Clare nodded at the sink. 'If you wash one.'

'Never mind. I'll grab some paper towels.' He moved to the dispenser and pulled out a handful. 'Quite a performance from our Erika, eh?'

'Yep. But her face fell to her feet when she heard Steve had died,' Clare said. 'She must know she's facing a potential murder charge.'

'Dunno,' Chris said. 'Him, yes. But I'd bet on her solicitor coming up with a story. She's just the type to wriggle out of it.' His eye fell on the laptop. 'What's that?'

'A laptop computer, Sergeant. We use it to store and extract information.'

'Very funny. What are you doing with it?'

'Max found it at the Freemans'.'

He stared. 'What – that?'

'Apparently so. Fancy a look?'

'Sure. Let me do the coffees and I'll join you.'

She regarded the pastie. 'Get a plate for that if you're bringing it into my office.'

He sighed and went to rinse the least worst plate under the hot tap.

Clare made her way to her office, the remains of last night's quiche in a Tupperware box. Chris joined her a minute later, having unearthed a tray from somewhere. He set this down on her desk while Clare bent to plug in the laptop.

It took a minute or two to come to life but finally the welcome screen appeared.

'Dammit,' Clare said. 'Password.' She sat back, thinking. 'Is Erika Freeman still in the station?'

'Yep. Jim thought we should hold her here at least until Rex's interview's over.'

'Right, then.' Clare rose from her chair. 'Let's see if she can give us the password.'

But Erika claimed to know nothing about the laptop. 'I think Rex unearthed it from somewhere,' she said, barely glancing at it. 'Look, I've not eaten since breakfast. Is there any chance I could have some food?'

Clare left her with a promise of sandwiches. Jim was busy tapping at his keyboard with his usual two-fingers method.

'Erika Freeman,' Clare began.

'If it's food it's sorted. I've sent one of the lads to the shop for a meal deal.' He smiled. 'Hope that's okay?'

'Perfect,' Clare said. 'But I'm after another favour. I can't get into the laptop and Erika claims to know nothing about it. I'm going to wait for a break in Rex's interview then ask him. But if he doesn't know…'

'You want it sent to Tech Support?'

'Please.'

'No problem. If I see Max I'll ask him to chap on your door.'

—

It was another half hour before Max appeared at Clare's door.

'He's consulting with his solicitor.'

'Sounds familiar. How's it going?'

'As you'd expect. Denied faking the burglary. Said he'd lost a really important document and they were hunting high and low for it. But he said they tidied up afterwards.'

'Then why wasn't it caught on camera? And why was there no footage of the real burglary?' Clare asked.

'I put that to him and the solicitor asked to speak to him alone. What did the wife say?'

Clare shook her head. 'Said it was a deep-fake. Someone did it to frame them.'

'Seriously?'

'Yup. I'm guessing if they'd realised we'd found the footage they'd have got their stories straight.'

Jim put his head round the door. 'That's them ready to resume.'

Max thanked Jim and his eye fell on the old laptop. 'That the one you want me to ask about?'

Clare pushed back her chair. 'Yes. I'll come in with you. See if he'll give us the password.'

Rex and Gemma Featherstone were talking quietly when Clare, Max and Nita entered the room. Rex's eyes narrowed when he saw Clare but he said nothing. Gemma sat forward, her eyes on Clare.

'I'll explain for the tape,' Clare said and Gemma nodded.

As they waited for Max to restart the recording, Clare studied the pair. Rex's face was drawn, his expression grave and Clare thought he appreciated the seriousness of his plight. *You ain't seen nothing yet,* she thought and she wished she could be in the room when they showed him the other videos.

Gemma, by contrast, was composed, unfazed by her surroundings and Clare reckoned they must have concocted a plausible story. Max indicated they were ready to resume and Clare introduced herself.

'I have only one matter to raise with Mr Freeman,' she said, and she placed the laptop on the desk in front of him. 'This laptop was found during a search of your house today.'

Rex looked at it then he raised his gaze to meet Clare's. 'I've never seen it before.'

'Are you sure?'

'Absolutely. Where was it found?'

She avoided the question. 'Do you know the password for it?'

A smile played at the corners of his lips. 'As it's not my laptop and I've never seen it, I hardly think you could expect me to know the password.'

'You don't know it?' Clare said.

'No I do not.'

She rose, picking the laptop back up. 'Not to worry. We'll find a way to access it. Thank you for your time, Mr Freeman.'

She gave him a smile but it wasn't returned. Was that a look of concern? He had to have seen that laptop before. Otherwise, what was it doing on his desk?

Sara was in the incident room, head bent over a pile of forms.

'Job for you,' Clare said, indicating the laptop.

Sara eyed it. 'Tech Support?'

'I'm afraid so.' Clare glanced at the forms. 'They'll have to wait. This is top priority.'

Sara sighed and took the laptop from Clare. 'I never seem to get to the bottom of my paperwork.'

'You and me both.'

She wandered back to her office, glancing at the interview room door as she passed. She was desperate to be in there, questioning Rex herself. But she had to give her team a chance to develop and this case felt like an open goal. They surely had enough to charge the Freemans with Steve's murder. She closed the office door behind her, glad of a chance to order her thoughts. That laptop didn't fit with the Freemans' glamorous lifestyle, their high-end electronic goods, so why had they found it on Rex's desk?

And then she remembered the old machine Jim had unearthed from his Cupboard of Many Things. The one Clare had used to check the contents of the flash drive. Maybe this was what Rex used when he didn't want to leave a trace. An old machine plus an anonymous browser like TOR and goodness knows what he could be up to.

She lifted the phone and dialled the number for Tech Support.

—

It was another two hours before Max and Nita appeared at Clare's door.

'You two look done in,' she said. 'Tough interview?'

Nita shrugged. 'He's an answer for everything, that one.'

'Did he change his story about the burglary?'

Max shook his head. 'Like I said, he claimed they were hunting for some important paperwork. He didn't install the camera and doesn't know anything about it. So he can't explain why it would record them pulling stuff out of drawers and not record the real burglary.'

'Because there wasn't a real burglary,' Clare said.

'He has a point, though,' Nita said. 'For all we know that camera may have had a connection problem, only kicking in intermittently. I know that's rubbish,' she added. 'We all know it. But if they produced a tech expert and put him in front of a jury…'

'I see what you mean,' Clare said. 'What about the other two clips?'

'He claims Jenny came to ask them to up the price for Dennis's cottage,' Max said.

Clare nodded. 'Same as Erika. What about Steve's visit?'

'He asked for a bit of time to consult with the solicitor,' Max went on. 'It was less than five minutes, though.'

'And?'

'He admitted putting a few pills in Steve's water bottle. Said Steve had been rude – threatened to bad mouth them to the press, accuse them of all sorts. Rex was annoyed so he put laxatives in Steve's bottle. He had some in a drawer. Claimed he bought them in Spain one holiday when he was constipated. He said they'd been in the drawer for a couple of years or more. After the way Steve had behaved he reckoned he deserved a dose of the runs.'

'Would the post-mortem show whether Steve had taken laxatives?' Nita asked.

Clare shook her head. 'I have absolutely no idea. I can ask Neil but it feels like a long shot.'

'Difficult to prove he was the one who put Fentanyl in the bottle,' Max said. 'It's a controlled drug, don't forget. Not that easy to come by.'

He had a point. Clare checked her watch. 'I'd better update Penny. I'm not sure we have enough to charge them but I'm inclined to give it a shot.' She picked up her phone and dialled Penny's number.

'It's not enough,' Penny said, after listening to Clare's account of the interviews. 'I'd be happy for you to charge them with the faked burglary, but definitely not the murder. You'll need more than video footage for that.'

Clare tried to argue her case. 'We have them on film putting drugs in Steve's water bottle. I honestly don't know what else we need.'

There was silence at the other end – a typical *Penny silence,* intended to prompt an apology from Clare but she was reaching the end of her rope with the Freemans' case.

'I really don't think we should release them,' she went on. 'I'm confident we'll be able to build a case and, in the meantime, they could be a flight risk.'

When Penny did speak her tone was icy. 'I disagree and it's my call, Inspector. Release them, please.'

Clare ended the call before Penny could. She slammed her phone down on the desk and took a few deep breaths to lower her heart rate. Mostly, Penny's decisions were realistic. Clare might want to hold on to a suspect but Penny would reason the evidence wasn't strong enough. But this? This was sheer nepotism. If anyone else had been filmed putting tablets in a water bottle later found to have contained a lethal dose of Fentanyl they'd be cooling their heels in a cell overnight, up in court the next day. But this couple seemed to have Penny wrapped round their little fingers and that really pissed Clare off.

She sat on, considering whether to charge them with the fake burglary. But Nita's point was a good one. It would be too easy for their defence to argue the camera could have been faulty. Besides, she wanted them for the murder and she was bloody well determined to have them. She sighed deeply. They'd have to be released. For now…

She found Jim going through a list of lost property.

'We'll have to let them go,' she said. 'Penny's orders.'

He put down his pen. 'Really? Not even the burglary?'

Clare hesitated. 'I could charge them with that but I think I'll hold off for now. See if we can get them for the murder.'

'Fair enough. Want me to do the needful?'

She smiled. 'Please. I'm not sure I can face either of them again today.' She scanned the front office. 'Where's Chris?'

Jim's brow creased. 'Not sure. I think he went out, maybe half an hour ago.'

'Probably eating Wagon Wheels in his car, somewhere,' Clare said. She left Jim to his unenviable task and went back to her office, feeling faintly dissatisfied. She'd started the day, believing she had enough to charge the Freemans with Steve Gibb's murder. Having to let them go was a bitter blow. *There are days,* she thought, *when I seriously wonder if this job is worth it.* There was still something niggling away in the back of her mind but, try as she might, she couldn't think what it was. Maybe if she stopped trying to remember it would come to her.

She decided to call Neil at the police mortuary to see if he could check Steve's post-mortem results for the presence of laxatives. But the phone rang out and she realised he was probably in the examination room. She tapped out a message then shut down her computer. It was almost five. Time to collect Benjy. Her desk phone began to ring as she reached the door and she stopped in the doorway for a second.

'Ach to hell with it,' and she let the door swing closed behind her. Whatever it was could wait until morning.

—

'It's not as bad as it looks,' Moira said when Benjy came to greet them at the door, one of his paws wrapped in a green crepe bandage, adhesive tape keeping it in place.

Clare bent to let the little dog lick her face. 'What happened?'

Moira waited until Clare stood up then led her into the sitting room. Bill was bent over the fire raking the embers with a poker. He rose and greeted her warmly.

'Poor wee lad,' he said, cocking his head at Benjy. 'Some idiot left a broken bottle in the car park at Magus Muir. We were heading for the path through the trees when he yelped and held up his paw.' Bill shook his head, his eyes full of remorse. 'I blame myself. Should have spotted it.'

'Bill!' Clare said. 'Of course it's not your fault. It's the idiots who smashed the glass.'

'Bill phoned me,' Moira said, an arm at Clare's back. 'I ran along in the car and we took him straight to the vet.' She looked down at the little dog. 'He was so good, you know.'

'Oh Moira,' Clare said. 'I'm so sorry. You must let me know what it cost.'

'Och, yes,' Moira said. 'We can sort that later. Meantime he's to keep this on for a few days. After that it should be okay. You just need to check it's not getting hot.'

Clare sank down on the sofa and Benjy padded over, his head settling on her lap. 'Did he need stitches?'

'No, thank goodness,' Moira said. 'There was a tiny sliver in his paw but they got it out. They gave me a pain killer to add to his morning meal for the next few days but there's no real damage.'

Benjy began licking her hand and she bent to kiss the top of his head, enjoying the warmth from his body. Tears pricked her eyes and she blinked them back.

She'd been so busy lately, she'd hardly had a minute for this little creature; and he deserved better. 'I'm so sorry,' she blurted out, unable to stem the tears.

'Here, now,' Bill said, coming to sit beside her. 'What's all this? It's just a wee cut on his paw. Could have happened any time.'

Tears were spilling onto her nose now. She felt Bill's arm on her shoulder. This simple gesture, the warmth of his hand against her, it was all it took for the last bit of self-control to slip away. The frustrations of the past week, the Freemans, the march and Penny – it all seemed to coalesce into an overwhelming tide of misery. She saw Moira's eyes on her, heard Bill's gentle voice in her ear but none of it seemed real. It was as if she was outside her own body, looking in, watching this person she didn't recognise lose her grip on a life she no longer knew. Moira was speaking now, Bill replying but the sheer relief of giving way to pent-up frustration blotted out all else.

She had no idea how long it continued, how long her racking sobs were the only sound in the room. All she knew was she'd reached the end of whatever had been sustaining her and the relief was enormous.

She felt Benjy's head against her knee then a jolt of pressure as he rose on his hind legs, his bandaged paw against her, and she wrapped her arms round his neck, grateful for his unconditional love.

She was suddenly aware of Moira at Bill's side, handing him a mug, steam rising from it.

'Here,' he said. 'Tea. It'll help.'

She accepted the mug, cradling it in shaking hands. Gradually her sobs subsided and Moira's worried face came into focus.

'I'm so sorry,' she said, mortified at the loss of control. She handed the mug back to Bill, reaching into her pocket for a tissue. 'I – it was just a rotten day.'

He eyed her. 'It's a wee bitty more than that, isn't it?' He waited until she'd blown her nose then offered the mug again.

She accepted it and sipped, the tea hot and comforting. Moira drew a chair up opposite, her eyes full of concern.

'Is it anything we can help with?' she said.

Clare shook her head, trying not to cry again. 'It's me,' she said. 'I'm making such a mess of everything. Work – it's so busy; I don't have time for it all and…' she broke off, conscious she was oversharing.

'That's settled, then!' Moira reached across and patted Clare on the knee. 'You're having your tea with us, and I won't take no for an answer. We'll feed you then Bill will see you home. Make sure you're okay.' She shook her head. 'You're worn out, that's your trouble. You need a break.'

'Likely missing that man of yours as well,' Bill added.

Their kindness was almost more than she could bear and she blinked away fresh tears. Benjy licked her hand again and she pulled the little dog towards her. The phone began to ring in her bag and she reached automatically for it.

'Do you have to?' Bill said, his voice gentle.

The ringing continued and she hesitated.

'They don't own you,' Bill said. 'You've put in a long shift today. Maybe let someone else have a shot, eh?'

She met Bill's gaze, saw the concern in his eyes and suddenly she wanted someone else to make the decision for her. Someone to pick up her phone and turn it off. Someone to dry her tears, to hold her and tell her it would be okay, that she wasn't messing everything up, that it was just a bad day. She wanted to be told they'd get justice for Jenny Gibb, that they'd reach the evidence threshold to charge the Freemans with Steve's murder and, most of all, that the housing plans would be abandoned and the protest march with it.

Moira was hovering, her face creased with worry. They were so kind, this lovely couple. The best friends and neighbours she could wish for. But they didn't get it. Didn't get the nature of her job, how under-resourced they were, how much the team needed her.

Then Al's words came back to her. The conversation they'd had the night before he'd left for Tulliallan.

'You don't need to fix everything yourself,' he'd said. 'Even if someone makes a worse job of it than you, sometimes you have to let them do it.'

He was right, of course. She didn't have to fix everything. She knew that. She reached into her bag, took out her phone and switched it to silent. Then she smiled at the couple and drew a hand across her eyes. 'Sorry,' she said. 'If that offer of a meal still stands, I'd love to stay.'

Day 9: Wednesday, 18th February

Chapter 31

'Where were you last night?' Chris asked when she walked into the station.

She glanced at him, her mind back on Benjy who she'd left with Bill and Moira. She'd been embarrassed after her bout of tears the night before but they'd waved this away, and assured her they'd take good care of Benjy. It hadn't stopped her feeling like the worst dog owner in the world, though, and she wondered how parents of toddlers felt, dropping them at nurseries before the sun had come up.

'Had a problem with Benjy,' she said.

Chris's eyes widened. 'Is he okay?'

'Yes, he's fine. But he'd cut his paw and Moira took him to the vet.' She shook her head. 'I was tired and it was a bit of a shock.' She weighed the phone in her hand. 'I saw you'd called. Sorry.'

'It's okay. Something I was chasing.'

She punched the combination into an internal door and pushed it open. 'Anything interesting?'

'Might be. I'm waiting on a call back.'

Clare opened her office door and switched on the light. 'Go on, then.'

But her desk phone began to ring. Diane from Tech Support. She held out a hand to Chris. 'Just let me take this.'

'Morning,' Diane said. She sounded indecently cheerful for eight in the morning. 'Got into your laptop.'

Clare switched her phone to speaker and put it down on the desk. Chris pulled a chair across and sat astride it, his arms resting on the back.

'Craig ran a password cracker overnight and we're in. I have it in front of me now so what would you like to know?'

Clare glanced at Chris. 'What did they want to know?'

'What sort of files are on it?' Chris said.

'Oh, hi, Chris,' Diane said. 'Right. There are loads of files. All sorts. Word documents, spreadsheets and a huge folder of video clips.'

'Eh?' All thoughts of Benjy and her tears the night before fell away. 'What sort of clips?'

'I've only checked a couple,' Diane said. 'But mainly spycam footage.'

Clare was suddenly alert. 'You're sure?'

'Oh, yes. Ceiling mounted. I'll stick them up on the network as soon as I come off this call.'

Clare looked at Chris. 'I knew that laptop was Rex's.'

Chris shook his head. 'Doesn't make sense. Faking the burglary's one thing but that clip of him putting the pills in Steve's bottle? No way he'd have allowed that to be filmed.' He leaned over to Clare's phone. 'Anything else, Diane?'

'Bookmarked websites. I'll put that on the network too.'

'What about the system information?' Clare asked. 'Does it have the owner's name?'

'Sorry. It's listed as *User*.'

Clare thought for a moment. 'Diane, is it possible to search the files for keywords?'

'Sure. What you thinking?'

'Could you try Rex please?'

Chris raised an eyebrow but she ignored him. If she could only prove it belonged to the Freemans.

They waited while Diane ran the search. It was almost a minute before she replied. 'Sorry, nothing.'

'Try Erika,' Chris said. 'With a k.'

Again, Diane repeated the search without luck.

'What about the video files? Can you check the properties to see if the owner's name's there?'

'Way ahead of you. I checked five or six. Nothing to help identify the owner. I reckon I can tie them to the spycam you sent down but that doesn't tell us whose footage it is. Best plan is to trawl through the documents. There might be something there. I'd offer to do it but...'

'I know,' Clare said. 'You must be snowed under.'

'Little bit.'

Clare thanked Diane for prioritising the laptop and ended the call. She turned to her computer and logged into the network. The files weren't there so she refreshed the folder a few times.

'What were you going to tell me?' she said as they waited for the files to appear.

'Oh, yeah. I had an idea.'

The files began to drop into the folder and Clare watched as the screen filled, mainly with video clips. She groaned. 'There are dozens of them.'

Chris's phone began to ring and he fished it out of his pocket, swiping to take the call. Clare was vaguely aware of his conversation as she scanned the rows of files. When they had finally finished loading, she clicked to sort them by type. As Diane had said there were dozens of MP4 files, several Word documents and three Excel spreadsheets. She opened one of the video files, tapping her fingers on the desk as she waited for it to load.

The footage was grainy at first, the light low. As Diane had said, it was taken from above, most likely a ceiling-mounted camera. A figure was moving about below and then it became lighter. *Must have switched on a light,* she murmured. She angled the screen so Chris could see but he was focused on his phone call, making notes on a scrap of paper. She closed the clip and opened the next file. It was the same room but in daylight this time, and she saw the room and the person in it more clearly. She peered at the screen, trying to catch a glimpse of the person's face. But it didn't look like Rex or Erika. The next six clips were of the same room so she skipped a couple of rows and opened another file. A different room appeared and she had the impression it was taken from further away – or did she mean higher up? An older Victorian property with a lofty ceiling, perhaps. A woman – at least she thought it was a woman – sat on a sofa, remote control in hand. She aimed it towards a wall-mounted TV, channel-hopping, Clare guessed. So there were cameras in at least two different houses. Would the Freemans' footage be here as well? She was scanning the files to see if any of the file names might relate to Rex and Erika's house when Chris put down his phone.

'You should see this,' she said.

'Never mind that. I've found your Fentanyl!'

She turned, hand still on the mouse. 'Seriously?'

'Think so.'

'Go on, then. Dish!'

'You know when we attended the Freemans' so-called burglary?'

'Yes.'

'Remember what Erika said about her mother?'

Suddenly Clare realised what had been bothering her for the past couple of days. Erika's mother had recently died. She thought back to the photo of the two women. The mother hadn't looked well. 'Did she—'

'Yep. She was in a lot of pain at the end. Some kind of cancer.'

'And she had Fentanyl?'

He grinned. 'She did.'

She returned the smile. 'Who's a clever sergeant, then? How did you find it?'

'I was thinking over that first day, when we visited the house, trying to recall if there was anything we'd missed about the burglary – maybe something to help us prove they were planning to kill Steve. For some reason, the mother's death popped into my head. So I did a bit of digging. Got her name and her GP practice.'

'And they told you?'

He shrugged. 'Took a bit of persuading. They were on about us getting a warrant so I pointed out this was a murder hunt and the mother was dead anyway.'

'And that did it?'

'Nearly. The receptionist said she'd have to speak to the practice manager and he'd gone for the day.' He nodded at his phone. 'That was him. Seems the mother died at home. Erika and the district nurse managed her end-of-life care between them.'

'Hmm. I'm guessing the nurse wouldn't have been in more than once a day – twice at most. Erika would have been in charge of her medicines.'

'Most likely. He's going to email over a copy of the last few prescriptions.'

Clare sat thinking. 'We need to tie up the date on the prescriptions with the date of death.'

'Yep. If she died a day or two after the last prescription was issued they'd have had a decent supply of Fentanyl left. I'll get in touch with the district nurse as well. She might remember how often Erika was handing out the Fentanyl.'

'Excellent work, Chris. Really great.'

He beamed again. 'I know. Probably deserves a doughnut. So, should we pick them up?'

Clare pondered this. 'Let's wait until we have the prescription and a copy of the death certificate. In fact, if you could do that now it'll give me peace to go through this lot.'

He glanced at the monitor, still angled towards him. 'What is it?'

'Spycam footage. Lots and lots of it.'

'Like the Freemans'?'

'Yes, only, I've not found theirs yet.'

He raised an eyebrow. 'So there are more cameras?'

Clare's eyes were on the screen. 'Looks that way.'

'Jeez! This is seriously weird.' He leaned over to watch the clip Clare had just opened. 'Who the hell's doing this? And how are they managing to stick all these cameras up?'

'Search me.'

He rose, scraping back his chair. 'I'll give you peace, then.'

Clare watched him go then turned back to the monitor and resumed ploughing through the video clips. It took half an hour to find footage from the Freemans' house. She dragged these into a separate folder and sat thinking. She was pretty sure the other clips were from different properties so what was going on here?

She scrolled back up to the Word documents and clicked to open the first. It had been saved as *Drumcarrow Letter*.

She scanned the contents and realised it was a letter to a care home attaching an application for a place. The name rang a bell then she remembered seeing the sign on the outskirts of town – a long, leafy drive leading to a low building in grey sandstone. She'd admired the grounds, a broad terrace in front of the home, wooden benches and huge parasols providing shade on sunnier days. If she had to end up in a care home one day, Clare thought she could do a lot worse. She wondered idly if it was private or local-authority run. Returning to the letter, she saw mention of fees. Private, then. Had Erika Freeman been planning to move her mother to Drumcarrow? Maybe she'd found looking after her at home too taxing and the mother had died before they could arrange the move.

The letter ran to two pages and she scrolled down to the second page, skipping over much of the content; and then she saw it.

The signatory.

Carol Merryweather.

Chapter 32

Chris drove while Clare explained.

'I think the laptop and flash drive must belong to Carol. The flash drive was found in her house, remember; and I bet that laptop was taken when she was burgled.'

'By Rex?'

'Has to be. How else would it have ended up on his desk?'

'But she said the flash drive wasn't hers,' Chris said.

Clare clicked her tongue in annoyance. 'Think about it. She might have thought we'd seize it in case the burglars had touched it and left some DNA. If she admitted it was hers and we'd examined the files, we'd have charged her. She had to say it wasn't hers.'

Chris yanked on the handbrake, making Clare wince. 'I wish you'd press the button in when you do that.'

He shrugged. 'I like the noise.'

She shook her head. 'You're just a six-foot toddler, aren't you?'

'So Sara tells me.' He looked along the road towards Feddinch's office. 'We going in, then?'

They emerged from the car and Clare noticed the temperature had risen. 'It's almost springlike,' she said, tucking the keys in her pocket.

'Don't you be taking off that woolly vest, Inspector. We're not out of the woods yet.'

'Thanks, Grandpa.' They had arrived outside the office. 'Ready?'

'Yep. All the same...'

She glanced at him. 'What?'

'Weird, isn't it?'

'No argument there.' She pushed open the door and the receptionist Melanie looked up. The smile left her eyes when she recognised them.

'Ms Merryweather?' Clare asked.

Melanie reached for her phone and spoke a few words. 'You can go through,' she said. 'There's no one with her.' She made a half-hearted effort to rise but Clare waved her back down. 'We know the way.'

Carol rose to greet them and offered refreshments.

'I'm afraid we won't have time for that,' Clare said. 'We'd be grateful if you'd accompany us to the station. There are some matters we'd like to ask you about.'

She blinked, her eyes on Clare and, for a moment, she didn't speak. Clare wondered if she might ask for an explanation but she simply lifted her phone without comment. They stood while she asked Melanie to cancel her appointments for the rest of the day. Then she tapped at her computer, shutting it down, and reached into her bottom drawer, taking out a small leather handbag.

'Am I under arrest?' she said, her voice tremulous.

'Not at this stage,' Clare said. 'But that may follow.'

She nodded. 'Should I call my solicitor?'

'If you jot down the details we'll call from the station.' Clare waited while Carol wrote the solicitor's number on a Post-it then she indicated a long navy coat hanging on a hook. 'Shall we?'

Carol stood, sweeping her gaze round the room, almost as if she knew it was a last look. She slipped on her coat, knotting a belt in front. Then she hesitated. 'Would you mind, I mean, could we maybe go out the back door? It's…'

Clare smiled. 'That's fine. Lead the way.'

They followed her out of the office and through another passageway. A door at the end led outside to a small square yard, laid in flagstones, the surrounding buildings towering either side. There was a dark blue wooden gate which she opened and they followed her out to a back alley that wound round the building. Seconds later, they were on South Street, Chris leading Carol towards the car.

As they drove the short distance back to the station, the sound of quiet sobbing was impossible to ignore. Clare turned and asked Carol if she was okay but she made no reply, a small cotton hankie clutched in her fingers. By the time they reached the station, Clare was becoming concerned.

'I think she should see a doctor before we interview her,' she said to Jim, her voice low. 'Is there any chance you can find one?'

'Leave it with me,' Jim said. 'Does she have a solicitor?'

Clare gave him the Post-it and went to show Carol to an interview room. Jim promised to keep an eye on the room camera. Clare thanked him and nodded at Chris. 'Let's have a chat in my office.'

'She wouldn't be the first to try and blub her way out of a charge,' he said, settling into a chair.

Clare considered this. 'I'm not so sure. She's pretty distressed. I think the impact of her actions is dawning on her.'

He shook his head. 'I don't even get why she did it.'

'Nor me. But I'm not prepared to put her under any kind of duress without a doctor saying she's up to it.'

'Fair enough.' He checked his watch. 'Could be a while. I'll see if I can track down the district nurse.'

—

It was almost two hours before the doctor tapped on Clare's door. She motioned him in and he sat down, his expression troubled.

'It's a distressing case,' he began. 'Psychologically, I think she's fit to be interviewed. But she is very upset. I'd advise you to keep sessions brief and to have her solicitor or a family member there for support.'

'What's actually wrong with her?' Clare asked.

The doctor was quiet for a moment. 'Her actions are quite unusual. Normally, people who spy on others are classed as voyeurs: they're sexually aroused by watching other people. I don't think that's the case here.' His brow furrowed. 'I'm not an expert but I think this is more about seeking emotional contagion through vicarious experiences.'

Clare raised an eyebrow and he gave a smile.

'Sorry. In layman's terms, I think she's unfulfilled and seeks to address this by spying on others. When she sees them experiencing an emotion she wants to share it – their joys, their sadnesses.'

'She's lonely?'

He nodded. 'I think so. She watches others going about their daily activities and she experiences a sense of belonging, as though she was watching her own friends or family.'

'Does she have anyone in her life?' Clare asked.

'She skirted around that,' the doctor said, 'but I get the impression she's quite a solitary person, probably not through choice.'

Clare sat back, thinking this over. 'We'd spoken to her on another matter and she seemed completely in command of herself – the model of efficiency.'

The doctor considered this. 'It may be a mask, one which exhausts her, leaving her little emotional bandwidth, hence her seeking it through others. My concern is, had she not been caught, her behaviour could have escalated. With voyeurs, their spying is initially from a distance. They watch through windows, follow people in the street without approaching them. But typically they become more dangerous. In Miss Merryweather's case, I'd suggest a full psychological assessment before any period of custody.' He glanced at his watch. 'I'm afraid I'm a bit pressed.'

Clare smiled. 'Sorry to have kept you. But thanks for coming out. It's good to know she has the capacity for a formal interview, even if we do have to go gently.'

Jim was waiting as she showed the doctor out.

'Solicitor's in for Carol Merryweather. They're ready when you are.'

'What's she like?' Clare asked. She'd have to tread carefully with Carol.

'Think she's been in before.' He checked his notepad. 'Rebecca Keith.'

Clare ran the name round her head as she went to find Chris. 'Do you remember a solicitor called Rebecca Keith?'

He sat back, brow creased. 'That couple – owned a jeweller's,' he said eventually. 'It's closed now. But it used to be a few doors along from Feddinch. Wasn't she their solicitor?'

'Ahh, gotcha,' Clare said. Her face fell. 'I remember her being quite tough – very protective of her clients.'

'In Carol Merryweather's case,' Chris said, 'she'll need to be.' He looked towards the interview room. 'What did the doc say?'

Clare's brow clouded. 'I've written it down. But basically she gets pleasure from spying on others.'

He stared. 'She's a voyeur?' but Clare shook her head.

'He reckons it's non-sexual. She's living vicariously through them.'

'Jeez. That's sad. Imagine having so little in your life.'

'Exactly. So we take it very gently. If she needs breaks, she has them.'

'Fair dos.'

'Got the footage?'

He tapped a tablet under his arm. 'Ready to go.'

'Come on, then. But gently does it.'

Chapter 33

Carol Merryweather was a head taller than her solicitor, Rebecca Keith, a small dark-haired woman Clare immediately recalled. Her eyes met Clare's and they exchanged polite nods. Despite her height, Carol seemed to have shrunk into herself. Her face was tear-streaked, her eyes pink with crying. She sat, arms wrapped across her front as though shielding herself from what she must surely know was to come.

Rebecca introduced herself and there was a brief exchange of pleasantries between her and Clare. Each time Rebecca spoke Carol's eyes were on her, as though she knew her fate lay in this capable woman's hands.

Chris began the recording and Clare invited everyone to introduce themselves. Carol was last to speak. She started to say her name but her voice cracked and she cleared her throat before trying again. Clare gave her an encouraging smile, hoping to put her at her ease. Finally she managed her name and Clare thought how starkly this contrasted with their first visit to Carol's office when she'd been every inch the confident business woman.

'May I call you Carol?' she said.

Carol gave a brief nod but didn't speak.

'Thank you,' Clare said. 'We'd like to question you about possible offences under Section One of the Computer Misuse Act 1990. Do you understand?'

Carol managed a faint *yes* and Clare continued.

'A flash drive was found on the floor of your house in Radernie Place, St Andrews. You initially told an officer it wasn't yours. I'd like to ask you to reconsider your answer.'

Rebecca clicked on her pen and sat forward. 'I'm not sure how Miss Merryweather can possibly say the flash drive is hers without examining the contents.'

'Of course.' Clare smiled and withdrew a photo from a folder. She passed it across the desk. 'This is a screenshot of the flash drive contents.' Carol's head was down and Clare tried to catch her eye. 'Perhaps you could look at it?'

She saw the rise and fall of Carol's chest. Rebecca saw it as well and she moved closer to her client, speaking in a soft voice. Then Carol lifted her gaze and looked at the photo. She sat without speaking, her eyes on the image. Finally, as Clare was about to prompt her, she cleared her throat.

'It's mine.'

'You confirm this is a screenshot of the contents on a flash drive belonging to you?'

'Yes.'

Clare thanked her and asked if she was okay to continue. Carol said she was and Clare went on.

'This is a photo of a laptop computer now in our possession.' She recited the production number and passed the photo across the table.

Carol stared, her mouth opening and closing but no words coming out. 'Where did you find this?' she said eventually. 'Who took it?'

'This is your laptop?' Clare asked.

'Again,' Rebecca said, her voice terse, 'I'm not sure how Miss Merryweather could possibly tell from a photo.'

'Agreed,' Clare said and she withdrew a third photo, showing the files saved to the laptop. 'As you'll see the list of files is almost identical to those found on the flash drive. In addition there are some letters signed in the name of Carol Merryweather.'

Colour began rising up Carol's neck. She reached for a plastic cup of water, her hand shaking. Clare watched her carefully. Her distress appeared genuine. 'Would you like a cup of tea?' she said. 'Or coffee?'

Rebecca gave Clare a brief nod of thanks and turned to Carol. 'A hot sweet drink might help.'

Chris paused the recording and left the room for a few minutes, returning with a tray bearing four plastic cups of tea. He handed these out and Carol wrapped her hands round one of the cups. Clare allowed her to have a few sips then restarted the recording.

'Where was the laptop?' Carol persisted. 'Where did you find it?'

Clare hesitated. She couldn't see it would help the interview to let Carol know it had been found at the Freemans', and it might compromise any charges against Rex and Erika. 'At the moment I'm not able to say. Do you admit it's yours?'

Finally, Carol nodded. 'Yes,' she said, her voice so small Clare asked her to repeat it for the recording.

'And when did you last see the laptop?'

'Last Saturday,' she said. 'It was on my coffee table before I went to a wedding in Dundee. When I was burgled,' she added.

'It was taken during the burglary?' Clare asked.

Carol shrugged. 'It must have been. It wasn't there when I got back from the wedding.'

'To be clear, then,' Clare said, 'both the flash drive and laptop shown to you in these photos belong to you.'

'Yes,' she said again. 'It's my flash drive and my laptop. It's all mine.' Her voice was rising and Clare watched carefully for any sign she was becoming distressed. She gave her a moment and eventually Carol seemed to have control of her emotions.

'Could I explain, please?' she said. 'In my own words – no questions. I just want to tell you.'

Clare smiled. 'Of course. But, if you need a break at any time, you only have to say.'

Carol flicked a glance at her but said nothing. She lifted the cup again and this time drained it. Then she dabbed the corners of her lips and took a deep breath in. 'I view a lot of houses,' she said. 'We do have other staff who go out to do valuations but I like to do the high-end ones myself; and some are very high-end.'

She stopped and Clare wondered if she was remembering the houses she'd visited.

'My own house,' she went on, 'it's fine, you know? It's a nice little semi. All I could afford on my own. Got it for a good price – one of the privileges of working in this industry. I had it decorated, bought a few bits of furniture. But I couldn't really afford to do anything fancy. It was hard enough just paying the mortgage.'

Clare gave a sympathetic nod and Carol continued.

'Neighbours are nice,' she said, 'and it's fine for me. But when I see some of these houses...'

She fell silent and, when it seemed Rebecca was about to prompt her, she carried on.

'My life,' she said, 'it hasn't quite turned out how I'd hoped.'

'Can you explain?' Clare said.

Carol took a breath in and out. 'My friends,' she said, 'we used to go out together. Have a few drinks, sometimes go to a club.' She smiled at the memory. 'They were all petite and pretty. I was tall and awkward. They got boyfriends, and I didn't.'

Chris shifted in his seat and Clare made a slight gesture with her hand. She didn't want Carol interrupted.

'It made a difference,' Carol went on. 'They married and had two incomes so they could afford nice houses, nice things. They had nice lives. As I said, my house is fine. It does me. But, St Andrews – well, you live here. You must know. It's full of gorgeous properties and people with the money to spend on them.' She nodded, as if assuring herself she'd summed it up correctly.

'It's quite simple,' she said. 'I want what they have; and I can't have it.'

'You're envious of what your clients can afford?'

'That's it exactly. And I get to see their houses when they're at their best – when they're ready to go on the market. All the clutter's tidied away, fresh coat of paint, lamps lit, flowers, freshly brewed coffee – all the usual tricks. It's an illusion but, for an hour or so, when I'm going round the house, I buy into it as well. Sometimes I imagine it's me showing *them* round the house – that it's mine.' Her eyes were shining now. 'Can you imagine what it must be like to live in one of these properties?' She shook her head. 'They probably don't realise how lucky they are.'

A change had come over Carol. There was a vitality, an energy about her now, and Clare realised why she was so successful in her professional life. She thought back to their first meeting. Carol had said she enjoyed helping people make their homes attractive to potential buyers. She could visualise her meeting clients for the first time, marvelling at their houses, suggesting small tweaks to make them even more appealing. Looking at Carol now, her mind wholly given over to the job she so clearly loved, Clare could see the doctor's assessment was spot on.

'That thrill, you know,' she went on, her eyes bright. 'It's lovely while it lasts. Sometimes I'd make an excuse to visit the houses again. And I tried to conduct as many viewings as my diary would allow. But, after a while, it wasn't enough. I wanted to know what the new owners did with the houses – if they'd redecorated – what their furniture was like – what kind of coffee machine they had. It was like a compulsion. I needed to know how they were living.'

She stopped suddenly and the light seemed to leave her eyes. 'I suppose, on some level, I wanted to be them.' She eyed Clare. 'That probably sounds pathetic. But it made me happy.'

Clare was about to speak but Carol went on. 'We get these people – professional viewers I call them. They've no intention of buying. They're just nosy. You see the same ones again and again. Sometimes I tell them the viewings are full because I know they're time wasters. It's an invasion of my clients' privacy but no one complains about them.'

Clare studied Carol wondering if she actually believed that viewing a house with no intention of buying was somehow worse than what she'd done. Maybe she really was detached from reality. But that wasn't within Clare's remit. That was for a psychiatrist to determine.

Mindful the doctor had warned against tiring Carol, she moved on. 'Did you install a hidden camera at the house in Hepburn Gardens, the house bought by Rex and Erika Freeman?'

Carol took a moment, as though savouring her last seconds of blamelessness, then she nodded. 'Yes. I did.'

'Can you tell us about that?'

'I saw the camera online,' Carol said. 'I'd never seen anything like it. Before I knew what I was doing I'd bought it – paid for twenty-four-hour delivery. When it arrived – I couldn't believe how realistic it was. I kept it for weeks, you know? Every day I'd come home from work and take it out of the box, examine it, imagine it on someone's ceiling. Eventually I rigged it up in my own house to see what it was like. The footage was excellent,' she went on. 'No sound but really clear video. So, I put it in the boot of my car with a few tools. I didn't really think I'd do it. But I liked knowing it was there.' She was looking beyond them now, as if lost in the memory.

Rebecca leaned towards Carol. 'Are you okay to continue?'

Carol smiled. 'It's a relief, to be honest.'

'When did you fit the first camera?' Clare asked.

She took a moment. 'About six months ago. Farmhouse west of the town.' Her face lit up at the memory. 'You should see it. Turkish rugs, beautiful artwork and a huge Aga in the kitchen. I couldn't resist.'

'How did you manage it?'

'They were supposed to be there when I did the valuation. But there was some family emergency, over in Glasgow so they handed a key into the office. Said they'd be gone all day. I went over and...' She paused, as if reliving the moment. 'I knew as soon as I stepped into the tiled porch that I was going to put the dummy alarm up. I knew I had to see that house again.'

'You didn't think it was dangerous?' Clare said, 'removing a working alarm?' But Carol shook her head.

'I didn't do that. I moved the existing alarm across the ceiling and put mine in its place. Still perfectly safe.'

Chris eyed her. 'You didn't think the owners would notice?'

'It happened a couple of times. I told them I'd checked the alarms and found one wasn't working so I reckoned it would be quicker to install a new one than to try and repair the existing one.' She shrugged. 'They seemed to take it at face value.'

Clare thought it was a risk. She could imagine Al getting a stepladder out to examine their alarms minutely if anyone had sold them a story like that. But she let Carol continue.

'I'm quite handy with tools,' she was saying. 'Comes with living alone. A ten-minute job. Once it was done, I couldn't wait to get home and check the footage. Honestly,' she went on, 'it was like being part of their family. Do you see?'

Clare didn't reply. She took a moment to order her thoughts then went on. 'How many cameras did you install altogether?'

Carol let her head fall back, eyes on the wall above Clare, as if running through all the times she'd done this. 'I think I ordered about thirty from Amazon, and I've still maybe ten or twelve left. So perhaps eighteen or twenty. Some houses I installed more than one.'

'Which houses were those?' Clare wanted her to admit installing both cameras in the Freemans' house. She wasn't disappointed.

'The first was the one you mentioned – Hepburn Gardens. Mr and Mrs Freeman.'

'Why that one? Was there a particular reason for targeting the couple?'

Carol's brow creased as though she didn't understand the question. 'It wasn't about them,' she said, eventually. 'It was the house. I can't describe how beautiful it is, even with some of their décor choices. It's probably the loveliest house I've sold.'

'Did you know Mr and Mrs Freeman prior to them buying the house?'

She shook her head. 'No. The owner was a dear man but rather frail. I offered to check his smoke alarms and he was only too glad to accept. I could see they were compliant but it gave me an excuse to get a stepladder out and put the dummy ones in place. I put one in the front room and one in the kitchen. I thought maybe I could see what the new owners did with the kitchen, whether they were foodies.' She nodded as she spoke. 'I was so looking forward to being part of their lives.'

Carol's expression darkened and Clare wondered what she was about to say.

'But it wasn't like that, was it? They didn't deserve that house. The burglary, for a start.' She turned to Rebecca. 'They were pulling things out of drawers, making it look as if they'd been burgled. Then you arrived,' she said to Clare and Chris. 'And I could see from the footage they pretended someone had broken in. People like that in such a lovely house.

'I couldn't report it of course,' she went on. 'Or I'd have had to confess about the camera. But when I saw them with the young couple…'

'Can you tell us who you mean?'

'The lad who died,' Carol said. 'It was in the paper. Steven Gibb. His wife was there first then he came round later. And I saw that man – Rex – I saw him put tablets into Mr Gibb's water bottle.' She shot an involuntary glance at the camera in the corner of the room. 'But, if you've seen the clips on the flash drive, you'll know about that.'

'What did you think was happening?'

Her eyes widened. 'Isn't it obvious? He must have poisoned Steven Gibb. Wasn't he found dead the next day?'

Clare eyed her. 'You could have sent us the flash drive anonymously.'

Carol's eyes were shining. 'That's what I planned to do. Then I had an idea.'

Rebecca's eyes were on Carol now. 'I think I'd like to chat with Carol before we go any further.'

Carol opened her mouth to protest but Clare held up a hand to stop her. She felt Chris's eyes on her but she ignored him. She was sure Carol had been about to say something important. But she was also mindful of the doctor's instructions not to push her; and there was something almost manic about her behaviour – up one minute, down the next. Such a contrast to the frightened woman who'd entered the station a few hours earlier. Anything she said could easily be contested by her defence advocate and disallowed by a judge. She needed to be sure Rebecca was happy for Carol to continue.

'We'll take a ten-minute break.'

Chris paused the recording and they left Carol and Rebecca to talk.

'How's it going?' Max asked when they wandered through to the incident room, Clare rubbing the back of her neck.

'Strange,' she said. 'Pretty intense.'

'Weird,' Chris corrected. 'She's like you with houses, only much much worse.'

'Seriously?' Max's knowledge of architecture was a running joke in the station.

'Yeah,' Chris went on. 'I reckon you two could be good pals.'

'Cut it out,' Clare said, her tone sharp. 'She's not well.'

'I respectfully disagree,' Chris said. 'I'd say she knew exactly what she was doing.'

'You going to charge her?' Max said and Clare nodded.

'Oh, yeah. We have to. It'll be up to her solicitor and advocate to put in a plea of mitigation.'

A wave from the door told Clare Carol was ready to continue and they made their way back to the interview room. Carol glanced up as they entered then lowered her head. Clare had the impression the fight had gone out of her and she wondered what they were about to learn.

Rebecca sat forward, ballpoint pen in hand. She waited until Chris had restarted the tape then she spoke. 'Miss Merryweather has some important information to convey. But she's concerned that, by doing so, she may incriminate herself. I have advised her that the importance of this information outweighs her own culpability. I also believe there are extenuating circumstances. Miss Merryweather is prepared to give you this information and we ask that you take her circumstances into account when you consider any possible charges.'

It was quite the speech, too vague for Clare to comprehend Rebecca's meaning. 'I can't give any guarantees,' she said. 'But we will bear in mind what you say and take everything into account when determining further steps.'

Rebecca seemed satisfied with this and she gave Carol a nod.

It took a moment for her to begin speaking. When she did, the tremor in her voice was unmistakeable. 'My mother,' she began, 'she's in a care home. Broomfaulds.'

She ran her tongue round her lips. 'Six months ago she had a stroke and she's gone downhill ever since. The home – it's not a fancy one – council run. The staff are lovely,' she went on. 'I can't fault them. But Mum – she's not happy. Before she was ill she used to visit a friend in another home – Drumcarrow. Mum's friend loved it and Mum often said, if she had to go into care, could she go there.' Carol spread her hands. 'I can't afford it. The fees are crippling as it is but places like Drumcarrow are out of the question.'

She swallowed hard then went on. 'The last few times I visited she begged me to take her away. Said if she couldn't go to Drumcarrow could she come and stay with me. But it's impossible. She needs round-the-clock care and I have to work to pay the bills.'

She met Clare's gaze and she saw Carol's eyes were misty.

'And then I saw that man.'

'Which man?'

'Rex Freeman. Like I said, I saw him on the video feed, putting pills into Steven Gibb's bottle. A whole strip. I'd no idea what they were but, when I heard he'd died, I thought it couldn't be a coincidence. It isn't, is it?' She looked from Clare to Chris, waiting for them to confirm it.

'What did you do?' Clare asked.

Carol exhaled. 'I thought about it and I copied the clip to the flash drive.' She let out a laugh. 'Actually I made three copies. One's still in my office desk. I still had Rex's mobile number in the office so I bought a pay-as-you-go phone from Tesco and I called him. Told him what I'd seen and, if he didn't want me to tell the police, he'd have to pay.'

'How much did you ask for?' Clare said.

'Fifty thousand. That would give Mum a year at Drumcarrow. The nurses at her present home think she probably won't live much beyond that. Fifty thousand would let her see out her days somewhere she'd be happy.'

'To be clear,' Clare said, 'for the tape, you asked Rex Freeman for fifty thousand pounds in return for not sharing the footage with us?'

'Yes.'

'How did he react?'

'Denied it at first. It was only when I explained it was me who'd installed the cameras that he agreed. Said it would take him a few days to get the money together.

I gave him a week. Soon as I came back from the wedding I knew it was him. Knew he'd been in my house.' She flashed a smile at Clare. 'He took my laptop, didn't he? He broke in and stole it, thinking he'd be safe.' She bit her lip, her head shaking slightly. 'He must have knocked the flash drive off the coffee table when he grabbed the laptop. If he was using a torch he probably didn't see it – most likely kicked it under the table without noticing.'

'Did you make contact with him after the burglary?'

Carol shook her head. 'The laptop was password protected. I knew he wouldn't be able to get into it. I thought I'd let the dust settle for a few days then get back in touch. Tell him I still had the footage.'

Chris shifted in his seat. 'You weren't worried he might harm you?'

She shrugged. 'I didn't think he had it in him. He's not the type. Putting pills in a water bottle's one thing. But I couldn't see him strangling me in my bed.'

Clare wouldn't have put anything past Rex Freeman but clearly Carol hadn't been thinking straight for quite some time. 'Just one more question,' she said.

Rebecca met Clare's eye, a warning in her expression but Clare turned to Carol. 'The laptop. It looks quite an old one. I don't suppose you have anything to prove it's yours?'

Carol smiled. 'Oh yes. I never throw out receipts. It's safely filed away. I can tell you exactly where it is.'

Chapter 34

'She's off to custody,' Clare said. 'There's a potential string of offences but she'll have to be examined by a psychiatrist before we can charge her.' She yawned and rubbed the back of her neck.

'Sounds pretty intense,' Max said.

'Yep. Definitely one of the strangest interviews I've done.'

'Want a real coffee? I've just ground some beans.'

A smile spread across her face. 'That sounds perfect. Thanks, Max.'

They wandered through to the kitchen, Chris having nipped out to the shops.

'You going to arrest the Freemans again?'

Clare frowned. 'Chris was waiting on a call back from the district nurse. Don't suppose she called while we were in with Carol?'

'Not that I heard.' He began spooning coffee into the cafetiere. 'Want me to ask Jim?'

'Nah. Wait till Chris gets back. He can chase it.'

The door opened and Jim looked in, his face creased with concern. 'Someone here you need to see.'

Clare studied his face. 'Who is it?'

'She says her name's Amber Morgan.'

Clare and Max exchanged glances.

'The first wife?' Max said and Clare nodded.

His eyes narrowed. 'Come to claim her inheritance?'

'Only one way to find out.'

Amber was well-named, with curly red hair, held back in a tortoiseshell clip. She was mid-thirties, Clare thought, fair-skinned with the palest of blue eyes. She was slim, casually dressed in dark jeans, a red Rab jacket over a navy top. The cool February air had heightened her colour and she looked like an advert for outdoor activities. She tucked a pair of black woollen gloves in a pocket and pulled her arms out of the jacket, leaving it behind her on the chair back.

'You're probably wondering why I'm here,' she said.

She wasn't Scottish, Clare thought. But was she English? There was a touch of something else in there – Welsh maybe? It didn't much matter but she did wonder how she'd come to be married to Steve Gibb.

Clare smiled. 'Maybe you could explain?'

'I heard about Steve,' Amber said. 'Dennis too.' She shook her head. 'Pretty tragic, the two of them dying so close together. What happened?'

What indeed, Clare thought. 'We're still investigating, but it does look as if both deaths are suspicious.'

Amber's eyes widened. 'I'm really sorry to hear that. Steve's – the woman he lives with – Jenny, isn't it? She must be devastated.'

Clare studied Amber's face, looking for anything to explain her sudden appearance. Was she here fishing for information on Jenny? She knew her name but it had been reported in the paper so that, alone, wasn't suspicious. But was it possible she was somehow involved in Dennis and Steve's deaths? As Steve's legal wife at the time of his death she probably stood to inherit. Or was there another reason she'd come?

'Yes,' Clare said, not giving anything away. 'She is very upset.'

'I'm not exactly sure why I'm here,' Amber went on, 'but I thought you might need some help to unravel it all.'

'That would be useful.' Clare glanced at Max. 'Do you mind if my colleague here takes some notes?'

Amber waved this away. ' 'Course. I've nothing to hide. What do you want to know?'

Clare took a moment to order her thoughts. 'Maybe start from when you and Steve were married.'

'Sure. I was working at a college in Hereford – in the admissions office. Steve came in one day. He was delivering for one of the printers in town. We had a rush job and he handed it in. It was lunchtime so I walked out with him and we ended up going for a drink. One thing led to another and we were married six months later. Spur of the moment thing,' she added. 'Seemed like a good idea at the time.'

'How long did the marriage last?'

'We were pretty much done by our second anniversary,' she said. 'It wasn't acrimonious. We parted on good terms. He had the offer of a job back in Scotland and I didn't want to leave mine.'

'You never divorced?' Clare asked.

Amber shrugged. 'We always meant to. But I'd had enough of being married. I wasn't about to do it again so, somehow, it kept slipping my mind.' She looked from Clare to Max. 'In case you're wondering, we are still married – *were* still married,' she corrected herself.

'Did Steve ever contact you about a divorce?'

Amber shook her head. 'I mean, he might have. But I left my job. Got another one in Bristol. Changed my phone number and didn't give him my new contact details. I reckoned if he did need to get in touch he'd find a way.'

'When did you last hear from him?'

She thought for a moment. 'Probably about five years ago. Just before I moved to Bristol.'

'And the nature of that communication?'

Amber smiled. 'Phone call. He was drunk. He used to do that, sometimes. When we were still together, I mean. He'd go out with the lads, have too many drinks then phone me up. Sometimes saying how much he loved me, other times demanding to know if I was having an affair. I wasn't,' she added, 'but he got like that when he'd had a few. It's one of the reasons we didn't last. His dad was the same. Drunks, the pair of them.'

'Goodness!' Clare could hardly keep the surprise out of her voice. 'I met Steve after his father's body was found. He seemed to be into fitness. Running marathons.'

'Crikey! Well good for him. I'm glad he managed to turn his life around, even if it was only for a few years. I'm guessing that was Jenny's doing.'

Clare wondered if Amber was fishing for information. As far as Jenny was concerned, she wasn't taking any chances.

'I know you said you heard about Steve.' She watched Amber carefully. 'But is there another reason you've come?'

For a moment Amber said nothing, her eyes avoiding Clare's. 'I suppose you think I've come for his money; but it's not that. I'm doing pretty well for myself now.

I don't need anything from Steve. I just thought…' she broke off and took a moment. 'My mum died a couple of years ago. Very sudden. Dad was already dead so it was just me and my brother. We had to clear out their house and there were so many things we knew nothing about. Photos of folk we didn't recognise, letters, all sorts, really; and there was no one to ask, you know? Their secrets had died with them. So, when I read about Steve's death, that he was survived by his wife Jenny, I thought she might want someone to talk to – someone who knew Steve. But I don't want to upset her. That's why I've come to you first. See what you thought.' She stopped and gave herself a little shake. 'That probably makes no sense. I just felt I should come.'

Clare thought about her own parents. One day, if things took the natural course, she and her sister Jude would be left with clearing out their house. What secrets might it hold? Might they discover things they never knew? Then she forced her mind back to Amber. Was there any harm in telling her about Steve's bigamy? It might be worth it to gauge her reaction. 'I can tell you,' she began, watching Amber carefully, 'Steve and Jenny went through a marriage ceremony and, until a few days ago, Jenny believed they were legally married.'

Amber's hand went to her mouth. 'Oh my God,' she said. 'How dreadful. Poor Jenny.' She shook her head. 'Losing Steve must have been bad enough but to find out they weren't even married.' She met Clare's eye. 'I feel so guilty now. If only I'd pressed on with a divorce.'

On balance, Clare thought Amber's reaction was genuine and she gave her a smile. 'It's not your fault. Steve's the one who knowingly entered into a bigamous marriage.'

Amber's brow creased. 'But I don't understand how he did it. Don't you need a divorce certificate or something?'

Clare glanced at Max. Was there any harm in telling Amber what Steve had done? It would come out soon enough. She had to protect Jenny at all costs but maybe Amber would know something about Brad. 'I can explain,' she said, 'but it must remain between us, for now.'

'Of course.'

'Steve used his brother's birth certificate to apply for a passport in Brad's name. Then he arranged a wedding in the Caribbean, away from family and friends. He told Jenny his real name was Bradley.'

Amber stared. 'He pretended to be Brad?'

'For the purposes of the wedding, we think so.'

Amber was quiet as she digested this. 'But Brad was married – oh, wait. They divorced, didn't they?' Her eyes narrowed, as if trying to recall. 'I never met either of them. He'd disappeared before Steve and I got together. But I did know he was divorced. Cindy, I think she was.'

Clare nodded. 'That's what we think.'

'Did Steve ever say where he thought his brother was?' Max asked.

'No. We assumed he'd jumped off a bridge, or something like that.' She looked at them both. 'You hear of it, don't you? And that River Tay – it's so wide. You might never find a body.'

It was true. The Tay Road Bridge was closed occasionally to let officers talk distressed people back from the edge. She tried to recall the statistics. Hadn't there been ten the previous year? Amber was right. Depending on the tide and whether the person had been seen entering the water, they might never be found.

'Was there any indication Brad was depressed? Or contemplating anything like that?' Max went on but Amber shook her head.

'Sorry. I've no idea. Steve didn't talk much about him and I didn't like to ask. As I said, it all happened before we met.'

Clare racked her brains. Was there anything else they could ask? Anything about Brad? But Amber seemed to know almost nothing about him. 'How long do you plan to be in the area?'

She took a moment. 'I'm not sure, to be honest. I'd like to go to the funeral, assuming there is one. But with his death being suspicious, might it be delayed?'

Clare smiled. 'It's possible. We should know soon but, at the moment, his body's still in the police mortuary.'

Amber nodded. 'Do you think Jenny might see me? I don't want to upset her.'

Clare hesitated. Amber seemed straightforward, her motives altruistic; and they knew the Freemans had poisoned Steve. Did Jenny have anything to fear from this woman? Then she thought about Brad Gibb. She couldn't ignore the fact that he and Amber could both inherit Dennis's cottage. They didn't kill Steve but were they involved somehow?

That anonymous call, accusing Steve of dealing Fentanyl – they'd thought the caller might have used a voice changing app. So it could have been Amber. But what would her motive have been? If Steve had been arrested would she have managed to get her hands on Dennis's money? Clare wasn't an expert on family law but, with such a long estrangement between the couple, it didn't seem likely.

And then she thought about Jenny. Was it possible meeting Amber might bring her some comfort? Maybe if it was a supervised visit…

She rose from her chair. 'I have an officer with her just now. Let me make a phone call and I'll come back to you.'

They left her in the interview room, Max following Clare to her office.

'What do you reckon?' she said when he'd closed the door.

'Seems genuine enough to me.'

'I agree. But I'm not taking any chances with Jenny's safety.' She picked up her phone. 'I'll give the FLO a call.'

Paul listened while Clare explained. To his credit, he didn't whistle or express surprise, and she wondered if Jenny was within earshot. 'Let me speak to her,' he said. 'I'll buzz you right back.'

He was as good as his word, calling Clare within a couple of minutes. 'She'll see her. But no promises about how long she'll let her stay; and she wants me there.'

Clare was glad to hear that. She wouldn't want Amber left alone with Jenny. 'I'll send her over in the next half hour,' she said. 'And make sure you don't leave them alone together.'

Paul said he'd stick to Amber like glue and Clare ended the call.

Max raised an eyebrow. 'Who is he and what has he done with the real Paul Henry?'

Clare laughed. 'He does seem to be less of an arse this time. Maybe he's grown up!'

Max got to his feet. 'Want me to run her along there?'

'Please. See her in and make sure Paul's there.' She fished in her pocket. 'Give Amber my card, would you? Tell her if she's anything further to say, or any concerns about Jenny to give me a call.'

As Max went to take Amber to Jenny's house, Chris came in, coffee in hand, a Wagon Wheel biscuit between his teeth.

'I hear I missed the real wife,' he said, putting the biscuit down on Clare's desk.

'Yep. Max is running her along to Jenny's.'

'Seriously? Isn't that a bit risky?'

'The FLO's there.'

'Wendy?'

Clare avoided his eye. 'Couldn't get her.'

'Who then? Oh don't tell me.'

Clare said nothing.

'You didn't bring that arse in again? Tell me you didn't?'

'Everyone deserves a second chance, Sergeant.'

He shook his head. 'He's the worst. You do know that, don't you?'

She regarded him. 'Maybe. But he does seem to have improved.'

'Hmm.' He bit into his Wagon Wheel, brushing crumbs off his jacket. 'I have news.'

'You do?'

'Yup.'

'The district nurse?'

'Yup again.' He took another bite.

'And?'

He chewed for a moment then swallowed and took a slug of coffee. 'Right. The Fentanyl prescriptions were issued once a week. But in the last couple of weeks of her life the district nurse set up a syringe driver. She popped in every day to renew the medication.'

'I'm sensing there's more.'

'There is. A further two Fentanyl prescriptions were issued *after* they were given the syringe driver. Apparently they were on a repeat and there was a breakdown in communication. They only stopped sending them when the old lady died.'

'No one noticed?'

'Nope. To be fair, the nurse did say Erika was pretty distracted, looking after her mother. She'd stayed with her day and night for the last month. Slept on a camp bed in her mother's room. Rex had been running back and forth to the pharmacy, dropping off prescriptions and stuff for Erika. It's not surprising they ended up with pills they didn't need. According to the nurse it's not unusual for relatives to return boxes of drugs when someone dies.'

'So they probably had two weeks' worth of Fentanyl left over.'

'Think so.'

'Enough to kill someone?'

'Oh yeah.'

She lifted the phone. 'I have to run this by Penny but I reckon we've enough to keep them in custody this time. Can you sort out a couple of cars?'

Chris went to find cars and officers and Clare dialled Penny's number.

Penny was quiet for a moment. 'Can we be sure the pills were collected from the pharmacy?'

Clare didn't know what to say to this. Was Penny being deliberately obstructive? 'I haven't checked that yet,' she admitted, 'but—'

'In that case I suggest you do before arresting the Freemans. Given what happened with their first arrest we wouldn't want to mess it up again.'

Clare didn't trust herself to speak and Penny ended the call.

Chris came in, jingling car keys in his hand.

'Hold the arrests,' she said.

'Oh you are joking. Don't tell me she's said no. How much more evidence does she want?'

Clare held up a hand. 'I know, I know! But she wants to be sure the drugs were collected from the pharmacy before we bring them back in. So get your backside round to Boots and check it out. In fact, get a printout so we have evidence to put before them.'

Chris went off, muttering about *fucking superintendents*. It was another hour before he phoned to say he had the printouts.

'*Now* can we bring them in? Or do you need written permission from Herself?'

'Go for it.'

Chapter 35

'She's not answering the door,' Chris said, 'but her car's here. I'm pretty sure she's in. There was definitely someone standing back from the window when we arrived.'

Clare paced her office, phone on speaker. 'What about him?'

'His car's not there. I reckon he's out.'

Clare thought back to the house and remembered large patio doors leading from the kitchen to the back garden. 'Try round the back. She might be in the kitchen.'

She listened, the sound of Chris walking round the side of the house coming through the phone speaker. She heard the creak of a gate and his feet crunching on gravel.

'Okay, round the back. I'll just look – hold on, she's here.' Clare heard him tap on the glass, calling Erika's name.

'What's she doing?'

'Sitting on the floor, back against the wall. Arms over her head.'

A knot of worry was forming in Clare's stomach. 'Chris, get in there. She might have taken something.'

The knocking on the glass grew louder. Clare heard them calling Erika's name then Chris came back on the phone.

'She's conscious. Wait – she's getting to her feet. I think she's coming to let us in.'

'Make sure she's okay before you arrest her.'

'Will do.'

The call ended and Clare put down her phone. The temperature had dropped and her office was chilly. She bent to turn the radiator up and stood against it, waiting for it to heat up.

She was cold and she was tired. It had been the most dispiriting investigation. Every murder was a tragedy for those involved but there was such sadness surrounding this case – from Jenny Gibb losing her husband, then finding out she wasn't even married, to Carol Merryweather, living a fantasy life through her rich clients. Then there was Erika Freeman. Why was she sitting on the kitchen floor, head buried in her arms? Was there something else they didn't know?

Heat began to spread from the radiator and she put her hands at her back to warm them, wondering if Erika had opened the door to Chris. There was nothing for it but to wait on his call.

Her thoughts turned to the march. Would it still go ahead? With Rex and Erika facing a murder charge surely the development would be halted; and no development might mean no march. Perhaps she could get in touch with the organisers. Ask them to call it off. But what about the people Penny was hoping to lure into the open? The professional agitators she planned to arrest during the march? They'd likely still come.

All at once she was overwhelmed with weariness. 'When this is over,' she said to the empty office, 'I am having a holiday!'

Her phone began ringing again. Chris. 'She's okay,' he said. 'We're bringing her in. I'll explain when we get there.'

—

Clare was concerned enough to call the duty doctor out again. Erika had entered the station, her head down, Chris's hand on her arm. The contrast to her previous visit was stark. She seemed to have shrunk into herself, as if her spirit had finally broken. Clare raised an eyebrow as Chris led her to an interview room and he shrugged, as if he wasn't sure what had caused such a change.

'You're certainly keeping me busy,' the doctor said when he arrived half an hour later. He put his bag down on a spare seat. 'What's the issue?'

'I honestly don't know,' Clare said. 'The lady in question is suspected of a serious crime. We've spoken to her a few times and she's always been fully in command of herself. But, today, she seems broken. It's a serious case so I want to be sure she's fit for interview.'

She showed the doctor to the interview room and left them to speak. 'Come to my office,' she said to Chris. 'Fill me in.'

They sat, either side of Clare's desk, Chris rubbing the back of his head. 'She let us in okay then she turned round and went to sit on the floor again. It was like she was saying *do what you want. Just leave me alone.*' He shook his head. 'She's not like the same woman.'

Clare nodded. 'I know what you mean. What about him?'

'Rex? He's done a runner. I put a shout out for his car registration. With luck he'll ping a few cameras.'

'Did she say so?'

He hesitated. 'Not exactly. I asked where he was and she just stared at me. *Gone,* she said. It's all we could get out of her.'

'Has he taken his passport?'

'Think so. Hers was in one of the desk drawers in their front room. No sign of his.'

Clare reached for the phone. 'I need to get onto ports and airports.'

'Already done,' Chris said. 'If his passport's scanned, he'll be detained. Likewise if the car checks into an airport car park.'

She sat, phone in hand. 'I don't get it. Why would he go and leave Erika behind?'

'Maybe she chose to stay,' Chris said. 'But even if she didn't want to go with him, why stay in the house? She must have realised we'd catch up with them eventually.'

'Like she was waiting for us?'

He nodded. 'Maybe.'

'Then it's even more important she gets a clean bill of health before we start to question her.'

Chris's phone began to ring and he snatched it up. He listened for a minute, grabbed a pen and began scribbling on Clare's notepad. 'What about after that?' he said, phone clamped to his ear.

Clare wished he'd put it on speaker but he seemed focused on the call.

'Dammit. Can we get anything from traffic cams?'

Again, Clare could hear faint sounds coming through the phone but she couldn't catch what the caller was saying.

'Gotcha,' Chris said. 'Can you alert Dundee cops?'

He listened again then ended the call. 'Rex's car crossed the Tay Road Bridge ten minutes ago.'

'Ten minutes? He could be anywhere by now.'

'He took the left slip road, heading west.'

Clare frowned. 'Where's he going?'

'Not to the airports,' Chris said. 'It's well out of his way for Edinburgh or Glasgow.'

'Unless he's heading for Aberdeen,' Clare suggested.

'Wrong direction. Too far, anyway.'

'Less busy, though.'

'I reckon he'll ditch the car somewhere in Dundee. Pick up a hire car. He might even jump on a train. It's not like we can monitor CCTV in all the stations. If it was me, I'd drive to Perth, park somewhere and catch a train to Glasgow. From there he could pretty much go anywhere.'

There was a tap on the door and the doctor came in, Max at his back. 'That's me done,' he said.

'How is she?' Clare asked.

'She's fine. Upset, worried – I doubt you'll get much out of her. But, medically, she's fit to be interviewed.'

Clare thanked the doctor and Max went to escort him to the front office.

Chris made to pocket his phone. 'Want to have a crack at her?'

But before Clare could answer, it began ringing again.

'Put it on speaker this time,' she said, and he clicked the button.

'Feeding back on your Lexus,' the voice said. 'If it had left the city it would likely have pinged one of the cameras.'

'So he's still in Dundee?' Chris said.

'His car probably is. As to him, I couldn't say.'

'Right,' Clare said when Chris put down his phone. 'Let's get cops to the bus and rail stations, phone round car hire places.'

'Taxis?'

'Good shout.'

Max appeared again. 'Doc's gone and Erika's solicitor's here. Jim thinks they'll be ready to start soon.'

For a moment, Clare was at a loss. Rex was somewhere in Dundee but they had absolutely no idea where; and, by the time they found out where he'd gone, he might have slipped away. 'We can't interview her just now,' she said. 'Finding him is priority.'

'She might be able to help,' Chris suggested.

Max looked from Clare to Chris and she realised he didn't know what they were talking about. Chris explained quickly about Rex being somewhere in Dundee.

'Big city,' Max said and they nodded.

'Let's see if she can help us,' Clare said.

She tapped on the interview room door and Garth Bryce, the Freemans' solicitor, glanced up, his expression not encouraging.

'We're still having a discussion,' he said.

'I'm sorry,' Clare said. 'But I need Mrs Freeman's help to find her husband. I'm happy to do it under caution. We can even tape it if you wish. But I need to do it now.'

He stared at her for a few seconds then turned to Erika who said nothing, her eyes on Clare.

'Erika,' she said, trying to keep a level tone. 'It's vitally important you tell us where Rex has gone. We know he's left you to take the blame. It's only fair we find him so we can ask you both the same questions.' She pulled out a chair and sank down opposite Erika, Chris and Max at her back. 'Can you help us? Do you know what he's planning?'

Erika eyed her for a long moment. Then she gave a slight nod. 'I think I do.'

Chapter 36

'Get onto Dundee Airport now,' Clare said as she ran back to her office. 'That plane is not to take off.'

Chris scrolled to find the number for the airport while Clare dialled Janey, a detective sergeant based at the Bell Street station in Dundee.

'Janey,' she said, not waiting for her to speak. 'I need you to get a couple of cars down to the airport urgently. Can you do that?'

'Sure.' She heard the sound of Janey moving through the office. 'What you after?'

'Man aged around forty – name of Rex Freeman. He has a part share in a Bulldog prop plane. He's wanted for murder and we think he might be planning to fly himself to northern France.'

She heard Janey shouting names across the room. The sound grew more echoey and Clare guessed she was running down the stairs. 'I can be there in five or six minutes,' she said. 'Have you called the airport?'

'Chris is onto them now.' She glanced at him and he shook his head. 'It's ringing out, Janey. The sooner you get there the better.'

'I'm at the car,' she said. 'Benny following.'

'Can you keep this call open please? I need to know what's happening.'

Something caught Clare's eye and she saw Jim was standing in her office doorway.

'Erika Freeman.'

She opened her mouth to say the interview would have to wait but he cut across her.

'The solicitor's said she wants to draft a statement.' He looked from Clare to Chris, both with phones clamped to their ears. 'I'm guessing that's okay for now?'

Clare was about to thank Jim when Janey came back on the phone. 'Bit of a snarl up in the Marketgait. I've blues and twos on and they're starting to get out of the way. Going to be another couple of minutes, though.'

Clare thought for a minute. 'Any patrol cars closer?'

'I'll put a shout out on the radio.'

She heard Janey speaking then a short silence before someone responded. But, it wasn't clear enough for her to hear through the phone.

'Car in the Perth Road just now,' Janey said. 'They'll head in from the other direction.'

'Finally!' Chris said into his phone. He introduced himself quickly and said he needed to speak urgently with Rex Freeman. 'I gather he might be about to take a plane out.'

There was a murmur of conversation on the other end then the voice said, 'Hold on.'

'Do not let him take off,' Chris said but the voice was replaced by a burst of tinny muzak.

'That's us through the jam,' Janey said. 'Passing the railway station now.'

Clare did a quick mental calculation. With blues and twos it would take two or three minutes tops to reach the airport. It was probably thirty or forty minutes since Rex had crossed the bridge. Five minutes would have taken him to the airport, if he'd stuck to the speed limit. But how long to get a plane fuelled and ready to go? Or were they already fuelled up? Would he know Erika might tell them his plans? Or would he think he had plenty of time and try not to attract attention?

'Yeah, hello,' Chris said. He was quiet for a minute, listening then she heard him interrupt the voice at the other end. 'Look we don't have time for this. It's vital he doesn't leave the airport. Can you keep him there?'

Clare's spirits rose. It sounded like Rex was there. They'd found him. But how close was he to getting into a plane and taking off?

'Jesus!' Chris shook his head. 'He's disappeared again. I'd be quicker getting in the car and driving over there myself.'

'ETA, Janey?' Clare said, one eye on Chris.

'Passing the railway bridge now,' she said. 'Twenty seconds.'

'Okay. It's possible he's already in a plane preparing to take off. If you can prevent that, great. But don't take any risks.' She put her hand over the phone. 'Chris, ask him to put you onto the tower, when he comes back. Tell them Rex is not to be given clearance to take off.'

'Pulling in the gate now,' Janey said. 'Benny's right behind me.'

She heard the sound of a car door slamming and Janey's breathing as she ran for the entrance. It wasn't a large facility, lacking the heavy security at international airports and she guessed Janey had abandoned her car at the front entrance.

'Put me on to the tower now,' Chris said. 'That plane cannot be allowed to take off.'

The voice began to speak but Chris was having none of it. 'THE TOWER!'

Janey was speaking to someone and she wondered if it was the same person Chris had called. 'Which way?' she said then called her thanks. Janey's breathing came through the phone again, thick and fast.

'Tell me you're joking,' Chris said into the phone.

Clare looked at him. What was happening?

Chris swore and turned to Clare. 'He took off five minutes ago.'

Clare felt utterly helpless. She was only fifteen miles away but she might as well have been at the other end of the country. The call to Janey was still connected and she could hear her firing questions at the airport staff.

'Seems he didn't lodge a flight plan,' Janey said when she came back on the phone. 'He's a regular, here. Often does the same routes. Told them he'd head south to Edinburgh then circle back via Stirling. Said he'd be about an hour.'

'Like hell,' Clare said. 'We have to find out where he's going.' She glanced at Chris. 'Did she say anything else when you picked her up?'

He shook his head. 'Only that he'd gone.'

She sat thinking for a minute then Janey cut across her thoughts. 'Anything else you want done here?'

Suddenly, she felt guilty. She'd taken two carloads of officers from whatever they'd been doing on a fool's errand. 'Thanks Janey. I really appreciate your help. We were so close.'

'Maybe if the traffic hadn't held us up.'

'I doubt it. If he'd seen you appearing from the terminal he'd have made a run for it.' She thought for a moment. 'If you could take statements from the staff there…'

'Will do. I'll email them over.'

'Sorry again,' Clare said.

'Ach not at all. It's ages since I've done a blues and twos. Keeps you sharp.'

Clare ended the call and sat back in her chair.

Max was hovering. 'Want me to interrupt? See if I can get anything more out of Erika?'

She gave Max a smile. 'Actually, that would be great. You've a nice way with folk. Might get more out of her than I would.'

'Leave it with me.'

She watched him go then turned back to Chris. 'Five minutes.'

He shrugged. 'Might have been more; and he'd likely have gunned the plane if he'd seen Janey heading for him.' A smile played on his lips. 'She's a tough cookie, that one. I'd probably have taken off if she was heading for me.'

Clare laughed, grateful for the moment of levity. 'They're a good bunch, the Bell Street lot.'

'Apart from their gaffer.'

'Oh her! Do not mention that name to me. If she'd let us keep the Freemans in custody this wouldn't have happened.'

The door opened and Max came in.

Clare searched his face. 'Well?'

'She's pretty sure it's northern France,' he said.

'We knew that. Can't she be more specific?'

'She's not sure but there's a private airfield south of Dunkirk. They've flown there before, albeit not in one go. Seems he knows the area. Speaks French, as well.'

Clare picked up a pen. 'Name?'

'Sorry. She hasn't a clue. I took out my phone and opened a map of northern France but all she knows is it's south of Dunkirk. As far as I could see, there are two or three that fit.' He held out his phone for Clare to see.

She stared at it. 'I don't even know how to pronounce them.' She looked up. 'How's your French, Max?'

They gathered round the phone, Max doing his best. '*Bonjour*,' he began, haltingly. '*Parlez-vous Anglais?*'

The voice came through the phone, uncompromising. '*Non.*'

'I'll use Google translate,' Chris said. 'Hold on.'

He tapped a few words into his phone and Google spat out a translation. While Max read this out, Chris typed the next part. The man on the other end seemed to understand but he replied so fast none of them could catch any of it.

Max tried again but the voice interrupted. '*Un instant, s'il vous plaît.*'

They heard a rustling at the other end then silence. 'I think he's gone to get someone else,' Max said. 'At least I *hope* he's gone for someone else.'

A moment later, a younger female voice spoke. The accent was French but the greeting raised their spirits. 'Hello?'

Max let out a breath. 'You speak English?'

'I do. How can I help you?'

'Do you work at the airfield?'

'Yes. I do.' She hesitated. 'I work on the computer.'

Max explained who he was and that they suspected a plane was heading for their airfield. There was a murmur of conversation at the other end then she came back on the phone.

'We haven't been notified of an incoming flight.'

Max looked helplessly at Clare. Her mind was racing. She didn't even know the right questions to ask. She should have gone to Dundee Airport – spoken to whoever was there herself.

'Can you ask her to let us know if they are notified?'

Max repeated the request and the woman agreed to call them. 'But we have a storm forecast,' she said. 'It might be advisable to contact your pilot. Advise him to reroute.'

He thanked her and ended the call. 'Is it worth calling other airfields in the area?' he said.

Clare's mind was racing. 'What's the journey time to France in one of these planes? Could he do it in one go?'

Max shrugged. 'According to Erika he usually stopped to refuel south of Rotherham.'

Clare considered this. 'Did she give you the name of the airfield?'

'No. But I'll find it. There can't be too many. They'll know if he's stopped there before.' He rose from his chair. 'I'll find it and give them a call.'

'Alert the police down there as well,' Clare said. 'If he does stop to refuel they'll need to detain him.'

She waited until Max had left then dialled the number for Dundee Airport. 'Can I speak to one of the trainers?'

'You want to arrange a lesson?'

'No, I just want to speak to someone. Urgently,' she added.

A few minutes later, she was speaking to a woman called Laura. Clare checked her notepad for the name of the plane and said she had some questions about it.

'Yes, I know that one,' Laura said. 'I saw it take off a little while ago. How can I help?'

'Would it be possible to fly that plane from Dundee to Dunkirk without refuelling?'

Laura was quiet for a moment. 'Bear with me.'

Clare waited and a couple of minutes later she came back on the phone. 'It's possible,' she said, 'but not something I'd advise. You'd have to fly economically – watch your speed. Wind would be a factor, too. He should have accounted for that in his flight plan. But, if he's heading for France, I doubt he'd risk it all the way. He'll likely refuel.'

'How long would it take if he did make it without refuelling?'

'I'd have to work it out,' Laura said. 'It depends on the route, weather – so many factors.'

'Ball park?'

'I'd say five or six hours.'

'Can we check? Is he likely to be in touch with the control tower?'

'Depends which frequency he's using,' Laura said. 'I'd try one of the tracker sites. If the plane has a functioning transponder you'll be able to find him.'

Clare raised an eyebrow and Chris shrugged.

'Try Flightradar24,' Laura said, laughing. 'It's the easiest to use. I'll give you my number,' she added, 'in case you need anything else.'

Clare turned to her computer and typed Flightradar24 into Google. The page loaded to show a map of the UK dotted with little yellow planes moving slowly in every direction. 'I'd no idea there were so many planes in the air at one time,' she said. 'Can we search on the plane number?'

'Worth a shot.' Chris ran a finger down his notepad and read the number out.

Clare typed it into the search box and details of the plane appeared on a side panel. She watched, fascinated as the small yellow icon moved slowly through Fife towards Edinburgh.

The door opened and Max came back in. 'That's Rotherham alerted,' he said. His eye fell on Clare's monitor. 'Oh cool. Is that his plane?'

'We think so.'

'How long to Rotherham?'

Clare scrolled out judging the distance between Dundee, Rotherham and Dunkirk. 'Maybe two or three hours.'

'Then you've time for this,' Max said. He passed her a few sheets of paper, secured by a paperclip. 'Erika Freeman's statement.'

Chapter 37

They gathered round Clare's desk, Chris on her left, Max standing behind. She spread the pages out and began to read.

> On Tuesday, 10th February I was persuaded by my husband Rex Freeman to stage a burglary at our home in Hepburn Gardens, St Andrews. Rex had been worried about opposition to our development in the town and he was afraid some of the more radical protestors might target us personally. Our home address was on the planning documents and we were both concerned. Rex suggested if we pretended we had been burgled we might be given police protection in the days leading up to the protest march. We did not seek to profit by making a false insurance claim and I deeply regret allowing Rex to persuade me to make a false report. I did this under duress and apologise unreservedly for it.

'Hah,' Chris said, tapping the statement. 'That's a heap of crap for starters.'

'I agree,' Clare said. 'But, frankly, with the other charges she's facing, the burglary's the least of her worries.' She bent her head and began to read again.

> Rex and I were keen to purchase a cottage belonging to Dennis Gibb to allow our development to proceed. Sadly Mr Gibb died and, as far

as we were aware, the cottage reverted to his son, Steven Gibb. On Friday, 13th February we were visited at home, first by Mrs Jennifer Gibb then separately by her husband, Steven Gibb. Mrs Gibb came to ask if we would consider increasing the price. If so, she would endeavour to persuade her husband to sell us the cottage. We told Mrs Gibb we could not afford to increase our offer and she left.

Later that same evening Steven Gibb arrived. His manner was aggressive, bordering on threatening and I was alarmed. Again, we declined to increase our offer. Mr Gibb then asked if he could use our toilet and I showed him where to go. I did not trust him so stood at the kitchen door to ensure he didn't enter any other rooms. While I was looking out for him I believe Rex put some tablets in Mr Gibb's water bottle. I was not wearing my glasses and when Rex told me they were laxatives I had no reason to doubt him. They had been bought a couple of years ago while on holiday in Spain. It was a petty thing to do but Rex was angry with Steven Gibb and wanted to teach him a lesson.

It was only later Rex admitted the tablets were Fentanyl, left over from my late mother's final illness. That night Rex made an anonymous phone call to the police 101 number, stating Steven Gibb was dealing in Fentanyl. I believe he hoped Steven would be arrested and blood tests would show the presence of the drug in his system, bearing out the content of the phone call. I do not believe Rex intended to kill Steven Gibb.

I would like to be quite clear that I had no part in planning to or drugging Mr Gibb. I did

> not know Rex had added Fentanyl to his water bottle and I did not collude with Rex in making the anonymous phone call. I was deeply shocked when Mr Gibb was found dead but I played no part in his death.

Clare sat back, taking this in. 'So Rex was the anonymous caller after all. It seems so obvious now.'

Chris shrugged. 'So she says.'

Clare eyed him. 'You think she's lying?'

'Economical with the truth,' he said. 'She's in it up to her neck. Rex has ditched her – God knows why – and she's trying to wriggle out of it, making out he was the Svengali in the relationship.'

'Question is,' Max said, 'will a jury believe her?'

'Not if they see the footage,' Chris said. 'I think it proves she was part of the poisoning.'

Clare moved the first page out of the way and began reading the second.

> This afternoon, Wednesday, 18th February, Rex received a phone call. He did not communicate the nature of the call to me. He announced his intention of going abroad and urged me to join him. He said in a week or two the fuss about Steven Gibb would have blown over and that we should go abroad in the meantime. It was my opinion he did not intend returning to Scotland. I believe the consequences of his actions had dawned on him and he had decided to flee the country. He asked me to go with him but I felt unable to do so. I believed it was my duty to explain what had happened; but, more importantly, I have recently buried my dearly loved mother. She died only a few weeks ago and I still miss her terribly. I could not countenance moving abroad with no prospect

of visiting her grave; and so I remain here, ready to help the police with their investigations.

I reiterate I am innocent of all offences for which I have been questioned. If I am guilty of anything it is of allowing my husband Rex to coerce me into activities which I now realise were ill-advised.

This is a true account of the events of the past nine days.

The statement was signed *Erika Jane Freeman* with the date alongside her signature.

Chris was first to break the silence. 'What a pile of crap. I don't believe a word of it.'

'The bit about her mother might be true,' Max said. 'I can't think of another reason she wouldn't go with Rex. She must realise they're both facing major jail time.'

'She certainly won't be visiting the mother's grave for a few years,' Chris said.

Clare pushed Erika's statement across the desk. 'You think she's guilty?'

'Definitely,' Chris said.

'So why didn't she go with him? It's not like the mother's still alive.'

Chris shrugged. 'I dunno. Maybe Max has a point. The nurse did say she was devoted to her mother. Sat up with her through the night. She only went to bed when the nurses came in to give her a break; and it has only been a few weeks.'

Clare picked up the statement again. 'That bit about Rex receiving a phone call. He takes a call then tells Erika they're leaving straight away.'

Chris nodded. 'Yeah. I wondered about that too. Who do you reckon called him?'

Clare met his eye. 'Maybe someone who wanted him to know we were on our way. Someone who thought he'd appreciate a bit of time to prepare for his arrest. Someone who held us up by demanding we check the Fentanyl was collected from the pharmacy.'

'You're not thinking…'

'Penny?' Clare pursed her lips. 'I wouldn't put it past her. I told you they were chummy. I'm not saying she did it so he could escape; more a heads-up so he knew to expect us.'

Max's brow creased. 'But that's completely unprofessional – criminal, even. Surely she wouldn't? If that part of Erika's statement is true, she's assisted him in escaping justice.'

'Yep,' Clare said. 'But I'm not sure we'll ever prove it.'

'We could check his phone records,' Max said but Clare shook her head.

'She's not daft. If she'd wanted to warn the Freemans, she wouldn't have used her own phone.'

Chris shook his head. 'I dunno. I've no time for Penny but I can't see her having a burner phone.'

'Might not be a burner,' Clare said. 'Not as such. She maybe has a spare in her desk, in case her own phone packs up.'

Chris eyed her. 'You'll never prove it. She's far too sharp, that one.'

Clare's face darkened. 'Yeah; but I'll know; and, if we don't pick up Rex Freeman, I'll make sure I'm not the only one who knows.'

The door opened and Jim came in. 'Carol Merryweather?'

Clare was suddenly alert. 'What about her?'

'Her mother's taken a turn for the worse. They're taking her from custody to be at her bedside. She's not expected to live the night.'

Clare thanked Jim then she clipped the pages of Erika's statement together and handed them to Chris. 'You two go and arrest her. We'll look at charges tomorrow. I can't think straight any more.'

She waited until they had left then turned back to her computer. Rex's plane was over the River Forth now, skirting round Edinburgh. Strictly speaking she should let Penny know

Rex had taken off and that Erika was in custody. But she wasn't in the mood for a Penny conversation. That could definitely keep.

She checked her watch and realised she'd have to do something about Benjy. If she waited until Rex landed in France it would be mid-evening; and she wanted to be on hand in the hope the French police would arrest him. It wasn't really fair to impose on Bill and Moira but the alternative was bringing him back here to the station. She knew he'd be far happier lying by their fireside. She'd have to hope they didn't mind too much. She lifted her phone and scrolled until she found their number.

Chapter 38

Clare phoned for a delivery of pizza which she carried through to the incident room. Erika Freeman had been taken to a cell in Dundee to spend the night and, for the next few hours, there was nothing they could do. It didn't look as if Rex had broken his journey at Rotherham so she handed the pizza boxes out and opened Flightradar24 on a laptop. Mindful of greasy fingers, she put it on one of the other desks where they could keep an eye on it.

Jim had found an officer in Cupar who spoke pretty good French and he was liaising with the three most likely airfields in France, local police on standby.

Clare fetched a pair of scissors from the kitchen and began cutting slices of pizza.

'I don't know why you persist in doing that,' Chris said. 'There's a perfectly good pizza wheel in the drawer.'

'They don't work.'

'Maybe for you. But normal people find them very useful.'

'Yeah, whatever.' She glanced at the laptop. 'According to Laura over at Dundee Airport he's flying into a headwind.' She shook her head. 'Can we try the control tower again?'

'No point,' Chris said. 'He's obviously not using the same frequency.'

'Laura said he'd have to alert the airfield in France. Otherwise, when he enters French airspace, they might send something up to intercept him.'

Clare's phone began to ring, a number she didn't recognise.

'DI Mackay.'

'Hi Inspector, it's Will Scott from Cupar station.'

Clare face lit up. The officer who'd been liaising with the airfields in France. 'Go ahead, Will.'

'He's radioed for permission to land,' Will said. 'Apparently he filed his flight plan while he was in the air. They've granted it but they've also warned him about the storm. He's flying straight into a solid headwind.'

'What does that mean?'

'They've advised an alternative course but he's said he's light on fuel so he might end up ditching before he reaches Dunkirk.'

'How will we know?' Clare asked.

'They're in touch and they're tracking him as well. They'll keep us posted.'

'They haven't told him the police are waiting?'

'No. He won't know until he lands. It's dark now so he won't even see their vehicles.'

Clare thanked Will and put down her phone.

Chris exhaled. 'I wouldn't fancy his chances up there tonight.'

'Let's hope he makes it,' Clare said. She lifted a slice of pizza and bit into it.

Her phone buzzed with a WhatsApp from Moira. She swiped to open the message and saw a photo of Benjy asleep in front of the fire.

> As you can see he's pretty happy! Good luck with work. See you tomorrow, if things calm down.

'That's one problem sorted at least,' Clare said, passing her phone to Chris to let him see Benjy.

'You're just like one of those mothers who can't look after their own kids.'

'Yup,' she said, refusing to take the bait. 'Got my very own social worker, as well.'

It was after ten when Will phoned again. 'Rex put out a mayday call about twenty minutes ago,' he said. 'He was low on fuel. Struggling to stay on the course he'd plotted. Wasn't sure he'd make it to land.'

'And?'

He hesitated. 'They lost track of the plane shortly after that. They've tried radioing but he's not responding.'

Clare blinked away tiredness. 'What does that mean, Will?'

'Looks like he's gone down.'

There wasn't a sound in the room as they waited for the inevitable.

'Over land?' Clare asked. She held her breath.

It took Will a second or two to reply. 'Strait of Dover. Last known position was five miles off the French coast.'

Clare opened her mouth to speak but her throat was tight. She had nothing but contempt for Rex Freeman, for the harm he'd done and for his cowardly attempt to escape justice. But the thought of him in that little plane, over choppy waters whipped up by storm force winds, realising he was running out of fuel – it didn't bear thinking about.

'They've alerted shipping,' Will went on. 'But, given the storm, it's unlikely they'll find anything tonight.'

'Five miles,' Clare repeated.

'Afraid so. Even a hundred yards in weather like this would be hopeless; and that's if he survived hitting the water.' He hesitated. 'They reckon he's gone, boss.'

The cottage was quiet when Clare arrived home. She missed the sound of Benjy's breath behind the door as he waited to launch himself at her. She'd thought briefly about collecting him from Moira but it was gone eleven by the time she'd left the station and she didn't want to disturb them. Plus, she was bone-weary, with another early start in prospect.

She climbed the stairs, tiredly, and went straight to the bathroom to clean her teeth. The bedroom was cold but she was too tired to care. She switched her electric blanket to high, pulled on her warmest pyjamas and climbed in under the duvet. Her thoughts drifted back to Rex Freeman, the terror he must have felt as the plane began its final descent towards the dark, churning waters of the English Channel. He was an experienced pilot. He'd have known his fate and she wondered how long it had taken for the plane to hit the water, how long it had taken him to drown. If he'd been alive when he ditched, the shock of the cold would have taken the breath from his body, robbed his limbs of the ability to move. She thought back to her own cold water survival training. His blood pressure would have spiked, hyperventilation would have had him gasping, his lungs filling with water as wave after wave washed over him. She pulled the duvet up around her ears and felt the heat of the blanket spread across her back.

She closed her eyes and tried to think of something more pleasant. But it was almost two hours before the image of Rex drowning receded enough for sleep to take over.

Day 10: Thursday, 19th February

Chapter 39

'Is it true?' Penny demanded. 'Rex Freeman is missing, feared drowned?'

Clare pulled out of the drive at Daisy Cottage and turned towards town, her phone on hands-free.

'Yes, we think so.'

'You didn't think to call me?'

Suddenly a deer loomed up in her headlights and she hit the brake, bringing the car to a screeching halt. The animal darted across the road, unhurt and she sat on for a few moments in case another followed.

'Sorry,' she said, putting the car into first and pulling away again. 'Deer cut across me.'

'You're not hurt?'

Clare bit back the irritation she felt. Penny always did this. She never asked *are you hurt?* Or *are you all right?* It was always a statement, never a question. *You're all right, I presume,* she'd say. Never asking, always presuming.

'I'm fine. Braked in time.'

'Good. So, to Rex. I'd have thought something so serious would have warranted a phone call at the very least.'

She was at the Bogward roundabout now and she signalled to turn right into the estate. 'It was very late,' she said. 'We didn't know they'd lost track of the plane until almost eleven.' That was a bit of a white lie. It had been closer to ten. But, after the day she'd had, the last thing she'd wanted to do was to call

Penny. And, besides, if Penny hadn't demanded she release Rex and Erika he'd be safely tucked up in a police cell.

'What about Erika? Has anyone told her?'

'I believe someone is speaking to her this morning.'

There was a pause then Penny said, 'I'll go down myself.'

'I'm sure she'll appreciate that,' Clare said. Privately, she was relieved. The last thing she wanted was a round trip to Dundee. Then she recalled Erika's statement from yesterday. 'Perhaps I should email you a copy of her statement first. You should probably read it before you speak to her.'

'Do that,' Penny said and she ended the call.

Clare drove on, sensing she'd won a rare victory. She wondered what Penny would make of Erika's statement, the phone call Rex had received now a matter of record. Either way, she planned to have Erika charged this morning. She'd be up in court on Friday and, hopefully, remanded in custody. She'd liked to have charged the pair of them but it looked as if Rex had escaped justice, albeit in the most dreadful way. She wondered how Erika would react?

Not my problem any more, she thought, drawing the car into the station car park. She stepped out and, for the first time in days, she felt lighter – as if a weight had been lifted from her shoulders. Presumably the march would be called off now, with the two major shareholders unavailable.

Jim was waiting for her at the front desk. 'Just had a phone call. Carol Merryweather's mother died last night, about two in the morning.'

She thanked Jim and headed for her office, her thoughts on Carol. She was facing some serious criminal charges and it had all been for nothing. The money she'd hoped to extract from Rex and Erika wouldn't be needed, now her mother was gone. Her career as an estate agent was over and she'd likely spend some time in prison, unless the judge took pity on her, suspending the sentence. Either way, she'd lose her job and probably her home.

Clare didn't condone what Carol had done. It had been an outrageous breach of trust and an invasion of privacy. But she couldn't help feeling sorry for her. She was clearly unwell. Maybe a psychiatrist's report would result in a more lenient sentence. For once, she hoped the judge would show some compassion.

Chris ambled in, a fried egg roll in his hand.

'Do not bring that in here,' she warned. 'I don't want the smell of egg in my office all day.'

'Hold on.'

He disappeared for a minute and returned, cheeks bulging, flour from the roll around his mouth.

'You haven't just eaten that?' she said.

He chewed for a minute and drew a hand across his mouth. 'Might have.'

She shook her head. 'You'll die before you're forty.'

'So you keep telling me, yet here I am.'

'I give up! Any news of Rex or his plane?'

'Nothing yet. But the wind's down now so the French coastguard's on it.'

'Might never find it.' She glanced at her Inbox as it loaded. 'Penny's going to break the news to Erika.'

Chris frowned. 'She seen the statement?'

'I'm about to email it over; and I'm going to ask for permission to cancel the march.'

'Makes sense.'

Clare tapped out the email and turned back to Chris. 'You not got any work to do?'

He shrugged. 'This and that.'

She opened her mouth to suggest he got on with it then her phone began to ring. A number she didn't recognise. 'DI Mackay.'

'It's Amber Morgan,' the voice said. 'Steve Gibb's first wife – well, his only wife, really.'

'Ah yes,' Clare said. 'What can I do for you?'

'Can I come and see you?' Amber asked. 'I'd like your advice.'

—

Amber arrived half an hour later and Clare led her to one of the comfier interview rooms. It had two small sofas and a low table instead of the usual bucket chairs and a desk, bolted to the floor. Clare invited her to sit and took a seat opposite.

'You wanted some advice.'

'Yes.' She hesitated and seemed to have difficulty deciding where to start. 'I went to see Jenny,' she said. 'And she's lovely. I can see why Steve fell for her.' The smile faded from her eyes. 'I hope they were happy.'

Clare eyed her. She'd been concerned for Jenny's safety, unsure if Amber might have her own agenda. But here, in Clare's office, she struck her as entirely straightforward. Maybe she could trust Amber. 'I think they were happy,' she said.

'That other police officer was there,' Amber went on.

Clare was glad to hear Paul had stayed with Jenny, making sure Amber wasn't a threat; but, given her past encounters with him, she hoped he hadn't said or done anything tactless. For once, her fears were groundless.

'He was really good with Jenny. Not over the top, just a good balance of sympathy and being practical. I was impressed.'

It was a pleasant surprise and Clare made a mental note to let Paul know.

'We had a good chat,' she said. 'But I could see Jenny was worried – about the house and everything. She told me their lives were insured and the policy's designed to pay off the mortgage but she's convinced herself the insurers won't pay out because of the bigamy. Paul – that officer – he tried to reassure her but she wasn't having it. So I said I'd ask you. See what you thought.'

The question threw Clare. She knew a fair bit about the law but how could she possibly advise Jenny? 'Has she spoken to her solicitor? That would be my suggestion.'

Amber nodded. 'I said that but she's too afraid to admit the bigamy to anyone. She's worried it might invalidate the policy.'

Clare considered this. She couldn't think why it would. Presumably the only time Steve had lied about his identity had been for the wedding. Hadn't Jenny said his driving licence was in his own name?

'Did she say which name was on the insurance policy?'

'It's Steve,' Amber said. 'The mortgage too.'

Clare thought back. Jenny had said something about the mortgage and insurance people not being as strict. Frankly Clare doubted that but, if they had used their driving licences when arranging the mortgage, the marriage certificate wouldn't have been needed.

Amber was still talking.

'Strictly speaking, I think I could make a case for inheriting Steve's half of their house, given we were still married. But I've told Jenny I'm not interested in that. If it turns out to be mine, legally, I'll happily sign it over to her.'

Clare gave her a smile. 'That's very generous of you.'

'Not at all,' Amber said. 'Jenny's put her heart and soul into that house. I've no moral right to it. But, I did have a suggestion for her.'

'Oh yes.' Clare was suddenly alert. She felt protective of Jenny, for all she'd been through. She hoped Amber wasn't trying to capitalise on Steve's death.

'Dennis's cottage – Jenny said Steve inherited it. As his legal wife I think it'll come to me.'

Clare sat back in her chair, considering this. Was Amber being greedy here? After all, she and Steve hadn't lived as man and wife for years. She eyed her but said nothing.

'I can see what you're thinking,' Amber said, 'and I assure you I'm not trying to do Jenny out of what's rightfully hers.

I'm happy to waive any rights to Steve's half of their house. Jenny will be mortgage-free and she can stay on there if she chooses. But I have an idea for Dennis's cottage.'

'Go on.'

'If it comes to me – and I know it might not – I'd like to share ownership with Jenny. Fifty-fifty. We can decide together if we sell it, or even do it up and rent it out. It could be a nice earner for us both and, to be honest, it would be a project for Jenny. You only have to look at their house to see she has nice taste. None of the décor was Steve's. I can promise you that. I think Jenny could make a go of something like that. We'd share the costs and the profit.'

Clare studied Amber's face for any sign she had a hidden agenda, but her expression was clear and guileless. 'Sounds great,' she said. 'So where do I come in?'

'I've not said any of this to Jenny yet. It's far too soon. She's still in shock. I'd like to chat to her about it before I head back down south; but I need to know if it would work, legally. I could do with some advice before I broach it; but I don't want to go to the expense of a solicitor. Not until I know if it's possible. You're a police officer. You know the law. Do you think her insurer will pay out? And is there likely to be any problem with me signing half of Dennis's cottage over to Jenny?'

Clare's brow creased. 'Honestly? I haven't a clue. I do know a bit about the law but not that sort. My knowledge is criminal law. It really would make sense for Jenny to speak to her solicitor – once she's got over the shock.'

Amber sighed. 'Yes, I suppose you're right. But I'm not sure when she'll be up to that, and I did want to speak to her before I head home.'

Clare thought for a moment. 'How long are you here for?'

'I can stay another week. Then I'll have to get back.'

She rose from her seat. 'Can you give me five minutes to make a call?'

Amber smiled. 'Sure. I'm in no rush.'

Clare walked back to her office, trying to come to a decision. There was someone she could call. Someone who knew the law inside out and backwards. Someone who would drop everything to help her. Someone she'd lived with years ago, when she'd been stationed in Glasgow. Someone she'd thought she would marry one day. Her ex-boyfriend, Tom.

'Clare!' As usual he sounded as if a call from her was the highlight of his day. 'What a lovely surprise. How are you?'

They exchanged polite remarks for a few minutes then she got to the point.

'I've an unusual situation,' she said. 'I wondered if you could give me some advice.' She began to explain but he stopped her.

'Let me get pen and paper. It sounds like I'd better take some notes.'

She waited and, when he was ready, she told him about Dennis's death. 'We think his son killed him,' she said, 'but I doubt we'll be able to prove it.'

Tom asked a few questions then she moved on to talk about Steve's bigamous marriage.

'Crikey,' he said. 'You weren't kidding when you said it was complicated. And you're sure the other son is dead?'

'No one's heard from him for the past ten years so I guess so. He's not been declared dead but I reckon if Jenny began proceedings it would be straightforward.'

She gave him a moment to make notes then told him Steve had also died, omitting the part about the Freemans drugging him. 'And now the legal wife has turned up.'

'It's like a soap opera,' he said. 'What a mess.'

'Yep.'

'Let me guess: the first wife, Amber is it? She wants the lot?'

'Quite the opposite.' Clare relayed her conversation with Amber. 'Seems she wants to do the decent thing.'

Tom fell silent, making notes she guessed. Then he cleared his throat. 'Let me see if I've got it right: Jenny, the second wife, is worried her life assurance will be invalidated because of the bigamous marriage?'

'Correct.'

'As far as that goes, you can set her mind at rest,' Tom said. 'From what you've told me, the only time he lied about his identity was at their wedding. Regarding the mortgage, they had a legitimate reason for a joint lives policy. Providing it's been legally underwritten, which I'm sure it was, she'll be fine. The policy will pay out.'

'And the first wife?' Clare asked. 'Amber?'

'She's renouncing any claim to the couple's home on Kilrymont Road, yes?'

'Correct.'

'Not that I think she'd have much of a case there, but it's reassuring for Jenny.'

'Indeed.'

'And Amber believes she'll inherit the father's cottage and wants to share it with Jenny?'

'Correct.'

'Okay,' Tom said. 'This is based solely on what you've told me. Steve inherited the father's cottage. Assuming he didn't make a will, there being no other relatives, I believe Amber will inherit that from him. Jenny could challenge this in court and may well win a share so what Amber proposes makes sense. Given it's neither of their homes, if it went to court, I think the court would see a fifty-fifty split as fair and sensible.'

Clare exhaled. 'Thanks so much, Tom. I don't suppose...'

'You want me to speak to her?'

'Would you?'

He laughed. 'For you, Clare, anything.'

She laughed with him but it was tempered with a wariness she'd felt since he'd first revealed the presence of cracks in his marriage. She was on the point of asking about Gillian, his wife, now working at a school down in Brighton, coming back to Glasgow every other weekend, but she decided against it. She didn't know how she would react if he said things weren't going well. She'd made a new life with Al, once her DCI, now her life partner. Tom was part of the past. But part of her suspected Tom didn't see it that way.

'She's in one of the interview rooms. I'll go through now.' She hesitated, her hand on the office door. 'And, Tom?'

'Yes?' His tone was eager and she felt a wave of guilt at no longer being part of his life.

'Thanks. I really appreciate it.'

—

Amber left twenty minutes later, promising Clare she'd pick her moment to speak to Jenny.

'Maybe encourage her to contact her insurers,' Clare advised. 'The sooner that policy pays out the better.'

Her Inbox was flashing with unread emails and she clicked to open Penny's reply.

Erika's statement seems fine.

I assume you'll charge her with defeating the ends of justice.

Pls phone if you want to discuss.

Re the march, there are other minor shareholders in the Freemans' company

so it goes ahead as planned.

Clare's heart sank. After working flat out, she'd been looking forward to a weekend off. However, the plans were in place so she'd just have to get on with it. Once the march was over, she'd take a few days off. Al had said she could take Benjy through to stay in his flat at Tulliallan. Maybe she'd do that. Have some lazy days, walking Benjy, curling up with a book or some junk TV. They could eat together in the evenings. She smiled at the idea. He'd be back tonight to work from home on Friday and she couldn't wait.

—

It was mid-afternoon when the call came in.

'Wreckage sighted off Calais,' Chris said. 'Looks like the same kind of plane. They're trying to get a photo of the number.'

Clare nodded. 'Not the ending we'd hoped for.'

'Nah. But it'll save the prison service the cost of keeping him.'

'Sympathetic as ever.' She glanced at her watch. 'You get off home. You're overdue an early finish.'

He didn't have to be told twice. 'We're going to the cinema tonight,' he said.

'Oh? What you seeing?'

'Dunno. Some French thing. Sara says it's good. I'll likely have a nap.'

She smiled. 'I don't blame you.'

The team were soon gone and Clare worked on, enjoying the peace that had descended on the station.

At four o'clock, she logged off her computer. 'Emergencies only,' she told Jim. 'I'll be back in about nine tomorrow.'

It was still light, the days beginning to stretch and she was soon on her way, stopping at an off-licence en route to buy Bill and Moira a bottle of wine.

The heating hadn't yet come on in the cottage and she went straight to the boiler to override the timer. Benjy went round the house, sniffing every corner, as though checking no one had been there in his absence.

She unearthed one of her mother's curries from the freezer and put it in the oven on a low heat. Then she lit the lamps and bent to set the woodburner, planning to make the house welcoming for Al when he arrived home. 'He'll probably die of the shock,' she told Benjy who wagged his tail in response.

She poured herself a large glass of red, deciding she deserved it and sat on the sofa, warming her feet in front of the fire. Benjy jumped up to join her and she put a hand round the little dog's neck, gently scratching behind his ears.

Headlights swept round the room and she rose from the sofa. Benjy went straight to the window, his tail wagging furiously. Al was home and that made them both very happy indeed.

Day 11: Friday, 20th February

Chapter 40

'Why were there dog hairs on my side of the bed?' Al asked, spooning coffee into the cafetiere.

Clare avoided his eye. 'No idea.'

'Thought we had an agreement about that.'

She glanced over at Benjy, emptying his dog bowl as if he hadn't seen food for weeks. 'Benjy must have found his way into the bedroom. When I was out at the bins,' she added.

'You're a dreadful liar, Clare Mackay.'

'Dunno what you mean.'

'Hmm. So you say.' He carried the cafetiere over to the table. Then he sat, regarding her. 'Sure you have to go in? You're looking pretty tired.'

'Yeah, I'd better. I want to make sure everything's in place for the march.' She eyed him. 'You heard any more?'

'No. But I did think…'

'Yes?'

'I might pick up a radio and hang about. Another pair of eyes, you know?'

She put a hand across the table and held his for a moment. 'Honestly, Al, I'm sure it'll be fine. You need your weekend.'

'And you need every officer you can lay your hands on. Plus, I won't be in uniform so I might spot stuff.'

Her brow creased. 'Like what?'

He shrugged. 'Anything, really. Petty crime, drunks.'

'God, I hope not,' she said. 'The last thing I need is to tie officers up dealing with pickpockets. I want them all on the spot.'

'Like I say, I probably won't be needed. Hopefully with the Freemans off the scene you might not get as many protestors.'

She drew a cup across the table and added milk to her coffee. 'The exhibition's still going ahead.'

'At the town hall?'

'Yeah. But the marchers won't be allowed over there. The route's from the West Sands to the top of North Street.'

'When's the fencing going up?'

'This afternoon.'

'Make sure it's secure.'

Clare sipped at her coffee, enjoying the caffeine hit. 'You heard any more about Penny's agitators?'

He shook his head. 'Doesn't mean they won't be there, though. She's going to pepper the crowd with undercover officers.'

Clare put down her coffee, her hands round the mug. 'I don't like it, Al. She's not been straight with me.'

He nodded. 'I know. But she's probably working on a need-to-know basis. The more folk who know about it, the more chance it leaks out.'

'She doesn't trust me.'

'I wouldn't put it like that.'

'Wouldn't you?' She shoved back her chair and took a last drink of coffee. 'That's exactly how I'd put it.'

—

She mulled this over as she drove into work. Penny didn't like her. She was convinced of that. Fine. The feeling was mutual. But she'd worked hard since coming to St Andrews. The least her superintendent owed her was a bit of respect.

The station was quiet, officers catching up on paperwork, others supervising deliveries of Heras fencing. She spread out the plans for the march on her desk, moving officers around until she was happy with the arrangements.

Jim tapped on her door just before lunchtime to let her know Carol Merryweather had been referred for psychiatric examination. She thanked him and turned to her Inbox, groaning with unread emails. There was a reminder about recommending officers for the Police Leadership and Development Programme, and her thoughts drifted to Sara. She was once of the best officers in the station yet, as far as Clare could recall, she'd never mentioned promotion. Was that the source of tension between her and Chris? Maybe she ought to raise it with Sara. Show her a bit of support.

Chris was in the incident room. 'I've a craving for a fudge doughnut,' she lied, a ten-pound note in hand. 'Fancy nipping out for a couple?'

He didn't have to be asked twice. She waited until he'd set off down the road then she approached Sara. 'Spare me a minute?'

Sara followed her to Clare's office, her expression wary.

'Don't worry,' Clare said, smiling. 'It's nothing bad.' She waited until Sara had taken a seat then she sat opposite. 'I'd like you to think seriously about the PLDP.'

Sara's brow clouded.

'I know promotion isn't for everyone,' Clare said. 'But you could complete the training to see how you get on. If you don't like it, fine. We won't take it any further. But I think it would be good for you – professionally, I mean.'

Sara avoided her eye. 'I'm not sure…'

Clare smiled again. 'Frankly, Sara, if I can pass the course, anyone can. You're one of the most capable officers I've ever met. I'd really like you to think about it.'

Sara met her eye. 'I could do the training? And it wouldn't matter if I didn't take it any further?'

'Of course, but you might change your mind once you'd completed it.'

She was quiet for a moment, as if turning it over in her mind.

'No pressure from me,' Clare said. 'But you're so capable, Sara. I'd love to see you use your talents.'

Sara's cheeks flushed. 'You really think so?'

'I do. And now, I won't keep you. I made Chris go out for doughnuts so we could speak in peace. I'd better put the kettle on.'

Sara escaped and Clare sat on, thinking about her young officer. They were like chalk and cheese, Chris and Sara, yet somehow it worked. They softened each other's edges and, thinking about the couple now, Clare was so glad they'd found each other.

—

By late afternoon, the fencing was up and traffic diversions in place. There was nothing more she could do until morning.

'Everyone in for seven,' she told them. 'Kevlar vests, and don't forget your thermals. You'll be hanging about for hours and it could be cold.' She watched them drift off home then she switched the phones to nearby Cupar station and headed for her car. It was a beautifully calm evening, a rosy glow out to the west as the sun made its final appearance of the day. She strolled across the car park and checked her watch. By this time tomorrow, it would pretty much be done. The marchers would drift off, buses ferrying their passengers back home. She couldn't wait for it to be over so she could spend some quality time with Al and Benjy. She clicked the remote control on her car and climbed in. It was time to go home.

Day 12: Saturday, 21st February

Chapter 41

The station was filled to capacity with officers, many of whom Clare had never met. They spilled out from the incident room to the front office and she stood between the two rooms, so they could all see her.

'You have your groups,' she said. 'If you're not sure where your starting post is ask one of the locals. Most of you will begin at the West Sands. Parking for buses is on the grass, beyond the surf shop and marchers are to be kept there until ten o'clock when you will lead them to North Street via Golf Place. We've allowed one hour for that so there's no rush. The organisers will address the marchers from eleven. They'll be behind barriers in front of the war memorial. That marks the end of the march.'

An officer Clare didn't recognise raised his hand. 'Do we have designated escape routes if there's a surge?'

Clare nodded. 'The barriers across North and South Castle Street can be pulled back to allow people to escape in either direction. Likewise Union Street further down. Group commanders have discretion here. The main thing is to keep alert. We don't want a crush so if it looks dangerous we'll open the most suitable exits.'

'What time are we expecting it to finish?' another officer asked.

'The speakers should be done by two in the afternoon. Buses have been asked to vacate by five. So officers at the rear should start shepherding marchers back towards the West Sands no later than three.'

There were a few more questions then she ended the briefing. They began drifting off to their posts and suddenly the station was almost empty.

'Time for a coffee?' Chris said.

Clare checked her watch. 'A quick one; but I want to be at the war memorial no later than nine.'

They sat either side of her desk, an uneasy silence between them.

'How many do you reckon we'll get?' Chris asked.

Clare considered this. 'Judging by the number of buses we're expecting, plus the local protest group, I'd say maybe two or three thousand.'

'I'd say more,' Chris said. 'Patch says there's a farmer south of the town has a board up on one of his fields, offering camping. He's put a row of Portaloos at one end. Hundred quid for two nights.'

Clare stared at him. 'How much?'

'I know! Patch says the field's crammed. Farmer was talking about opening up another one.'

'Jeez. Does he have a licence for that?'

Chris shrugged. 'Doesn't much matter. They'll be gone by Monday. Nice work if you can get it.'

'You're not kidding.' She checked her watch again. 'Drink up. I want to get down there. Make sure the fencing's secure at the top of North Street.'

-

A small group was gathered at the war memorial, sipping drinks from stainless-steel travel mugs. There was a wooden dais, for the speakers she presumed, a loud hailer resting on it. One of the group looked familiar but she couldn't think why; and then it came. Nicholas Stewart. He'd led a protest against a bottled water plant on the outskirts of town a few years ago. She'd never forget it. The group had assembled to disrupt a charity fun run and, in the ensuing chaos, a baby had been stolen from its pram. She hoped today would pass off without any similar incidents.

'Mr Stewart.' Clare moved forward, hand outstretched.

'Inspector,' he beamed. 'How lovely to see you. I can tell we'll be in safe hands with you in charge.'

'I hope so.' She gestured at the dais and loud hailer. 'Would you mind talking me through your plans for addressing the crowd? We've allowed three hours then we'll begin shepherding them back down the street. I presume that'll be enough time.'

He smiled. 'Plenty of time.' He gestured at the small group, still sipping their drinks. 'We've four speakers, in total, all with different points to make. Half an hour each should be plenty.' He looked up at the sky. 'And it looks like the weather will be with us.'

Clare followed his gaze. The early clouds were drifting off, leaving the sky a pale blue. 'Going to be cold, though,' she said and he nodded.

She followed him over to the group and introduced herself. They chatted for a few minutes then her radio crackled.

'Buses are starting to arrive,' Max said. 'There's a dozen here already. Plus a large group of locals.'

She thanked Max and asked him to keep her informed. There was nothing else to do so she wandered down North Street, assuring herself the escape route barriers could be pulled back in an emergency. The events of the past weeks were playing in her head like a newsreel. That first encounter with the Freemans at their house following what turned out to be a faked burglary; Dennis and Steve's murders, Carol Merryweather and her hidden cameras – and now the march was here – the event that took her full circle back to the Freemans and their development. She couldn't help thinking, without the couple, none of it would have happened.

With traffic restrictions the street was eerily quiet, almost as if they were soldiers waiting for battle to begin. Was that what the day would be – a battle? Hopefully the measures she'd taken would ensure any trouble was stopped before it really started.

Her phone buzzed and she saw it was Al.

'Hi, you.'

'How's it going?' he asked.

'Pretty boring at the moment,' she said. 'But there's a fair crowd at the West Sands already.'

'I'll walk Benjy then head over. Do a bit of mingling.'

'Got your *All Cops are Bastards* T-shirt on?'

'It's not funny, Clare. I hear on the grapevine some of those on their way are known to us already. Be careful, okay?'

'Sure.' They chatted on for a few more minutes, Clare checking the barriers as she went. As she reached Golf Place, she heard the noise. Curiosity took her down towards The Links where she had a clear view across the sands. She stopped in her tracks. A procession of buses was making its way along the road bordering the sands. Hadn't Max said there were a dozen there already? There must be easily that number again – far more than they'd been notified of. The sands themselves were filled with people milling about. She could hear the sound of drums, whistles and what she thought was an air horn, the kind of sounds that came with professional protestors. It was too far away to make out any of the faces but there was no mistaking the weight of numbers. An anxious feeling began to develop in the pit of her stomach. This was far bigger than any of them had anticipated.

She took out her phone and dialled Penny's number. It went to voicemail. She waited for the prompt then turned her back on the beach, sheltering her phone from the wind.

'This is far bigger than we can cope with,' she said. 'I need more officers to guarantee public safety. Please send whatever you can.'

She dialled Max next but the noise from the marchers made it impossible to speak and she ended the call. She began walking quickly, following the route, speaking to officers stationed at each point.

Her phone started to ring and she saw it was Chris. 'This is huge,' he said. 'If they're not peaceful we could have a problem. The TV are here too.'

She thought for a moment. Public safety was priority. They had to control the pace of the march, keeping them in a tight group. 'Okay,' she said. 'I want two lines of officers across the front of the march and a single line down each side. Move a few up from the back if necessary. Use your discretion.'

She reached the top of North Street just before ten. They'd be on their way in a minute. Tension hung in the air and suddenly she felt oddly vulnerable, with just a handful of officers stationed at the break-out points. A few people hung out of windows overlooking the street and she hoped there would be little for them to see.

And then she heard the strains of the marchers, distant at first, shouts, chants and whistles. A drum beat, deep and regular punctured the air making Clare think of a funeral; and every second was bringing it closer.

Chapter 42

Clare stood just inside the cordon where the speakers were preparing to address the crowd. A short woman in a padded coat and knitted hat was to be first and she stepped onto the dais, helped by Nicholas Stewart. She picked up the loud hailer and stood, waiting for the crowd to move closer.

Clare watched as the lines of officers slowed their pace, alerting those behind they had almost reached the cordon. Banners fluttered in the wind and chants of *High Cost Housing – No No No!* rang round the street.

The marchers seemed largely good-natured and Clare began to think it might just be okay. Max, leading a team at the rear, had radioed to say all was well there. A helicopter hovered overhead but, with the sun in her eyes, she couldn't see any markings. Was this Penny's doing? Or was it press? Chris had said there were TV reporters. A march this size in such a small town was bound to make the national news.

The woman in the padded coat put the loud hailer to her lips and began. 'St Andrews needs affordable housing,' she called, her voice reedy and robotic. 'Housing in our town is now more expensive than any other coastal town in Scotland. Our own young people have no hope of buying their own homes, and rents are through the roof. We need affordable homes. We do not need another over-priced housing development.'

Clare tuned out, scanning the street for any sign of trouble. The march had come to a halt now, chants and drumbeats filling the air; and then she saw them, just one or two at first, peppered through the crowd, faces masked, hoods pulled over their heads making identification impossible. Black flags were held aloft, fluttering in the wind – the symbol of anarchism. Clare's throat tightened as the chanting grew louder and closer, the dark-clad figures weaving their way to the front.

They were in trouble now. She knew it but she didn't know what to do about it. She reached for her radio, to warn officers manning the escape points but she was thrown by the sound of breaking glass. Her head whirled round, looking for the culprit, but it was impossible to pick them out of the crowd. There were shouts now, angry cries, and then the surge began. The officers in front locked arms and dug their heels in.

Patch held firm giving support to those on either side and Clare marvelled at her strength. She could see masked figures, hands to their ears and she guessed they were receiving instructions through earpieces. Penny's officers? Or the people she was hunting?

There were more sounds of breaking glass now and she scanned the crowd, trying to gauge what would come next. Behind her the speakers stood, rooted to the spot and she began ushering them towards The Pends Gate House.

'Make for South Street, then Abbey Street,' she shouted, hoping they could hear her over the chanting. 'Get right away from here.'

They moved quickly and she watched, checking they'd escaped safely. Then she turned back. Marchers in the middle of the crowd were pushing forward and she was afraid those at the front would be trampled underfoot. She clicked her radio and gave the order to open the escape routes then she jumped on the dais and snatched up the loud hailer, left behind by the terrified speakers.

'You must disperse,' she called, to jeers and blasts from airhorns. 'Turn around and make your way slowly down North Street.'

Something missed her head by inches. A brick or a rock – she wasn't sure what. Suddenly the air was filled with missiles flying in all directions. And among the masked protestors, the flag wavers and the missile throwers she could see the faces of terrified locals, caught up in a protest that was fast becoming a riot.

The Heras fencing was pulled back and, gradually, the mass of bodies began to thin as people fled the chaos. But a determined band of masked rioters remained, surging forward. Batons were drawn now and slowly the police lines began to gain ground. The protestors were still shouting, chanting anti-police slogans but they were moving back. Overhead, the helicopter hovered and Clare hoped whoever was up there had cameras. She wanted to nail every single one of these bastards.

It was as if the next few seconds happened in slow motion. They were regaining control. She continued issuing instructions through the loud hailer, her officers making slow but determined progress down North Street.

The figure came out of nowhere. He ran against the flow, fighting his way through the others. He was masked but his eyes flashed with a hatred that stopped Clare in her tracks. Then he raised his hand, drawing it back. It happened so quickly she scarcely had time to register. Something was flying through the air – at speed; and then it stopped. It stopped, and it felled one of her officers.

For a second, Clare froze. The masked man froze and the officer hit the ground, the sickening crack of a head connecting with concrete.

More by instinct than presence of mind, she pressed the emergency button on her radio. 'Officer down,' she cried. 'Officer down. Top end of North Street, St Andrews. Ambulance and urgent assistance.' Then she released the button.

She couldn't see who the object had hit, three or four colleagues crowded round the injured officer, others driving the crowd back. Her head whirled round desperately, checking for them all: Chris, Sara, Max and Patch – even Al was in there, somewhere. But she couldn't see any of them. The crowd round the injured officer was too dense. She sent up a silent prayer for her colleagues – her friends – as she tried to force her way through.

The roar made her spin round and she saw another man charging towards her. Batons were raised as a figure in a khaki parka threw himself at the masked man, bringing him down. Before the assailant could react, the parka-clad man was on top of him, knees in his back. Then he raised his gaze to meet Clare's.

'I've got him,' he said. 'I'll keep him here. See to your officer.'

She stood, rooted to the spot, her eyes on the man, and on the figure beneath him, writhing on the ground.

'I've got him,' he said again. 'Go!' A couple of uniforms from Cupar rushed up and she left them in charge of the masked man and fought her way through to the injured officer, the sound of CPR being administered filling her ears.

'Nine – ten – eleven – twelve...' a voice she thought she recognised. One of the Glenrothes cops? She struggled through, pushing the others out of the way and she saw him bent over the figure on the ground, his hands clasped as he pressed down, keeping a steady rhythm. But still she couldn't see and, again, she pushed forward, exhorting her colleagues to let her through. She had to know.

The officers parted and she tried to focus on the figure on the ground. Her heart felt as if it was forcing its way up her chest, preventing her from breathing. She let the loud hailer fall and sank to her knees.

'Oh no no no, oh please God no.'

The ringing in her ears screened out the siren, as the ambulance came closer.

The counting began again. 'One – two – three – four,' and suddenly the siren filled the air, blue lights bouncing off the warm sandstone buildings.

Strong hands tried to pull her back and she fought them off until she heard Al's voice in her ear.

'Step back,' he said. 'Let them do their job.'

His hands were under her arms but her legs wouldn't support her and she felt him raise her to her feet, gripping her tightly. He held her close, whispering in her ear. Some nonsense about it being all right. But anyone looking at the figure on the ground, the dark pool spreading out from the head, knew it wouldn't be all right.

She heard the sound of feet running and a minute later a defibrillator was produced. Al had pulled Clare right back now and she hung limply, all her weight on him as the paramedics began shocking the figure on the ground.

A murmur of conversation punctuated the periodic shocks then, 'Got a pulse.'

A trolley was wheeled across and they bent, preparing to lift the figure onto it. Clare stumbled forward and saw there was a bandage round the officer's head now. Would it be enough to stem the bleeding? All her training told her it didn't look good but they'd found a pulse. Maybe it would be all right.

'It will be okay, won't it?' she said, her eyes searching Al's face for answers.

He pulled her head into his shoulder and kissed her hair, murmuring softly.

And then the doors were slammed, the siren started up again and the ambulance taking Sara to hospital pulled slowly away.

Chapter 43

The arrival of the ambulance and the arrest of the masked man had somehow drained the crowd of energy and they began making their way slowly back down North Street. Max had driven a distraught Chris to Ninewells A&E, promising to let Clare know as soon as there was any news. She'd wanted to follow them but Al had gently suggested she hold off.

'You won't get near Sara for ages,' he said. 'They'll be working on her. She might even go to theatre.'

'But I should be with Chris.'

'And you will be. But, for now, you've a job to do here.'

He was right, of course. She knew that.

Turning from the dark patch on the ground, she surveyed the street. She recognised Penny's officers now, one or two of them marching masked figures towards police vans, others talking on radios. A clutch of officers was standing a little way off, eyes on Clare, waiting for instruction and she sent two of them to check on the speakers who'd fled to Abbey Street.

'Tell them they can bring their vehicles as far as the arch,' she said. 'Let them clear their stuff away.' She directed the others to follow the marchers to their buses on the West Sands. They were largely subdued now and she didn't anticipate any trouble. But she needed them safely out of the way.

Patch and one of the Cupar officers had handcuffed the masked man and were waiting on a van to take him back to the station.

'He'd better see a doctor,' Clare said, her voice mechanical. She was going through the motions, on automatic pilot. But none of it felt real. 'And take a statement.'

The parka man's eyes were on her and, for some reason, she was drawn to him. She shrugged Al's arm off and walked across. 'I don't know how to thank you,' she said. 'With such a crowd, we'd never have detained him.'

He shook his head. 'Only what any decent person would have done.'

There was something familiar, something about his eyes and she searched them for a clue. It was there but she couldn't grasp it. He was thirty-ish, or he might have been older, his lean weatherbeaten face evidence of a life spent outdoors. But she was drawn back to those eyes – dark blue, shaded by thick eyebrows. She was about to turn away when it hit her and she knew now why he was so familiar. She'd looked into those same eyes a few days earlier when she'd spoken to Steve Gibb.

'You're Brad, aren't you?' she said. 'Bradley Gibb.'

For a moment he didn't speak. A smile played at the corners of his mouth. 'Not officially.'

'Has someone taken a statement?'

He met Clare's eye but he didn't answer.

'You gave a false name.'

Again, he said nothing.

'We'll need your witness statement. Guys like him don't plead guilty.'

He waved this away. 'There are hundreds of witnesses. Your officers for a start. They all saw it. And I'm betting that eye in the sky caught it on camera. Pretty horrible for the family but it'll put him away.'

She stood, taking in his face. 'You really are Bradley Gibb?'

'No comment.'

She shook her head. 'Why are you here?'

'Heard about my dad, and Steve. Thought I should pay my respects. I want to be at the funerals – just at the back. I won't make myself known to them; and I don't want you telling them I'm alive. I don't want anything of my dad's – or Steve's. His wife's welcome to the lot. I just thought I should be here. Soon as the funerals are over I'll head off again.'

Clare studied him. 'Where, though? Where will you go?'

He shrugged. 'Here and there.' He stepped back and gave Clare a smile. 'Better see to your troops.'

She watched him melt into the crowd then her eyes fell on the figure on the ground, his hands cuffed behind his back. She thought about Sara, lying prone, blood pooling around her head and a fire began burning within her.

Suddenly Al was there, at her side again. 'Don't,' he said. 'It's what they want. Don't give him the satisfaction.'

Her phone began to ring and she glanced at the display. Max. Her hands were shaking, the lump in her throat so large she thought it might choke her. She handed the phone to Al and he swiped to take the call.

She watched, her eyes never leaving his face. She saw his expression, heard the words, took the phone wordlessly as he handed it back. She waited, knowing what he was going to say but cherishing every second until he said it. If she didn't hear it she wouldn't know and maybe it wouldn't be true.

He cleared his throat and put his hands on her arms. 'I'm so sorry, Clare. Sara died before they reached Ninewells. They worked on her for almost an hour but the head wound was catastrophic.' He pulled her into a hug and she stood, wooden, frozen. Sara dead? It wasn't possible. It couldn't be true. That lovely young woman, one of the most promising officers she'd ever met and, more importantly, Chris's cherished wife. How would he ever get over it?

A police van drove slowly up the street and Clare watched as the masked man was led into the back.

Al moved to block Clare's view. Empty of emotion, she let him. Then he spoke into the radio, issuing instructions. She had no idea what he was saying. All she could think about was Chris.

'Sorted,' Al said, putting his phone away. 'One of the Cupar inspectors is going to supervise dispersal of the marchers. The fences will be taken down once they're safely on the buses.'

She heard the words, knew what he was saying but she was numb, unable to react.

'Come on,' he said. 'I'm parked at the harbour. We'd better head for the hospital.'

Chapter 44

Chris was sitting in a side room, his eyes red-rimmed, staring at the wall opposite. A large plastic bag was at his feet, knotted at the neck and Clare avoided looking at it. She didn't want to see what Sara had been reduced to – little more than a bag of clothes and possessions.

He turned his head as Clare opened the door then looked away again.

'Is it okay if we come in?' she said, her voice low.

He nodded but didn't speak.

She moved carefully into the room as though trying not to disturb the air, Al at her back. There was a pair of chairs opposite Chris and she pulled one towards her and sat down. Chris's arms were on the desk in front of him and she reached across and put a hand on his. He drew back quickly and she wondered if he was afraid of being touched, as if accepting this small gesture of empathy might fracture the brittle exterior he'd built around himself.

Instinctively Clare moved her own hand back, giving him the space he obviously needed. She wanted nothing more than to take him in her arms and hold him so so tightly. 'Chris,' she began, her own voice hoarse with emotion, 'I'm so dreadfully sorry.'

'We both are,' Al said. 'And we're here, for anything – anything at all.'

Chris gave a slight nod of his head and Clare tried again.

'Have you had something to drink?'

He made no reply and Clare jerked her head at Al. He took the cue and went quietly from the room.

Left alone with Chris, she tried again. 'What can we do? Would you like me to call her parents?'

He shook his head. 'Hospital's done that.'

Clare nodded. That at least he'd been spared. 'Are they coming over?'

'No. They're waiting until she's been moved to the undertaker's.'

Clare was glad to hear that. Far better to see Sara in calmer surroundings than the busy teaching hospital where her life had officially ended. 'She was one of the finest officers it's been my privilege to know,' she said.

Chris's head was down now and she saw tears begin to spill. *Good,* she thought. *He needs to cry.* She stood and put an arm round his shoulders. He leaned in and she wrapped her other arm round him, feeling tears turn to racking sobs. After a few minutes, she sensed Al was at the door then she heard it close quietly again and she was grateful for his understanding.

Finally, Chris drew back and put his hands up to his face, wiping his eyes. She waited while he composed himself then resumed her seat.

'We were so lucky,' she said, 'having Sara in our lives,' and he nodded.

'She deserved better than me.'

'Don't you dare say that,' Clare said. 'You were perfect for each other. Like two sides of the same coin.'

He managed a smile. 'More like chalk and cheese.'

Clare returned the smile. 'Who doesn't love a bit of chalk with their cheese?'

He met Clare's eye. 'Can I tell you something?'

'Anything you like.'

'We'd been trying for a baby.'

For a moment, Clare wondered if Sara had been pregnant. Suddenly her throat felt tight. How on earth would she comfort Chris at the loss of his wife and his unborn child?

He seemed to guess and shook his head. 'It hadn't happened.' He sniffed and fished in his pocket for a tissue, blowing his nose. 'Sara – she wanted us to see our GP but I wasn't keen. Maybe if I had gone, maybe if she'd been pregnant she wouldn't have been on duty today, and I'd still have her.'

Suddenly Clare understood. She realised why the pair had seemed so tense over the past few weeks. She'd sensed something had been wrong. Now she knew and her heart went out to them.

'We were going to move,' he went on. 'Finally have that house with a garden.' He sank back in his chair. 'We'll never have it now.' Fresh tears began coursing down his face and she let him cry. There was nothing else for him to do.

The door opened again and Al came quietly in, a cardboard tray of coffee cups in his hand. He eyed Chris then put the tray on the table.

'Chris,' he said, his voice gentle, 'I'm going to help the staff with the paperwork – if that's okay?' He glanced at Clare. 'They've said you can go in to see Sara again. If you'd like to.'

Chris nodded and Al pushed one of the coffees across the table. 'Maybe have this first.'

The coffee was lukewarm but Clare was glad of it. They drank in silence then Chris set his cup down and rose heavily.

'I'd like to see her now.'

They followed a nurse down a corridor and into a side room, Clare stopping at the door. 'Would you like me to come in with you?' but Chris shook his head.

She watched him push the door open slowly, the nurse with him. Seconds later the nurse emerged and gave Clare a nod.

'I'll be at the desk if you need me.'

Clare watched her go then leaned against the wall, next to the door, her mind on Chris, spending the last precious moments with his wife. As she stood, she thought about the hospital, its patients and visitors, the births and deaths. She'd been here with Chris, more times than she could remember, visiting victims of crime and, occasionally, the perpetrators themselves; but never had she experienced anything so painful. She wondered if she'd ever be able to come here again without remembering the acuteness of Chris's suffering.

She had no idea how long she stood there, waiting for Chris. Al appeared, the paperwork done and he nodded at the room.

'Still in with her?'

'Yes.' She checked her watch. 'Twenty minutes, now.'

'Maybe it's time…'

She nodded and steeled herself to go in but the door opened and Chris came out, his face expressionless.

'I'd better go,' he said. 'They'll be wanting to – you know.'

Clare nodded. Then she looked back at the room. 'Would you mind?'

He met her eye. 'Of course not. Sara would love to see you.'

She tried to speak but her throat was too tight so she waited, watching Al lead Chris back to the room where they'd found him. Then she turned to the door and pushed it open.

Sara lay on her back, a white sheet across her body. Her eyes were closed and the bandage had been removed. With the back of her head against the pillow there was no visible sign of the injury that had robbed her of life – just a bruise where the rock had struck her on the temple. There was a quiet dignity in the way the hospital staff had laid her out and Clare was grateful for that. She stood looking at the face of this lovely young woman, so full of life when she'd arrived for duty that morning. A life that now was gone. Clare had seen many dead bodies in the course of her working life but never had she faced anything like this. From nowhere a choking convulsing sob overtook her and she allowed herself to be overwhelmed by grief and despair.

Day 13: Sunday, 22nd February

Chapter 45

Al had wanted her to take the day off but she positively refused. 'I need to speak to them all,' she said. 'Obviously not Chris, but the rest of them. Something like this,' she shook her head. 'It'll have knocked them for six.'

He eyed her. 'It's knocked you for six as well.'

She forced a smile. 'I know. But it has to be done.'

He drove her in and insisted on coming into the station with her.

Jim was at the front desk, in his usual position, his face ashen. He seemed to have aged ten years overnight. Clare went forward and, unusually, he came out from behind the public enquiry counter and took her in his arms. It took all her self-control not to give way to tears as he held her in a bear hug.

'That poor lassie,' he said, his eyes misty. 'And Chris. What'll he do?'

Clare nodded, not trusting herself to speak. She indicated her office. 'I'd better…' and she escaped before the tears began to flow.

Al made two mugs of coffee and brought them into her office.

'How many are in?' she said.

'Half a dozen. More on the way. Max passed your message round.'

She checked her watch. 'I'll have this then I'll see them.'

'Sure?' he said. 'I could do it for you?'

She stretched out and took his hand in hers. 'Thanks, Al. But it goes with the territory.'

Half an hour later, she entered the incident room and every pair of eyes turned to see her. Their expressions were a mixture of concern and pain, a few officers sniffing into hankies. Al came in behind her and took a seat at the back. She moved to the front of the room and perched on a desk.

She took a moment, cleared her throat then looked round. 'For anyone who hasn't heard, our colleague Sara lost her life yesterday. She was hit on the temple by a missile thrown by someone in the crowd. She fell back and sustained a further head injury.' Clare stopped for a moment to let them take this in. 'CPR was administered where she fell and paramedics managed to start her heart. Sadly, she arrested again en route to hospital and, this time, they were unable to save her.'

She broke off again, trying to recall what she had planned to say. 'A book of condolence will be opened and I will arrange for flowers to be sent to Chris and to Sara's parents. No doubt we'll speak in the coming days and weeks about suitable tributes but that's not for now. For the moment—'

The door opened and Clare turned to see Superintendent Penny Meakin. She hesitated then came into the room, closing the door quietly behind her. Clare blinked, as if not believing what she was seeing. Of all the times.

'Good morning,' Penny began, in what Clare thought was a carefully measured tone. The kind of tone they used for delivering a death message. She was moving across the room, about to assume her position at the front next to Clare.

Like hell, Clare thought. A fire began burning within her, all the anger she had felt at Sara's murder, at the piddling number of officers Penny had spared her and, most of all, at Penny using the march to flush out the professional rioters. From the back of the room Al was shaking his head. *Don't do it,* he was saying. But there was no power on earth could contain Clare's anger.

'You!' she said, jabbing her finger in Penny's direction. 'You have the cheek to come in here like you've done nothing wrong.'

They were staring at her now, her officers. Penny too, but she didn't care. She was past reason. 'You come in here after what you've done?'

'Inspector,' Penny began but Clare cut across her. She wasn't about to let her speak, to salve her conscience with a carefully worded tribute to Sara. Not a fucking chance!

'This is all your fault.' Clare was in her face now, jabbing a finger in her chest. Al was on his feet, striding across the room. 'You knew I had concerns about policing the march. You knew I didn't have enough officers and you KNEW there were career criminals among the crowd. You knew it and you wanted them there so you could have your undercover cops arrest them. And everyone would say *Well done, Penny. What a great job, Penny.* Only it wasn't a great job, was it, *ma'am*?' Clare managed to imbue the term of respect with absolute contempt. 'It wasn't a great job because one of my finest officers died.'

Al had his arm on Clare's now but she shrugged it off. Penny looked beyond Clare, her expression severe.

'I hadn't thought you so indiscreet,' she said to Al.

The room was deathly silent. No one moved a muscle. Al took a breath in and out, then he spoke, his voice level.

'And I hadn't thought you capable of putting your own plans above officer safety.'

The colour drained from Penny's face and for a few seconds she didn't speak. Clare watched, aware every eye in the room was on Penny and she didn't spare her a second of it. She stood, waiting for Penny's response. Finally it came, the tremor in her voice unmistakable.

'You would do well to remember my rank,' she said to Clare.

Clare raised an eyebrow. 'I'd refer you to the words of Scotland's national poet, Robert Burns, ma'am. *The rank is but the guinea's stamp.* Frankly, if kowtowing to you is part of this job,

I'll take a P45 any day.' She marched to the door and yanked it open. 'And now, if you don't mind, I have the welfare of my team to consider.'

Penny stood, her eyes burning into Clare's then she spun on her heel and marched out of the room, her shoes clipping the linoleum. Clare's eyes were on her back, waiting until the front door slid closed then she turned back to face her team.

For a second there was silence then a burst of applause as every officer in the room rose to their feet.

—

Chris met them at the door and Clare took him in a hug. Then she stood back and studied his face. His eyes were hollow, red-rimmed with crying. He was a shadow of the bouncy, biscuit-loving officer she held so dear.

He led them into the sitting room. Sara's parents were there, and they rose to greet Clare, the effort of standing almost beyond them. She introduced Al and spoke to each of them in turn, holding their hands in hers.

Chris hovered behind her. 'Umm, tea?'

Al gave Chris's arm a squeeze. 'Why don't I make it?'

She sensed Chris's awkwardness. 'Give him a hand,' she said, nodding at Al. 'He'll only mess up your cupboards.'

Chris escaped into the kitchen, Al following him. She heard the murmur of conversation and she was glad Al had come with her. He'd be good for Chris. Clare was too close.

She chatted to Sara's parents for a few minutes, telling them what a fine officer she had been, how she'd recommended Sara work towards a promotion. Sara's mother's eyes filled with fresh tears at that, her dad nodding wordlessly.

'The minister's just been,' he said, when Clare ran out of conversation. 'We're having a proper church funeral. Christopher says there's a lovely cemetery near Drumoig. Sara always fancied a house there so it seems the right spot.' He let his head drop. 'She'll never have that house now.'

Chris and Al returned bearing a tray with mugs and biscuits. Clare waited until they had handed out the mugs then she put a hand on Chris's arm.

'It hardly seems enough to say how sorry I am but…'

'It's fine,' Chris said. 'Honestly, it's all anyone says. And I know they mean well but,' he met Clare's eyes and she saw resignation in his, 'it doesn't help, does it? Nothing helps.'

They stayed another half hour, chatting about Sara then Clare rose. 'We've been here long enough,' she said. 'But I'll come again.'

Chris led them to the door and she gave his arm a squeeze.

'Well done,' she said. 'Every minute you do, every hour – I know it doesn't feel like it but you're doing well.'

He gave a slight shrug. 'I wish they'd go home. I need some time to myself.'

'Maybe say that,' Al suggested. 'They probably think you need the company.'

He nodded. 'Yeah. I'll do that.'

She pulled him into another hug then stepped back. 'I'll be in touch.' And, with that, she left him to his grief.

—

Al suggested she went straight home and she was too tired to argue. They drove in silence but, as they pulled in at Daisy Cottage, she put a hand on his arm.

'I owe you an apology.'

'Eh?'

'Penny. I dropped you right in it. Telling her I knew about her plan to expose the professional rioters.'

He shook his head. 'I don't care. She's not my boss now and, for all she knows, I could have told you about it last night, after the march.' He clicked his seat belt button, allowing it to slide past his front. 'And if she even mentions disciplinary,' he said, one hand on the door, 'I'll bury her. Professionally,' he added.

Two weeks later

Chapter 46

'In the midst of life we are in death,' the minister intoned.

Clare had been to enough funerals to be familiar with the text and she zoned out, her eyes taking in the view. From the elevated site rich farmland was laid out before them, a patchwork of fields criss-crossed by fences and dykes. Chris had been right. It was the loveliest spot.

She stole a glance at him as he moved forward to take a cord from the undertaker. Al stood a little behind, waiting for his cord, his back ramrod straight, a stark contrast to Sara's father who seemed even more of a husk than when she'd seen him in Chris and Sara's house, the day after her death.

Sara's mum stood, supported by another relative Clare recognised from the couple's wedding. As the coffin was lowered gently into the earth her sobs rent the air and Clare felt her own eyes fill up. She dabbed at the corners with her index finger, blinking back tears. Above all, today, she needed to be strong. She had kept her composure in front of her officers and she wasn't about to let it drop now. They stood, stiff as soldiers in dress uniforms, eyes resolutely forward. She was so proud of how they'd conducted themselves and astonished at the turnout. The farmer who owned the land surrounding the cemetery had opened his field for parking and she'd seen three or four buses snaking along the narrow road. Buses full of officers from different parts of Scotland. They'd all come for Sara, a stirring sight as they made their way up the narrow road, silent and dignified.

She was relieved Penny had stayed away. Chris had sent a message requesting she shouldn't attend and Clare had passed it on to Penny's PA with barely concealed relish. Al had heard a rumour Penny was exploring transfer possibilities, more officers than Clare laying the blame for Sara's death at her door. Clare knew, of course, the real culprit was the masked man, languishing on remand in Perth prison. Thankfully, the press helicopter hovering over North Street had caught his deadly assault on camera, evidence Clare was satisfied would lead to a conviction and, hopefully, a heavy sentence. But the resentment she felt towards Penny still burned bright within her.

The cord-bearers were stepping back now, Chris's face a mask of control. She wondered if his GP had given him something to help him through the funeral. But today was only the start. He had a lifetime of living without Sara to get through, the acuteness of early grief fading to an aching sorrow. Time would help. She knew that. But would he withdraw the resignation he had tendered on her last visit? She'd refused to accept it, hoping he'd reflect and change his mind. But he'd seemed determined, an obduracy she'd not seen in him before.

She'd discussed her own future with Al, the last few weeks among the most miserable of her working life. But, if Penny's actions had taught her one thing, it was the importance of good leadership and, now more than ever, she had to be there for her team. She just hoped Chris would relent and remain one of them.

Al moved to put a hand on Chris's shoulder then stepped back to let him say a final goodbye to the wife he'd loved so dearly.

The minister was shaking hands, his face softened as he delivered words of comfort to Sara's family. A buzzing reached their ears and Clare lifted her gaze to see a propeller plane flying out to the west. And, as she looked, a shaft of sun came through the clouds, landing on the ground where they stood. It felt to Clare like a symbol of hope. Life would never be the same for any of them, especially Chris. But as she watched the progress of the plane, the sunlight glancing off the wings, she knew that one day – maybe not soon – but one day, they would all smile again.

Acknowledgements

Every time I sit down to plan a book I realise how much of a team effort it really is and I'm so grateful to everyone who has supported me during the writing of *Watch Them Fall*. Louise Cullen, Matt Webster-Moore, Deborah Blake and Catriona Camacho's skilled editing advice helped make the original word salad into a book I'm now so proud of, and Blacksheep's stunning cover is the icing on the cake.

Throughout the creation of this book I was supported, as ever, by my amazing agent, Elizabeth Counsell and the whole team at Northbank Talent Management. The 'back room boys' at Canelo have also worked tirelessly and I'm so grateful to Kate, Hannah and especially Alicia for all they do.

For technical information I'm so lucky to be able to rely on the knowledge of Liz Anderson, Ruth Darbyshire, my brothers Iain and Kenneth, and my son Euan. Not everyone who was kind enough to advise me wanted to be named in the book so I'd like to extend my grateful thanks to every single one of you (and send my apologies for the late night emails with bizarre questions!)

Writing can be a lonely activity and without the friendship and support of my writing friends it would be a lot less fun. Special thanks go to Sheila Bugler, Emma Christie, Catherine Cooper, Heather Critchlow, Jeanette Hewitt, Rachel Lynch, Angela Nurse, Louisa Scarr, Victoria Scott, Daniel Sellers, Ellee Seymour, Barnaby Walter, Sarah Ward and Michael Wood. Our group messages make me howl with laughter and keep me going as I grind out the words.

To every reader, blogger and bookseller a huge thank-you for putting your faith in Clare & co. I hope you'll enjoy this latest outing.

Finally, the biggest thank you goes to my lovely family and close friends. You put up with so much when I'm tussling with a book and your love and encouragements sustains me more than I can say. Fish, chips and prosecco on me!

Do you love crime fiction and are always on the lookout for brilliant authors?

Canelo Crime is home to some of the most exciting novels around. Thousands of readers are already enjoying our compulsive stories. Are you ready to find your new favourite writer?

Find out more and sign up to our newsletter at canelocrime.com